IMPEACHMENT DAY

A Novel

by
Bert Black

IceBiker logo cartoon by Andy Singer and copyrighted by Andy Singer. Used by permission.

Cover design by Shelley Johnson of Johnson Creative.

Impeachment Day is a work of fiction. Names, characters, places, and incidents are either the product of the author's imagination or used fictitiously. Any resemblance to actual persons, living or dead, or to actual events or specific locales is entirely coincidental.

ISBN: 978-0-9850676-4-9

IceBiker Press

Minneapolis, MN

Impeachment Day is dedicated to the memory of my late wife, who was the best and most courageous person I ever knew. She taught me how to live and inspired me to write, and it is she who is responsible for whatever is good about this book.

ACKNOWLEDGMENTS

In addition to my late wife, Judy, several other people have reviewed and improved my manuscript. In particular I would like to thank my brother Roy Black and his wife Ann Hobson; Charles Salzberg from the New York Writers Workshop; Patti Frazee and Gordon Thomas, my publication and editorial gurus; fellow lawyers Peter Christian and Caitlin Grom; and friend and colleague Terrie Wheeler.

CHAPTER 1

Everyone who later remembered seeing him said they knew something wasn't quite right. "A proper Santa Claus should not drive to the mall wearing his red suit," one prim old lady told the first FBI agent to arrive on scene. She looked like an elderly Mary Poppins, had a splendid British accent, and placed sharp and reproachful emphasis on the word "not," as if the investigators were somehow complicit in this terrible breach of Santa etiquette. Why, what if her small grandchildren ever saw such a thing! It could forever end their fantasies about airborne sleighs and home-baked cookies left by the fireplace, not to mention countless other talismans of their innocence.

Other witnesses did not share these apocalyptic fears about loss of childhood credulity, but when questioned they all were quick to agree that even at the time the whole thing had seemed at least a little strange. Shouldn't shopping mall Santas change backstage, like in an employee locker room or something? Maybe so, the chief investigator said. Maybe. But perhaps this guy was behind schedule. Maybe he had to don his costume at home or on the go. She instructed her team to check out all possibilities.

There was, however, no reported sign that this Santa was in any kind of rush. A high school art teacher at the mall to buy a gift for her boyfriend recalled that the traditional details were perfect.

Wire-rimmed spectacles positioned precisely at the end of his nose. A long, floppy hat with the fur-tufted tip hanging just so over the front of his left shoulder. A bushy beard and mustache too thick and pure white to be real, but flawlessly affixed, as if painted on by Norman Rockwell. And, the teacher added, he'd manifested no tension or anxiety about being late for work, no glances at a watch or phone, no scowls at the line of cars waiting ahead of him to enter the self-parking part of the garage. He'd even waved and flashed a cheery smile at the valet attendants who stood nearby to serve more affluent or impatient drivers.

Most people quickly passed him by without a second thought or even the briefest of second looks. And, in truth, there really wasn't much to hold their attention. He was driving a nondescript old SUV, once white but now streaked with rust and dirt, and of all who saw him in it only one of the parking valets noticed the back part was filled with brightly wrapped Christmas presents. The SUV was big, the valet said. "A Chevy Suburban maybe. And the rear seats were down to make room for all the boxes, stacked up high, almost to the roof. Packed in tight like bricks." With ill-concealed pride the valet noted that most of the year he worked construction, so he knew all about the transport of bricks and other heavy loads. "Yeah," he added, "whatever they were, they weighed a lot. Had the springs and shocks damn near bottomed out."

So, the investigators asked, had he and Santa spoken to each other?

"No," the valet said. "No. I just waved back. Probably smiled at him. I thought it was kinda funny he was actually bringing gifts with him to work. Figured maybe for his family."

And what did he look like? On this question the valet and most other witnesses generally agreed. Santa wasn't white and probably not black either. An immigrant, perhaps. Maybe Mexican, or Middle Eastern, or Indian, or Pakistani. Northern Virginia was an upscale melting pot, and the mall at Tysons Corner welcomed all shoppers and hired Santas of all hues and all religions.

Thus the now suspect Saint Nick had not seemed out of place. Nor was his behavior odd in any way. He waited patiently for a parking spot on the second of seven garage levels and then stepped out of the big old SUV and ambled toward the glass doors that opened into a big anchor department store. His gait, though slow, had the easy grace of an athlete, not the rolling waddle of a real-life fat man. Along the way he stopped and stooped to greet children, and bellowed hearty ho-hos and Merry Christmases with a faint accent no one could identify exactly. Most people said they'd focused more on the glasses, which seemingly defied gravity and stayed precariously in place no matter how he moved his head.

Videos later retrieved from surveillance cameras showed that once he entered the mall he quickened his pace and headed for a narrow, dimly lit hall that led to a little-used employee restroom. One of the last people to see him remembered how he looked over his shoulder before veering off from the main mall promenade, and images from a security camera mounted high outside the restroom door caught him alone. He stopped and looked up at the lens, and then reached deep within the padding of his costume to pull out a telescoping pole with a can of spray paint mounted on the end. He extended the pole, pulled on a string, and blinded the camera by painting over the lens. And after that there was nothing. A security officer watched the spray painting on a monitor and went to apprehend the red-clad vandal, but he never returned and was presumed among the dead.

AN EMPTY PORCELAIN coffee cup rattled on its saucer, shaken by a brief vibration too slight to jiggle anything bigger or more substantial. What was that? Sally Macalester gave it an irate look for interrupting her thoughts. Had even the coffee service turned against her? No. At least not yet. Her scowl softened into a smile at her own paranoia. She forgave the cup, refilled it from a matching dark blue porcelain pot, and after a long and contemplative sip went back to reading the latest impeachment charges against her. Nonsense, like all the others. With any luck they, too, would die quickly in committee.

But whatever she did, the last election's peculiar outcome continued to dog her. During each of her eleven months in office at least one member of Congress had filed formal papers declaring her impeachably unfit to serve. One month it was for vetoing abolition of the EPA, another month for nominating a gay person for the Supreme Court, yet another for attending the opening session of the United Nations. How any of these supposed sins could meet the Constitutional test of treason, bribery, or some other high crime or misdemeanor was never clear but also seemed not to matter. She blew out a long sigh, swiveled around in her chair, and gazed pensively at the leafless trees on the South Lawn.

The second interruption came only minutes later when her secretary announced on the speakerphone that the Secret Service wanted the President to move right away to the security and safety of the basement operations center.

"What?"

"They want us in the pea-ock. Right away."

Sally's eyes rolled at the acronymic shorthand, a dangerously contagious form of communication endemic to the Washington bureaucracy and against which there was no defense or immunity once a person set foot inside the beltway that looped around DC. To the Secret Service she was POTUS—President of the United States. At least so long as she could beat back the impeachers. Her code name was Gopher because she came from Minneapolis and played sports for the University of Minnesota Golden Gophers. The PEOC was the Presidential Emergency Operations Center, located in the netherworld beneath the East Wing. Most normal people called it the bunker.

"Why do we have to go there now?"

There was no answer from the secretary, and after a brief and inaudible discussion in the background another voice, deep and male, came over the speaker. It was the agent in charge of the Secret Service White House detail, who said four bombs had just exploded at four different shopping malls. By all reports very big bombs at very big, high-end malls. One was at Tysons Corner, across the Potomac in Virginia. Hadn't the President felt the rumble?

She glanced again at the offending coffee cup and answered with the kind of dead-calm coolness for which she'd been famous in the Senate and on the campaign trail. Way back in grade school teachers tabbed her a natural leader, and when she fulfilled their predictions later in life people marveled how her toughness never became hard or sharp, and her niceness never squishy or weak. She always had the quickest mind and quickest wit in the room. Even her most rabid opponents called her the perfect politician, and they meant it as a compliment.

"Where else?" she now asked.

"New Jersey and Denver and . . ." The voice paused. "Just

got another report. Now it's up to six. Virginia, New Jersey, Colorado, Arizona, Texas, and somewhere near San Francisco. Ms. President, we don't know what's next. You need to go to the op center. You don't have any choice."

Of course as President and Commander in Chief she had every choice. But she uttered no objection or complaint and joined her secretary and the Secret Service man for the walk from the West Wing down to the basement and through the tunnel to the subterranean safe room on the other side of the White House. As they hustled along she turned to her secretary and told her to call the Director of National Intelligence and the Secretary of Defense. "Have them get over here right away, or be available on the phone if they can't make it." She paused a second and then added the Directors of the FBI and the CIA to the list, and the Chairman of the Joint Chiefs. The Vice President, she knew, would have to call in because he was back home in Arizona.

"Anything else?" the secretary asked. She was a youngish grandmother with a pink round face on the verge of plumpness, and intense gray eyes that never smiled. She had long since learned to sweat every detail for her boss.

Sally stopped a few steps short of the PEOC door to ponder. "Yes. You need to call everyone we invited to watch the football game this evening and tell them the party's off." She took two more steps and stopped again. "But when you call Senator Nelson tell her to come over anyway. Bring her down here as soon as she checks in at the East Gate."

In the Senate they were called the Minnesota Twins, which rather aggravated Jane Nelson because she represented Wisconsin. But she and Sally had indeed grown up together in the same Minneapolis neighborhood. And they were longtime best of friends, even though they went to different high schools and in sports suspended friendship to do battle without quarter, courtesy, or humor. The competition ended only when they chose to join forces at the U and together led its volleyball team to three Big Ten titles and one national championship. So except for lack of kinship they had more in common than most sisters.

They also looked a lot like twins; both six feet tall, fair-skinned, and athletically attractive. Very attractive. They even wore their hair alike, no-nonsense Midwest straight and well short of shoulder length. People sometimes said the only difference was Jane's hair was red and her eyes a keen and startling green. Sally had light brown hair, almost blonde, and her eyes were the pale blue of ice or tempered steel. She would have been anyone's pick as the Scandinavian Lutheran of the two, and Jane the half Irish Catholic, not the other way around. Only after graduation did they separate, when Jane got married and her husband took a teaching job in Madison and she trailed along to go to law school at the U's archrival.

She was in a limo headed downtown on the avenue named for her adopted state when she heard a muffled boom to the south. She and the driver, a spaghetti-thin Haitian, exchanged quizzical looks via the rearview mirror. He shrugged, turned his eyes back to driving, and muttered in a thick Creole accent about the problems created by construction sites. She took out her iPhone to monitor the news. Nothing except reports about the throngs at the malls on the last Saturday before Christmas. *Amazing*, she thought. She'd grown up with the Internet as an everyday part of life, and never expected traditional shopping to persist in the face of online competition. But just as movie theaters kept going despite television, brick-and-mortar stores continued despite electronic shopping. According to a Wall Street Journal article she'd read on her phone that morning, in-store Christmas sales already had broken every historical record, and there were still five days left.

By now the limo had gone past the back entrance to the Naval Observatory, but it was still north of Georgetown. Jane was thinking maybe she'd have time to stop at one of her favorite little stores when an alert flashed across the tiny iPhone screen. "Bombs destroy four malls. Thousands feared killed." Her right hand, which held the phone, dropped to her lap, and for an instant she froze with indecision. Should she return to her condo in Chevy Chase? Keep going to the White House? Maybe go to her office? Or something else? She told the driver to pull over while she thought it through, and first thing called her family, already back in Wisconsin for the holidays.

"You all okay?" she asked her teenage son.

Of course they were. What the heck was wrong?

"Four malls just got blown up. You guys make sure you have

enough food, and fill up some water bottles. Make a quick dash to the store if you have to, then just stay home and watch the news."

"Yes ma'am." He started to ask more, but Jane's wife-and-mother time was up. She said she loved them all and missed them dearly, but right now she had to talk with the President.

Not a second after the first call ended the ringer on the phone went off. She had it set to sound like an old-fashioned telephone, and its loudness took the driver by surprise. He glanced again at the mirror and frowned, but said nothing. The new call was from Sally's secretary. Had the Senator heard the news?

"About the malls? Yes."

"Well, the football party is off, obviously. So's the game. But the President wants you here anyway. Come to the east entrance. They're all in the PEOC."

"The what?"

"The bunker. Get here fast as you can."

ROGERS, the Homeland Security Secretary, kept his eyes on the PEOC's wall of TV monitors as he spoke. "Shit. Unbelievable. Holy shit. Eight all at once." That was the latest count, and it seemed to be holding steady. Once a skinny college kid who lived on two meals a day when he could afford it, his diet grew richer as his metabolism slowed in middle age, and he long since had gone completely soft. His blood pressure spiked under any stress, and at the moment he was very red.

The President, who usually tolerated no profanity, ignored or didn't hear him. Nicknamed Bumble, he was the former governor of a state she needed to strike the bargain that led to her election. His appointment was one of many unfortunate by-products of the deal. But immediately after the first report on the bombs Sally had taken full hands-on command, and right now, whatever Bumble's failings, there wasn't much he could do or screw up. Before anyone arrived in the PEOC, and while the bomb count was still rising, she'd given orders to pretty much shut the country down. Sort of.

She bypassed Bumble and went straight to the career people who really ran his department. The senior administrator had been in the transportation department back in 2001, and recalled how on the infamous 9/11 George Bush quickly grounded all civilian aircraft after hijacked planes crashed into the World Trade Center and the Pentagon. "Should we do it again?" he asked.

"Yes," Sally said impatiently. "But that's the least of our worries. We're not sure how they blew up the malls, but it wasn't planes. Truck or car bombs, I'd bet. Had to be to do so much damage. Remember what one truck bomb did in Oklahoma City back in the nineties, and whatever hit the malls was much worse." First reports said the big buildings were completely flattened, and everything for blocks around as well. The death toll had to be in the tens of thousands. Like Dresden in World War II, one old-time newsman said on TV.

"So," Sally continued, "if there's more bombs coming or already in place, the last thing we want to do is keep people from driving to get away. We need to empty every mall and every other place there might be a crowd. I'm not worried about planes flying, but I am worried about crowds of people at airports. We don't have security checks for the parking ramps, so who knows if there might be car bombs there too." That was the only reason to shut the airports down.

"So just send everybody home?" The administrator couldn't quite grasp anything that simple.

"Exactly. My guess is most people don't have to be told, but let's get on TV and the radio and the Net. And have every governor call out the National Guard to help direct traffic. Have them set up food distribution points and put helicopters on standby to use instead of fire trucks and ambulances. Nothing's going to move very fast for a while, not even with sirens and flashing lights."

Thus did shopping crash to an immediate halt. Basketball and football and hockey games finished early. Christmas pageants never reached their end, and moviegoers were left hanging when theater screens went suddenly dark. Most people already at grandma's house decided to stay, and a few people who were at work decided just to hunker down in place. But everybody else scrambled onto the road. No one needed any Presidential urging to flee from crowded places. All streets and highways were gridlocked. Millions of immobile cars and trucks were strung together in endless ribbons of frustration and carbon monoxide.

The small group now gathered in the bunker with Sally watched the news with rest of the country. Watched continuously looped videos of the shattered malls, and live coverage of National

Guard troops who helicoptered in to clear traffic jams and allow emergency convoys to pass. Watched fights break out on the George Washington Bridge in New York and the Golden Gate in San Francisco. And watched looters attack grocery stores in New Orleans, and a survivalist militia outside Boise take potshots at Army trucks transporting emergency supplies. Thank God the attackers' aim was poor and the captain on the scene had enough sense to press on without starting a firefight in the middle of a crowd.

Rogers continued to mumble the number eight and run through the list of bombed-out malls in an endless litany of doom. His entire head was flushed, all the way to the top of his shiny and nearly hairless scalp, and he had one arm of his glasses stuck into his mouth, as if sucking on it might provide nourishment or yield a clue or answer. Shit, he swore. Two bombs apiece in each of the country's major time zones. Huge explosions timed simultaneously to maximize the psychological impact, and likely to make sure one bomb did not serve as a warning about the others and thus reduce the death toll.

Four o'clock Eastern Time in nearby Tysons Corner. The same time at a mall in Orange, New Jersey. Three o'clock Central Time at North Park Mall in Dallas and the Mall of America in Minnesota. *Of course the Mall of America*, Sally thought ruefully. The name was too symbolic, and the mall too big for a terrorist to pass up. And for her it was all too close to home. Two o'clock Mountain Time in Colorado and Arizona, and an hour past noon Pacific Time in Bellevue, Washington, and at a mall between San Jose and San Francisco.

The explosions and timing were both far worse than anything in Iraq or Afghanistan during the worst of the bad old days back in the century's first and second decades. In those never-ending foreign wars the really big bombs came only one or two at a time, and never this big and this well coordinated. Even on 9/11 one of the planes never reached its target. Here there apparently hadn't been a single slip up. All the bombs seemingly arrived and exploded on time, and all the bombers got away without leaving any immediate trail or trace. The planning and execution were obviously the work of some evil genius, yet no one claimed credit, and the powers that be had no idea where to look or how to catch the perpetrators.

Edwin DeSales, the National Intelligence Director, snapped at Rogers like a Doberman about to dispose of a pesky Chihuahua. "We all fucking know it's eight. Forget about counting the booms. Who sent the damn bombs?"

The rudeness if not the question shocked the room into an unstable silence. Everyone sat poised for an unexpected fight, though they also remained eager for the answer. DeSales, after all, never cursed. He was a hereditary if not genetic diplomat. Both his parents had been ambassadors, and he'd attended the best private schools in three different countries and grew up speaking five languages as his native tongues. He had the long nose and lean face of a British aristocrat, dressed like a wealthy banker, and spoke like a tenured Harvard professor (a position he'd several times declined). He graciously condescended to all yet somehow offended no one, and he never, ever faced a question he could not answer. Until now.

Dismissively he looked away from Rogers and spoke directly to Sally. "You see, Ms. President, this plot was thick and complicated. Not at all easy to pull off. Not the work of some stray lunatic with a few pounds of explosives and a grudge against the West. Nothing like that at all. But we can't find a clue about who it was. We might have missed the e-mail and telephone traffic beforehand, but we've scoured our databases and still can't find a thing."

Years after the infamous Edward Snowden affair, the NSA defied all reforms and still scooped up almost everything from any suspect country, person, or organization. Yet there was no trace of an operation so complex it would have stretched the limits of the most advanced military. "I'm not sure our SEALs could have pulled this off," DeSales said. "Certainly not without some kind of traceable communication or traceable movement of the explosives. So we're pretty sure it wasn't any government, and we've deprived terrorists of all their old safe spots. So that's not it either."

In the wake of multiple invasions and the toppling and replacement of multiple dictators, poverty and anarchy still fueled terrorists' fervor in the fractured Islamic Middle East, but while they regularly inflicted horrendous carnage close to home, outside the region the they were starved of the means to do much of anything. Nothing beyond an occasional assassination or a relatively small bomb that, except for the immediate victims, resulted only in a brief spate of intense consternation and news coverage.

The sickening brutality of ISIS had ultimately forced grudging cooperation from China and Russia, as well as Saudi Arabia, Egypt, and other Arab states. With their help, Israel and the West now tracked damn near every terrorist effort to obtain or ship the weapons and supplies of mass destruction. Even North Korea, finally free of the Kims, was making nice with the South and cooperating. Iran was the only remaining outlier, and DeSales said there was no sign of recent threats from that quarter either.

So there it was. They were faced with a total mystery, except the CIA director, on the phone from his own safe room in Langley, loudly disagreed. His name was Jack Gronkowski, and he was a holdover from Sally's Republican predecessor. Another compromise choice she now regretted like an unfilled cavity turned to a toothache. "It's Iran," he said, as if it were a matter of easy mathematical proof. "Has to be. Out to get even for what we did two years ago." It had to be vengeance for the great raid that finally did away with Iran's reactors and nuclear bombs. The Israelis had mounted the raid after they caught Iran violating its deal to stop refining weapons-grade plutonium, but the Iranians blamed the U.S. for helping out.

DeSales shot right back. "And that's why we've got ten satellites over them all the time, why you guys have more spies there than anywhere else. And they all tell us the Iranians know less than we do about the malls." Wiretaps and other listening devices had picked up frantic conversations among bad guys all over the world, and they were asking the same who and why questions as everyone else, only the answers they sought weren't how to catch the phantom perpetrators, but whether or not to take credit for their unexpected handiwork.

Sally cut short Gronkowski's angry riposte and asked the FBI Director what he thought. He, too, was on the phone. "Every other big attack," he said, "we've had some warning. We may have missed it, like for 9/11, but it was there when we went back to look. And usually someone jumps up to take credit. But like Ed says, this one is so off the charts no one can figure it out. We can't, and all the usual suspects are just as confused. Taking out a mall is nothing new. Think back to Kenya in 2013. But eight at once, with a lot more destruction and not a single clue . . ." His voice trailed off for a few seconds and then he turned to possible domestic threats. There weren't all that many homegrown terrorist groups, he said, and the Bureau figured it had most all of them infiltrated and under close watch. Certainly any group with the kind of resources this attack had taken. "Heck, most of the immigrant Muslim communities cooperate with us. They don't want their kids turning into suicide bombers."

"So what about another Tim McVeigh?" It was the Vice President, Carlos Castaneda, who'd called in from his home in Phoenix. His election, like Sally's, was a great anomaly. He had not been her running mate, and was never a friend. She would have expected him to back Gronkowski's Iran theory, but until his comment on McVeigh he'd been silent.

"Not likely," the FBI Director said. The super-patriot anti-government types generally didn't have the brains required to strike a match, though several militias already had emerged from their scurvy holes to take vengeance on every minority and politically suspect person they could find. If the end of days had not actually come, they would take the opportunity to bring it on themselves. Already they'd attacked ten blacks, eight Asians, two gay couples, and a liberal talk show host, and crude makeshift bombs had caused minor damage to a mosque, two synagogues, three Starbucks, and a branch of the Federal Reserve. The primitive stupidity of their efforts only highlighted why the true mall culprits could not be them.

The President wearily motioned for an aide to turn off the sound on the TVs, as if banishing the words might also banish the reality. "I've got to talk to the country again," she said. "Right away. Before things get really bad." Then she asked for suggestions about what they should do.

Nelson, her friend and former colleague in the Senate, had an immediate response. "Say you're making Wally responsible for security, for making sure we're safe. So we can start getting back to normal. Have him organize a search to make sure there's no more bombs. Maybe have him run the investigation." Everyone would back the choice, she said. As bad as things were, with fights already breaking out and riots looming as a real threat, there wouldn't be any political blowback. Not even from the Tea Party.

Wallace Stromdahl was the only person the whole country would trust.

"I don't need Walleye."

"No, but the country does. People will listen when he says what to do, and they'll believe him. Like no one else. And you shouldn't call him Walleye. He hates it."

The President half smiled. "He didn't when I gave him the name."

Nelson ignored the aside and stuck to the main point. The situation was way too serious a thing to leave to fifty different governors and fifty different National Guards, she said. "It's just like in New Orleans after Hurricane Katrina nearly wiped out the city. We had to bring in Federal troops under a trusted general. And this is a million times bigger. It's the whole country. If we lose control there's no telling what kind of fear and violence we'll see." And, she repeated the general had to be Stromdahl. He was a national hero for his countless exploits. The Chairman of the Joint Chiefs, a colorless Air Force general who made her name in logistics and had only weeks to retirement, nodded her vigorous agreement on giving the job to him.

"I never needed Walleye," Sally said. Actually, once she did, or thought she did. But that was long, long ago, and for very different reasons.

CHAPTER 2

The twenty-foot container passed through customs and an agriculture inspection without a hitch, likely never even opened by the overworked inspectors. And why should they worry? It was just a simple shipment of dried dates; sent from Yemen Fruits Ltd. in Aden to Mid East Foods Inc., located a mere thirty miles from the Newark docks. The fees and costs had been paid in advance, and the consignment papers made clear the container should be taken to a warehouse lot near the port. The food company would come to pick it up in due course.

Thing was, no one ever replied to the e-mail message about its arrival, and the shipping papers didn't provide a phone number. So there it sat. In mid-December the warehouse manager wasn't too worried about spoilage, and he never bothered to check the web to find the phone number. The container was a minor aggravation that slipped from his mind until the mall bombs, and then he couldn't get through to the police, the Port Authority, the FBI, or anyone else. Not even on a hotline set up for tips and clues. He might as well have been trying to file a claim with his health insurance provider.

On Sunday morning, the twenty-first, he finally called Linda Ferrell, an inspector for the Department of Agriculture and the wife of a childhood friend from Newark's Ironbound neighborhood. He and the friend were pure Italian, but Linda was black and from the Bronx. After her marriage she'd moved to the Ironbound, where she overcame these vast ethnic and geographic differences to become the acknowledged second mom for every kid on the block who was not her own.

"Can't be," she told the warehouse manager. Yemen had never exported ten tons of dates in a single year, not once. Much less a single ten-ton shipment. She was the unofficial Middle East expert for the port, so she knew. Half-joking, she added that she was the date expert too. Then she went stone cold serious as they pondered what might really be inside the container.

AN **FBI** AGENT and a contingent from the Newark bomb squad met them at the warehouse half an hour later with a truckload of equipment and a well-trained German Shepherd named Schnapps. The dog sniffed around, woofed weakly once or twice, and looked up at his handler as if aggravated a false alarm had disturbed his weekend day of rest. Only repeated tugs on his leash kept him moving, until he reached the door end of the container, where a cracked rubber gasket hung off to the side like a limp piece of stale celery. In an instant he lost his lassitude, reversed the dynamics of the leash, and lunged at the gap left by the gasket. When given a foot of slack he wedged his snout into the narrow crack with the full ferocity of his ancestral wolf genes, oblivious to any treat or entreaty.

The FBI agent, a graying by-the-book Bureau veteran, pasty-faced, balding, and physically average in every way, called Washington immediately. Maybe another one, he told the director. Maybe bigger than the mall bombs. They couldn't blow it up in place because the blast might level a large part of the city. And they couldn't risk disarming it because they might fail with the same explosive result. Best to clear the area, try gently to move it, and if that worked take it elsewhere for disposal. The director called the President who told the governor to get the container on a barge and tow it out to sea. The governor immediately agreed and ordered the National Guard to evacuate everything and everybody along the route back to the waterside terminal.

But what if the movement did set it off; what if there was one bump or jostle too many? There were a hundred what ifs. "Then you gonna find out what if you goin' to heaven or goin' to hell," the warehouse manager said. He was a vigorous sixty-year-old who looked like he'd come straight from the docks in Naples. No more than five foot six, barrel chested and stoutly built, he wore a well-trimmed mustache, chomped cigars, and took poorly to contradiction.

"I'll get it onto a truck," he said. "With the big front-end loader." He pointed toward a yellow tractor with huge fat tires and a forklift on the front. "Then I'll drive it to the dock."

"No," the agent demurred. Too dangerous.

The manager brushed past him without a moment's pause. "You ain't got no other way. And no one else to do it."

They dressed him head-to-toe in body armor, but everyone knew that if a twenty-ton bomb went off, more than four times as big as the Oklahoma City device, this meager protection from flying shrapnel wouldn't do much good. The manager took it all off as soon as he got into the loader's cab, tossed away his unlit cigar stub, and wheeled the machine into position. Everyone else had either cleared out completely or hunkered down a half mile away in a deep drainage ditch by the road, where they lay in the muddy, icy water with hands over their ears to save what they could of their hearing if the manager failed.

The loader's big diesel engine revved fast and then lugged down in a cloud of oily fumes as the lift forks slid into the slots on the underside of the container and hoisted it up. So far so good. The manager crept it over to the truck chassis and gently lowered it. Too gently, or maybe not lined up quite right. Whatever the cause, it didn't snap into place with the proper metal-on-metal clunk. He raised it again and moved the loader two inches closer to the truck to get things better aligned. Slowly, slowly he eased the container downward for another try, till it was only a hand's width above the chassis rails. Then he hopped down to double check the positioning. Everything looked in perfect order, and he remounted the loader, raised the forks a bit, then lowered the big metal box into place. But once more there was no confirmatory clunking sound, and he could see the locking mechanism had not engaged.

In the ditch Linda and the FBI agent grew impatient and popped up their heads to check out his progress. They exchanged glances, but said nothing before ducking back down. In her head she ran through the Lord's Prayer and wondered if she should shift her body so she could get her hands into the classic supplicant's position.

The manager got down to check a second time. The position was good, and all else was in order. The only issue was momentum and the only cure was increased downward velocity. He gave the container a rueful look, paused a moment, and climbed back onto the loader. He shifted his butt to get comfortable, took a deep breath, and raised the container yet again. After another pause he let it drop down full tilt. The metal-on-metal sound was loud enough to reach the drainage ditch, where everyone squeezed even closer into the mud and squeezed harder on their ears. But no explosion followed. The manager turned off the loader, jumped down a third time, and fastened all the clamps and chains to keep the container on the chassis rails. On the way out from the lot he flashed a thumbs up to Linda and the FBI agent and the others in the ditch, and stopped to allow a military police escort to move in and form up around the truck.

AT THE WHARF all things superfluous had been moved as far away from the waiting barge as possible. A single gantry crane remained in place, one end of its giant horizontal boom over the truck, the other end over the barge. A device called a spreader dropped down, latched onto the container, and hoisted it off the chassis like a shoebox full of feathers. Electric motors whirred as the gantry's traveler rolled along the rails on the bottom of the boom and swung the container over the barge and lowered it to the deck.

The barge was lashed to the bow of a Coast Guard tugboat, and a smaller tug stood off a few hundred yards, ready to give aid if necessary. From a far corner of the wharf parking lot the warehouse manager watched the loading operation, and when the gantry completed its work he sprinted to the edge of the dock and jumped aboard the big tug as the crew cast off the lines.

"Where are you going?" the FBI agent demanded.

"Kind of thought I'd come along and see it through," he said with a smile. No one tried to stop him.

Linda and two bomb squad members already were on board. She'd convinced the agent and his bosses back in Washington that they shouldn't just blow up the container or simply dump it into the deep. Better, she said, to open it on the long-shot hope they'd find some clue about the origin of the other bombs. She knew for sure it didn't hold dates. At least not from Yemen. And with her knowledge of Arabic and other Middle Eastern languages she could interpret if they found any documents or labels on the contents.

THEY CAST ANCHOR five miles off the coast and the smaller tug moved past to go farther out to sea and out of harm's way. The two bomb squad members jumped from the larger tug onto the barge and cut the lock on the container's door, but when they tried to undo the latch it wouldn't budge. Again the warehouse manager went into action. He joined them on the barge and pulled a special key from his pocket that released an inner lock on the latch. He started to pull the door open, but the bomb specialists stopped him. Who knew what booby trap that might spring. Instead, they tied one end of a long cable to the handle and returned to the boat, to which the other end was already secured, looped around a large cleat. The boat backed away a good five hundred yards before the line went taut and the door popped open. All exhaled when there came no explosion.

The water astern the tug churned angrily as the wheelman reversed the propellers to move forward again, toward the barge. He glided the tug alongside, and the FBI agent, one member of the bomb squad, and Linda scrambled off. She surprised them when she easily and lightly made the leap. Not more than five-two and dressed in a shapeless uniform and bulky body armor, she looked sort of fat and dumpy. A nondescript middle-aged woman with a roundish face and close-cropped kinky African hair. A person no one would remember. But she ran every morning, no matter the season, and in warmer weather played one-on-one back-alley basketball against her teenage son, and her body was harder than the armor. It was the agent, not she, who landed funny and twisted an ankle. She gave him a hand up and together they gingerly approached the container to inspect its contents.

At first glance the shipment appeared exactly in accordance with the bill of lading. They could see two pallets of burlap bags, one pallet stacked on the other, and they smelled a faintly sweet odor, something like a mix of molasses, alcohol, and linseed oil. Dates, Linda said matter-of-factly. Then she walked over to take a closer look. The writing on the bags was in Arabic script, but the language was Farsi. From Iran, not Yemen. And where one or two of the bags had slipped a little they could see a bit of white paper or plastic peeking through from the core of the top pallet.

"Wonder what that is," she said. "Think we can pull out the first stack of pallets so we can take a closer look?"

They signaled for the tug to come back, tied the cable to the two visible pallets, and repeated the backing-away maneuver, though it took more of a pull to get the cargo to budge. Once again all exhaled, and once again Linda and her two companions went back aboard the barge to take a look. Because of the agent's gimpy ankle, this time he was lowered with a rope and harness. When they peered again into the container all they saw was another two-pallet stack exactly like the first.

"Should we keep pulling them out?" the agent asked.

Linda shook her head no. She nodded at the two stacked pallets they'd already removed and the barely visible whiteness where there should only have been brown burlap. "Let's just see if the dates are hiding something else."

The tug used its boom to place an explosion blanket over the suspect dates. Then it took everyone back on board and the boom lowered a remotely controlled robot onto the barge. It crept under the blanket and used its tin-snips shears to cut the straps on the top pallet. The image from the robot's camera eye showed several bags of dates slipping off the outside of the stack, and revealed something very different on the inside—paper bags of prilled ammonium nitrate, explosive grade. Again the labeling was in Farsi. But whatever the explosives' origin, there was no detonator. This wasn't a bomb, but the makings of a bomb. Or many bombs.

CHAPTER 3

L uke Rumbo was high and happy. With a loopy smile fixed on his otherwise flaccid face, he lay buck naked on his back with his hands behind his head as he admired the equally unclothed Lisa Larkin. Oblivious of his gaze, she stood in front of a full-length mirror mounted on the broadcast booth wall, leaning forward and intently combing out her long and tangled blonde hair. The view from behind was almost enough to get Luke up for a repeat performance on the quilt-covered futon that served as their bed. Lisa inspired him that way even though he wasn't fit for much sex with anyone and hadn't been for years. Without Viagra he was a total dud. North of fifty and well past overweight, he drank and smoked to excess, and despised exercise even more than he hated Democrats or Sally Macalester and her damned New American Progressives. NAPsters, or the kidNAP party, as he liked to put it. Because that's what they'd done to the country.

Nothing sent him into his habitual orbit of spite and outrage more quickly than an article about Macalester's workouts or bike rides, or one of her chirpy cheerful speeches about health and fitness. A diet and exercise Nazi, he told his radio audience; a dictator bound and determined to force all overweight Americans to live on a perpetual fat farm, with every calorie counted and every mile of jogging carefully logged. Socialism at its worst.

A frightening threat to the freedom of every beer-swilling, beef-eating, crew cut true American like him. When he really got into it, which was fairly often, he declared she should be deported to Sweden or some other haven for socialist heresy. Or forced to subsist on acorns and gruel.

And anyway, who said fatty food was bad? That was just left wing political correctness, the kind of bias Luke had suffered all of his chubby life. Now he'd made it big and kept company with celebrities and the high and mighty, not to mention the likes of the lovely Lisa. And his diet still consisted of well-marbled steaks, few if any vegetables, and free-flowing booze. He still had three eggs and six slices of bacon every morning for breakfast, still smoked and inhaled big thick cigars, and still was doing just fine, thank you.

Fat, fine, and happy in Birmingham, his hometown; right where he began his career as a disk jockey for a religious revival radio station. When he shifted to political commentary and went national he stayed in Alabama because he hated New York and L.A. And because Lisa, the true brains behind his success, wouldn't leave her husband to join him. She managed his schedule, and his website, and all the other media through which she sold his books and video clips and posters and T-shirts and anything else she could conjure up to profit from the Rumbo name and likeness.

Her husband was pastor at the state's biggest Pentecostal church, and inadvertently started it all some years before when he volunteered Lisa to do a Sunday afternoon program with Luke. What better way to clear her out of the house so he could pursue his own dalliance du jour. But at the station she and Luke were alone together and didn't really have much else to do. So they would put incoming calls on automatic hold, play ten songs at a time, then smoke dope and ball away to their hearts' content on the futon Luke kept behind his broadcast booth stool.

She continued coming for the drugs and later the money. He deluded himself that she came for sex. Thus was the gig strangely good for both of them. And now it was better than ever. He and Lisa ran their empire from offices and a studio in the basement of his super-size golf course mansion. For old times' sake they kept the futon from the radio station and continued to do one or two Sunday gospel shows a month.

And that's where they were when the phone light started

blinking the day after the mall bombings. Inside the booth they used a light instead of a ring tone to avoid disrupting the program. He gave the blinks an irate look and let them expire. But within seconds they started again. And again when he continued to ignore them. Only on the fourth call did he sit up to check out the caller ID. It was Hiram Heilman, a Republican Tea Party stalwart from South Carolina who was the Senate Majority Leader and a frequent guest on Luke's regular weekday radio program on the Wolfe Network.

First elected in 2014, Heilman was a tireless advocate for returning government to the nineteenth century. No income taxes; no Social Security; no national health care or child labor laws; no popular election of Senators. No unions and no regulation of any kind. No. No. No. Far as he was concerned, except for the armed forces every part of the government should be blown to smithereens. Man was meant to live in total freedom, not under the oppressive thumb of bureaucracy. That was the original intent of both the Constitution and the Bible, and if ever the two conflicted, the Bible should be supreme. Not because Heilman believed it. Quite the contrary, he was an atheist through and through, a non-believer of the solipsist Ayn Rand variety. But he delighted in ferreting out Biblical passages that supported his views on his own intrinsic superiority.

Luke, on the other hand, was a true believer who preached with a zealous sincerity that short-circuited logic and brushed off annoying contradictions. His radio show was called Luke's Truth, and both his followers and detractors called it the Gospel According to Luke, albeit with vastly different degrees of sarcasm. When he saw the Majority Leader's name and number on the phone's little screen he shook his head in disgust and resignation and got up from the futon like a flabby beached whale. It was not a pretty sight. He took a seat on one of the broadcast stools and reluctantly answered. "What the hell do you want on a Sunday afternoon?" As he spoke he waved at the naked Lisa, who had laid back down on the futon for some further amorous activities. She smiled, struck a seductive pussycat pose, and motioned for him to hang up and come join her.

"Turn on the TV and you'll see," Heilman said.

"What?"

"The FBI and the Coast Guard found explosives for another bomb."

"Where?"

"Newark. In a container from Yemen. Least that's where it went onto the ship. Looks like it's really a little present from Iran. Turn on your TV."

Rumbo took a quick break to queue up the next ten songs and tell his audience what they were. Then he switched off the microphone, switched on the television, and watched the madhouse scene at the Newark waterfront. A curious Lisa pulled on her panties and a sweatshirt and came over to sit on the other stool while she watched too.

"You got it on," Heilman demanded.

"Yeah. When did all this happen?"

"Maybe an hour or two ago. Not much yet from the White House, but things are getting out of control pretty damn fast. May be our chance."

"For what?"

"Make the impeachment stick."

Rumbo frowned and pointed out that like it or not, the odds were far better the country would rally around the President than turn against her.

"Not if she dithers over it," Heilman said. "And not if we play this right."

A soprano? The President wasn't getting it. How could they tell what a dead person had sounded like before he died? And how could a guy be a soprano anyway?

"No. His name was Salvatore Soprano. And the other guy was named Gotti. They were stuffed into the trunk of a black Caddy in the garage at the train station in Newark. Honest. I couldn't make this up."

Yes, you could, she thought. Their first summer together he tried to tell her there was such a thing as a freshwater shark and a Canadian gorilla. That was also the summer he introduced her to fishing, and she gave him his fishy nickname. But a Marine Corps Commandant wouldn't make up stuff like that. Not even Walleye Stromdahl. Not in the middle of a report to the United States Cabinet on securing and reassuring the nation and getting the wheels of Christmas commerce turning again. No terrorists were going to stop Christmas.

That's what she'd told the country the day before in a TV speech delivered an hour or so before the FBI discovered the contents of the Newark container. General Stromdahl would be responsible for security and safety and the U.S. would come out of this latest challenge stronger than ever. And let there be no doubt they would find the guilty and respond with the fateful lightning of a terrible swift sword. But she also warned that private justice was no justice at all, and they needed more evidence before they could strike back. The Luke Rumbo crowd hated that. They believed strongly that wherever the bombs had come from should be nuked into oblivion. And if no one could figure out where wherever was, well just pick some unwholesome place to nuke and be done with it. Mostly they thought the target should be Iran.

At the emergency Cabinet meeting on Monday afternoon Stromdahl reported that his men had removed all cars left behind in just about every mall and airport and train station parking garage in the country. Didn't find more bombs, he said, but they had solved several other crimes, like the missing Mafiosi. And they'd stumbled on some other weird stuff too. Like stashes of illegal drugs, bundles of cash, three boxes of long-play phonograph records, and two parrots trained to squawk obscenities.

But the massive search had worked, he said, and malls everywhere were open again or set to reopen very soon, with inspectors and bomb-sniffing dogs in place. And his troops, mostly National Guard, but some regular Army and Marines, too, had set up remote ground-level parking lots where a blast would do little harm beyond taking out a few more cars. The plan was for buses to shuttle shoppers to and from the mall of their choice, and it was already up and working as well as could be expected. Well enough to accommodate the tiny number of people brave or foolish enough to venture out again. The incident in Newark had reduced that category to nearly no one.

Despite the President's vow to save Christmas, the only thing really alive was online commerce. Otherwise shopping was moribund to dead as the nervous country looked over its collective shoulder at anything and everything that seemed odd or out of place. Every backpack or briefcase left behind on a bus or subway train had become a suspect bomb; every stranger a suspect terrorist. And stores were emptier than the Sahara during a heat wave.

AS THE CABINET members and their various aides and assistants filed out the President asked Stromdahl to stay behind. She sat at the middle of the long table, with her back to the room's wall of French doors. At her invitation he moved to a chair directly opposite. Even sitting down he was an imposing figure, with eight rows of ribbons on his chest, and huge shoulders that more than filled out his forest green uniform.

The Cabinet were a less impressive lot, a motley crew cobbled together in the deal that got Sally enough votes when the Electoral College deadlocked and the House of Representatives had to decide the Presidential winner of the last election. First time since John Quincy Adams in 1824, and no one really understood all the Constitutional and political arithmetic. Panelists on one of the Sunday morning cable news shows had nearly come to blows over it.

Voter votes, it turned out, made little difference. In a three-way race the Progressives won fifty-one percent of the Presidential popular vote, compared with twenty percent for the Democrats and twenty-nine for the Republicans. But the damned electors got split up 220 for Sally and 145 and 173 for the donkey and the elephant. So no one had the required absolute majority. And that's where things went totally kaflooey. According to the Constitution's Twelfth Amendment, each Congressional delegation in the House got one vote, which meant Delaware, Vermont, and Wyoming counted the same as California, New York, and Texas. And because the Progressives hadn't been able to field candidates in every district, and hadn't done so well against incumbent representatives, they held only twenty percent of the seats and controlled only Minnesota, where the party got its start. The other states and the District of Columbia were split twenty-four to the Republicans, nineteen to the Democrats, and seven with delegations in which no party held a majority. Overall the Republicans still held more than half of the seats and would get to elect the Speaker.

TV and Internet commentators floundered vainly to explain all the permutations, combinations, and variations, but the bottom line logic was not hard to see. For any candidate to gain a majority of the states, one of the old parties had to strike a deal with the other or with the party-crashing NAPsters. Depriving Sally of the Presidency after she'd won the popular vote was not likely, but getting there required some hardcore backroom deals. In the end, she agreed to retain several Republican appointees of the Tea Party variety from the prior administration, like Gronkowski at the CIA. In return three Republican states and four of the no-majority states joined all the Democratic states and Progressive Minnesota to get her one past the magic number of twenty-six. She also had to take on a few less-than-stellar Democrats, like the hapless Rogers. Compromise, at best, was the least onerous alternative.

Most rank-and-file Republicans, however, were bitterly opposed to this deal, and from the outset of her administration they howled for impeachment, in large part because the Vice President wasn't Sally's running mate but rather, the Republican candidate. An inexplicable loose end in the Twelfth Amendment gave the Senate the power to select the VP if the electors couldn't, and the Senate remained solidly in Republican hands. So there sat Castaneda ready to take over, undo everything Sally had accomplished, and give free rein to the Tea Party to drive the country into ruin.

In the years since the hapless second Bush and the high hopes for Obama, elections had veered back and forth between Democrats who promised much but couldn't govern or deliver, and Republicans who promised only that they weren't Democrats and didn't believe in government at all. If government couldn't function, the Tea Partiers said, why not just do away with it? Blow it up and be done with it. And if Congress couldn't figure out a way to elect a President, so what. Those among the Republicans who thought themselves more cerebral and philosophical touted Ayn Rand's *Atlas Shrugged* like the third testament of the Bible, and hewed like apostles to her belief that all government was an encroachment on liberty. "Leave us alone and let the productive among us thrive," they chanted. "Reward the makers and not the takers."

Occasionally a foolhardy Democrat would try to reason with them. Weren't humans a cooperative species as well as competitive individuals? Shouldn't the government levy taxes to spend on things like education and health care that would enable people to become makers? Shouldn't it also spend on welfare programs to help people through rough patches and back to makerhood? No, no, no, the Tea Partiers shrieked. That was all for the magic of the laissez-faire marketplace, and if occasionally it collapsed in a great depression or recession, well, that was simply "creative destruction."

When Jane Nelson and Sally served in the Senate together Jane regularly marveled at how anyone could be so obstinately wrong. "They forget," she'd tell Sally at lunch in the Senate dining room, "that all people are takers as children, and most when they retire. And their damn heroic makers get wiped out along with the takers when the market collapses. Or when plagues caused by poverty infect the entire world." And worst of all, history taught that worldwide war could follow such calamities.

Yes, Sally would say. But Jane was forgetting that the vast majority of Tea Partiers didn't give a hoot about maker-taker philosophical purity. Their movement was rooted in gut level but not irrational revulsion for the elitist nagging of the nanny state, coupled with totally loopy belief in flat earth follies like creation science, rejection of climate change, and conspiracy theories about the malign purposes of the Trilateral Commission and secret legions of black helicopters. And there also was the religion thing. Most Tea Partiers saw the United States as a Christian bastion against a cynically secular Europe and the Islamic hordes of the Middle East and Asia. All the unsaved peoples of the world who would go straight to hell come judgment day. How this devotion to Jesus Christ and the Bible squared with Ayn Rand's atheism and the greed and excess of unfettered free market capitalism was never made very clear and rarely discussed.

The spiritual if not real leader of the Tea Party Republicans was now Rumbo, whose rants defied logic or consistency but won hands down for their tone and target. One day he yelped at the President for interfering with free enterprise because the government inspected things like meat and milk. A blatant communist plot. Then the next day, as if the first rant never happened, he blamed the Democrats and NAPsters for a salmonella outbreak caused by a grocery wholesaler who illegally sold buttermilk bottled without inspection. How could a well-run Food and Drug Administration miss such a thing!

When a blogging online liberal pundit pointed out the

disconnect between the "no inspection" and "inspect more" positions, Rumbo explained on his next show that if people didn't depend on the FDA they'd do the inspecting themselves and no bad food would ever be sold. And if something rotten somehow slipped through, well, the market would punish the seller. That's what God intended in a world of truly free individuals limited only by His word and His will. Government inspection made things worse, not better, and people ought to get rid of it and get right with God. So there.

Sally rarely listened to Rumbo, but Jane Nelson, as a Senator from Wisconsin, was attuned to all things milk and dairy, and she went ballistic about the attack on inspectors. "So," she told the President, "he'd crash the sales of dairy products because no one could be sure they're safe." The idea of letting the market punish unsafe producers was just fine, except it was hard on the kids who sent a market signal only by dying from bad milk. Luke, they agreed, was a disaster; the kind of thing that sorely tested forbearance for free speech.

His stock in trade was a whiny simpering mocking imitation of anyone in favor of regulation, fairness, civil rights (except for corporations), environmental protection, diversity, or a healthy diet. Only sniveling hand-wringing weaklings would even suggest such things. Then his voice would go deep and strong as he told his listeners that the real America was a place for God-fearing Christian capitalists, and anyone who didn't like it could leave. But of course he also was for freedom and individual choice. Just so long as the choices were rightwing and right.

For months he and Heilman had been pushing to impeach and convict Sally and then move on to Castaneda. "And now," she told the Commandant, "they think they can really pull it off."

Stromdahl nodded yes. He knew the impeachment and conviction math. Remembered it from high school civics if nothing else. A majority in the House to impeach, and two-thirds in the Senate to convict.

"The House part is pretty easy," Sally said. "Remember, they once even impeached Bill Clinton. But conviction is a lot tougher. They've only got sixty Senate seats, so they'd need at least seven Democrats. For now I'm safe. But Heilman and Rumbo are playing the Iran thing to the hilt. Rumbo says he's morally certain the Iranians did the bombs. His words, not mine. Morally certain, mind you. Says they were out to get even for the reactor raid. Says they got help from Jihad in Yemen, which also is out to get even. Because we killed Akbar with a missile from a drone. So if I don't bomb 'em back, it's like treason."

"Lots of people saying it was Akbar. Not just Rumbo. Maybe he's right for once, at least on that." Stromdahl didn't remind her of his own connection to Akbar, the late leader of the Jihad in Yemen terrorists and one of the great disappointments of his life.

"Yeah," Sally continued. "And maybe Saddam Hussein had nukes and chemical weapons in Iraq. Maybe the sun will rise in the west. Maybe the Cubs will win the World Series. Maybe. All we've got is maybes. I don't want to go to war over maybe again." Thing was, no one had any idea who really did the bombs. Or who sent the container. This wasn't like 9/11, where al Qaeda jumped up to take credit. But Rumbo and Heilman had their acolytes convinced it was for sure all cooked up by Iran, and the U.S. should nuke 'em back to some time before Genesis. And if Sally didn't act pretty soon Congress should get rid of her and turn the country over to someone with the balls to do it immediately.

"Rumbo says the House can do an impeachment in less than a week if it wants to. And the Senate can finish it off in just a few days more. Says that's what we need to do if I don't launch on Iran. He and Heilman want me gone as soon as possible after the Christmas break."

"So I've seen in the news," Stromdahl said. Even if he didn't listen to Rumbo, the Republican push for impeachment was all over TV and the Internet.

She glanced past him at the portrait of FDR and Churchill that she'd selected for the Cabinet room's west wall. Rumbo, she said, loved to wrap himself in pseudo-Churchillian rhetoric about readiness to fight tyranny. "He says it's time for us to use our hydrogen bombs as God intended. Why else did He give them to us? Wants to zap Iran, then amend the Constitution to make us officially capitalist and Christian so we also can zap all the liberals and pinkos here."

Stromdahl whistled softly. "So unless we find out who really blew things up they'll have you gone and the rest of us fighting World War III. And we all damn well better become regular churchgoers. They'll dismantle the government except for some kind of bureau to make sure everyone shows up for services on Sunday."

She flashed a quick weak smile at the hyperbole that wasn't really all that hyperbolic. "That's what I'm afraid of. Rumbo's telling the world the container shows how incompetent we are. Says other containers obviously did get through, and that's what got used to make the mall bombs. And he says we've been trying to make nice with Iran. That's why I need to be fired. Maybe burned at the stake." Again she smiled. "Well, not that. But they would if they could."

Of course there was no precedent for such immediate removal of a President, but neither was there any precedent for the likes of Rumbo, not even the late Limbaugh or Beck. If the wacky impeachment scheme worked and the Senate got to vote on charges against Sally, the Republicans and some scared and disaffected Democrats could send her packing. Some of the old-time Dems remained mad as hell at her for splitting from the party to form her own, and they might just go along on conviction.

Stromdahl shook his head at how things were zooming out of control. Mohanjani, the new Iranian president, was crazier than a cockroach on crack and acting for all the world like he wanted to get nuked into martyrdom. Only hours after the mall explosions he gave a speech praising Allah's just punishment of the infidels for the big raid on Iran's reactors two years before. And while he denied complicity in the mall bombings, no one believed him.

"Who knows," the President said. "I don't think they actually planned it all, but they've been giving bad stuff to bad people for a long time. Thing is, probably not this bad stuff. Only Gronkowski believes for sure they did it, but he's no different from Rumbo. He hasn't got any evidence. Nothing. Not one source who says so. Not one intercepted message. Nothing from Iran, and nothing from al Qaeda or ISIS or any of the other jihadi zealot groups."

Again Stromdahl asked what had her convinced it wasn't Iran.

"I don't know for sure. What I do know is the container is the best lead we have, and I want your guys to track down who actually did send it."

He held up his right hand to fend her off, and shook his head no. "That's not exactly part of our mission. Actually, it's kinda against the law."

Sally looked directly at him. "Walleye, I need you to do this. Just track down who sent the container. You speak Arabic. You've got Marines who speak Arabic. That was your big thing years ago. So send some of them to Yemen."

Marines weren't spooks, he said. Let the CIA do it.

"Look, you know Gronkowski's a Republican flack I had to keep as director. A real Tea Party nut when he was in the House. But it was all part of the great compromise we had to make for me to get elected and get my Cabinet confirmed." As she spoke she held up her hands to put air quotes around "great compromise," which she now saw more as the great disaster.

Gronkowski had transformed the CIA from the professional agency that once tracked down Bin Laden, and it had become instead the playground for political hacks out to prove whatever fit their ideology. At the moment that meant justifying a war against Iran, and for darn sure it did not mean helping a non-Republican President. Walleye was the only good choice to track down the truth.

He shook his head once more and grinned. So now he was Walleye again. He thought back to when he came to visit her while she was the hotshot young mayor of Minneapolis and he was a wounded war vet hoping he'd get well enough to get on with his life. Back then no tabloid gossips cared at all about who either of them slept with, and they spent a long weekend at her downtown condo, mostly in bed. It was not the last time, but was the most intense; the end of any innocent hope their lives could ever fit together in some kind of normal way.

She did not return the grin and gave no hint she shared his memories of their past, or that she held onto any second thoughts about what might have been. "We don't have time to worry about the rules right now. Impeachment probably makes it out of committee this time, and who knows what happens in the Senate. But if we nuke Iran the whole world could blow up. Remember, the big raid maybe wasn't really such a big success."

He said nothing, but nodded to signify he didn't need reminding. The Iranian reactor raid was shrouded in all kinds of rumors. Israel had done it, of course, but with lots of American equipment and maybe with CIA help, and maybe some of the nuclear fuel was lost in transit. The raiders swooped in with special long-range helicopters carrying a reinforced regiment. After two

Israeli airstrikes some years before, the Iranians had rebuilt their reactors in deep caverns immune to air attack, so it was no longer possible to act without putting boots on the ground. The raiders had to blow off heavy steel and concrete entrance doors just to get into the tunnel openings, and once inside they met intense armed resistance. But they made it through and managed to cart off all the fuel rods to prevent another resurrection of the rogue program. And at that point the story got very murky.

Press accounts based on unattributed sources in the Middle East said two of the helicopters carrying the nuclear material out of Iran never quite made it back. Supposedly they went down somewhere on the border between Jordan and Iraq. The CIA claimed it didn't know what was true and what wasn't, and sure as hell did not know where the fuel was. The Israelis wouldn't admit they'd lost it for fear of looking inept and weak, and the Iranians wouldn't admit they had it for fear of inciting another raid.

Stromdahl pondered it all for a few seconds more, then came back to her original request. "And say I do send someone to Yemen, what happens if it's my little investigation that blows up?"

"Then we never had this conversation. You decided to do it on your own. And I'll prosecute the hell out of you." Sally didn't say it out loud, but they both understood the thought lacked one more phrase—"Or the next President will."

"And suppose it all works, but the truth gets out. Which it will."

"Easy. You get to retire with another medal to go with your court martial. I'll make sure you get a medal."

"Thanks."

Her face reshaped itself into a big wide smile. He was welcome, she said. For all their past ups and downs, they trusted each other completely. Neither of them had ever married, but they still felt more for one another than most spouses. Each was the other's ideal, and yet they both had come to understand that their different callings would always pull them apart.

He got up to leave, but she had one more question, important if not urgent. Why had he not accepted her invitation to the White House theater to watch the big game? After years of debate, the NCAA was at long last holding a full-fledged sixteen-team football playoff, and Minnesota miraculously had made it into the field. The idea was to use four of the traditional bowl games on New Year's Day for the quarterfinal round, then do the semis on the first weekend after January 7, and the final game eight days after that, on a Monday night. The first-round games had been set for the weekend before Christmas, with Minnesota scheduled to play Temple on Saturday. Given the U's mostly unfortunate football history, no alum wanted to delay a party on the hope the team would advance further. This game could be the only playoff appearance Minnesota would ever make.

"Well, I would've come," he said, "but we already had a headquarters party planned for Minnesota Marines." Marines with ties to Temple also were invited.

Just like him, she thought. The damn Marines had always come first. It was the worst thing about him and also the best, and right now she was very thankful he'd chosen the Corps instead of her.

CHAPTER 4

By all accounts he should have been a Thor, not a Wallace. A Thor, like his father and grandfather and countless generations back in Norway. That was clear from his almost white blond hair, light skin, and piercing ice blue eyes. And also from the strong Norwegian undertone in his Minnesota accent. A Viking through and through, with a jutting jaw that gave him a look of stern authority but also made him something less than handsome.

The two Thors before him both thundered in the sky flying fighter planes for the Marines, and therein lay the deviation from past naming practices. Wally was named after his father's best friend, who died in a dogfight over North Vietnam. Thus did the Corps displace his heritage while remaining his destiny. He, too, would be a fighter pilot.

But in college his genes intervened and grew him to Thor-like size. He came to the U and its football team as a skinny pass-catching walk-on and left as a defensive end good enough to play on Sunday. And too big for the military by two inches and more than fifty pounds. He beat the rap only because he'd signed up for the Platoon Leaders Course as a freshman and got a special dispensation after the growth spurt, but serving as a pilot in the Air Wing was absolutely off-limits to someone of his size and bulk.

So he shifted to the infantry and couldn't wait to go on active duty. To heck with the NFL. He'd already missed the 1990 Gulf War and Saddam's "Mother of All Battles," and didn't want to miss the next one, whatever its parentage. The Marines had a plain and simple mission that now was his—seek out, close with, and destroy the enemy. Nothing more and nothing less. Then came 9/11, and it all turned far more complicated. The United States would invade Afghanistan not only to destroy al Qaeda and the Taliban, but also to remake a land that thrived on destroying outsiders.

By then Wally was Captain Stromdahl, in charge of a rifle company. His battalion commander was a lieutenant colonel from Oklahoma who took it all in stride. He said war was like riding a bronco. A horse might buck left nine times out of ten, but the rider damn well better be ready for the one time right. Or for some combination twist never seen before. "Look, you adapt or you die. And just pray to God you keep adapting right. But we're Marines. Tell us the mission and we'll get it done."

THE MISSION that eventually set Stromdahl on the path to becoming Commandant began in the Arabian Sea in the wee hours of a cold December morning in 2001. Ten helicopters carrying his company lifted off from a carrier deck in darkness and flew due north almost straight into a monsoon blowing from the north northeast, dry and cold and steady. Not a storm, but a constant wind that slowed their progress and forced the choppers to refuel in midair over western Pakistan. The Marines on board knew they'd finally entered Afghan air space when all lights disappeared below. Had to be the Registan Desert, the big blank space on their maps.

A squadron of attack helicopters joined them once they crossed the border and covered the remaining journey and the landing zone at the northern edge of the desert. Come first light the company was five hundred miles from the sea and on its own after the attack birds departed. Their objective was a mud brick square compound, about a hundred yards on a side, with ten-foot walls and twenty-foot watchtowers, one at each corner. The intelligence report said it was unoccupied, and in fact they took it without seeing a soul or firing a shot.

Its original purpose was not clear, but it seemed new if not modern. The bricks were solid and uncracked, and the mortar fresh and uncrumbled. Inside there was an asphalt parking area only recently swept clean of the constantly drifting sand. Yet there were no barracks and no water supply or armory or magazine. Only three small trailer offices and two pre-fab steel warehouses, the shiny metallic construction as out of place in the desert as an igloo or a snowmobile. Maybe an army base, maybe a drug collection depot, Captain Stromdahl reported over the radio. As if the distinction were real or made any difference. The ragtag Taliban militia supported itself by feeding the West's craving for opium, so the walled compound easily could be simultaneously military and commercial.

And no matter what the intended function, it was now Camp Porcupine, the first in-country operating base for the 2001 invasion. The starting point for a planned push to take Kandahar City, a hundred miles farther inland and smack dab in the heartland of the Taliban. The camp was on the left bank of the Dori River, which flowed east to west and kept the Registan region dry by intercepting all the rivers that flowed southwest out of the mountains on the Dori's right bank—the Arghastan, the Tarnak, the Arghandab. Green-banked streams that drained valleys squeezed between sere and jagged ridgelines. The Dori was not green. Like the edge of a sponge it soaked up water and made it disappear.

Stromdahl surveyed the walls and towers and quickly ordered his men to start turning them into a proper fort. They piled sand against the inside of the walls so Marines could stand high enough to see over the top. The only entrance was a thick plank gate in the northern wall, the one that faced the river, and to its right (looking outward) they built up an especially large mound for the heavy tripod used to fire anti-tank missiles called TOWs. They had ten missiles, just in case, but figured the worst thing they'd confront might be a truck or two. Supposedly the Taliban's inherited Soviet heavy weapons had fallen into total disrepair.

Two or three hundred yards upstream of the compound was a ford across the Dori, a shallow spot where the sandy bottom was augmented with a thick concrete slab. And not far above the ford was a small village, just coming to life as the Marines commenced their construction work. The smoke plumes from the chimneys all bent southward with the wind, but eddy currents in the air wafted traces of the pungent odors of burning wood and spicy cooking sideways as well, and piqued the appetites of men who'd gone more than sixteen hours without a proper meal.

A short strip of asphalt pavement, fresh and black and unweathered, ran from the southern end of the ford to the compound's gate. On the other side of the river a longer two-lane band of black ran northward and disappeared into the foothills. Only a rutted trace of compacted mud and sand connected the village to the crossing.

NO ONE FROM THE VILLAGE came to greet them, so the Afghan interpreter who'd flown in with the Marines walked over to look around. When he returned he said the villagers were scared. "They are all women and children who dare not speak with you."

The interpreter was a bearded leather-faced man of indeterminate age, skinny as a rail and never without a cigarette. On the helicopter flight across Pakistan and the desert it took two Marines to keep him from lighting up and blowing the chopper out of the sky. When they pointed at the boxes of ammunition he shrugged and held his hands out, palms upward, as if begging the question. Why the big deal? In his country every day was an explosion risk no matter what a person did.

Stromdahl listened to his report and said the Marines better go take a look themselves. Accompanied by a squad from one of the company's platoons, he and the first sergeant and the interpreter walked over to introduce themselves and inquire about local Taliban activity. A cigarette again dangled from the interpreter's lips as he trudged through the sand. But now that he was on the ground his disdain for risk had disappeared, and he cautioned them to stay off the beaten track lest they set off a mine.

The village looked little different from the surrounding terrain. Except for their square shapes and the crude wooden doors and shutters, the mud huts could just as well have been giant anthills mounded up from the native soil. There were no glass windows or electric lines or generators or cars or signs of any other technology developed since the first publication of the Koran. Not even any streets or a discernable layout or plan. The anthill huts were scattered like the tents of nomads in a temporary camp pitched helter-skelter in the dark.

Between the village and the river were fallow fields, apparently sustained by irrigation during the growing season, but in the winter gone as dry and barren as the untilled desert. In his head Stromdahl did some quick Minnesota farming math. There were only fifty huts, but no way could the small cultivated area provide food for even that many families. Evidently agriculture was not their means of survival. The first sergeant, a short and wiry African American raised on a farm in Mississippi, saw the same thing, and also the absence of livestock. Only two or three desultory goats, who roamed among the huts, and one lonely donkey tethered to a stake.

And as they walked past the first of the huts they noticed that the interpreter was almost right. There were no men in sight until a black-turbaned, white-bearded great-grandfather type stepped out of one of the huts. He had a left eye, a left leg, and a right arm and told the interpreter he'd lost their opposing counterparts years before while fighting the Russians.

"Tell him we're here to protect them from the Taliban," Stromdahl ordered the leather-faced interpreter. "Tell him we're here to help them."

"Captain sir, he himself is a great Talib hero." The interpreter took the cigarette from his mouth and spat to emphasize his disagreement. "And even those who are not Taliban may not want your help."

Behind the old man Stromdahl saw two or three shrouded women scurrying from one hut to another, and two small girls peering at him from around a corner. Otherwise there was no sign of human life.

THE LARGEST BUILDING in the village was a dilapidated single-story school with two classrooms, one for older boys and one for younger. Before the Taliban it served several other villages too, and part of the Marines' mission was to get it up and running again under a new system. One wing for boys, one for girls. The Secretary of Defense saw it as a kind of rough-and-ready American frontier schooling that would remake Afghanistan if not the world. Never mind that his own education about the place he sought to change went little further than reading Rudyard Kipling in grade school. And he'd skipped or forgotten the cautionary tale of "Arithmetic on the Frontier," a poem about the failure of modern technology when deployed against fierce Afghan tribes. No, he and President Bush would make their own history. He wanted to begin the school project right away to send a message far and wide that American troops brought peace and progress, a new dawn for an ancient land.

Only two weeks after taking control of the camp Stromdahl was ready to get started with the co-education plan. "Not good," the interpreter said. He flatly refused to explain it to the old man with one arm and one leg and one eye, and walked away without another word.

The first sergeant watched his retreating back and spoke with matter-of-fact solemnity. "He's right Skipper. You know that."

Stromdahl, too, watched the interpreter's retreat, and answered as a colleague, not a commander. "Top, I got no choice. I told 'em it won't work. They wouldn't listen. They're already sending us a teacher."

"God save him."

"Her. She's coming today. This is a big showcase project."

THEY ARRIVED that afternoon on one of the resupply helicopters. A Navy lieutenant, a Marine corporal, and Meena, who was to be the new school's first teacher. The lieutenant went back with the helicopter. Over Stromdahl's objection, Meena and the young female corporal stayed.

"Those are my orders, sir," the corporal said.

"From who?"

"Washington, sir. We're supposed to stay at the school."

She never asked for it, but Stromdahl sent a rifle squad with her for security, twelve Marines in all, not counting the female corporal. "Dig in," he told them.

That evening the first sergeant walked around the camp's perimeter, then over to the school to inspect. The sun was low in the west and the sky was ominously dark and fast growing darker. To the north the gray clouds merged with the gray rock of the mountains. The Marine positions were all in order, but as he walked back inside the walls of Camp Porcupine he thought of the old Dylan song his father used to sing. *A Hard Rain's A-Gonna Fall.*

CHAPTER 5

On the banks of the Dori darkness and silence were total. Clouds obscured the moon and stars, and this night there was no wind. The Marines on watch swept the ground surrounding their base with night vision goggles and binoculars, and poked each other to stay awake. Inside the compound Stromdahl had his headquarters in a sandbagged corner of one of the steel warehouse buildings. A sort of inner keep in case the mud brick walls were breached. He slept fully dressed on a thin foam pad laid on the concrete floor, with only his pack for a pillow and a lightweight blanket for warmth. His boots were on but unlaced to allow his feet to swell without cutting off circulation. Not two yards away the executive officer and a radioman monitored reports from the walls and watchtowers, and from the Marines at the school. Nothing.

At a quarter past one in the morning the radio suddenly crackled to life with a report from Tower One, on the northeast corner, closest to the village and the ford. "We got enemy headed our way. Still on the other side of the river."

The radioman shook Stromdahl awake. "Something from the north."

He sat up and grabbed the headset to talk directly with the Marines in the tower. "What you got?" the earphones popped as the lieutenant in the tower pressed the button to reply, but the not-so-distant sound of big engines and clanking tank treads interrupted and gave a wordless answer. How many, Stromdahl asked.

"A bunch. We can see like a hundred men. At least. And more coming. Three, no, four tanks." The Taliban troops were spread out in a wide formation, the lieutenant said. They could wade across the river, but the tanks were rolling down the road, headed for the concrete bottom at the ford that would keep them from bogging down in the sandy bottom.

Stromdahl turned to the first sergeant. "Get everyone up. Move. And get the anti-tank platoon to the wall. Now." He tied his bootlaces and said he was going to the tower to get a better view. The XO, he said, should stay put and contact the Navy carrier to report the attack and call in air support. "And tell the mortar platoon to put up illumination rounds."

Back on the radio he told the lieutenant in the tower that once the illumes were up he should direct mortar fire on the enemy to slow their advance or stop it, and only moments later the crumping explosions of the high-arcing rounds shattered the night with the first sounds of hell. Then came the sharper boom of a tank's smoothbore cannon and the loud burst of a projectile when it struck the wall, almost immediately followed by the crackle of rifle fire and the burping bursts of machine guns. And also the whistling descent of mortar rounds fired back by the Taliban. They too were well armed.

"Incoming!! Incoming!!"

Stromdahl ignored the warning cry and reached the tower just in time to see the first tank crossing the river. "Fire," he ordered the TOW platoon over the radio. If they could destroy the tank in midstream it would block the ford and keep the other three on the north bank. "Fire!"

Nothing happened, and through a pair of night binoculars he could see the tank turn toward the village and the school. Shit. Suddenly the TOW blasted out of its tube, and the sky flashed briefly when it struck the tank and set off a secondary explosion. One down, three to go.

The TOW platoon frantically reloaded so they could hit the second tank and still block the ford, but in their haste they fired high, and the distance was too short to allow a correction with the wire guidance system. The rocket sailed long and detonated harmlessly when it struck the ground; a small flash, a puff of smoke and dust, and nothing more. And now the second tank was headed straight for the entrance gate. It paused and fired, and the projectile slammed into the wooden planks, this time wounding two Marines and creating a gaping hole. Then it crashed through the gate and turned and fired point blank at the TOW tripod.

THE TANK was inside the compound, two more were racing toward the ford, and with the TOW gone all the Marines had to stop them were shoulder-fired rockets, the modern version of the World War II bazooka and not much more reliable or effective against modern tanks. The Marines in the tower had two of them. Stromdahl grabbed one and a lance corporal took the other, and together they raced out to do battle, hoping against hope they could avoid the tank's machine guns and get close enough for a kill.

Already a dozen Taliban foot soldiers were near the gate and more were on their heels, and the roaring firefight drowned out speech and scrambled thoughts and drove even a Marine or two to shake with panic. The smoke of burning cordite hung just above the ground in tattered sulfurous clouds that looked and smelled like sour dragon's breath from a fantasy film gone wrong, and through the murky darkness the enemy horde pressed forward behind the tank that was already within the walls. The tank had to be destroyed.

"Let's go," Stromdahl told the lance corporal.

Without a word or any hesitation the young man ran to follow the captain. He made it ten yards at most before a round caught him in the leg and he went down. Stromdahl winced at the spurting blood, waved over a Navy Hospital Corpsman, then picked up the second bazooka rocket and continued on his own to dodge and run toward the tank. When he got within a hundred feet he dropped to one knee, sighted on the turret, and watched the round bounce off. *Shit*.

Immediately he picked up the second rocket and fired at the treads. This time he scored an explosive hit. The tank wouldn't move any farther, but the turret was still working, and the barrel was pointed right at the headquarters bunker in the corner of the warehouse. If that went they'd lose good communications with the Navy and couldn't coordinate air support.

All Stromdahl had left was two hand grenades and zero time. He took a deep breath and ran toward the left side of the tank, hoping against hope neither the driver nor the men in the turret would see him. Five, strides, ten strides, twenty, and he was there. He climbed on top of the hull just as the cannon fired a projectile that missed the warehouse and hit the south wall of the enclosure. Reloading and re-sighting would take a good crew less than a minute. That's what Stromdahl's life was down to. His life and all the Marines he commanded. If he could shimmy out along the barrel to the muzzle end he could insert the grenades. Ten seconds gone.

Suddenly the turret hatch popped open like the top of a deadly jack-in-the-box, and the Taliban jack was only feet away and looking straight at Stromdahl, his face an ugly patchwork of fear and hate. Stromdahl ripped open his snapped holster, yanked out his pistol, and pulled on the slide to chamber a round. The Taliban too had reached for a pistol, raised it, and fired first, but just as the turret lurched five degrees clockwise. He missed, and before he could re-steady his weapon after the recoil Stromdahl's bullet hit him square between the eyes. Twenty seconds gone.

But now the crew knew a Marine was attached to the hull of the tank like a barnacle. The barrel began to move up and down and side-to-side to knock him off, which gave him a bit more time but also kept him from moving to take advantage of it. At least the dead man's body blocked the hatch and kept anyone else from coming out to shoot at him. Stromdahl went flat on his stomach to dodge the tube and waited for his chance. Then it stopped moving. The crew must have gone back to reloading and the clock was ticking again. He got onto his hands and knees, reached the base end of the barrel, and began to inch his way toward the muzzle. He started out on top of the tube, but it began to move again and the motion almost flopped him off. *They must be ready to fire*, he thought. Only a few seconds left.

He clung to the tube from below with both his arms and legs, like a chimp shimmying out on a tree limb. Five more seconds gone. Why hadn't they fired yet? At last he made it to the barrel's business end. He held on tight as he could with his left arm so he could let loose with his right hand, which he used to stuff both grenades down the bore. Then he jumped down and ran like hell.

The explosion caught him in midstride, less than ten yards from where he first hit the ground. It went off like a truck bomb and sent shrapnel flying everywhere. Only much later did he think to wonder how his hearing survived. The pressure from the blast blew him another dozen yards forward and knocked him flat on his face, and when he tried to get up he realized he'd been hit pretty bad. The electric-sharp pain in his right leg collapsed him to the ground like a karate chop, and he saw a jagged four-inch sliver of steel obscenely embedded in his calf, like a crude meat cleaver.

He rolled onto his back and somehow kept from screaming while he listened to the screams of other Marines who'd been hit. Jaws clenched, he sat up and tried to pull out the shrapnel, but it remained almost red hot and he fell back to the ground. The other screams were increasing in number and intensity, but the Marines manning the mounded ramparts nearest to the gate were still returning fire, and for the moment had repelled the enemy.

He turned onto his stomach and crawled toward them, and when he made it to the mound four or five hands reached down to help him up. The captain's hit, someone shouted. Another Marine threw up after looking at the wound, and the corpsman who came to help went into a panic and started screaming completely out of control. "The captain's hit bad. He ain't gonna make it."

The captain, however, had other ideas. He grabbed the corpsman's leg and then his belt, and pulled him down so their heads were only inches apart. "Shut the fuck up and get that fucking piece of metal out of me. I ain't dyin' and neither are you. You hear me?"

The corpsman nodded, but did nothing.

Stromdahl tightened his grip and shouted again. "Move, God dammit," he commanded. "Move and get it out. Now!"

Zombie-like the corpsman nodded and went to work on the leg. The metal shard had now cooled enough to touch, but he couldn't grasp the jagged edges to pull it out. A Marine tossed him a T-shirt, which he wrapped around it to protect his hands. And then he pulled and out it came, much easier than he'd expected. Miraculously it hadn't broken any bones or severed an artery, and though Stromdahl could put no weight on the leg he managed to stand up long enough to survey the battlefield. He saw both of the remaining tanks had crossed the river and stopped where they could fire at the walls while out of bazooka range. And in the light from the muzzle flashes and the illume rounds he could see a Taliban assault wave running toward them.

"WE GOTTA CRAWL out there to get those tanks," Stromdahl told the nearest sergeant. "Who's gonna come with me?"

The Marines at first stared in mute disbelief. It was a suicide mission at best, and the captain could barely walk. Another projectile slammed into the wall not twenty feet away, and they all instinctively ducked to avoid the shower of dust and deadly metal fragments.

"I'll go," the sergeant said. No one else spoke, but every hand went up to signify "me too."

Stromdahl took a lance corporal and two privates and told the sergeant to direct cover fire and have the mortars stop putting up illumination. Then he laid out his orders. "Look, it's gonna be dark. They'll never expect us to go out there, and we've got night vision and they don't except maybe in the tanks. And we gotta crawl anyway so my leg won't make any difference."

They took only rifles and pistols and one shoulder-fired rocket each, dropped over the wall on a rope and set off across the parched sand. Before they'd moved fifty feet the tanks fired twice each. It wouldn't take long for them to reduce the entire north wall to rubble. But at least the flashes made it easy to keep them in sight. And also revealed Taliban foot soldiers within spitting distance. The four Marines froze in place and waited for them to pass, then resumed their crawl. In the first hundred yards they had to stop three times as the enemy slipped by, but Stromdahl had been right. No one expected Marines to be moving forward outside the walls.

The second hundred yards and the third went without incident except for the periodic firing from the tanks, the sound of rifle and machine gun fire, and the occasional crumping of a mortar round. At last one of the tanks was close enough for them to take a shot, close enough that they could smell the diesel fumes. But Stromdahl whispered that they should wait. The lance corporal and one private were to crawl to the second tank so they could take them both out together and allow neither a chance to escape.

"We'll give you five minutes. Go ahead and fire when you're ready. We'll follow right up."

The five minutes passed, then another two and both tanks remained unscathed. Stromdahl was just about to fire on his own when he heard the rocket's hiss to his left. The sky lit up with a big explosion. Half the mission accomplished. Immediately the first tank spooked and started to move back toward the ford. He fired at the treads to stop it. This time the tactic failed. The round glanced off harmlessly. The private fired too and also failed.

No longer did they have the advantage of night vision. No longer was their position unknown. Orders barked in Pashto and the sounds of men moving fast surrounded them. Rifles fired and the flashes lit them up as they scrambled to a small swale and hunkered down. Then a brief silence. Then more rifle fire.

Again a brief silence, followed again by the sound of men moving toward them. And then a grenade bounced into the swale. In the grip of instinct, Stromdahl dove away. The private dove the other way and landed on top of the grenade. Without pause he reached under his chest and flung it backhand out of the swale. It blew up half a second later but caused no harm.

Stromdahl rose up to fire in the direction the grenade had come from. At least three rifles on full automatic burped back. They all missed. He crouched back down, grabbed the private by the arm, and prepared to crawl out the other side of the swale. A grenade sailed over them and blew up harmlessly twenty feet away. Another grenade landed between them. The private dove again, this time too slowly. The blast lifted his body five feet into the air. The force of it hit Stromdahl on the left side of his face and he fell backwards. He touched his cheek to check the damage and felt bits of bone and flesh. The private's, not his.

In front of him he could hear voices and the labored breathing of the enemy closing in. To survive he had to move and slip away. He crawled out of the swale and made it only four feet before the bullet hit his leg, two or three inches above the earlier wound and not half an inch below his knee. This time he knew right away that bones were broken. It also fleeted through his mind how strange it was that weapons if not lightning could strike twice in nearly the same place.

He rolled into another depression, and lay ready to go down fighting. Bullets flew overhead, and two grenades went off not twenty feet away. Near misses. The leg now throbbed as if every nerve had caught fire, and he passed out from the pain and loss of blood. When he woke up he was in a helicopter headed for the aircraft carrier, which had a team of trauma surgeons on standby waiting for the casualties.

The corpsman sitting next to his stretcher shouted so he could be heard above the noise of the engine. "You're gonna make it, sir. We got the tanks and most of the enemy." Right after Stromdahl passed out a squadron of fighter jets had swooped in for close air support, followed by a wave of attack choppers. One helicopter went down to a stinger missile, but the air power had won the day. The Taliban attackers were caught in the open, and few survived.

Stromdahl's eyes asked the next question. What about his men?

"You all took about fifty wounded," the corpsman said. He wasn't sure how many dead. Stromdahl shut his eyes and shook his head. At least one, he knew. The private who'd fallen on the grenade and sacrificed himself so his captain could continue fighting.

CHAPTER 6

The snow began to fall after dinnertime on Tuesday, the twenty-third, and it didn't end until the wee hours of the twenty-fourth. Eighteen inches in all, and the temperature dipped twenty degrees below freezing. Samir Al-Mahdi woke up at five, about an hour after it stopped, roused from sleep by the growling engines and scraping blades of snowplows on Wisconsin Avenue. An eerie quiet followed after they passed, and he got out of bed, walked to the window of the second-story bedroom, and pushed up two slats of the Venetian blind. Nothing was moving, and a block off Wisconsin on Volta Place the unplowed fluffy white blanket deadened any sound. Wow, he said softly. Wow. The Washington weather channel had said four inches, not this. Parked cars had become gentle bumps in the universal whiteness, and the leafless oaks and maples looked as if they'd been draped in delicate white lace.

Ayan sat up in bed and tugged the quilt around her body to keep warm. She was naturally ample, curvy yet trim. In her late thirties, she could still pass for a twenty-something student, but unlike her husband, she never worried about exercise. He was a lean six-footer who couldn't go a day without the gym, a compulsion that drove her crazy. Why the hell, on a short weekend getaway to San Francisco, had he spent hours changing hotels to find one with a proper fitness center, and then more hours pumping iron? But she did like the results. In the faint illumination from a plug-in nightlight she could see the taut muscles in his butt and back. Neither of them had bothered to put on their pajamas again after shedding them earlier for sex. "What's wrong?" she asked.

He kept looking outside. "Nothing. Nothing at all. But we're gonna have a white Christmas for a change." His hand dropped from the blind and he rejoined her under the quilt. Propped up on his elbows he took in her long hair and luminous almond eyes, and one breast invitingly uncovered by the quilt. He thought how nice it was their son and daughter had gone to visit grandparents for the holidays. "It's really deep. Like back home. Great day to stay in bed." He flopped down as if to emphasize the point.

She remained sitting up. "So you're not meeting him today. Good."

He raised his torso with half a sit-up, supported himself on his elbows, and looked back at the window. "Guess I can still walk there after breakfast. We're supposed to meet at eight. Guess I'll still go." He turned to face her again and reached over to pull her down and closer.

She rolled the other way and gave him a push. "Go ahead then. But you can fix your own damn breakfast before you leave. And please make sure to lock the door."

BACK HOME in Michigan he would have broken out the snowshoes and the parka with the periscope hood. Here he settled for an old pair of combat boots, a Navy pea jacket, and a bright green toboggan hat pulled down tight to cover his ears and the top of his neck.

The walk to Georgetown University usually took no more than fifteen minutes, but this morning he allowed half an hour. He stayed in the middle of the unplowed streets, where a few vehicles with foolish drivers or four-wheel drive had packed down the snow at least a little bit. His route was the same as always. West on Volta to 35th, then south to O Street, then west again to the main gate, at which he paused to scan the big lawn in front of Healy Hall. The white expanse was smooth and pristine. His footprints would be the first.

He breathed deeply to savor the cold, clear air and hiked smartly through the virgin snow toward the library at the south end of the lawn. It was an industrial strength thing more than half a century old, built of raw concrete with a blocky faux bell tower at one end. Only the most scholastically pure lovers of architecture saw in it any charm, and Samir was not among them. Why did the West's zeal for originality and disdain for tradition so often produce such monstrosities? The closer he got the more apparent became its ugliness, but from the inside at least he'd no longer have to look at it. He pressed onward, swinging his arms as if propelled by invisible ski poles. He was out of breath when he reached the main entrance. And he was alone. *Shit.*

Then, after half a minute, came a loud whisper from behind a tree not twenty feet away. "Samy, go on in and open the back door for me. Prop it open and go ahead on up to the fifth floor." Samy knew that meant the seminar room where in the past they'd regularly met for one of the advanced classes he taught. The academically arid subject was language, culture, and reality, and there was none of this cloak-and-dagger secrecy crap. The whole idea was to mix together potential enemies and turn them into something else, and the sad part was how few non-academics had any interest.

SAMY DID as he was told, and when Stromdahl walked in he was sitting at the room's only table with his back to the windows and his eyes fixed on the open door. Stromdahl pulled the door closed and took a chair directly across from him. Dressed in jeans and a yellow anorak with a hood that hid his close-cropped Marine Corps hair, he looked nothing like a general. Maybe just a big maintenance man or, less likely, one of the school's basketball players trying to hit the books on the day before Christmas.

The table was as severely utilitarian as the unfinished concrete walls. A simple slab of varnished but unstained oak supported by brushed stainless steel legs. The swivel chairs were thinly upholstered plastic shells, dark gray in color and mounted on stainless pedestals that matched the table legs. The carpet, too, was gray, though much lighter. Based on the chemical smell and lack of wear, apparently it was new.

No artwork adorned the walls, only two large whiteboards, both blank and clean, but the view out the windows exceeded any art. First-time visitors took it in like eager tourists atop the Washington Monument or the Statue of Liberty or some other high observation spot at the end of an elevator ride or a climb up a long, dark stairway. A sudden panorama, expected but still awesome and surprising. When people looked downward and to the south they'd see Key Bridge and the Potomac. If they raised their gaze a bit they'd see the office towers of Roslyn across the river, just beyond the far end of the bridge. To the west and upstream a person could see all the way to Chain Bridge, but not quite to the CIA headquarters in Langley, which was close to the river but not directly on it.

Samy spoke first to preempt the purpose of the meeting and end it so he could get back to his wife and try making up. "No. I won't do it. Whatever it is, I won't."

Stromdahl briefly stood up to remove his heavy jacket and hang it on the back of the empty chair to his left. Underneath he was wearing an old Minnesota maroon sweatshirt with a cartoon caricature of Goldie the Gopher. "Do what?" he said as he sat down again. "I haven't asked you to do anything except meet and talk. And you're already here."

Samy shook his head and laughed. He, too, was dressed in jeans and a sweatshirt, though his was gray with no lettering or logo. And while his hair was clipped short, it came nowhere near Stromdahl's buzz cut. "Skipper, that's bullshit. You always told us the Marines were no talk all action. So tell me what's going down." Skipper was a sort of post-Marine Corps compromise he'd arrived at to avoid "sir" and "general," yet still show proper respect. In the Marines a captain commanding a company is often called the skipper, and though Stromdahl was a major when Samy first met him, and now wore four stars, the title nonetheless seemed to work.

"So what you hear from back home?"

"Dearborn or Yemen? Dearborn's home, but I'll bet that's not your question."

"What you hear from Yemen lately?"

"About the container and the bombs?"

A nod told him to continue.

"My father's uncle Anwar said it might be Sami Akbar."

"What?"

"Said it might be Sami A."

"Said he did which? Sent the container or did the bombing?"

"Anwar says both."

"But Akbar's dead. They got him with a drone eighteen months ago. You mean Akbar's people? Right?"

Al-Mahdi scoffed and waved his hand to bat away the foolishness. "No. I mean Sami A himself. Who says he's dead? CIA?"

"CIA and everyone else." This was the first Stromdahl had heard any doubt about Akbar's demise. Even Ed DeSales, always a skeptic, seemed convinced. He said the NSA hadn't heard a peep about or from Akbar since the drone.

"Yeah, but all the intel comes from the informer who directed the strike, and last time I called Uncle Anwar he told me that's shit. The informer guy actually worked for Sami A and directed the strike against one of his main rivals. Helped Sami disappear and got rid of his biggest local enemy at the same time. And he's plenty smart enough to avoid any electronic communication if he really wants to hide." It was, Al-Mahdi pointed out, exactly what they'd expect from the other Samir, the one who spelled his nickname with an "i" to make sure he would not be mistaken for a Samuel. The wide receiver who caught Samy's passes when they played together for West Dearborn High. Samy to Sami, just like Benny Friedman and Bennie Oosterbaan, the 1920s Michigan teammates who radically changed the college passing game with their Benny to Bennie completions.

Stromdahl contemplated the news and stuck his tongue against the inside of his left cheek while he mulled it over. "But your uncle said 'might be Sami.' What does that mean?"

"Oh he's certain Sami's still alive and with us, and I've no reason to doubt he's right about that. About the bombs he's just giving me the latest rumors. Most people in Yemen want to believe Jihad in Yemen did the bombing. Hell, they're proud of it."

"Proud, huh?"

"That's the way it is."

Another contemplative pause. "Changes a lot, you know. If he's alive. Maybe this is how he decided to come out of hiding. You know what the CIA's saying now?"

"About Iran?"

"Right."

Again Al-Mahdi waved his hand to dismiss any reliance on the CIA, which only the day before claimed to have found the people who sent and shipped the container. The agency said its agents had teamed up with the Yemeni secret police to track down four suspects, two each from the fruit company and the shipping company in Aden. In short order the agents extracted signed confessions that the miscreants had been put up to it by Iranians, and that they belonged to Jihad in Yemen.

"Iranians doesn't mean it was the government," Samy said. "And my uncle says the word on the street is the Jihadists did it all on their own. Both the shipping and the bombing. But remember, more than half the people in Yemen are Sunni, and they don't much like the Iranians or any other Shiites. So who knows what the police and the CIA beat out of these guys. Or even if they were really in Jihad." Or, in always-fractured Yemen, who the police really were and what the CIA had to do with it.

"So what do you think?"

Al-Mahdi shrugged. "Look, nobody knows for sure what happened. Akbar is a Sunni, but the big deal with Jihad in Yemen is it takes in people from any sect. That's his thing. Always got along fine with me and the other Shiites in Dearborn. Used to tell us if a Jew and a Christian like Friedman and Oosterbaan could play football together, why couldn't all Muslims cooperate. Now he thinks he's the next great prophet, the one who's going to unite the Islamic world. He'll be caliph of us all."

"Would he blow up the Mall of America?"

Samy squinted and contemplated the question. "So far they've only attacked Americans in Muslim countries. Nothing over here or in Europe. Won't work with al Qaeda because they're anti-Shiite. Same for ISIS and al-Nusra and all the other Qaeda spinoffs. But maybe the idea we'd target him with a drone kinda pissed him off. Maybe now he is out to get even."

"Wouldn't he want to make sure we knew it was him, then? Why hasn't he taken credit?"

"Hell, Skipper, I don't know. I haven't seen Sami or spoken with him in almost twenty years." He paused a few seconds. "But what I do know for damn sure is I don't give a rip what the CIA says anymore. Not since Gronkowski took over."

Stromdahl stood up and walked over to the window wall. He spoke while staring westward in the general direction of the Agency's headquarters. "Samy, we've got to find out what really happened, who's really behind the bombs." After a few seconds he returned to his seat and looked square into Al-Mahdi's eyes.

"Look, I'm not sure exactly how, but the container has something to do with the malls. It's the key. And if we don't figure it out, the crazies over here who want to nuke Iran are going to take over and we'll have a war that could blow up half the world. I need for you to go to Yemen to track down who sent it and why."

"What! Like how the hell am I supposed to do that?"

Stromdahl tilted his head a bit to the side and held his hands interlaced in front of his stomach. "You speak the language. You have the right accent. You've been there a million times. You've still got family there. Who else is going to do it?"

"And what if I find it was Iran? Then things blow up anyway."

"Maybe. But if we find some real proof on Iran we can get the Russians to help us. And the Chinese. And Europe. And then we won't go nuclear. The crazies here are just itching to pull the atomic trigger, like they think they can solve everything with one big bang. They say it'll help Israel, but the Israelis know better. It's their neighborhood, too, and they'd like to keep living there."

Samy shook his head no. "What did I say when you walked in?"

Stromdahl ignored the refusal and pressed on. He now needed the good Samy more than ever. And the recruitment would not be as easy as the first time. Then he had a grand plan and a grand mission. Now he was just fishing for the truth, and maybe asking Al-Mahdi to get the goods on the bad Sami, his one-time best friend and teammate.

IF ASKED WHAT had led him to Dearborn and Al-Mahdi in the first place, Stromdahl probably would have traced it to the female corporal from Camp Porcupine and what she had told him about the battle a few months after it was over. Her name was Linda Ferrell. He had met her a second time when they were both in rehab. Back then his big worry was walking again, a chance he'd almost lost when he got back to the aircraft carrier and into the clutches of the Navy doctors.

The two surgeons in the carrier's operating room wanted to amputate his leg right away. Shattered beyond repair, they said. No chance to save it. But they made the mistake of speaking in his presence while he was still awake and their backs were turned. Before they saw him move he'd pulled the IV tubes from his arm and loosened the straps that held him onto the gurney. Without a bit of clothing to hide his bulging torso or the shredded leg, he hopped behind them and yanked them up simultaneously by their collars; much more forcefully than he'd yanked on the corpsman back at Camp Porcupine.

"If I wake up without a leg, I'll kill you both. I swear it." He was leaning back against a bulkhead for support, but his grip had tightened, and one of the doctors was struggling to breathe. When a sailor ran over to help, the look from Stromdahl stopped him cold. "You too," he glared.

He glanced down at the bleeding flesh below his knee. Hamburger. But everything remained attached and he was going to keep it that way. The doctor who could still breathe tried to reason with him. "Only guys who might save it are at Navy Med. But by the time you got there the swelling and stiffness would make it impossible." He wiggled to free himself a little and tried to cajole Stromdahl into a morphine shot to deaden the pain before they put him under for the bone saw.

It didn't work. Stromdahl banged him against a hatch and said he wasn't taking a single injection till he was on a plane heading home. Okay, the doctor muttered, and even under duress he sounded sincere. Okay, okay. But for Stromdahl to have any chance, he would have to keep the leg elevated for the entire trip. And he could take no sedation for the pain.

"How long to get there?"

"Least a day. You'll have to change planes in Germany."

He relaxed his grip on both collars, but not completely. "Now that's better. Set it up and get me fucking outta here. Ice the damn thing down and get me on the plane." From his football days he knew how to handle injuries as well as anyone. This one was nothing new or different.

CORPORAL FERRELL had wounds from head to toe, but the only big problem was her shoulder, shredded almost as bad as Stromdahl's knee and leg. Though he didn't know it, she, too, was on the plane to Germany and then the second plane back to the States. And her story was no less heroic than his.

For the fiercely anti-female Taliban, the school had been more of a target than the mud-walled compound, which probably was why the lead tank had headed for the village and ignored the fort. But the first sergeant had made the Marines assigned to guard the building dig in deep, and they held their own for half an hour. Then three went down when a rocket hit their bunker, and two more when grenades found their foxholes. Soon there were only four left, plus Linda, who was the only noncom still in action. She grabbed the rifle of one of the fallen and joined the others to return fire. She also got on the radio and directed mortars and machine guns from the compound, which slowed the charge, and allowed them to hold on even longer.

Inside the remains of the building Meena and five girls who were sleeping over hugged the earthen floor and turned the desks on their sides, as if the inch-thick wood might stop the bullets. Meena was hit in the head and died instantly, and two of the girls were severely wounded. Yet except for the young teacher they all survived.

The Marines were less lucky. In the end ten were killed and Linda and the other two were both shot up badly. But they continued firing back, often at point-blank range. The bodies piled in front of them provided cover that let them keep fighting. And just when they were down to their last two clips of ammunition the planes arrived and the enemy fled. A corpsman found Linda not far from Meena's body, passed out from loss of blood, but still alive.

THE NAVY MED hospital in Bethesda sat atop a grassy knoll. The main building was a concrete tower so gleaming white it looked like a marble monument or some kind of outsized temple. Stromdahl and Ferrell were on the sixteenth floor, which had a solarium placed on the west side to maximize exposure to the afternoon sun. "Like a damn greenhouse," an old gunnery sergeant groused. "Like they think we're plants and need light to grow or something." He'd lost a leg to a roadside bomb near Kandahar, and no amount of sun would ever grow him a new one. Which was no big deal, he said, because he'd been wanting to retire even before the blast, and didn't really need two legs anymore. He spent his days hobbling the halls on crutches or napping in one of the solarium's wicker chairs, an overly cheerful short timer suddenly and strangely at peace with the world.

Stromdahl and Ferrell didn't have it so good. They now lived lives of reconstructive and rehabilitative pain and only occasionally got to bask in the restorative sunlight. Not until their third week did they realize they were together again. It was a Saturday afternoon, and they'd temporarily escaped from their therapists to the solarium. Both of them were watching the Gunny flirt with his nurses. Who, he asked, wanted to come take care of him when he retired to Montana? It was clear that medical attention, cooking, and housework were not the subject of his inquiry.

"Gunny's old school," Stromdahl laughed. "The kind you hate to lose." He said it to one of the nurses, who rolled her eyes at the blatant sexism, but when he spoke Linda recognized his voice and saw he was the captain she'd briefly met a month earlier.

"Sir, were you at Camp Porcupine?"

For the first time he looked at her closely, and replied with an exclamation. "Damn! You're the corporal who came with the schoolteacher." He stared at her chest to make out her name.

"Yes sir. Corporal Ferrell, sir."

"I heard you saved the day."

"No sir. I survived the night. A lot didn't."

It took them a few days to get past the formalities of rank and the traumas of their memories, and only then did they really talk about all that had happened. Late one afternoon, again in the solarium, she told him about Meena, who was only seventeen, and trusted the Marines would keep her safe. "We were together for five days before we came to Porcupine, and she was really neat. She and her mother ran away to Pakistan after she got caught with a book. At first we couldn't understand each other. A year in language school just gets you started. But I learned more Pashto from her in less than a week than all my time in Monterey."

Stromdahl was sitting with a book on his lap, just staring at the cold, clear winter sky when she first spoke. "I was never much for languages," he mused. "Some Norwegian, maybe. Went there five or six summers when I was a kid. Stayed with cousins. But they all wanted to learn English. So I picked up less of their language than I should have." He chuckled at the memory. "Kinda pissed off my granddad when I got back home the first time."

She continued as if he hadn't spoken. "Know what she told me? Right when the shooting started?"

No. How could he?

"She said the girls had warned her. They told her the interpreter was Taliban. He set it all up."

"So why didn't she tell us?"

Linda teared up, and her voice quavered. "She did. I just didn't understand. She tried to tell me about the attack, and I didn't get it. And now they want to give me a medal." She was sobbing out of control, totally overcome with guilt about all who had died, but especially the woman who would have saved them if only they had listened better. And if they'd tried harder to understand.

THE MEDALS TURNED out to be a big deal for both of them. He had to talk her into taking the Navy Cross, and the Commandant himself came to talk Stromdahl into accepting the Medal of Honor. He and the private who fell on the grenade got it, but not the other two who ventured out from the compound to destroy the tanks. And not Corporal Ferrell.

"Makes no sense," he told the Commandant. "They killed their tank and they get the Navy Cross. We screwed up and missed ours, and we get the Medal of Honor. And without Ferrell everyone at the school would have been killed. It's not right."

They were alone together in the office of the admiral who ran Navy Med. The Commandant was a precise and compact Annapolis grad whose big worry was the anti-war fallout if someone like Stromdahl refused a medal. He was seated at the desk, and Stromdahl, with the help of crutches, stood before him, in uniform for the first time since the battle. All pressed and proper except for the slit in the right trouser leg to allow room for the fixator wrapped around the leg like some kind of strange combination of scaffolding and a bird cage. On the inside the leg and knee were held together with a million plates and screws, and the x-rays looked like pictures of an odds-and-ends bin from a hardware store.

The Commandant knitted his fingers together and pushed his thumbs against his chin, his face taut with well-controlled but ill-concealed displeasure. After a short silence, he put his hands back down flat on the desk and audibly exhaled. "Captain, you were the leader," he said. "You inspired the others. And killing a tank is not the same as jumping on a grenade." It came out as more of an order than an argument intended to persuade. Commandants weren't much into arguing and persuading.

Stromdahl didn't budge or speak. He relented only when the dead private's mother said she would refuse her son's medal unless the captain accepted his. She came to see him when he was recovering from his third surgery. Her name was Amelia Hernandez, and she had the residual traces of a Mexican accent from the south of Texas. She was a small, careworn woman. Not much older than Stromdahl, and already she'd raised and lost her oldest child. The boy had been so proud of being a Marine, she told him. And he revered his company commander like a god. "Luis would have run through a stone wall for you," she said when they met in his hospital room.

He reached up from the bed and took her hand. "I think he did a lot more than that." They both were crying, and after she left he called Marine Headquarters to say he'd changed his mind.

CHAPTER 7

The carnage of Camp Porcupine and the madness of the medals almost drove him out of the Corps. "Like the Charge of the Light Brigade," he told Sally when she called to check on him. "Sent us out there with slingshots, then called it a victory and sold us all as heroes. Bullshit."

"Well, if I remember right, David had a slingshot and he was a big-time hero. Right? And he won. Like you did."

"He won because his slingshot worked. All we did was shoot pebbles at tanks and chase the goats across the road. Our guys are still out there fighting. Hell, still tryin' to find the enemy. It's bullshit."

She didn't quite know what to say next, and so for several seconds said nothing. In the years between their senior year split and his deployment to Afghanistan they had not talked often. Every few months at most, like when he called after she got elected to the city council while still in law school at the U, and again when she ran for mayor at the precocious age of twenty-eight and won. And when he made captain his mother told her mother, who nagged Sally to at least send congratulations in an e-mail. All four parents had figured they'd get married, and the mothers never quite gave up on the dream of multiple grandchildren crashing every academic and athletic record in Minnesota, if not the world.

SALLY'S FATHER was less enthusiastic. He always hoped she'd find a Catholic. Not that his own family history was any paradigm of ethnic or religious purity. His great-grandfather was a Scottish Presbyterian of indifferent piety who emigrated to America at the age of seventeen to escape the legal consequences of a drinking binge in Glasgow.

In order to avoid getting shipped back, Robert Macalester quickly declared his intent to become an American citizen, and as a reward for this newfound love of the U.S., a year later he got drafted into the Union Army. A Minié ball at Gettysburg nearly cost him an arm, and while recovering in a makeshift Army hospital near the battlefield he met a wounded corporal from Minnesota who told him about the flourmills at St. Anthony Falls. Right downtown in Minneapolis, the corporal said, on both banks of the Mississippi. And much in need of skilled workers. He was certain an apprentice millwright from Scotland could easily find employment there as a full-fledged journeyman.

Robert settled into his new job but remained single until 1881, when at the age of thirty-nine he converted to Catholicism and married the daughter of an Italian co-worker. That was the same year Pillsbury, his employer, opened its "A" Mill on the east bank of the river. The biggest mill in the biggest flour-producing city in the whole wide world. Boom times for all, but also bad. Labor became a commodity like wheat or corn or sand, and the long dusty hours toiling to serve the milling machines were unsoftened by any personal contact with the owners. And the machines, always dangerous and never forgiving, could in an instant snatch off a man's hand or arm, or kill him outright.

Thus did Robert go on strike, and thus did he find himself out of work and scraping by on whatever odd jobs he could get. Broke, broken, and dispirited, he died a few years later, a few days short of fifty. But his son, Robert Jr., trod undeterred in his footsteps and grew up to become a union organizer and a founding member of the Farmer-Labor Party. He married an Eastern Orthodox Lithuanian, and this time it was she who converted. Their son, Sally's grandfather, helped unionize the autoworkers at the Ford plant in St. Paul and worked with a young Hubert Humphrey to merge the Democratic and Farmer-Labor Parties. He married a Baptist who refused to convert.

So on the paternal side of Sally's family tree there was no

great history of marriage to birthright Catholics. In truth, her father was the only exception to the non-Catholic spouse rule. His parents, the Catholic and the Baptist, had struck a deal whereby their first child would be raised Catholic, the second Baptist, and so forth. Sally's father was the eldest of an eventual seven, and she often wondered if it was not this odd religious schism that made him so committed to the Church he inherited only based on birth order. He went to high school at De LaSalle and college at St. Thomas, and his first real foray away from the bosom of his faith was grad school at Harvard, where he met Sally's mother at Easter mass.

The newly married couple returned to Minnesota, where he taught labor economics at the University and made five quixotic runs at the DFL nomination to represent his district in Congress. The district included the U and was just about the most liberal place on the planet. He railed against the moral decline of America and ran as an anti-abortion Democrat, and always got less than five percent of the vote. But he never departed from his Democratic and union roots. His wife would have divorced him if he had, and probably would have done him grave bodily harm as well. She was the one girl in a family of eleven raised by Irish immigrant parents who left the Emerald Isle right after World War II, and her views on the Church were far more selective and practical than his. In twentieth century America three children were quite enough, she said, and she had no problem using birth control to stay within this limit. She assured her husband the Pope would never find out.

This mix of religious and cultural memes doomed Sally to politics and independence as surely as Walleye Stromdahl's genes doomed him to be tall, and his family history doomed him to be a Marine. Maybe that's why the two of them could never bend the tracks of their lives to converge.

HER CALL to Navy Med was, for once, purely Sally's doing, not something urged on her by her mother. Just to make sure Walleye was going to be all right, of course. Nothing more. They were done, pulled apart by the competing demands of law school and the Corps, and ambitions that would never play second fiddle to anyone. So when she popped out the invitation to come to Minneapolis it surprised her more than him. He said he'd had it with the Corps and thought maybe he wanted to leave, and she said well then, come visit to get away from it all and think things through. What she really hoped for she didn't know, or wouldn't admit.

"You can stay with me. I got a new condo on the East Bank, just north of the U. Corner unit on the fifteenth floor. You can see the whole city across the river."

"Yeah?"

"Yeah. You can take the guest room. Just chill. Go drive around campus. Take a walk if you can. Like old times. Maybe what you need." What else was he going to do?

Go see his family, of course. On the dairy farm north of Bemidji, where the Mississippi begins and Paul Bunyan supposedly once lived.

Had he told them yet he was coming?

No.

"Then come to Minneapolis instead. What you gonna do in Bemidji in March? The thaw doesn't start there till the Fourth of July."

WHEN SHE PICKED him up at the airport Friday afternoon she could not believe how thin he was; how his uniform flopped around his body like an unstaked tent about to blow to the ground in a wind storm. And because of the crutches she had to carry his bag and help him into the car. It was only ten degrees above zero, and wind-driven snow beat against the windshield as she inched along in the evening traffic.

Back at the condo he sat in the love seat by the fireplace while she started to make dinner. A special curry recipe he always liked when they lived together off campus, something their Pakistani neighbor had taught her to do. Stromdahl stared intently at the burning birch logs and poked them once or twice to keep the flames high. She put the curry on the stovetop and came to sit next to him, a foot away with no contact and not a thing to say.

He finally reached over and took her hand and said thanks for having him. He prodded the fire again and leaned back as much as his leg allowed. He still wore a fixator and couldn't move it much. Another minute or two passed, and then he asked how she liked being mayor.

She tugged her hand free, wrapped her arm around his neck

and pulled him close for a long, deep kiss. Then she pushed him back a few inches and said being mayor was great. She loved it. Minneapolis was a great city. He should come back and live there.

He looked her straight in the eyes and let his hand slip from behind her neck down her side, and then along her arm, so they were holding hands again. Then he turned his head back to the fire, used his free arm to poke the logs once more, and stared at the flames. "Not sure what's next," he said. "Maybe go live on a beach in Mexico."

She laughed. They'd once gone to Cancun on spring break, and he hated it. The weather turned bad and he wasn't much into recreational drinking or nightclubs. And when they rented a car to go see Mayan ruins he got lost and almost ran off the road in the dark. So they'd spent a lot of time in bed, and for that they didn't need to go to Mexico. "Really," she said as tactfully as possible. "You really goin' back to Mexico?"

He said nothing and clambered up on his crutches to go look out the window at the brightly lit buildings across the Mississippi in downtown Minneapolis. She was right. He could see the clock tower on City Hall. And the big white balloon roof of the Metrodome, where he'd played so many football games. One year Minnesota had Michigan and Ohio State at home when they were both having down years and somehow managed to beat them both. It was the U's best season while he was there, but the team still finished only 8-5 after losing its bowl game.

When he turned around to rejoin her on the love seat she was gone. Her blouse lay on the cushion, her bra on the floor a few feet away. The trail of discarded clothes led straight to her bedroom, where the door was open and only the nightlight was on. He followed her in, leaned the crutches against the wall, and fell into bed beside her. She helped him undress, and snuggled up close for a big hug and a bigger kiss, then lay on top of him, her breasts within inches of his face as she ran her fingers across his close-cropped head.

It took them a few minutes and lots of nervous laughter to figure out how to deal with the fixator, but they managed. And when they were done he fell fast asleep and she got up to dispose of the overcooked curry and try to figure out what the hell she'd just done.

In between sex and sleep they left the condo only twice that weekend. Once for the promised ride around the campus and once to go to a movie at the theatre on Main Street, only a block from her building. Not till Sunday morning did she raise again the question of what he might do when he healed up and left the Marines. His answer set off all the old conflict and discord.

"I think I'm staying in to fix it," he said.

They were lying together in bed, naked after making love, and she sat up and stared down at him and tried hard to neither cry nor yell nor throw him out. And even then, at some level she was half-glad. The Corps is what he loved most, and he'd never be happy without it. She'd lost out again, but it was a fight she couldn't really win. She got up and put on a pair of jeans and a sweatshirt, then sat down on the edge of the bed, where he lay propped up on two pillows with his hands clasped behind his head, trying like hell to avoid her eyes.

He felt like shit, certain she'd think he'd deceived her when he accepted her invitation, which wasn't true. He had come back with every hope they could start again, and he deeply wished they could. But the memory of Luis Hernandez haunted every second of his life and compelled him to make right what had gone so wrong on the south bank of the Dori. And much as he loved her, that's what he had to do.

She bent over and gave him a mother-in-law's kiss, and he got up and pulled on a pair of pants baggy enough to accommodate the damned fixator. He didn't bother with a shirt. "Come on," she said. "Let's have breakfast."

In the kitchen she boiled water for the coffee maker and for instant oatmeal, and watched as he sprinkled brown sugar and raisins onto the gooey blob in the bowl before he added milk. When they started living together he'd told her that back on the farm his mother always called it Paul Bunyan cereal to make it seem more palatable, and the breakfast habit if not the hokey name had stuck with him just as the oatmeal stuck to his ribs. Sally couldn't stand the stuff and even now wrinkled her nose.

"So what exactly you gonna do?" she asked.

He took a long drink of coffee, set down the cup, and fixed his eyes on the tabletop as he tried to say his answer right. "The medal's a crock," he began. "A helluva lot more than I deserve. But it lets me pick what I do next. The Commandant wants me to go to the White House as an aide, but I figure I'll go to personnel in headquarters to do some recruiting."

"There's a shortage of Marines?" By every account she'd read, all the military services were swamped with volunteers after the 9/11 attacks. Especially the Corps. Even pro athletes were signing up. Why the heck would he go into recruiting?

At this he began to warm to the task before him, and to explaining it to his one-time soul mate. "Yeah, we get plenty of volunteers, but not many who speak Arabic or Pashto or Dari. Not many who can smell the food and tell you if it's local. Or hear an accent and tell if it's not." Or who would know when an interpreter was about to betray them. He told her the story of Corporal Ferrell, who could speak the language but didn't understand the ebb and flow and texture of the places it was spoken.

"So where do you plan to recruit people who do?"

Dearborn, he said. Dearbornistan, where half the families originally came from the Middle East. It was 2002 and the next invasion was clearly in view. Iraq. And this time he wanted to have Marines who could read the cultural terrain as well as they could read a contour map. He was going to learn Arabic and he also was going to recruit people who could speak it without a Midwest accent.

THE STAFF SERGEANT in charge of the Dearborn recruiting station gave him an odd look, part skeptical, part bemused, and wished him luck. "They don't join. Not their thing. Hell, I think half of 'em thought 9/11 was a good thing."

The newly promoted Major Stromdahl shook his head no. "If we act like we don't want them, know what, they won't want us."

The sergeant, whose name was Adams, was almost as big as Stromdahl. He was a New York City African American, dyed-in-the-wool cynical and tough as a grizzly's toenails. "Yes sir," he said, "but that ain't always true. The Corps didn't want black folks, and we fought like hell to get in. And we don't take gays, but they're fighting like hell to get in. So I'll do whatever you say, but I'm not thinking we'll make much of a dent just by makin' nice if folks don't want any part of us."

"Not just making nice. Giving them a chance to be special, to teach us so we don't piss people off because we don't understand them. Ever read *Moby Dick*?"

Adams nodded his head yes. At least he started it. Three times for his English course in junior college. "Didn't pass," he said. "Part of the reason I ended up in the Corps." And anyway, what did *Moby Dick* have to do with recruiting Arabs into the military?

"Ah. Thought you might ask. You know Queequeg was the harpooner, right? From an island in the Pacific?"

"Yeah."

"You remember the wheelbarrow?"

"Wheelbarrow?"

"Yeah. Queequeg told the story to Ishmael. How he was given a wheelbarrow to get his sailing chest onto a ship, and how he didn't know what it was for. So he lashed the chest to the barrow, then picked up the whole shebang and carried it aboard instead of using the wheel."

"So?"

"So Ishmael asks if people laughed, and Queequeg says no. And then he told another story about how a ship's captain came to his island and washed his hands in a sacred bowl of coconut milk. 'My people didn't laugh,' he said. 'It wasn't funny.'"

Sergeant Adams nodded his understanding. He might have flunked *Moby Dick* in school, but he got the story now. And he got the Major's message, if not all the proper pronunciation. "So you're lookin' for some Key Kegs to keep us outta the coconut milk when we go bustin' into villages. That the idea?"

STROMDAHL FIRST MET the two Samirs in the West Dearborn High gym, right after basketball practice. Adams came along to introduce him. "If you're really serious 'bout this shit, they're your top-two recruiting targets," he said as they drove over.

"How so?"

Easy. The standard reasons were all there. High school athletes who were well liked by all. As American as could be. Al-Mahdi's grandfather had served in the Army during World War II, and his father in the Marines during Vietnam. The grandfather had come over from Yemen in the late 20s, just a year before the Wall Street crash, and except for the war he spent his entire working life on the Ford assembly line. His son, Samy's father, also worked at Ford.

"What about their Arabic?"

Adams took his right hand from the wheel, and his thumb

went straight up. "They've both gone back to Yemen pretty regular to visit family. So they're fluent as hell." He went silent for a second or two as he pulled into a visitor's parking space in the school parking lot, then continued talking as they walked to the building's front door. "The one you really want most is Akbar. Born over there, but came here when he was three or four. And he's all gung ho 'bout the Corps, 'cept he says he might go to Western Michigan and try out for the football team instead."

They checked in with the vice principal, who sent them straight to the gym. "That them over there?" Stromdahl pointed to two young men sitting by themselves in the first row of the only section of bleachers pulled down from the gym walls during practice. A few of the other players were still shooting baskets, and one of the two in the bleachers caught a stray ball and threw it back to his teammates. When he turned his head after tossing the ball he spotted the Marine uniforms and waved them over.

"That's them," Adams affirmed.

One of the Samirs stood up and stuck out his hand. "Samir Al-Mahdi," he told Stromdahl. He pointed to his seated companion. "He's Samir Akbar." Al-Mahdi explained that even though both last names technically began with "A," their coaches called him "Samy M" and Akbar "Sami A." "That's how we know who they're yelling at."

"Sarge here tells me you all might want to become Marines."

Samy and Sami replied in unison. "Depends."

"He tell you we got a special mission in mind?"

"Told us you were coming. Said it was a big deal for an officer to be recruiting us." This time only Al-Mahdi spoke.

Adams jumped in with his newfound understanding of the major's objective. "You all read *Moby Dick* yet?" he asked.

Neither of them had, and Akbar had never even heard of it. So Stromdahl made the point more directly. The Marines needed people who understood all the quirks and habits of the Middle East and the Islamic world. People who would not blunder and offend, and who could keep other Marines from blundering and offending. "We want to have someone like that with every platoon. On every patrol. Everywhere we go."

"Like spies?" Sami A did not like that idea.

"No. More like teachers." It was the first time Stromdahl had put it that way. Teachers. That's what he was looking for. People who could teach both ways; teach both their fellow Marines and the strange foreign peoples the Marines wanted to befriend.

"So we gotta go to boot camp and all?" This prospect did not entice Al-Mahdi.

"Like all Marines," the sergeant jumped in sternly. In the Corps there were no shortcuts. After boot camp they'd have to go through infantry training too.

"Do we get dress blues," Akbar asked.

"Only if you make Pfc right out of boot camp."

Later that year both of them did.

CHAPTER 8

After meeting in the Georgetown library with Samy Al-Mahdi on the morning of the twenty-fourth, Stromdahl took a narrow path that led from the campus down a steep, rocky hillside to Canal Road. There were stairs only on the worst parts, and the snow made footing doubly treacherous everywhere. He grabbed tree branches and the stairway railings to keep his balance, and even so slipped and fell twice. When he reached the bottom he went east to where Canal merged into M Street, then slogged across through the slush and continued southward about a hundred yards to a gravel trail that paralleled the Chesapeake and Ohio Canal along its north bank. Snow covered the trail, and only a few footprints, spaced far apart, marred the whiteness. Runners, he figured.

Before railroads rendered it obsolete and the passage of time rendered it quaint, the canal was supposed to follow the Potomac to its source deep in the Appalachians, then cross the mountains to reach the Ohio. It never got beyond Cumberland, in Western Maryland, but continued operating until 1924. Here in Georgetown it ran between the drab brick-and-concrete backsides of buildings old and new, which hemmed it in like the walls of a ravine. About four blocks east of the university it went under

Wisconsin Avenue, and then in quick succession through Lock 4 and Lock 3, near Thomas Jefferson Street.

There was a small park with several benches next to Lock 3, and when Stromdahl reached it he checked to make sure he was alone and swiped the snow from one of the benches with his right arm. Then he pulled out his mini-tablet device and sat down to read the latest issue of *Sports Illustrated* while he waited. He preferred something a little bigger than just a smart phone; something big enough to accommodate his oversize fingers, yet small enough to carry in a coat pocket. Unlike some of his earlier devices, this one had both phone and tablet capabilities.

Not five minutes after he sat down a man dressed like a winter ad from the L.L. Bean website carefully traversed the ice-slick section of the trail that sloped downward from Jefferson Street to the canal. He wore a leather bomber hat with flaps that covered his ears, a dark blue down-filled jacket, and a pair of heavy brown corduroy pants. And, of course, the famous boots with leather uppers and rubber covering on the bottom part.

The man looked to be a tad over six feet tall and had a classic Nordic face. He was athletic but not bulky, likely in his late forties or early fifties. He swiveled his head to confirm there was no one else but the two of them in the immediate area, brushed additional snow off the bench to make more space, and sat down next to Stromdahl. Once seated he peered over to see what was on the tablet. "So Minnesota gonna win it all?"

Stromdahl continued to read and answered without turning to look at his new bench mate. "Of course. No way we'll lose." He shut down the tablet, stuck it back into his coat pocket, and stood up. Only then did he make eye contact. "Merry Christmas, Sven. Let's go for a little walk. Get away from anyone who might be curious." He pointed to the west, back toward the university, to indicate the direction they should take.

Sven Swenson nodded his agreement with a look on his face that betrayed the mix of aggravation and curiosity running through his mind. It was only hours from Christmas Eve. His daughter and new grandson were in town. And he didn't need this spy-novel melodrama bullshit. What was wrong with his office? Or Wally's? After all, Wally was the Marine Corps Commandant, and Swenson was Chief of Naval Operations.

He'd only agreed to the meeting because the two of them went back a long way, with a lot more in common than not. He came from Michigan, ancestrally via Sweden and academically via the University of Michigan and the Naval Academy as a transfer student. About two years after the invasion of Iraq he'd just made Commander and was serving at the Pentagon when a mutual friend introduced him to another Midwestern Scandinavian, a Marine Lt. Colonel and former Minnesota football player.

Stromdahl remembered it all quite well, especially how the friend assumed a Swedish Swenson and a Norwegian Stromdahl would naturally hit it off. At their introductory cafeteria lunch his mind flashed to the old ditty taught at an early age to everyone in his family. A thousand Swedes ran through the weeds, chased by one Norwegian. He kept it to himself, however, and silently started eating his soup.

Swenson was less reticent about their differences in ethnic origin, and right away preemptively blurted out the Swedish counter version of the ditty. "A Swede there was, ran through the weeds, chasing ten Norwegians."

Stromdahl kept spooning his soup and didn't rise to the bait. Whatever wars they'd fought against each other in Europe, in the New World all Scandinavians more or less banded together. Hell, his sister had married a Swede, and the most serious and best of the few drunks in Stromdahl's life was when he matched shots of aquavit with his new brother-in-law at the bachelor party. Besides, he couldn't help but like Swenson, who could have passed for a Norwegian sea captain and had a mind as tough and sharp as a Swedish steel knife blade. At the time of their first meeting they were both newly returned from the war in Iraq and shared an intense commitment to finding better strategies for combat in the Middle East. As Stromdahl liked to say, fewer footprints, heavier steps.

It took them several years to develop their doctrine and sell it to the brass. And by then they were the brass. The idea was simple—small forces equipped with overwhelming weapons and deployed only in a small area and for a small quantum of time. It proved perfect for the fragmented landscape left behind in the countries the U.S. once tried to occupy or control. Since Bush's failed attempt to remake Iraq in the image of Texas, and Obama's equally failed efforts to hold the mess together, the country had split into three separate and loosely affiliated parts, which mercifully did violence mostly to each other and not their neighbors or the United States. At least not yet. Afghanistan, Pakistan, and Syria were even worse, nominally still unified countries, but divided into ill-defined fractious pieces, led by warlords who formed endlessly fluid alliances and fought ceaselessly with each other over even more fluid borders.

The feuding tribes and regions were without any real government that could sustain fighter jets or fancy radars or even tanks or big artillery. ISIS had a few tanks and big guns, but could not really maintain them. So a properly supported and reinforced Marine company or battalion could take and hold any piece of ground it chose, and if missions were limited in time and locality, the enemy could not respond. At the very most it might require a division.

The objective was not to re-make Muslim countries, only to keep the bad ones at bay until they evolved into something better. And if they didn't evolve, to do nothing that would make things worse. The Bush crowd had never grasped the reality of terrorism—that it could be minimized and kept at the gate, but never destroyed. At least not simply with military might. This kind of war required the wisdom and judgment to strike just the right balance. Too much force only increased hatred of the West, too little created disrespect and scorn. And in between there was no perfection.

"THE BIGGEST FLAW was always Iran," Swenson said as they retraced in reverse Stromdahl's route along the towpath. "And now it's finally bit us in the ass." Throughout the Bush and Obama Wars, Iran remained intact, adept at making its own weapons or buying from facilitators like China or on the black market. It was a country always spoiling for a fight. And nothing changed when American troops departed its neighbors, Iraq and Afghanistan. That's what finally led to the ill-fated Israeli reactor raid and more recently the malls. Swenson held not a shred of doubt.

Stromdahl stopped, made a snowball, and flung it against a windowless brick wall on the other side of the canal. "That's Rumbo's story," he said. "And the Republicans', but the evidence ain't really all that great. Look, it's easy to blame Mohanjani. Almost too easy. Why rush in to start a nuclear war when we can wait and make sure?"

"So that's what you dragged me out here for? Just to line up my vote when the Joint Chiefs meet next week? Wally, it's cold as hell. My family's in town. I'm gonna be late for Christmas Eve dinner. Get to the damn point." They had not resumed walking, and Swenson glanced back toward Wisconsin Avenue and the two locks. He took half a step in that direction but no more.

Stromdahl bent over to pick up the makings of another snowball, but this time simply crunched the snow together and held it in his right hand. He took a deep breath and then took the leap out of bounds. "Sven, who did you vote for last time?"

Swenson stared at him and waited to let a young couple jog past, headed westward. "Bad question. Is this all about Sally Macalester? She put you up to this?" He knew about Stromdahl's past history with the President. How they went way back to their college days, drifted apart for a while, and then went off and on for years and years after Stromdahl's return from Afghanistan. Even when she was in the Senate. Mayor Macalester had come to visit him in 2005 during his first tour at the Pentagon, and they'd all gone out to dinner together. Sally, Wally, Swenson, and his wife.

"Yeah, I guess it's about Sal. But not her and me. I gotta know. Did you vote for her?"

The CNO shook his head yes, but his eyes had the wary look of an animal backed into a corner, simultaneously watching its attacker and looking for an escape route. "Yes I did. And if you're tryin' to convince me the impeachment stuff's a crock, I agree. Obviously. And I'm with you on going slow with Iran till we've got all the facts. But that's not exactly what we're here for, is it?"

"Yes and no. Big thing is Gronkowski and the CIA aren't pushing on any theory but Mohanjani and Iran. And . . ." He paused a second or two, uncertain how best to broach the mission he'd taken on for the President and his plan to send Samir Al-Mahdi to Yemen.

Swenson didn't give him time to gather up the loose ends of the explanation. "Yeah, they decided it's Iran because they caught the bastards who sent the container. And because the bastards admitted the Iranians put them up to it."

"Come on. Three days after the mall bombs and they already know for certain who did it? You know that's crap. Are you really ready to go nuclear on Iran because the CIA got a few stringers to beat confessions out of some sorry-ass shipping clerks in Yemen?

The NSA hasn't got a thing to back them up. Nothing. DeSales says they're pretty well tapped into Iran, and they haven't picked up anything except they're asking each other who did it, just like we are."

"So Yemen's run by thugs. What's new? They got rid of one guy back in 2011 and then had a coup in 2015, which lasted till we and the Saudis arranged for a new thug a few years ago. But they're our allies over there, and we're stuck with them. I can't fix that. Neither can you. And I said I was all for going slow, and waiting for NSA to corroborate. But look, the story makes sense, doesn't it? Iran's pissed because of the reactor raid. The Jihad guys are pissed because of Akbar. They team up and boom go the malls. Yes, I want more evidence, but I'll bet that's where we end up."

"Except Akbar's alive."

"What?" Swenson's look softened with the first hint he might want to listen instead of get out of the cold and back to his family.

"Akbar's alive."

"Who told you that?" He said it like a parent trying to correct a badly mistaken child.

"Samir Al-Mahdi."

"The Georgetown guy?"

"Yeah."

"How the hell does he know?"

"His family's from Yemen, so he's got his ear to the ground. Or he talks to people who do. Used to be a Marine. One of the Arab-Americans I recruited. Maybe the best one. He and Akbar grew up together in Dearborn."

Swenson's look went hard again. "Yeah, and you recruited Akbar too." Sami A's history of betrayal was known to anyone who even vaguely followed the news. The All-American kid who joined the Marines to help fight terrorism, then became a terrorist himself. Legend had it he was a fanatical Islamic zealot who intended all along to defect once he became a trained killer courtesy of the Corps.

"I did recruit him," Stromdahl admitted. "And I'd probably do it again. I don't know what went wrong. He's the only one, you know. The others worked out better than we ever expected."

Swenson conceded the point. But while the "teachers" had performed brilliantly in the field, their larger mission had failed, and Stromdahl's vision was never realized. When they went on combat patrols with a platoon the number of ambushes and firefights dropped to nearly zero, and the locals treated the Marines almost like cousins. Thing was, there never were enough of these Arab-American cousins to go around, and in the end even they couldn't overcome the anger and resentment always directed at an occupying army. If they were like relatives it was distant relatives at best. They were welcome for a brief visit, but not as permanent guests. Certainly not when they were there to prop up the corrupt "uncles" who were robbing people blind.

Stromdahl dropped the second snowball and jabbed the air with his finger as he strove to get their discussion back on track. Deciding the success or failure of the "teachers" was not the reason for dragging Sven Swenson out into the cold, he said.

"What is it then?"

"I'm sending Al-Mahdi to Yemen to find out what really happened. And I need your help."

"What? Al-Mahdi's going to Yemen? For us?" Swenson's mouth fell half-open, but no further sound emerged for what seemed forever, and his eyes went first wide with amazement, then narrow with skepticism. Had old football injuries to the head finally caught up with the Commandant?

"You heard right. You got a better idea?"

"Yeah. Lots of better ideas. Like first of all anything but sending in an untrained professor who's great buds with a prime suspect. What could possibly go wrong?!"

"No. That's exactly the person we need. Someone who has at least a chance at learning the truth."

Swenson's face softened ever so slightly, and he blew out a huge sigh. "So you want the SEALs to sneak him in? That it?" The question contained no hint this request would be considered, much less granted.

"No. He'll fly commercial, on his nickel, not ours. To keep it all secret and deniable. But I need help keeping in touch with him. And getting him out alive if we have to."

The look on Swenson's face softened a bit more, but only into a sour frown that demanded more details.

"I need a ship or two in the Gulf of Aden to relay messages. And I want a Marine company on board, ready to go in and retrieve him if things get too hot. Maybe take out the bad guys if he finds them."

Swenson shook his head no, and added some choice words

about his friend's sanity and likely court martial. He turned to walk back to the locks, but when Stromdahl shouted for him to wait, he stopped and retraced the few steps he'd taken.

"Listen, Sven, I probably am nuts. And maybe in the end it was Iran that blew up the malls and we do go to war. But either way, if we can prove what happened, we'll have the world on our side. Then we can avoid using nukes. Right now Al-Mahdi's our best chance at getting some proof." He paused as the shock and rejection started to drain from the CNO's face. "And you're right. It's about Sally too. If they toss her out and put in their new constitution this isn't my country anymore. Yours either."

Swenson looked around to double check their solitude. "Wally, this country was never yours or mine to own. Professionally we belong to it, not the other way around. And both of us took an oath to defend it, and the Constitution."

"And now the crazies want to kill the Constitution. That's just the point. They want to pull a coup and scrap what we have and give us a new one based on *Atlas Shrugged* and the Bible."

"No. You're wrong. They're not pulling a coup. They're going by the rules. Exactly what the Constitution allows. That's their right. What you and I are sworn to defend. You want us to do a coup. You know that's wrong."

"So you got no problem if twenty percent of the country pulls off a shitty little legal trick that turns us all into a rightwing nuthouse theocracy? You can accept that?"

"No, of course not. But I get only one vote. Same as anyone else. You're tellin' me we have to break the Constitution to save it. That's a paradox I don't need." He turned and this time started walking more resolutely back to the east.

Stromdahl ran and grabbed him by the shoulder to arrest his escape. "Sven, wait a minute."

Swenson did not resist, and once again rejoined the debate. But his face betrayed neither capitulation nor resignation. Wally damn well better make it quick.

"Listen, you remember when we were in Command and Staff College and they brought in that asshole law professor from Harvard?"

Yes, of course he did. The professor was all bent out of shape that sometimes torture might be necessary, and so there shouldn't be an absolute rule against it. He'd posed the hypothetical of a terrorist who planted an atomic bomb in Manhattan, timed to explode within hours. Wouldn't it be better to torture the location out of him rather than let millions of people die?

Most of the class fell into the trap of debating whether some torture should be legalized. Only Stromdahl and Swenson took a different tack. "If it was my choice," Stromdahl had said, "I'd squeeze the truth from the son of a bitch any way I could, and then hope for leniency at my court martial. But I'd never change the law. I don't want to live in a country where torture is legal."

"So," Swenson now said, "you're saying we send the Marines into Yemen and you and I take the hit if we get caught? That it?"

"Pretty much. Except I don't think there's much 'if' about it. We can probably count on the truth coming out, and then a court martial, not a medal. But it's not a coup if we don't take over the government. It's not a coup if we take our punishment for breaking the rules. It's not a coup to make sure the truth is known instead of hidden by the big lie. How is this any different from a Marine who jumps on top of a grenade to save people? We get embarrassed, maybe go to jail. The Marine dies. Which is worse?"

The CNO stuck out his lower lip and pondered the choices now thrust upon him. By the book he should turn Stromdahl in and be done with it. That he wouldn't do. Using a Navy ship to relay messages as part of an unofficial spying mission was definitely illegal, but also probably not such a big deal. Sending in the Marines would be an act of war, and the court martial likely would not be lenient. Nor, he thought, would the country.

He spoke only after completing this internal calculation. "Wally, you can have your ships. We'll help with the communications. But you and I can't decide when to send in the Marines. That's the President's job, and I gather she's not in on this."

"Not officially. Leave it at that."

"Well then, that's where I have to leave it. You got the ships. You got whatever comm gear you need. But nothing more."

Stromdahl looked down at his feet and kicked the snow. At some level he knew Swenson was right. Bending rules was one thing. But the Constitution, if not holy writ, was sacrosanct, a set of principles that could be changed if necessary, and interpreted by the Supreme Court. But never compromised. He could make do with Swenson's offer, he said. It would be fine. He took his right glove off and stuck out his hand to seal the deal, and Swenson did the same.

When the CNO moved to drop the handshake, Stromdahl held on a second more and put his gloved left hand on Swenson's shoulder and thanked him a second time. Not for the ships, but for refusing the Marines. "Sven, it's a paradox I don't need either."

Swenson smiled. "I know," he said. "And I promise you'll never have to worry about a court martial, because no matter how big and mean you are, I will personally kill you if this goes bad." He added that he'd beat the murder rap by claiming justifiable homicide.

STROMDAHL HAD NOW accomplished two of his missions in Georgetown, but there was a third. After he and Swenson parted ways back at the Lock 3 park he hiked up the Wisconsin Avenue hill into the heart of the shopping district. The shop he sought was on the east side of the avenue, in the long block north of Q Street.

On Sally's 2005 visit to Washington they'd strolled hand-in-hand along the same route, also in the wintertime. They had a mid-morning snack of buttery croissants and cappuccinos at a coffee shop so small the smells seemed doubly concentrated. Customers got the jitters just by taking a deep breath. Then, jolted by the caffeine, they continued their walk and poked into boutiques and antique shops. Near the end of their sojourn they came upon the Box and Clock Chalet. The front window was filled with kitschy cuckoo clocks and cheap music boxes, and he wanted to walk on, but she said it looked like fun and dragged him inside.

At the rear of the shop was a locked case filled with antiques, and she fell in love with a walnut box inlaid with an intricate pattern of ivory, pearl, and lighter woods. The movement played Strauss's "Blue Danube" waltz. The price was five thousand dollars, and she reluctantly handed it back to the store's owner and said maybe when she made her first million.

According to the Internet, the shop was still there, and its website showed an almost identical box at a much higher-than-identical price. The owner was still there as well, and actually remembered long, tall Sally. Only her looks. He had no inkling who she was then or that the woman he'd waited on was now President. He also remembered Stromdahl. "You were in the Marines, right?"

"Yes," he laughed. "Yes, I was."

CHAPTER 9

"You're sending Al-Mahdi?" The question clearly went to the wisdom of the decision, not the simple facts.

"Yeah."

"The guy at Georgetown? The one who writes all the books?"

"Yeah. Who else?"

The President shook her head. Samy's publications were a litany of criticism about U.S. occupations in the Middle East and its once-blind support of supposedly stable dictators. Most people thought he was an apologist for the Islamic terrorists, if not himself a closet bomb thrower. But most had not read the books. The only best seller was his autobiography about growing up Arab-American and his honorable service in the Marine Corps, where his last commanding general tried mightily to send him to Officer Candidate School.

"I chose college instead," he wrote in the introduction, "so I could teach. I wanted to help the people of my country understand the people from my grandparents' country." That's mostly what he tried to do while in the Corps, but there it hadn't worked out too well.

Thus did he understand the enormity of his self-appointed task, and perhaps its ultimate impossibility. At the end of the book he wrote that he was only an intermediary, a man of neither world. "In America I have the looks of an Arab and the traces of an Arab accent, and in Yemen I am merely a fluent foreigner." And yet his last sentences were full of optimism. "I work at a Catholic university that has a business school building donated by a Muslim like me, and which bears his name. I know the two religions can work in harmony. Together they can find a greater understanding of the world than either alone has achieved." Once upon a time he would have said a greater understanding of God, but that was in his past.

Sally had read the best seller and the other books too, and she didn't doubt Samy's sincerity. But neither did she trust what he'd do if forced to choose sides instead of mediate. Surely Stromdahl's investigation and her survival in office didn't come down to a one-man mission by the high school buddy of Samir Akbar, mastermind of countless attacks on American troops and embassies and corporations in the Middle East before the CIA finally took him out.

Stromdahl squirmed in his chair and said Akbar wasn't exactly dead yet. It was a few minutes past four in the afternoon on Christmas Day and they were in Sally's private second-floor office, just the two of them. He hadn't come to the White House for this meeting, only for dinner. She'd asked him to join her parents and siblings and seemingly countless aunts, uncles, nephews, nieces, and cousins for their first White House Christmas. The family filled the big oval Yellow Room on the second floor, drinking holiday punch, admiring the handmade decorations on the tree, and generally swapping well-embellished tall tales about their varied history. The invitation to the Commandant was not Sally's idea but her mother's.

He'd showed up on time, dressed in a brown tweed jacket and a red and green Norwegian Christmas sweater, and brought with him a present wrapped in shiny silver paper dotted with green holly leaves and red holly berries. Most definitely he was not prepared for work, except he had to tell the President about Al-Mahdi. When he whispered to her that he had someone lined up to go to Yemen she was eager to hear all about it, and did not want any of the family to get curious and catch a whiff of what was going on. She set his unopened gift on an end table, grabbed his hand and tugged him out of the room. Her mother, a perpetually cheerful and optimistic retired high school teacher, saw it all and assumed only the best. After more than twenty years she might yet succeed in marrying off her daughter.

"Akbar's what?!" Sally now demanded.

"What I said. Still alive. That's what Samy told me yesterday."

He could see in her face the lightning-quick progression from shock to understanding. In an instant her eyes went big with surprise, then beady small with anger; her jaw slack with disbelief, then set with resolve. It was clear, she said, that if he was still alive Akbar had sent the bombers to avenge whatever slights and insults had driven him to take up terrorism. But if the enemy was now known, the means for retaliation were not. There was no place to invade or bomb, no easily captured person to flay and hang, and thus no way to stave off the Republicans. The government in Yemen, never stable but still a semi-friendly dictatorship after several changes, was already hot after Jihad in Yemen, and sending U.S. troops would more likely cause its fall than prop it up. All of which would only hinder Akbar's capture.

Stromdahl held up his hand to halt her rush to judgment, which was starting to sound too much like the Tea Party. "Slow down. Al-Mahdi says he's certain Akbar's alive and well, but the rest is only rumors spread by people who want it to be him, just like Rumbo wants it to be Iran. Over there in Yemen they think Akbar's a hero and this would be the most heroic thing he's ever done. It's all part of the myth. And myth isn't reality. Not this myth any more than Rumbo's Iran myth."

Her eyes rolled to the ceiling. What was all that supposed to mean? The bomber's old buddy was covering for him, she said. The same old buddy now chosen to do the investigation. In a rare lapse, she broke the no-expletive rule. "Fucking sweet. I can't fucking believe it."

Stromdahl was about to point out that Al-Mahdi never would have mentioned the misdirected drone attack and Akbar's survival if he was in fact trying to cover up for terrorists, but they were interrupted by a knock on the door. "The FBI people are here," a young female aide said. "Should I bring them in?"

"No. We'll meet them downstairs in the Oval Office. Be there in a few minutes."

"What's going on?" Stromdahl asked. "Do I need to leave?"

"No. I told the FBI to come over soon as they had anything to report. Even today. And since I've made you responsible for most everything relating to the mall bombs you need to hear it too. Just as well you're here already."

"So I'm not fired?" He said it with the faintest of smiles, a hint he was kidding. But he wasn't really sure.

She replied with no smile at all. "No. Not yet."

UNLIKE THE **CIA,** the FBI lacked anyone to torture, and in any event didn't have arrangements for rendering suspects to obliging foreign torturers. And unlike the CIA's Gronkowski, who was a certifiable Tea Party nut case, the FBI Director tried to find the truth rather than create it, which probably is why Rumbo kept arguing that the Bureau's investigation didn't matter. The Jihadists in Yemen had confessed all, Rumbo said, and that left no doubt both the container and the bombs were ultimately the work of Iran with a likely assist from Akbar. What difference did it make which specific individuals actually mixed the explosives and drove the bombs to the malls? Of course whoever it was had to be captured and promptly executed, but no need to delay the nuking of Iran over such trivial details.

The Bureau was led by Danny O'Brien, an unflinchingly ethical Washington rarity, admired and trusted by Democrats and old-line Republicans alike. And now the New Progressives too. He served two terms as a moderate Republican Congressman from Pennsylvania before the Tea Party did him in. President Obama then appointed him to the Federal bench, and Sally's Republican predecessor later made him FBI Director. He wore a Marine Corps honorable discharge pin on his lapel and looked like he could still lead an infantry platoon or take the field again as a pint-size quarterback for Princeton. He was only about five six, and in his day was hailed as the flying leprechaun, a sort of Ivy League Doug Flutie type, except he had a classic case of red hair and freckles. And nowhere near as big an arm as Flutie.

Stromdahl beamed at the lapel pin and took an instant liking to O'Brien, who seemed totally without bullshit. He came into the Oval Office with four senior agents, but handled the report himself. Only in the last few hours, he explained, had rescue operations ended at the malls, and until then the investigators couldn't go full bore. But already they'd made some interesting discoveries. And with eight crime scenes to comb through he was certain they would find something crucial that the bombers had not intended to leave behind.

"Tell us what you've found so far," the President said.

"Depends on which mall you're talking about. But let me start with what seems to be common to all of them. We've retrieved surveillance videos from six, and we've found the remains of the bomb vehicles at five. Looks like they were set off with phone calls, not timers. Maybe one call for all of them. That's why they were so well coordinated." He said it also looked as if the bombers used big old SUVs. All that the investigators had found were Chevy Suburbans or Ford Expeditions. Some of the last gassers made before the switch to hybrids and electrics.

Was that important, Sally asked.

"Yes. Actually real important. But if you'll indulge me, Ms. President, I'll get to that in a minute."

She didn't speak, but her silence said to go on.

"So, as you'd expect, once we knew what kind of vehicles were used, we went to the videos from the surveillance cameras in the garages. We've been able to do that at four of the five malls where we found the SUVs. And that's where it gets really strange. There was only one person in each vehicle. At least that we could see from the videos. The driver. And not much room for anyone else. All the rear seats were down and they were all packed solid with what looks like presents. No doubt the bombs. Probably bigger than what McVeigh and Nichols used in Oklahoma."

"What's so strange about a single driver?" Stromdahl asked. "Some reason we should expect more?"

"No, but just hang on. Here's the thing. Each of the drivers was in a Santa suit."

"A what?" Stromdahl and the President spoke at once.

"A Santa suit. They were dressed up like Santa Clauses. And what's more important, they looked sort of Middle Eastern or Asian or maybe Mexican or South American. But it's hard to tell much more with the fake beards and all." O'Brien allowed himself a slight smile. "These were some fancy Santa suits."

Sally shook her head and spoke softly, more to herself than anyone else. "So Santa blows up Christmas. Whose idea was that?"

"Don't know yet. But from what we've found at two of the malls it gets even more strange. Each of the drivers we know about arrived half an hour or so before his bomb went off. We've got tapes of them going inside the malls, and these two went to out-of-the-way employee restrooms where we think they changed into something less conspicuous before getting away."

Stromdahl asked if there were cameras by the restroom doors that might have caught them on the way out. That would provide a better idea what they looked like.

"Good question. Yes. But before going in they disabled the cameras. So we've got no shots of them coming out. They knew where to cut some wires for one. For the other, the Santa had a spray can on a pole that he used to paint over the lens."

"How do you know that?"

"Easy. We've got the video of him doing it. And a mall security guard spotted him on the TV monitor and went to check on it."

"So did the guard get a better look at the guy?"

"I guess. But there's no way we'll ever know for sure. He was shot dead in the restroom before the bomb went off. We found the body in the rubble right before I came over here. It was at Tysons Corner."

The President briefly frowned as she recalled again the rattling coffee cup. Stromdahl thought back to the SUVs, and asked if they had license plates, or serial numbers from the engine blocks. Could they trace them back to find the owners?

"Yes. We've done that already. They weren't rented or bought or anything like that. They were all stolen. Months ago. In eight different states. The vehicles, not the plates."

What did that mean?

"What I said. The plates weren't stolen. They were fakes. Someone managed to manufacture fakes. And they were pretty darn smart about it. Used numbers for nearly identical SUVs that were legally licensed, so if anyone checked them through the computer there'd be no problem. These guys covered every base to make sure the thefts wouldn't be traced. And they picked the perfect vehicles. Like I said, that's important. There's a lot of Suburbans and Expeditions still around, in fairly good shape and not used much here since the electrics have come on the market. They're easy to steal and no one cares all that much. And they can carry a big load."

"So they've covered all their tracks," Stromdahl said.

O'Brien shook his head no. He was certain they'd find some forgotten loose end that would lead them to the bombers. "We just have to keep looking. But whoever did this had a lot of time, a lot of money, and a lot of people to throw at us. Look, this was really, really well planned. By some people who really, really didn't want us to know who they were. And that's like no terrorists we've seen before. Not even al Qaeda at its peak. Or ISIS later on. If al Qaeda could have pulled off something like this, they would've taken credit for sure."

Did he have anything more, Sally asked.

"One other thing, Ms. President, but it's something perhaps best for you and me to talk about alone." He looked at the four agents and Stromdahl, a clear invitation for the President to ask them to leave.

She motioned toward the door, but told Stromdahl to wait outside.

Ten minutes later O'Brien emerged, grim and focused. "The President said you should go back in," he told Stromdahl, who stood off to the side, only a few feet from the door. The little Director walked on by, then paused and turned back toward the man who was a legend to all living Marines. The greatest Commandant ever, some said. At least since Archibald Henderson, who was the first. A flicker of a smile softened O'Brien's face and he extended a hand upward to make up for the fourteen-inch height difference. "I've always wanted to meet you, general. A real honor. Semper Fi."

TAKE A SEAT, Sally said when he walked back in. Things were worse than they thought.

"What things?"

"Impeachment. Hiram Heilman's been out selling his story. Asked O'Brien to sign off on some kind of CIA report saying there's no doubt Iranians did the bombs. The FBI Lab says they were made with ammonium nitrate, like the Oklahoma City bomb, except whoever did the malls added a few other things to make them even more powerful. So Heilman wants the FBI to leap to the next conclusion and say it's clear the Iranians sent the nitrates from Yemen and then targeted the malls to kill as many people as possible. That's the Tea Party story and they're stickin' to it. And, of course, that means I should be bombing Iran or else."

"What did O'Brien do?"

"What you'd guess. He told the good Senator to take a hike. Said he had an investigation to do and didn't appreciate interference from political hacks. That's why he wanted you all out of the room. He doesn't want this to go public. Doesn't want the Bureau caught up in a political dogfight. I made it clear you'll be coordinating things for me, and he'll be reporting to you from now on."

"So did Heilman back down?"

"He did. Claimed he was just doing his job as chairman of the oversight committee."

"Right."

"Yeah. Right. But they're pushing to have me gone before February. They insist it's an impeachable offense for me not to go to war when the country's attacked."

"Anything else?"

"Yeah. I asked O'Brien who he thought did the bombs. Told him about Akbar and asked if it could be Jihad in Yemen. He doesn't know. But he keeps coming back to how well organized this was. How complicated. How different from every other terrorist attack. Our law enforcement people watch things closer now. It's harder to get around our security. A lot harder. And he points out most of the bad guys are actually pretty stupid. Every year or so someone tries to blow up their shoes or underwear or something on an airplane, and so far they've always screwed it up."

"And we've been lucky," Stromdahl said.

"Yes, we've been very lucky. But O'Brien thinks the malls went way beyond anything anyone's ever tried. Even 9/11. That was brilliantly simple. This was brilliantly complex. Smuggling in sixty or seventy tons of explosives is no mean trick."

"Maybe they bought it here. Or made it here."

"I asked him that. He says not very likely. These bombs were made with nitrates, and ever since Tim McVeigh and Oklahoma City bulk sales are closely regulated, even though most of the stuff is used as fertilizer. The FBI and the Ag Department people have gone back to double check for any possible slip ups, and they didn't find anything big enough to account for even a fraction of what was needed. And manufacture of that much explosive-grade nitrate outside a big commercial chemical plant would be almost impossible to do, and certainly to conceal.

"But none of this makes any difference to Rumbo and Heilman. They don't care who did it. Heilman said as much to O'Brien. Told him that if we blow up Iran everything in the neighborhood goes up too. So one way or another we'll hit the right target."

Stromdahl let out a small whistle. "Kind of like an atomic shotgun fired in the dark at any noise we hear. God save us if they take over."

"God save the whole planet."

CHAPTER 10

Time and gentrification had bypassed the Cardiac Arrest, a burger joint on the fringe of Georgetown, south of both M Street and the canal, and only a hundred yards or so from the river. It was located in the middle of a dingy row of old three- and four-story brick buildings, once shops with offices and apartments above, now mostly abandoned except for the first floors. The row fronted on a narrow cobblestone street permanently darkened by an elevated freeway and the closely spaced steel pillars that supported it. On the other side of the street were a small riverside park and a parking lot, newly paved and painted with bright yellow lines.

In the shadow of the freeway the restaurant's neon sign gleamed brightly round-the-clock. It had two columns of vertical lettering—one for Cardiac, one for Arrest. Inside, equally harsh fluorescent tubes lit up six tables and a four-seat bar, all topped with red Formica faded nearly to pink. The chairs were metal, and the backless bar stools wobbled on chromed pedestals permanently anchored with gnarly lag bolts.

The CA took its name from its hamburgers, which oozed red juices and melted cheese with every bite. The kind where the chef mops the grill with the buns to soak up the leavings and never cooks the meat more than medium rare. They were the best burgers in the city. And so, despite the eatery's location and the neon sign's full disclosure of health risk, the waiting line was almost always long.

The day after Christmas was no exception. The temperature had warmed into the upper forties, the snow was melting, and shoppers were out and about looking for bargains or returning gifts. But at two thirty, in the lull between lunch and dinner, the joint was nearly empty and Stromdahl got a table right away. He ordered a large draft beer and one of the famous burgers, complete with American cheese, lettuce, slices of tomato and onion, and lots of ketchup. And a big mound of French fries. When Samy walked in at ten till three the Commandant was the only customer. He was two bites into his feast and leaning over the plate so the drippings would fall on the fries and not go to waste.

At first Samy didn't recognize him. Despite the milder weather he again wore his bulky yellow jacket, but this time with a red sock hat pulled over his ears to hide his lack of hair. He'd unzipped the jacket, but otherwise kept on his outerwear, and except that he was clean-shaven, in this setting he looked more like a truck driver or street person than a Marine. Or maybe the bulky "maintenance man" from the Georgetown library two days before, now taking a late lunch break. "Have a seat," Stromdahl said. "Want half of this thing?" He put the hamburger back on the paper plate, cut it in two, and offered up the unbitten portion.

"No thanks, Skipper." *Since when had the great Wallace Stromdahl started eating greaseburgers?*

Without a trace of guilt or contrition, Stromdahl said he'd chosen the perfect venue for their meeting—a place where no one would expect either of them to set foot. With ostentatious gusto he savored another bite and said cholesterol was allowed during the holidays. Required even. "I changed the regulations myself. Just now."

Samy grinned, reached over and took a single French fry from the edge of the plate, where the drippings hadn't yet contaminated it. He popped it into his mouth and looked around to make sure no one was within earshot. They were alone except for the cook and the waiter huddled near the door, toting up the lunch hour take in the cash register drawer. They were a middle-aged male gay couple, from all appearances married in life as well as business.

One of them started to come over to take Samy's order, but Stromdahl waved him off.

So why this second meeting, Samy asked. "I got the tickets like you told me. With my own credit card. I'm assuming you'll pay me back someday. I leave on the late flight tonight."

"You still sure you want to go?" Stromdahl asked.

"We went through that already. Something more than the greaseburger regs change just now?"

Stromdahl glanced down at the unfinished burger half still on the plate, then lifted his gaze to speak. "Sort of. I can't promise any back up to come get you. You'll be on your own. Completely."

Samy's face tightened with perplexity at the sudden solicitude for his safety. There hadn't been any such a promise in the first place. "What backup you think I might need?"

The Skipper looked at his plate again and said nothing. One part of him recalled Luis Hernandez, dead because of an overambitious mission, too little equipment, and maybe too much courage. Another part fixed on the hard-edged reality of military life. Mission first, men second. But he wasn't exactly sending in a Marine this time. Samy was not an expendable military asset.

"Don't know," he finally said. There followed another uncomfortable silence before he continued. "Look, if this has anything to do with the mall bombs, the folks you'll be asking about don't want us to know who they are. And even if there's no connection between the container and the malls, it wasn't any good guys trying to smuggle in tons of explosives."

"Skipper, that's no secret. But they're not likely anywhere close to Aden anymore. Far as the world knows, I'm just going to see my family near Sana'a, do a little research, and take a two-day trip down to the gulf to ask a few questions and take some pictures for a book I'm writing. Not a big deal. Believe me. Ayan will kill me if I don't make it back. And I'll be with my granddad's brother. The one who told me about Akbar. In Yemen he's better protection than all the Marines in the Corps."

Stromdahl looked over at the two men counting their cash, then back at Samy. "And what if you find out Akbar's the one we're looking for? You gonna be able to live with that?"

This time it was Samy who looked away before answering, and as he stared out the front window a group of twentysomethings came in and took nearby seats. "You done eating?" he asked abruptly.

"Yeah. Let's get outta here. Take a walk along the river. I got something I have to give you before you leave." Stromdahl also needed an answer to the last question.

THEY DIDN'T HAVE to worry much about solitude in the riverside park. The footpaths remained slushy wet, and a nasty raw wind had started blowing down the Potomac Valley, just a few ticks above freezing and heavy with humidity. They found a bench that faced downstream, toward the Watergate and the Kennedy Center, and hunched up to ward off the damp chill at their backs.

"Here," Stromdahl said. "Before I forget." He handed Samy a well-worn black phone. "Use this to report what you find. It's setup with your real phone number, but the signal is scrambled. There'll be two Navy ships in the gulf that can send messages straight to us at headquarters. And relay our messages back. Either text or voice. All secure."

Samy took it gingerly and eyed it like an exotic spider. "I thought we were all hush-hush. How'd the Navy get involved?"

"Just say I got some connections."

Samy raised his eyebrows and swallowed any further questions, then put the phone in his pocket and pulled out his own to text Ayan that he was running late. "We're supposed to go out to dinner," he said. "Before she drives me to Dulles. You and the Marines aren't scoring many points with her lately."

"Did we ever?"

He laughed. "Not really."

"So answer my question. What happens if you find out this was all Sami A?"

"I've thought about that. A lot. Even before you asked me to go."

"And?"

"If you're asking will I tell you the truth if it's Sami, the answer's yes."

"No matter what?"

"No matter what. Look, you remember that Kaczynski guy who died in prison a few years ago?"

"Sure. The Unabomber. I remember when they caught him.

Right after I graduated from the U. I get the point. His brother turned him in."

"Yeah. So I'll get you whatever truth I can find. But don't ask me to help take him out. He's the closest thing I had to a brother growing up in Dearborn."

DEARBORN, JUST WEST OF DETROIT, was where early in his life he first began to sort through the jumble of ideas and disciplines that became the raw material for his life's work as an academic and author: religion, history, and science; language, race, and ethnicity; and philosophy, politics, and polemics. Dearborn was a melting pot that itself was an unmelted rough-edged chunk of another world, American yet not, Arab yet not, Islamic yet not. The first Arabs to arrive were actually Christians from Lebanon, recruited to work for Ford in the industrial vastness of the River Rouge plant, located only a few miles to the southeast at the confluence of the Detroit River and the Rouge. But Lebanese Muslims soon followed, and with them immigrants from Syria, Iraq, and Yemen. They settled mostly east of Southfield Freeway in well-worn neighborhoods of small old houses and big old cars. Not slums, but always a bit raggedy around the edges. Both cars and houses were chronically on the verge of major repair or repainting.

By the 1990s, when the two Samirs were in grade school, Warren Avenue, east of where it crossed Southfield, had taken on the look of Beirut or Damascus. Five miles of small single-story shops and service stations on a cracked and decaying street lined with cracked and decaying sidewalks. The buildings were interspersed with down-at-the-heels industrial plants and dusty weed-choked lots used for parking or dumping, and after dark for the sale of drugs. But the multiple small businesses defied the blight of their surroundings with garish bright paint—yellows and electric blues, purples, and flamboyant greens—that made them foreign and faintly exotic even without the Arabic lettering of their signage and the smells of honeyed pastries and roasting lamb drifting through the air from the bakeries and restaurants.

Dearborn's mosques were divided into Sunni and Shia, much like its churches were divided into Protestant and Catholic, and until the sectarian conflict from the Middle East began to seep into the city's Islamic religious life, the Muslim coexistence was as peaceful as for the various Christian denominations. Tribal origins faded as all Arabs banded together to maintain their identity while they became American. Not exactly Swedes and Norwegians in northern Minnesota, but also not the Hatfields and McCoys, or the warring tribes that once had Yemen split into two countries and constantly threatened to reopen the schism.

The Al-Mahdis were Shiites and the Akbars were Sunnis, but Samy and Sami often went to mosque together and mixed with Christians and the few Jews in their school as well as with their Muslim brethren. Were there some scale to measure and compare assimilation, almost anyone would have placed the two of them on the high end. They were exemplars of peaceful diversity. And geographically they both lived west of Southfield, and went to West Dearborn High School where they had to fit in because, unlike at the original Dearborn High, Muslims were not the majority. But Samy Al-Mahdi was naturally American and Anglicized his nickname with a "y," while Sami Akbar was naturalized and more conflicted, and always insisted that his nickname had to end in "i." And when he returned from a summer in Yemen just in time for football practice his senior year he was not the same. No more beer, no more dating, and lots more time with the local imam.

AS AL-MAHDI and Stromdahl stood up from the bench and turned to leave the park, Samy stopped to look upstream at Key Bridge, which loomed high above them, a connection across the river that once separated the two warring parts of the United States. "You know," he said, "when I think back on it now, Sami A was never really comfortable here. Kind of like he was caught between two places. Stuck on a bridge and couldn't figure out which end was home. His father's father was an imam, you know. Back in Yemen. In Tarim, where half the people think they're descended from Muhammad. Very religious. And his father came to America and became a drunk."

"Well he sure as hell was more gung ho than you. He's the one who finally dragged you into enlisting if I remember right."

"True. I guess he had some doubts to banish, especially when he came back from Yemen for his last year in high school. Like he needed to prove to himself that despite it all he was still American. I just had growing up to do."

They were walking now, north toward M Street. The sun

was low in the sky behind them and to their left, and in the long shadows the wind blew colder and bit harder. Hard enough they had to speak up, but not so much they had to shout. Not hard enough to make them hurry to find warmth.

"What turned him bad?" The question had hung between them for years, a sore point never before touched or mentioned so explicitly.

Samy looked to his left at Stromdahl, and also into the cold and wind. He paused and thought a second or two about his answer. "I wouldn't say he ever turned bad. Wrong. Not bad. Iraq forced a choice on him, and he didn't choose us."

"He did fine in Iraq. Got promoted twice and got a medal."

"And hated what he saw and heard. Sent me texts and e-mails about it all the time. Like he'd be standing right there and the other guys would start yacking about hajis and ragheads and all that shit. Dumb shit. Oh, you're American, they'd say. You understand 'cause you're American. Then they'd turn around and razz him when he wouldn't drink. For the Mormons there was no problem, of course, but not for him. I got the same thing, but they stopped when I asked. Maybe I was in a better unit or something. For him they never stopped, even when he saved their butts by sweet talking intel from the locals. Even when he pulled two of 'em out of a burning Humvee. You tell me what that shit was all about."

They'd had the discussion about hajis and ragheads and the dumb side of the Marines many times before. But never so much about Akbar. For Stromdahl the beauty of the Corps was how its discipline and esprit enabled heroic service. Like a football team except the stakes were life and death. And like a football team, the off-field problems of the troops sometimes messed up the mission.

That's exactly the problem, Al-Mahdi always said. War was heroic, policing an occupation anything but. And using Marines to do it was like using a great football team to clean up the other side's stadium after a game. With opposing fans throwing rocks and bottles from the stands. And in Akbar's company he was treated like a rock thrower even though he wasn't.

"But that's not what all happened," Stromdahl said. "They gave him a silver star for the Humvee. Come on. And I inspected his company half a dozen times to check on the teachers and he never complained once. Not even when I took him aside especially to ask. In Arabic."

Yeah, Samy thought. Stromdahl had ninety percent of the story right, but no one but Akbar himself really knew about the ten percent that probably counted most. The part after the two friends got back to Camp Lejeune from Iraq and went home on leave together for Al-Mahdi's wedding. Two weeks later they returned to duty. And the first weekend after that Sami A was gone and never seen or heard from again. Except on the Internet, calling down God's wrath on the West and boasting of his exploits. Like blowing up a destroyer with a missile stolen from the Saudis, and blowing up two embassies with trucks supposedly carrying groceries. Jihad in Yemen had nothing but large ambitions and did nothing but large and deadly explosions.

Twenty children killed at the embassy in Cairo, and not a word of apology or contrition. Nothing. Akbar said he was a prophet descended from the prophet. His goal was to unite all Muslims under a new caliphate, first to rule the Middle East, then the world. He was smart and charismatic and American enough to know his enemy, and convinced he walked with God. A madman with military skills far beyond the corporal's rank he held in the Marines.

Chapter 11

Like the phone he'd given Samy, Stromdahl's mini-tablet was no ordinary device. About the size of a slender paperback book, it had been customized by Marine Corps techies who added a self-destruct feature that kicked in if anyone made more than three attempts to log on with the wrong password. Stromdahl had learned to live with this bit of hyper-security, but only the hard way, after blowing up an earlier tablet himself when he kept forgetting to capitalize the second "r" and type in the dash in "GopherRifleman-6." He quickly changed to a shorter and simpler password.

Saturday morning, two days after Christmas, he turned on the latest tablet without incident and checked his messages before embarking on a too-long-delayed December bike ride. Monthly rides had been a self-imposed ritual for him ever since his junior year at the U. Sally got him started biking, but it was he who turned defiance of Minnesota's weather into a vendetta against the cold and ice. Every month he rode at least once, plus every equinox and solstice. Not a religious or spiritual or astrological thing, he told Sally. "It's about discipline and resolve. You gotta make yourself love hardship." He was certain it would all pay off some day on some faraway battlefield.

They were eating lunch at the student union a week into

December, and he was about to take off for a ride in the snow. In near-zero weather the flakes fell like crystalline powder and drifted in the frostbite wind. Great, he said. Snow and ice just added to the challenge. She looked out the window, then back at him and said he better not bring his damn bike into their apartment till he'd cleaned it off outside. Marine Corps training, she thought, did strange things to the mind.

After graduation, he continued his riding rituals, whatever their sanity and logic. He did it even in combat zones, where bikes were few and rideable roads fewer, and even during his rehab at Navy Med, where he convinced a physical therapist to let him ride fifty feet down a hallway. In all his years since the U he'd never missed a month, and the only time he ever missed a season's first day was this winter because of the mall bombs. He was not about to lose what was left of December as well.

An orderly brought the bike around to the back door of the mansion that had served as the Marine Corps Commandant's residence for more than two centuries. Stromdahl wasn't the first bike rider to live there, but he almost certainly was the most militant about it. He straddled the frame, cleated into the left pedal, and then checked his electronic messages. With a few deft finger drags he determined there was nothing that required immediate attention and jabbed the air with a gleeful fist pump. Today would be the day, despite all that had happened, when he finally could check off the last month of the year from his bicycle to do list. And better yet, he'd easily get back in time for the rescheduled Minnesota football game against Temple.

The country needed football to help get back to normal, Sally had said on TV when the new date was announced. To Stromdahl she'd expressed a view more akin to gallows humor or theater of the absurd. "Football's like all spectator sports. Absolutely essential precisely because it's so meaningless. The more time we waste watching it the less time we have to do real harm."

For him playing did mean a lot more than the watching, but he was no more willing to miss viewing a Minnesota post-season game than miss his monthly ride. It could be the most meaningful event in the U's entire history. Fighting terrorism and impeachment could damn well wait a few hours for both his biking and his Gophers.

He stuck the tablet into the back pocket of his Marine Corps biking jersey and set off for a spin along his regular route—west down the Mall, then multiple laps around East Potomac Park Golf Course on the Hains Point peninsula. Two MPs always came along, also in Marine Corps jerseys, but not the traditional biking tights. Instead they wore cargo shorts to conceal their pistols. The security detail usually stuck with Stromdahl like super glue, and he'd been forced into some pretty big and barely white lies to ditch them for his recent trips to Georgetown.

They were on their second lap at the Point when the tablet started buzzing and vibrating. It was a text message from Danny O'Brien, who cryptically reported "interesting news" and suggested a meeting right away. "We're changing our route," the Commandant told his bodyguards.

Where to? The MPs did not like unplanned forays, and were under standing orders to discourage them.

Not far, he said. Just to the Hoover Building on Pennsylvania Avenue. Not far at all.

THE MPS TOOK the bikes inside and out of sight while Stromdahl got escorted to the Director's office on the top floor. Even on a Saturday O'Brien was dressed in his usual dark blue suit and a Princeton rep tie. The investigation, he said, was starting to yield some clues and potential leads.

The FBI investigators had started with the usual obvious questions. Who had seen the Santas at the malls? Did anyone speak with them? Or get a close enough look to make an identification? And despite the long lapse since their theft, did anyone recall anything about the SUVs? The problem wasn't a lack of witnesses, but the fakes who wanted their moment of fame or just to prank the system. There were hundreds of calls and e-mails about flying sleighs carrying bombs, and at least a dozen hapless crazies came forward to confess impossibly lurid details.

The real witnesses, like parking valets and people who encountered the Santas on their walk into or out of the malls, told a story of little contact with the suspects. One valet recalled that the SUV at his mall was clearly overloaded. It bothered him at the time that Christmas presents should weigh so much, but to his great regret he did nothing to check out his suspicions.

Other than drivers in Santa suits, little else seemed particularly odd or out of place. Certainly nothing earthshaking. Three people from the Mall of America recalled that their Santa's beard was smudged and dirty. And almost everyone who heard the Santas bellow out Merry Christmas remembered that they sounded a little off. They couldn't place the accent, but it wasn't American. Except, that is, at North Park in Dallas, where Santa sounded almost like a local. The witnesses there were especially impressed with how much he smiled and how friendly he seemed. And also apparently forgetful. The investigators found a wig and beard and red hat in the storeroom where he'd changed. The FBI was doing DNA tests on the real hairs inside the wig in the hope there might be some genetic anomaly that would allow the investigation to focus more precisely on a specific race or ethnic origin.

And then there was the main reason for O'Brien's message. He said a suspicious tractor-trailer had been reported only hours before by a retired accountant who lived on a farm fifteen miles west of Baltimore and a mile or so north of Interstate 70. "He told one of my agents that he saw it a week ago, early in the morning on the Saturday the bombs went off. Said he was out on a walk with his dogs when he spotted it backed in behind an abandoned barn, about two hundred yards from the highway."

"What's a semi got to do with anything? I thought the bombs were in SUVs."

"Let me finish. The truck looked odd, and it didn't belong there. So the accountant guy, he got curious, but didn't want to get too close. He just stayed in the trees and watched."

"And?"

"And he saw two SUVs roll out the back of the trailer and drive off. And then the semi driver loaded the ramp back into its slot underneath the trailer and drove off too. The accountant told us the SUVs were a Ford and a Chevy. He was sure of that 'cause he could see the logos on the front grills. He thinks it was a big Suburban Chevy and a big Ford Expedition. And they both looked like they had heavy loads."

Stromdahl was now paying very, very close attention. "So we know they used a Suburban at Tysons Corner, and an Expedition in New Jersey, right?"

"Exactly."

"Did this guy see the damn license plates?"

"No such luck. He told the agents that he didn't look. Said he just shrugged it all off and pretty much forgot about it until he saw on the news how old SUVs had been used to cart the bombs to the malls. That's when he called us. But one thing did stick in his mind. There wasn't any lettering or logo on either the trailer or the tractor. Nothing except the required DOT stuff. And the rig was dark blue, like Duke Blue Devil blue."

O'Brien allowed himself a slight grin when he related the Blue Devil part of the story. "The agent who interviewed him said this guy really hated Duke from back in the days when Maryland was in the ACC and they played every year. It was the color that really got his attention."

Stromdahl also grinned briefly at the sports angle, but immediately got back to the main point. "What did the SUV drivers look like? Were they in Santa suits?"

"He never saw them outside the vehicles, but he's now convinced at least one of them had a white beard. Could be just his memory catching up with the story on the news, but it all seems to fit with what we've found so far."

"What about the semi driver?"

"Never got a good look at him either. Said the guy wore a baseball hat and had on sunglasses. Probably wasn't African or African American. Couldn't remember anything more."

So how could they pull on this thread to unravel more of the case? How could they trace the tractor-trailer without any clue but its color? The questions poured from Stromdahl as if the investigation were his and not the FBI's, which it sort of was since his vague Presidential appointment as general overseer.

O'Brien grinned and motioned for him to calm down. "We're checking," he said. "Checking every possible angle."

"Like what?"

"Like we're reviewing all surveillance camera images of trucks going through toll booths or weigh stations on I-70 and I-95 to see if we can come up with a license number. We're checking everything within about two hundred miles."

Stromdahl shook his head and said do it for the whole damn country. "Every toll booth and every weigh station and every other place that might have caught a picture of truck traffic rolling through. Go back a month if they save stuff that long. We gotta figure out where that truck started its trip. And when."

"That'll take a while."

No choice, Stromdahl said. "Do I-70 and I-95 first, but then do everything else. Every damn thing you can think of."

They would, O'Brien promised, but he doubted the license number would help very much. Probably another fake that would lead them nowhere. The DOT numbers too. The better hope was to find someone else besides the accountant who'd seen the truck in transit and maybe could describe the driver.

"Right. But that's not where I'm goin' with this."

"What do you mean?"

"Look, suppose we get a license number for a truck that fits this description. Suppose we get it from a weigh station on I-70 in Maryland, then we check that license number and find it went through a station in say Alabama two days before. That would sort of tell us the starting point—probably where they made the bombs. It would pretty much have to be at least as far south and at least as far west as Alabama. And even if we just spotted a plain blue truck in Alabama it would give something to help focus our search."

"Lots of ifs in there. And that would mean just about the whole Southwest. Plus Alabama, Mississippi, and Louisiana."

"Yeah. I know." Stromdahl was about to say a lot of people were dead and maybe the country's fate on the line too, then thought better of such melodrama. Instead he ventured another idea about what more they should do. "Let me give you some more ifs. Let's assume for some reason they used bigger trucks like the blue semi to get all the SUVs close to their targets. Maybe because the SUVs were so overloaded. Maybe just to make things harder for us to track down. Could be lots of reasons. Anyway, if I'm right, that barn wasn't the only place where an SUV with a bomb got dropped off by a big truck. And maybe someone else saw the unloading operation."

"So we should tell the media types to get the word out."

"Bingo."

O'Brien nodded his agreement and pondered where they were in the bigger picture of trying to solve the case. "You think it was Akbar? Maybe recruited some old homies from Dearborn?" That would explain where the perpetrators had found enough people to do all their dirty work. And maybe the Santas' slight accents.

And also, Stromdahl said, it would explain how Akbar might have pulled it all off while hiding in some cave in Yemen. But where in the States had they kept the stolen SUVs? Where had they made the license plates? Where had they stored the nitrates? How could all those things be done in secret and without a trace? At an abandoned old factory in Dearborn? Somehow that didn't quite fit. Maybe Samir Al-Mahdi would find a better lead.

CHAPTER 12

Throughout the week after the mall bombings, even on Christmas Day, the Tea Party talk shows were rife with suggestions for a final solution to terrorism. Callers mostly wanted to incinerate every non-English speaking segment of the globe, and to expel all non-citizens from the U.S. and anyone with a funny-sounding name, whether citizen or not. Onward Christian Soldiers! There seemed some sentiment for sparing Europe and maybe Israel and Japan, and for setting up a kangaroo court to assure the propriety of the name-based expulsions, but beyond that no place or person should be safe from America's righteous vengeance.

Then on the evening of the twenty-eighth, the Sunday after Christmas, the Wolfe TV Network broadcast a four-hour "impeachment special" from New York, hosted by Rumbo and featuring Senator Heilman and half a dozen others out for the President's political if not actual scalp. Rumbo, whose sagging jowls and bulbous nose were made for radio, didn't often do TV, but this show was maybe the most important performance of his life. So important that he'd reluctantly come to New York and interrupted the annual holiday meeting of the Rumbo, Inc. shareholders at his beach house in Boca Raton. He and Lisa were the only shareholders, of course, but the meetings gave them a fig leaf explanation for why she spent Christmas away from home and husband. She told everyone she and Luke were on a crucial business trip, absolutely necessary to wrap up year-end financial details. The first few years she took a room in a nearby hotel in case somebody checked on her, but for the last five she hadn't bothered. Her husband the preacher had his own special holiday retreat with his own special friends, and he was grateful for her absence.

Heilman spoke first on the impeachment show, like a prosecutor giving an opening statement. The CIA had solid proof it was Iran. Two years of threats and bluster after the reactor raid. Plenty of motive. Large capacity to make ammonium nitrate and other chemicals of mass destruction. Plenty of means. And the shipping container in Newark was clearly from Iran, and would have gotten through customs had not the country been on super-alert precisely because the contents of other containers had already been used to such deadly effect. Plenty of opportunity. The latest FBI discoveries about Santas and semi trucks changed none of this evidence and only made the case stronger. The fact that at least one of the Santas spoke English like an American showed that the Iranians had been clever enough to find pinko sympathizers in the U.S. One more reason why expulsions and executions of strange and odd people had to be part of the plan.

But despite this overwhelming proof, Sally Macalester had done nothing except tell the country not to rush to judgment and then ask the United Nations to help with the investigation. Why on earth bring in the United Nations! And why hold back judgment when the truth was so evident and clear! Though not exactly in the Constitution, failure to defend had to be an impeachable offense. It was tantamount to treason.

Yes, Rumbo agreed. Impeachment was a slam dunk. The others on the show—another Senator, three Congressmen, and two comely blonde Tea Party TV talking heads—vigorously chimed their accord too. The President had to go. Even without the bombs her sins were impeachable beyond a doubt. Despite her ostensible Catholic roots she was a Godless socialist out to destroy both Christianity and Capitalism, the two "C's" at the heart of America's pre-ordained exceptional existence.

"She's been at it since day one," Rumbo rumbled. "Since she was on the city council and then mayor in Minneapolis. She pulled some trick to use gasoline tax money to build bikeways.

Bikeways, mind you. Not roads. And we're not talking the usual separate lanes or paved trails. Oh no! She had to really go all out on the spending. Talk about brick outhouses. She wasted taxpayer dollars on elevated bikeways downtown. All over Minneapolis. Can you believe it! Bike-els!"

And then when she was a Senator she came up with her ridiculous plan to hasten the country's "switch" to electric cars and trucks. Imagine, Rumbo intoned. What could be more un-American than an electric pickup truck? No throaty V-8 growl, just a pussycat purr when doing a man's work. It was some kind of homosexual commie plot and had to be stopped.

Of course her idea was anything but radical, as Jane Nelson always pointed out to the President's critics. Sally wanted to have thirty percent of the spaces in every big parking lot or garage equipped with a plug-in option that would allow drivers to get their cars recharged while they were shopping or getting their teeth cleaned at the dentist's office or whatever. An electric meter would put the cost on the user's credit card.

"Easy and simple," Jane told a Wolfe Network correspondent. "And we've got studies that show it overcomes most of the reluctance about electrics." While they still took longer to recharge than it did to refill a tank with gasoline or diesel, the extra time didn't matter so much if people had things to do while they waited. In actuality, the recharging option often would be less bothersome than pumping fuel.

Plug-in parking found support in all the polls, and increasing sales of electric vehicles gave rock-solid tangible economic evidence that it was working. But the oil industry would have none of it. "No way," a senior VP said during what he thought was a closed session at his company's annual shareholder meeting. He didn't realize that two reporters had slipped in. They stood very quietly at the back of the room recording his every word.

"Gas station pumps are the heart of our business, and the heart of America," the VP said. And in case anyone failed to get his drift, he pointed out that the human heart also was a pump. "What the country really needs is free-flowing oil in our pipeline arteries. And the best way to prevent shortages and blockages ain't electricity. What we need is more control over supplies from the Middle East. We need to get Iran in line with everyone else. That way we can sell product both here and overseas, and keep making record profits." New demand in India and China had sent prices soaring, and the last thing the industry needed was electric competition.

Oilmen and their companies poured billions into both Republican and Democratic campaign coffers to stop Senator Macalester's plan, and that's when she and Senator Nelson decided to start the New American Progressives. Forget the never-ending blood feuds over abortion rights and gay marriage and health care and taxes. If the two big parties couldn't come together on an easy common sense solution to the energy problem they would never be able to do anything.

STROMDAHL WATCHED the Sunday impeachment special while he pounded out miles on a treadmill in the gym at the Commandant's Mansion, which was part of the Marine Barracks complex at Eighth and Eye Streets in Southeast DC. Outside it was snowing again, and in deference to a nagging cough he decided to forego his usual daily jog. The in-home gym was about the only thing he really liked about the mansion, which was too ornate and too big for an old farm boy without a family. But to Sally he bragged that his house, not hers, was the oldest government residence in Washington. It went back to 1801, and since then it had been continuously occupied, whereas the White House was burned down during the War of 1812.

One upping each other had always been a constant thing with them, as never ending as their disagreements about sports, politics, philosophy, and nearly any other topic of discussion. They were proof positive that opposites attract in both relationships and magnetics. In college their debates often came close to a contact sport. But despite his family's Republican traditions, when he had to choose for her or against her on Minnesota absentee ballots in the Senate and Presidential elections, he checked the Macalester box without hesitation. And before that he followed from afar her Minneapolis campaigns for city council and mayor and was proud as hell when she won.

Right now he was mad as hell at Rumbo's slurs against her. The bikeway criticism especially pissed him off, and he shouted an obscenity or two at the TV screen to vent his anger. Year-round bike riding in Minneapolis had gone up more than a hundred fold when the new enclosed and elevated system was completed, and it relieved traffic congestion and saved millions of gallons of gasoline. Winter riding was no longer limited to nuts with strange ideas about bikes and solstices. And when the med school at the U did a health study, it found the average weight for adult Minneapolitans had dropped five pounds. Heart attacks and strokes also declined. It was this kind of practical success that propelled Sally into the Senate and the Presidency. Everyone in Minnesota agreed she was a more than worthy successor to the tradition of Hubert Humphrey, who also had been mayor before going on to Senator and Vice President.

But Rumbo and his cohorts were into political and theological purity, not practical results, and an hour or so of their impeachment bombast on TV was about all Stromdahl could take. He clicked off the TV in disgust and upped the speed on the treadmill to work off his frustration with a final sprint. Bikes, he recalled, had always been a big deal with Sally.

She was on a bike the first time he noticed her. It was early their sophomore year, in September, when the weather was near perfect and half the student body rode to and from class. He spotted her as she pedaled away from the library on her old fifteen-speed Trek and headed down the campus mall towards the student union. Perched on top of the high seat, she leaned gracefully forward over the dropped handlebars and effortlessly stretched out her long legs to make it move. She wore only a tank top, short shorts and a pair of tennis shoes, and looked sexy as hell.

Who's that, he asked a teammate who was standing with him.

"Sally something. Plays on the volleyball team. Don't know how you've missed her."

Neither did Stromdahl. He looked up the women's volleyball team roster to find her last name and wheedled her class schedule out of a friend who worked in the registrar's office. And because the semester was only in its first week, he managed to transfer into her English class and sat next to her once or twice.

"Don't you play volleyball?" he asked.

"Sometimes," she muttered.

Undeterred, he started riding his old mountain bike to class, and with carefully planned nonchalance managed accidently to pull up next to her while she was stopped at a light. "Great day, isn't it. I'm in your English class. Remember? Wanna take a ride along the river?"

Without a word she sped off and quickly left him far behind.

The next bicycle encounter went much better. He'd aggravated her enough that she asked around about him and was pleasantly surprised he had not tried to impress her with his status on the football team. And he did meet one of her big criteria for a potential date. He was significantly taller than she was.

"I'm doing a training ride to Saint Paul," she challenged him as they left class one day. "Come along and see if you can keep up." Had she pushed it, he couldn't even have stayed close, but she rode slowly enough that he could at least keep her in sight. They followed the Mississippi's East Bank all the way to the Twin Cities' other downtown, crossed the river on the High Bridge and came back on the West Bank. That night they ate together in the cafeteria, and thereafter saw each other almost daily for the rest of their time in school. For most of those days they lived together as well, and she even started going to football games and occasionally to Lutheran services with him on Sunday.

Renewed church attendance was a big change for her. Religiously she was her mother's child, not her rigidly Catholic father's, and until Walleye came along she'd stopped going to services of any kind. Her conversion from the church—or more accurately withdrawal—occurred in the middle of her junior year of high school. Guided by her ever-practical mother she started on the pill, and in school she learned about evolution and read a biography of Thomas Jefferson that did not sugarcoat his antagonism toward all organized religion. God became an hypothesis for her instead of a belief, and skepticism quickly supplanted faith.

She told Walleye she was a Darwinian. "It's like some grand intelligence set it all in motion," she said, "and She or He or It is sort of watching to see how it all turns out." The two of them were in their college apartment, completely undressed and sitting on the living room floor. They were leaning against the front of the sofa and each other. In the aftermath intimacy of wild "can't wait to get to bed" lovemaking on the carpet, her head was on his shoulder and she was trying to share her deepest thoughts about the world's destiny and their place in it.

"So where does morality come from, any sense of right or

wrong?" he said. "If there's not a God who cares what we do, why should we?" Like his church, he didn't dispute the biology of evolution, but neither would he give up a righteous God. Or a chance for another romp on the carpet. He was trying to push her down as he spoke.

She moved a few inches away from him and sat up straight, the better to give her answer unimpeded by his efforts at more foreplay and sex. "Evolution," she said. "It all comes from evolution. Our genes make us a cooperative species. So we have common beliefs as part of cooperation. Like belief in God. Just like we evolved language." She was trying to be very serious even though his focus was far more carnal and immediate.

"Well," he said, "I gotta tell you there's a lot evolving left to do." To himself he thought warfare and the Marine Corps were a lot more evolved than widespread cooperation, and that had nothing to do with genetics. Then he put his arm around Sally's chest and before she could resume her explanation he tugged her downward. With only token resistance she answered his kiss as they lay back on the rug.

When they were done and lying side by side he propped himself up on his elbows and looked down on her face. "You know you have to be wrong."

"What?"

"You're wrong about evolution and religion. If there's a 'believe in God gene,' you don't have it. You're living refutation of your own theory."

"No. You're wrong. I do believe there's a higher source for everything. Call it a deity if you want. But you'll never find it in any church. I've evolved beyond that." As she spoke she cuddled close and slowly slid her hand downward along his stomach. Thus diverted he never asked the obvious next question. If each person was free to define her own deity, how did that explain cooperation through common belief.

AFTER HIS SUNDAY TREADMILL RUN Stromdahl toweled off the sweat and was headed for the shower when a corporal came into the gym with a message from the duty officer. "Sir, we got a call from a Sergeant Ferrell in Newark, and the lieutenant on duty thought you might want to return it right away."

"What did he say that's so important?" Stromdahl, still cranky over the lies about Sally and not at all patient, spoke with a sharp hint of sarcasm. This better be good.

"She, sir, not he. And I don't know sir. Something about the bombs and all. I think she's the ag inspector who found the bomb stuff in the container."

He thanked the corporal and made a mental note to have a word with the lieutenant about sending more coherent messages. Or maybe a more coherent messenger. But for the first time it dawned on him that the Ferrell he'd heard about on the news might be the young Marine from Afghanistan and Navy Med. She no doubt had received a promotion before leaving the Corps.

"Corporal, wait a minute," he called to the messenger, who had done a smart about-face and was halfway out the door. "I want you to get in touch with Ferrell and tell her to go to the Coast Guard headquarters in Newark. Then you call the Coast Guard so they know she's coming and tell them to let us know when she gets there so we can talk with her on a secure line. Got it?"

"Yes sir. Aye, aye sir." There was another smart about-face but no salute. Marines don't salute indoors.

"And Corporal, let me know as soon as we reach her."

Half an hour later he took the call in his study, a dark and book-lined room filled with heavy mahogany tables and chairs that went back to a time, before television, when every upper-class dinner ended with cigars and brandy and lots of harrumphing about the sad state of the non-English speaking world. Except for traditional Marine Corps parsimony, no one could explain how this furniture had outlived its original postprandial purpose, but changing it would take a Commandant far more concerned than Stromdahl with the niceties of interior design.

And whatever their esthetic shortcomings, the chairs were comfortable. His favorite was overstuffed, upholstered in well-worn maroon leather, and big enough to swallow up even someone of his size. Incongruously dressed in jeans and a Golden Gopher sweatshirt, he leaned back and crossed his left leg over his right. "Hello," he said. "Are you the Ferrell from Camp Porcupine?"

"Yes sir. I got out of the Marines years ago. Work for the Department of Agriculture now."

"So I hear. I hear you were outstanding with the container. What I'd expect from a Marine."

"Thank you sir. But maybe not so outstanding. I should have called last week. I should have seen it then."

"Seen what?"

"That it's not the way the bombers got their stuff. Can't be. I didn't realize how wrong that is till I heard Senator Heilman just now on Rumbo's program. I had to turn it off. They're not making any sense."

What's new? Stromdahl thought. What was she driving at, he asked.

"Sir, this was the dumbest smuggling anyone's ever tried. If that's how the bombers tried to get explosives into the country, it's not real likely it ever could have worked." There was no such company as Mid East Foods, which should have been a red flag warning. And if the inspectors had opened the container like they were supposed to do, and usually did, they would have found the ammonium nitrate two or three weeks earlier. People smart enough to organize eight simultaneous bombs could not have been stupid enough to set up such nearly certain failure.

But what about the Persian dates and Farsi labels on the nitrate bags?

"Sir, you can buy dates almost anywhere in the Middle East. And anyone can stencil labels in Farsi."

"So you think . . ." He spoke slowly, unsure where he wanted to go, and she finished the sentence for him.

"I think someone's trying to make it look like the explosives came from Iran when they didn't."

"Why?"

"Well, just think about it. If we'd discovered Iranian explosives a couple of weeks before the malls, everyone would have made the connection right away when the bombs went off. There wouldn't be any question." And there wouldn't be any Iran either, because the Air Force would have obliterated it.

He asked if she'd told the FBI.

No, she said.

"Why not?"

"Sir, I tried to reach 'em, but all I got was voicemail. Like I was calling my Internet company to make a complaint. I called you because the President put you in charge of security and all after the malls. And because I hoped you'd remember me and call me back."

WHEN HE GOT through to Sally a few minutes later she was in the Oval Office meeting with Senator Nelson on how to beat back the impeachers. "So if Ferrell's right, we've got a whole new problem," Nelson shouted. She and the President were on a speakerphone, and she spoke about three decibels too loud to make certain it picked up her voice.

Stromdahl winced and moved the receiver away from his ear, then moved it back to reply. "Well, more like a different answer to our questions," he said. And certainly another reason to hold back any attack on the Iranians.

Nelson dropped a decibel or two and sounded skeptical and hesitant; like a dog lover confronted with an unwanted cat. Who would try to start a war between the U.S. and Iran, she asked.

He laughed. "Oh, we share lots of enemies. There's plenty of people who'd be more than happy if we and the Iranians fried each other. Taliban. Al Qaeda. Half the militants in Pakistan. You name it."

"They won't be so happy if they get fried in the same fire," Sally joined in. No government was that crazy, and not many terrorists either. She took a second or two to regroup her thoughts, then added another idea. It had to be someone or some group that understood the U.S. Someone who knew both the harm and the outrage bombing malls at Christmastime would cause. And someone with the wherewithal to plan the attacks and pull them off.

Stromdahl said nothing, but saw where she was going. Back to Akbar, who was her prime suspect ever since she learned he was still alive. Except for the domestic rightwing super-patriot wackos who hated Iran and all Muslims, the only known terrorist group run by an American was Jihad in Yemen. Akbar was a Sunni with no great love for Shiite Iran, and he had plenty of extra motivation to kill Americans after the failed CIA effort to take him out. And based on his unfortunate past successes in the Middle East, he knew all too well how to do it.

"Wait a minute," Nelson said. "Wait a damn minute. You're assuming it was Muslims. What about *Nagaf*?"

Nagaf?

"Yeah. The ultra crazy Jews in Israel. The ones the Israeli government's so hot to round up since the peace treaty with the Palestinians."

THE WORD MEANT smite in Hebrew, and that had been Howie Fabelman's plan, why he took *Nagaf* as the name for his movement. Israel, he said, should smite its way to the grandeur and glory promised by God. The Bible was clear. Yahweh had given the Jews all the lands between the Euphrates and the Mediterranean. All of Syria, Lebanon, Jordan, Iraq, and Iran. A big chunk of Arabia too. Maybe some of Afghanistan and Pakistan. And God had appointed Howie as the instrument to achieve this Greater Israel. Yahweh spoke with him often, and he had no doubt about his mission.

He was born in Manhattan and studied physics and computer science at Queens College, but it was events in Brooklyn that set him on the path of murder and mayhem. In 2004, at twenty-five, he ran off to Israel after he and two buddies beat and killed a Palestinian who threw rocks at orthodox Jews in the borough's Williamsburg section. The rocks caused a few bruises. The beating was slow and sadistic. They stuffed a rag into the victim's mouth to stifle his screams and then removed fingernails and toe nails and inflicted cigarette burns and pushed painful objects into every orifice before delivering a fatal blow to the head and dumping the body in front of a mosque. Every police officer and coroner who saw it threw up, and the district attorney fainted outright.

Once in Israel, Howie hid out with militant Jewish settlers on the West Bank, and found among them recruits enough for an army more vicious than Hamas. They took as their motto a hundred lives for every eye or tooth, and in practice needed no provocation or pretext at all to blow up Muslim school buses, hospitals, nursing homes, or nurseries. They were out to kill Muslims, as Yahweh commanded. When asked how he thought he could control a hostile population many times bigger than Israel's in the lands he proposed to conquer and occupy, he answered succinctly that the only good Muslim was a dead Muslim. In high school he had learned his American history well, and he figured the biggest mistake the United States made in settling the West was allowing any Indians to survive. *Nagaf* would smite its way past that kind of problem.

Until Fabelman's capture by the Israeli security forces he gave only one interview, and it nearly ended in death for the reporter, who asked how *Nagaf* was any different from the Nazis, or Howie any different from Hitler. *Nagaf* was doing God's work, Fabelman said, and he grabbed the reporter by the neck and shook him violently until one of his storm troopers had the temerity to intervene.

Only a single, solitary rightwing extremist in the Israeli government questioned the prosecutor's decision to ask for the death penalty, and had it been carried out Howie would have been only the second person ever executed by the Jewish state. The other was Adolph Eichmann. But Fabelman died prematurely when his followers attacked the prison where he was being held and he was hit by a stray bullet. Since then *Nagaf* had gone into remission, with only an occasional small attack to remind the world it had not been completely extirpated, but lately there were signs it had become more active. There were reports the United States had become a target because Sally's Republican predecessor had brokered the establishment of a genuine Palestinian state and the return of much of the land seized over the years by Jewish militants.

Though the transition was still underway, the treaty was one of the few achievements of an otherwise lackluster administration. All rocket and suicide attacks against Israel had ceased, and to everyone's shock and delight, the Israeli government and the new Palestinian government had already commenced discussions about joint economic development and efforts to conserve water and protect the environment. Many people in the U.S. wondered why Republicans and Democrats couldn't get along so well.

"So," Stromdahl said, "question is, which version of God has decided we and the Iranians have to die? Allah or Yahweh?"

"No," Sally said. "The real question is who thinks God has been directing them against us here on earth. This thing was cooked up inside someone's head, not in heaven."

CHAPTER 13

The day after Christmas and two days before the Sunday TV impeachment special, Ayan Al-Mahdi dropped off her husband at Dulles Airport for his flight to Cairo en route to Yemen. During his brief time at Cairo International he slipped into a long white *thawb* robe and put a white *keffiyeh* on his head, secured with a black rope circlet called an *agal*. Since his first meeting with Stromdahl he had not shaved, and though his beard was still short and stubbly, he appeared little different from the hundred other Yemeni men making their way home from more prosperous parts of the world. Half an hour past midnight local time on Sunday morning he passed through Yemeni customs without incident or even a comment on his American passport.

He needed at least the beginnings of a beard to appease his great uncle Anwar, who was the venerable chief of the Dabwa Tribe. Unbent by the burdens of eighty years, seven wives, and countless children and grandchildren of both the regular and great variety, Anwar lacked only some stone tablets and a staff to pass for Moses in a movie. In real life, he presided over three high mountain valleys about forty miles and three hours northwest of Sana'a. Places straight from the time of the Koran in architecture, agriculture, and religious outlook. For him the holy book was about immediate, tangible reality, not myth or legend, and it required little if any interpretation by mere humans. At the Georgetown faculty club Samy sometimes joked that Anwar took his religion the way Scotsmen took their whisky: unblended, uncut, and deadly serious. A bit of humor he never attempted to repeat on his many trips to the abstemious Middle East.

He first traveled to his ancestral homeland with his father the summer after he finished the third grade, shortly after the nominal end of what was then the most recent civil war between the northern and southern parts of Yemen. His image of the country had been shaped by what he'd seen on TV. Despite a family photo album filled with glossy prints of smiling relatives, terraced green fields, and solid homes of stone and brick, he thought he was going to a place of desiccated sand and wartime disaster. An oil-free and destitute corner of the Arabian Peninsula where people had little to do during the day except lay about and chew a plant called *qat* to achieve euphoria.

But while poor in oil, Yemen was rich in history and tradition, and in the part closest to Africa it had a climate that seemed nothing short of magic in the desert. Here the mountains bent the westerly winds upward and wrung from them all the moisture absorbed on their track across the Mediterranean and the Red Sea. Proof of Allah's blessing, Anwar said. The mountains were supposedly the birthplace of the Queen of Sheba and the launching site for Noah's Ark. And since those Biblical events nothing had changed except for the coming of Muhammad and more recently Kalashnikov rifles and an occasional automobile. Most houses had no glass in the windows and no locks on the doors. And dark nights were completely quiet and unspoiled by artificial light or the sound of machinery. In this timeless land of milk and honey people of necessity lived closer to heaven and closer to God, and the Dabwa and other northern tribes called it the paradise of Arabia.

Samy thought it was the paradise of the world, and wanted to stay when his father's two-week vacation time was up. So it was that Anwar's family took him in for the rest of the summer, and so it was he returned to Dearborn filled with religious purity and fervor, and a determination to be Yemeni and Islamic first and American second, if at all. He showed up at Detroit's Metro Airport wearing a *thawb* and skullcap and carrying a Koran. His father was not pleased.

The counterreformation began immediately, on the way

home from the airport when they stopped at a McDonald's. Mr. Al-Mahdi went to the drive-through window and ordered one Big Mac, one large fries, and one vanilla shake, their traditional lunch when the two of them went out together to do Saturday errands. Samy looked puzzled. Why only one order? Was his father not hungry?

"Heck no. I'm starved. But this stuff's not *halal*. You'll have to wait till we get home. Course that might not be so *halal* either. You may have to go shopping on your own. Got any money?"

Mercifully his mother was a little less draconian and direct in her methods. She figured neighborhood peer pressure would in the long run be more effective than starvation, and for a time even cooked *halal*, or at least claimed to do so. And while she didn't use the abstract and overly refined language of academia, she also started the discussion of tradition and cultural context that later would become Samy's life work. Eventually his father joined in too; more of a closet academic than he ever would admit.

For Mr. Al-Mahdi it came down to two simple questions. Was human progress good or bad? And why had Allah waited until thousands of years in the progression of human history before revealing ultimate truth through Muhammad and the Koran? Had He then frozen progress in the seventh and eighth centuries? The answers, he told his son, were not so easy, but by coming to America, Samy's grandfather had chosen progress over poverty. And he also chose to be American, which meant the family had a Christmas tree though they went to mosque, and Samy's grandmother worked in a beauty shop but wore a headscarf. They ate no pork and drank no alcohol, but otherwise pretty much ignored the rules of *halal*.

Samy eventually came to his own accommodation, or more accurately spent his life trying to figure it out. Much like Sally, he concluded a profoundly great and perfect intelligence must be responsible for the universe, but man was no more central to creation than a chipmunk or a grain of sand. And so he did not believe in God except as a human attempt to describe and understand the creator. How else, he said, could one account for the diversity and sloppiness in religious texts, which were mostly hodge-podge collections with multiple authors and written over multiple centuries in multiple languages.

But he also could not deny the importance of God in human

history and the development of cooperation in complex societies, or at least the importance of belief in God. If belief held men together and caused them to do good, then it was God. If it caused them to do evil, then it was sin and Satan. And so, because he believed in belief but not in God, he remained selectively religious; a believer in Islam but not in Allah. As an academic, he took his degrees in history and religion but toiled in the liminal interstices between these fields and the sciences of evolution, anthropology, and psychology. He was convinced that somewhere in this space resided a rational explanation for man's conception of God and need for organized religion. And all along he clung to his Shia heritage and traditions like the bans on pork and alcohol, which were harmless or even beneficial.

The rules on cutting or not cutting various parts of the human body were another matter, however, as he tried to explain to Uncle Anwar when he took his fourth trip to Yemen at the age of sixteen, clean-shaven and full of the innocence and arrogance possible only in a teenager. Why should Allah care about hair on a man's face or the covering on his head? And why was it that male facial hair could not be cut, but female genitalia had to be? Why would a perfect and all-powerful Allah create people who required such carefully calibrated maintenance and modification?

Anwar excused the blasphemy only because he understood his great nephew had been damaged by his time in America. But he made clear that Allah's will was not to be questioned, and Samy had darn well better grow a beard forthwith, no matter how hot the summer heat.

AT THE SANA'A air terminal in the wee hours of Sunday morning (still Saturday night in the U.S.) Anwar scowled at the short stubble on Samy's face, but said nothing. For all his religious fervor he had no quarrel with non-believers who lived in non-Islamic parts of the world. He knew only that in his part of the world, blessed in climate and blessed in peace during the recent wars, people would show their thanks by remaining pious. And peace in the mountainous redoubt would be maintained, praise Allah, with a stock of heavy weapons both bought and stolen, and with men adept and well trained in their use. The irony of embracing these deadly parts of modern technology to protect ancient tradition totally escaped him.

With Anwar at the airport were three of Samy's younger cousins, men in their early twenties who alertly surveyed their surroundings as they all walked out to four pickup trucks armed with heavy machine guns mounted in their beds, and a fifth with an anti-tank rocket launcher. The trucks were all Toyotas, small by American standards, but in third world places like Yemen nearly ubiquitous as the war chariot of choice. And they ran on gas because electricity was an intermittent commodity at best. There were none of Sally Macalester's pet project charging stations. Eight men stood guard over the vehicles, all with Kalashnikovs in their hands and well-honed traditional daggers called *jambiahs* in their belts.

"We cannot go to the village until daylight," Anwar said as he and Samy climbed into the backseat of the one truck with an extended cab. The dangers of the road were too great to travel in the dark. Instead they would spend the few hours till Sunday's dawn with a son who lived in Wadi Dahr.

Samy smiled at the news. "My father's cousin, who lives near the imam's palace?"

"Yes. You remember well."

Of course he did. How could he forget the cousin who had treated him so well on his first trip to Yemen. And how could anyone forget the palace. The Shia imams who had ruled from Sana'a went back to the first centuries of Islam, when their realm included all of what was now modern Yemen and more. In those days the economic base was coffee, marketed through the Red Sea port of Mocha. In later times foreign coffee competition did in the economy, and the imams became little more than leaders of the resistance against invaders like the Turks and Wahhabis. But through it all they lasted almost a thousand years, until the death of Imam bin Yahya in 1962 and the Egyptian-inspired revolt that established the Yemen Arab Republic, otherwise known as North Yemen. Ever since the North and South variously joined or fought one another, like a conflicted couple bouncing back and forth between the altar and divorce court.

But all revered the Wadi Dahr summer palace as a symbol of Yemen's glorious past. Built atop a massive natural pillar of red tan sandstone, it stood like a giant chess piece rook at the wadi's edge. The masonry, for all its bulk and heft, appeared lacy and graceful, almost delicate. It was a lookout point over the flat plain to its south, yet dwarfed by sandstone cliffs to its immediate north. Here architecture merged with nature in perfect harmony. A spectacle more stupendous than Mad King Ludwig's fairy tale confection at Neuschwanstein in Bavaria. Proof positive of the divinely inspired superiority of Islam. Neuschwanstein was the stuff of Disney. Wadi Dahr was the stuff of Allah.

The house of Anwar's son was less than a kilometer from the famous palace. It was, of course, far more modest, but nonetheless built of the same red rock and with the same lace-like trim and ornamentation. Only the son, a younger and stouter version of his father, was awake when they arrived at half past one. He led them with a smoky flickering candle to a room not large but big enough for them all to sleep on the floor. Blankets had already been spread out, and for Anwar, in deference to his age, there was a single cot against one wall. The windows were glazed but uncovered with shades or drapes, and the morning sun would wake them early.

After their host went back to bed Samy approached Anwar and waited for him to complete his prayers. "Uncle," he said, "there's a trip I need to take before we go to the village."

"To where?"

"To the south. To Aden. And I need your help."

"Why?"

Samy glanced around the room. In the faint starlight seeping through the windows he looked at the men all laid down and positioning themselves for sleep. "Let us take a little walk and I'll tell you more."

AT FIRST Anwar resisted. The South was never safe, and Aden in particular was a den of multiple iniquities. A city once controlled by the British and once home to Royal Navy and Air Force bases, it was thoroughly contaminated by the West.

"Uncle," Samy told him, "I do this only to save us all from a holocaust. Because of the bombs back home, the Crusader crazies in America are ready to obliterate the entire region, and we have to stop them."

"By you going to Aden?"

"By me finding out who really did the bombs."

Though he didn't quite get the reasoning, Anwar eventually agreed. But they would need more supplies and men for such a journey. First thing in the morning Anwar would send two men back home to assemble and organize the required materiel and reinforcements.

THE LARGER CONVOY, now ten pickup trucks and two SUVs, finally headed south from Wadi Dahr in the middle of the afternoon on Sunday, December 28. They traveled until dark, spent the night at Yarim, and early Monday drove farther south through Ibb, then southeast to their final objective. It was a force formidable enough that neither local bandits nor the army made any attempt to stop them, and they saw no sign of either until they'd almost reached the coast. The time was half past ten in the morning on December 29.

On a map the port of Aden looks like two giant lobster claws reaching south to clutch a piece of the sea. Seen in three dimensions from the air, the crustacean appendages become former volcanic islands, each attached to the mainland by a wide isthmus. An oil refinery and the city of Little Aden occupy the western claw. An extinct volcano dominates the island part of the eastern claw, and the ancient and original city of Aden is located inside the half-collapsed cone of its crater. The open side, where a piece of the cone long ago went missing, faces southward and seaward, toward the Gulf of Aden, and the gap affords access to the old harbor, in which picture-postcard dhows bob gently in the breeze. The modern port facilities at Al Maala are outside the crater, on the north side of the eastern claw in a harbor that is both larger and more sheltered from the open water.

The new harbor is bounded on its east end by the connective terra firma of the isthmus, a flat, windswept strip six miles long and two miles wide. Near the midpoint is Aden International Airport, the former Royal Air Force base. Because the runway takes up the entire width of the isthmus, a four-lane causeway skirts around its west end and runs northward all the way to the mainland, where an army checkpoint now awaited the Dabwa convoy. It controlled all traffic to both the airport and the docks at Al Maala, and the soldiers' standing orders forbade passage for the kind of heavy weaponry Anwar had brought from Wadi Dahr. He and his men knew about both the checkpoint and its rules, and they pulled into a moribund construction site half a mile before they reached it. Only Anwar and Samy, plus a driver and two bodyguards, continued south in a single shiny white and nearly new Toyota SUV.

PAPERS, THE CORPORAL at the checkpoint demanded. Dutifully the four Yemenis produced their IDs. Samy handed over his passport, which took the corporal by great surprise.

"American?"

Anwar instantly intervened to answer and explain. "My brother's grandson. A famous professor who writes about Yemen and wants pictures of the old Steamer Point. The reason for our trip."

Samy could only hope his surprise didn't show too much. He had no idea what Steamer Point was, and did not learn until Anwar told him it was the name given to a long-defunct British coaling station outside and to the west of the big crater. He also had no camera, which might make things a bit sticky if someone asked to see it. What the hell was Anwar thinking!

The corporal remained skeptically impassive. A military policeman through and through. Why would five people drive more than three hundred kilometers for a few pictures? And how did they make it from Sana'a in a single unarmed vehicle? But when Samy spoke in perfect Arabic the policeman's scowl changed to a grin and he half-joked that maybe his picture, too, should appear in the book. To their relief he seemed pleased when Samy used the camera feature on the old black phone and showed him the image on its small screen.

Once through the checkpoint they drove past the airport and on to the south end of the isthmus, then turned right into Al Maala on a wide boulevard lined with six- and seven-story office and apartment buildings, which despite their clean pastel colors were sadly Soviet in their shoddy drabness. Yemen Fruit, Ltd. had its office on the first floor of one building, and the shipping company office was only a block away on the first floor of another.

They found both offices burned out, boarded up, and totally devoid of life. At the shipping company the driver stopped and one of the bodyguards went to inquire at an insurance office next door about what had happened. The plump little insurance broker greeted him with the jovial smile of a born Rotarian and salesman, but at the first whiff of a question about his former neighbors his face went cold with panic. He hustled the bodyguard back out the door, lowered the blinds, and stuck a "closed" sign in the window. And as he hurried to his car he wouldn't even glance at the SUV or show his face to its occupants.

"Let's get out of here," Samy said. They'd been in the city only half an hour, and that now seemed too much time.

"Go on to the docks," Anwar ordered.

Samy didn't speak, but his eyes said no. They needed to get the hell out of Aden as fast as possible.

"And what of your quest to save us all from the Crusader holocaust?"

"Not making any progress here, am I?"

"Let us go to the docks and maybe you will find your progress."

THERE WAS BUT a single ship moored along the quay, a rusty tramp of Korean origin and Liberian registry. A crane that appeared oversize for the task was busy unloading it under the watchful eye of a short and slender supervisor with a neatly trimmed beard. He was dressed in well-pressed khakis and wore a bright yellow hard hat. When he saw Anwar walking toward him from the SUV he waved for an assistant to come take charge and then led his visitor to an air-conditioned equipment shed where they could talk privately and in comfort.

After fifteen minutes Anwar emerged, got into the SUV, and said to go back the way they'd come, and to stop at a western-style supermarket he'd seen south of the airport. It was past noon, he was hungry, and they needed supplies for the trip home.

"What was that about?" Samy asked.

Anwar pulled nervously on his beard, kept his eyes on the road, and ignored the question. They didn't want to miss the market, he said. Only when he was certain his instructions had been understood did he turn to his great nephew to tell him the true tale of what had happened to the hapless clerks and their bombed-out offices. And how their colleagues had fled to join Samir Akbar.

Chapter 14

"ho?"

"Ferguson. Sounds to me like Ferguson. He still alive?"

"Haven't heard he died. I probably would have." Jake Ferguson's death would not likely be either peaceful or inconspicuous. Stromdahl jotted himself a note to check with O'Brien later in the day. It was only four in the morning in DC on Monday the twenty-ninth, and he'd taken the call in his bedroom. "So who told you all this?" he asked Samy on the phone. The connection through the Navy ships, a satellite, and then Navy headquarters was adequate but not great, and he had to repeat the question twice.

"A guy at the harbor talked with my uncle. A cousin, I think. From our tribe. Anyway, he said a guy with prematurely white hair and a sort of lightning bolt scar on his cheek came along with the police goons and helped torture thc clerks. Said the white-haired guy was really the one in charge."

"Which cheek was the scar on?"

"Harbor guy didn't know. But he said White Hair killed the clerks after he and the goons had their fun. Cut their fingers off one by one. Then other parts. Then slit their throats. That sounds like Ferguson. Did the CIA use him to do its investigation?"

"Don't know." *But probably so*, Stromdahl thought. Gronkowski was a big Ferguson backer. He paused a couple of seconds, then asked Samy if the torture and killings had been done at the now-burned-out offices.

"No. Police station. White Hair and one goon came back and blew both places up. By then everyone else in the offices had run off to go hide with Akbar. Guess my uncle was right." Samy said the last with a bitter mix of triumph and sorrow. The news dispelled any doubts about the reliability of Uncle Anwar's earlier report, but it also meant Akbar had gone even further across the line between piety and zealous madness. What had turned Samy's old football teammate into a terrorist ten times crazier and more lethal than bin Laden?

Stromdahl sensed the regret in Samy's voice, but left it alone. "How the hell does your uncle's cousin know all this," he asked. "I take it he wasn't there."

"No secret who went into the offices and took the clerks away. Or came back to blow things up. The whole street saw them."

"And the other stuff?"

"Like who did the killing and how? They burned the bodies, but it got so bad one of the goons couldn't take it. Don't know who he told, but the word got out. Maybe they wanted the word to get out." He let the thought hang in the air, and when Stromdahl said nothing he added what was going through both their minds. That, too, sounded like Ferguson's sort of thing.

"So where are you now?"

"Some kind of supermarket near the airport. I'm outside waiting in an SUV. My uncle's buying stuff for the trip back." As Samy spoke Stromdahl heard the sound of truck doors opening and an engine starting in the background. The noise nearly drowned out the already poor connection.

"What's going on?"

No answer.

"What's going on?"

"They just got back." Static and noise.

"What?"

"We're leaving now."

Stromdahl was about to ask where they were going when the background noise turned to gunfire and wild shouting. Not the rattling crack of rifles, but the deep rumble of heavy machine guns. At least two of them.

"Samy, you still there?"

No response.

"Samy!"

Again, not a word. Only the sound of more incoherent shouting and the roar of a revving engine punctuated by more heavy gunfire. And then the phone went completely silent. Not a simple clicked-off silence but a raspy, scratchy squeal followed by a steady low hiss, as if it had been crushed and was breathing its last breath before death.

JAKE FERGUSON NEVER did understand the civilized world. Not in Iraq nor anywhere else. By 2006 the Marine Corps faced military failure in Anbar Province, which comprised the western third of Iraq and was nothing but sand dunes and desert except for a narrow green band along the Euphrates River, where all the big battles were fought. Places like Fallujah, where the river meandered within forty miles of Baghdad and the Tigris. Then upstream north and west to Ramadi, Hit, and Haditha, and finally Al Qu'im, just before the Syrian border. The Marines took and retook every one of these cities and every town and hamlet in between. They never lost but also never won, and so they didn't stop fighting until everyone realized they couldn't kill their way to victory. Everyone except Lieutenant Colonel Ferguson.

He commanded the battalion charged with securing Haditha and the big dam above the city, which provided most of the province's electricity. In the flat land through which the Euphrates gently flowed toward its union with the Tigris, impoundment of the muddy water required an earthen dike six miles long, a vulnerable terrorist target almost impossible to defend. Responsibility for its protection would have driven a saner man crazy, but like Howie Fabelman and *Nagaf*, Ferguson had infinite faith in the power of brutality and violence. He was hard-bitten, hardcore, and not about to back away from anything. Every day he sent his men patrolling across the top of the dam and through the farms and villages along the river's palm-lined banks, and every day the body count went higher. For both the good guys and the bad.

Then on a sweltering Thursday in August a convoy of five Humvees drove into an ambush in the tall grass of a marshy area downstream of the dam. A land mine blew the lead vehicle off the road and killed two of its four occupants. The driver and the lance corporal riding shotgun survived, but were dragged off by the attackers before the other Marines had a chance to fan out and mount a rescue assault. Two days later what remained of them was found in the middle of the same road, left by the enemy as a grisly warning.

Corporal Samir Al-Mahdi, on his second tour in Iraq, had joined the battalion only two days before, and had not yet realized the full intensity of Ferguson's perversion. The colonel proudly proclaimed he was at war with Islam, just like the blue coat cavalry had gone to war against the Indians in the American West, and he thought of Samy as something like a benign pet Indian scout.

"Find out what village those bastards came from," he ordered. "We're gonna take 'em out."

Naïve and unwarned, Samy did his bidding. The people from the village, just south of Haditha, trusted his Arabic and his name and told him there were five al Qaeda among them, three Saudis and two Yemenis, all much hated for their primitive religiosity and violence. They had led the attack and tortured the two captured Marines.

"Outstanding work, Corporal," Ferguson told him. "Fucking outstanding." Maybe Stromdahl's teacher idea wasn't so stupid after all.

That night the colonel led the raid himself, he and ten men handpicked for their shared belief about how to handle the insurgency. They returned at six in the morning, covered with blood.

The bodies of the five members of al Qaeda were found shortly after sunrise, hanging upside down from palm trees by the river, body parts missing and throats slit; bled out like slaughtered animals and scalped as if the victims of Apaches. Ten more bodies were found floating in the river, equally abused; supposedly the people who lived in the houses where the others had been hiding. Among them were the two young men who had confided in Samy.

At the time Stromdahl was commanding another battalion, responsible for the area around Hit. It took Samy two hours to reach him by radio. "Sir, I can't say why, but you need to get up here. Right away."

In the mundane black-and-white of a document or text message the request would have grabbed attention. Corporals did not give orders to lieutenants, much less lieutenant colonels. But the auditory tone, even clipped of its character by the narrow bandwidth of the military radio, told far more than the words. In Samy's voice Stromdahl heard not the horror of combat, but something much worse. Maybe the horror of the real hell. And revulsion at unintended complicity with the real devil.

And now, in Aden, the devil Ferguson had come back and the phone connection to Samy had been broken. Stromdahl clicked off his phone reluctantly, then, despite the early hour, he clicked it on again and called Sven Swenson.

"WALLY, I SAID no back up. Besides, we got no one within a thousand miles we could send in. And what the hell could they do anyway? Where the hell would they look? If the phone was working we could get a fix on where he was. At least where the phone was. But it's completely dead."

"How do you know that?"

"I sent a text message to the duty officer just now, while we were talking. He says they've lost the signal. It's supposed to keep sending even when it's turned off, as long as there's any juice left in the battery. But we're not picking up a thing." To his credit, Swenson was sympathetic, and not scrambling to cover his ass, but the mess with Al-Mahdi's secret mission to Yemen was already bad enough and he wasn't going to make it any worse. He bit his lip and stopped just short of "I told you so."

Stromdahl paused a second to do the quick and cold-blooded mental triage required for survival in combat and politics. "All right," he said. "I get it on Samy. But what the fuck was Ferguson doing there?"

"You sure it was him?"

"How many younger white-haired guys are there with big ole scars on their faces?"

Swenson had to agree, and recalled the story behind Ferguson's disfigurement. He was a first lieutenant on shore patrol duty in Malta when a drunk sailor and a drunk Marine got into a fight in a Valetta bar. The Marine broke off the bottom part of a glass beer bottle and used the sharp-edged remainder to slash out one of the sailor's eyes. Ferguson, who was built like a linebacker and had the disposition of an angry rhino, stepped in between them, took a slash to his right cheek, and then clocked the son of a bitch with a blow that broke his jaw into seven pieces. In the ambulance on the way to the hospital the lieutenant was pissed as hell and said he got cut only because he hadn't realized the Marine was left handed. "Otherwise I woulda rammed that bottle up his fuckin' ass." The incident and his comment made him briefly legendary in both the Navy and the Corps.

"He oughta be buried under the brig for what he did in Anbar," Stromdahl continued. "Shoulda been hung by his balls for it."

"That's the kind of thing he would do, not you."

"In his case I'd have made an exception." Stromdahl remained deeply bitter at how Ferguson beat the rap at his court martial on some bullshit technicality, and even more bitter over what happened afterwards. A disgusted Commandant quickly cashiered him out of the Corps, but the only option was to dump him on society with an honorable discharge. Immediately he became the darling of the anti-Muslim rightwingers who warned of Islamo-Fascism and a deep dark plot to impose Sharia law on the United States. Like *Nagaf*, they believed the only good Muslim was a dead Muslim.

"I might have strung him up too," Swenson conceded. "But I've no idea who sent him to Aden. Sure as hell wasn't us." By "us" he meant the military. He couldn't speak for the CIA or Gronkowski, who back in 2006 was one of the Congressmen who wanted to give Ferguson a medal.

"So where is he now?" Stromdahl asked O'Brien just after lunch later on Monday. They'd already spoken at seven thirty, as soon as the Director got into his office, and the FBI had quickly made inquiries into Ferguson's current whereabouts.

"Good question."

"I know that. What's the answer? Red Sand?"

"No. He left there five years ago. Too crazy even for them." Red Sand Security was the brainchild of a retired Air Force General named Runyon who never got over the Cold War and saw commies everywhere. When he left the military he recruited younger but like-minded veterans from the SEALs and Special Forces and Marine Corps Recon. The toughest of the tough, the ones who needed constant enemies and constant action to survive.

Red Sand paid them four times what they made in the service and let them cowboy around the world pretty much unrestrained by any laws or government supervision. The Republicans in power when Runyon started the company quickly got him contracts with the CIA and State Department, and he became an overnight multi-multi-millionaire.

Except for the bad publicity fallout from the exercise of too much force or the display of too much arrogance, neither he nor his new clients gave much of a damn how Red Sand got results. But Ferguson couldn't abide by even those loose rules. Back in Iraq as a contractor, he soon gained fame for shooting up civilians and seizing their property, and once again departed under a cloud.

"So you talked with Red Sand," Stromdahl asked.

"I spoke with Old Man Runyon himself. Listen to him and you'd think Jake was some kind of martyr. They only let him go when the Democrats took control of the House and held hearings on the whole private security business."

"Which gets me back to my first question. Where is he now?"

"Well, maybe Aden, if you believe Al-Mahdi's uncle's cousin. At least last week. Real question is, who's he working for now? And for that I've got no answer, except I don't think Runyon told me one tenth of what he knows."

"What's he leaving out?"

"My best guess is they set up some kind of secret subsidiary to do their really dirty work. And I'd guess the first choice to run it would be Jake."

BACK IN YEMEN, while Stromdahl was on the phone with Admiral Swenson, Samir Al-Mahdi and his uncle bounced back and forth on the SUV's floor mats like flotsam tossed by a storm. When the first spray of gunfire ripped through the rear window and out the windshield it missed them both. Proof positive of Allah's divine intervention, Anwar later said, and even Sami had trouble attributing it all to chance and luck. In the lull before the second burst they instinctively dove downward, Anwar first despite his age. Once down, their arms and legs became hopelessly tangled as the scientific laws of inertia and centrifugal force shuffled them rudely from side to side while the SUV zigzagged north at a hundred miles an hour.

The other three occupants of the vehicle, perhaps not so

favored by Allah, did not fare as well. The bodyguard in the shotgun seat died instantly from a bullet to the head, and the second bodyguard, who was in the narrow fold-away seat in the rear, slumped over badly wounded. The driver, too, survived, but a ricochet off a doorframe shattered his left shoulder. The impact threw him forward into the steering wheel and nearly knocked him out. He was a small, spare man, yet hard and tough, and he fought through the pain and hung onto consciousness and the wheel to get away from the market's parking lot. After he got back on the road he floored the gas pedal and with his one good arm yanked the wheel from left to right to evade the gunfire from three pickups in hot pursuit. The windblast through the shattered windshield no doubt helped keep him from passing out.

Samy had the black phone held to his ear when the attack began, but when he dove down it flew from his grip and went skittering under the front passenger seat, only to emerge on the other side where it wedged beneath the lifeless bodyguard. The dead weight on the touch pad sent the electronics into chaos and cut off the call to Stromdahl. Just how the various bounces and jounces had meshed to produce such an exquisitely strange outcome was anybody's guess, but Anwar, always carefully selective about attributions to Allah, this time agreed with Samy that it was a matter of chance. Allah, after all, was on their side.

The second burst of bullets missed completely. The pickups all had bed-mounted heavy caliber machine guns, but in pursuit only the truck closest to the Toyota could shoot because it blocked the line of fire for the other two. Its gunner blazed profligately away, and the fearsome muzzle flashes shot out like long-tongued flames from a welding torch turned on full blast. But the gunner might as well have fired blanks. He hadn't much idea how to aim or handle the recoil from his weapon. And the driver only made things worse by slowing down to allow for easier aiming and then suddenly speeding up as the white SUV started to pull away. Every burst the gunner fired went high and wide.

Thus did the deadly caravan careen northward onto the causeway at the east end of the harbor, past the west end of the airport's runway, and towards the army checkpoint, where the injured driver hoped to find salvation. He had the advantage of a bigger engine and more nimble handling, but his wounds and loss of blood sapped his strength and attention, and the zigzagging became ever more random and erratic. The lead pickup drove within a few feet, and its driver tried to position it so the gunner would have an unmissable shot, but he had to back off to avoid a crash with oncoming traffic. He regrouped, came close once more, but again had to fall back. The checkpoint was only a mile away, and the SUV and its desperate driver were going to make it.

On the floor Sami and his uncle continued to tumble back and forth, aware only of the machine gun blasts and the increasingly extreme zigs and zags and a decrease in speed when the driver reached the checkpoint. But there was no salvation. At the sound of the approaching gunfire the soldiers vanished, either complicit or fearful they were outnumbered and outgunned. Most likely all of the above. The wounded driver slowed down, saw the checkpoint was abandoned, and once again floored the gas. The pickups had fallen back a few hundred yards, ready to turn and flee from the army, but when the pursuers saw their prey continue north they too sped back up and quickly closed the gap.

And so the chase continued through the residential streets of a mainland district called Shaykh Uthman, with the pickups drawing closer as the SUV's driver lost blood and struggled not to pass out. In total disregard of oncoming traffic, the lead pickup finally managed to pull alongside to the left, and the gunner trained his weapon straight at the driver's head. He pulled the trigger and there was a click and then there was silence. Again he pulled, and again nothing but a click. And again and again, until he saw his ammo box was empty, at which point he shook his fist at the sky and dropped back to let his comrades take up the hunt.

The next pickup now pulled up behind the Toyota and fired more accurately. Three rounds ricocheted off the heavy framing around the rear door, and the rest sailed through the space between the seat tops and the ceiling, except for one that came in a little lower and grazed the right ear of the fading driver, so near gone he probably never noticed. He gripped the wheel with all the might remaining in his right hand and squinted to keep the road in focus. His zigzagging became a completely random weave as he veered from one side of the road to the other and finally crashed into a light stanchion.

The collision bounced Samy and Uncle Anwar forward into the seatbacks, but the upholstery absorbed their momentum and they dropped back to the floorboard with unbroken bones and little more than bruises. Outside and out of their view the three pickups converged for the kill. The two with remaining ammunition fired simultaneous bursts that finished off the driver. The spray of blood inside the SUV clouded the air like red mist, and Samy and Anwar could taste the sickening salty sweetness. They both went fetal and awaited their fate.

They heard the truck doors opening, and the sound of rifle bolts pulled back to chamber rounds. They didn't hear any footsteps on the ground, but they knew the men were coming. Anwar was praying loudly, and Samy was trying to curl into a tighter ball. And then they heard two huge explosions, and through the shot-out windows of their vehicle they felt the pressure and heat from the blasts. Two of the pickups had vaporized into fireballs, and the men who remained alive and standing dropped their weapons and jumped into the third as it turned around and raced away to the south. A sudden silence followed the booms, broken within seconds by the sound of the approaching Dabwa convoy and then the rapid jabbering of the tribesmen who were both ecstatic and awestruck at the destruction they had wrought with their anti-tank rockets. At the moment it mattered not that one of the pursuing pickups managed to escape.

Anwar lost hearing in one ear, but Samy's fetal curl kept his hearing intact. Woozy but in command, Anwar climbed out from the remains of the SUV and ordered his men to set up a secure perimeter while they tended to the surviving bodyguard and assessed the damage. He also pulled out his phone and called the cousin at the docks to warn him. If he was still alive.

From what Samy could hear, apparently he was indeed unharmed and already under very deep cover. "He will leave Aden by boat," Anwar said after clicking off the phone.

"Where will he go?"

"He will sail to a safer haven in the north, on the Red Sea." Anwar paused and pointed vaguely to the northwest, then looked squarely into Samy's eyes. "And tell me, my nephew, who it is that so badly wants to hide the truth that they would take such risk to kill us all? Is it your Crusader Americans or the Persians?"

"I have no idea. Probably not the CIA, which does the Crusaders' bidding." Samy had no doubt the agency could be murderously ruthless, but he didn't think it was capable of reacting so fast to anything like his last-minute trip to Yemen.

And why would they kill him anyway? "More probably Samir Akbar," he said.

Anwar frowned his disagreement.

"So then it was Iranians." If not Akbar, that seemed the only logical choice. Except it didn't ring true, and they both knew it. "Or maybe Ferguson," Samy added softly.

"I thought you said this Ferguson worked for the CIA, which you say is not a likely suspect."

"Yes, but he wouldn't work under their control. No one controls what that bastard does."

CHAPTER 15

On the air Luke Rumbo claimed deep knowledge of the Bible and the Constitution. Philosophy and history too, and if need be, science, economics, or any other field he felt an urge to cite in spinning his tale of the way things ought to be. But the Bible and the Constitution were his two sacred texts, the one inerrant and the other inerrantly inspired. Luke was a big believer in sticking with the original intent of the founding fathers, as if they possessed a divinely guided single mind when they wrote the Constitution in 1787. Had the Supreme Court stuck with original intent there'd be no need for the complete Constitutional overhaul he and the Tea Party were now pushing, a purging of heresies like the early Christians' purging of the Gnostics.

When a caller asked about the founders' acceptance of slavery and the Civil War that resulted three score and fourteen years later, Luke dismissed these issues as mere details, inconvenient and not of great consequence. Amendments to the Constitution did give him slight pause, because they suggested some flaw in the sacred document and the original intenders' thinking. But he saw the first ten amendments in the Bill of Rights as a seamless extension of the original seven articles, sort of like the New Testament following upon the Old. They were adopted only three years after the initial ratification in 1788, and introduced by none other than James Madison, a leader at the original Constitutional Convention.

And even more important, they were clearly aimed at limiting the power of the Federal government, not the states. According to Luke, the states were left free to establish rules based on religion if they wanted. The founders, he said, understood that Christian practices differed from one state to another, and their only point in the First Amendment's guarantee of religious freedom was to prevent attempts at imposing a uniform national version of the country's fundamental Christian faith. Christianity itself was never in doubt. The Supreme Court didn't see things that way, but what the heck. The Court was just wrong.

Like the Bill of Rights, the Eleventh and Twelfth Amendments were of no great concern. The Eleventh dealt with judicial procedures and the Twelfth aligned the election process with the reality of political parties, and both were adopted close enough in time to 1787 that original intent could be inferred. It was the three post-Civil War amendments that caused him real consternation. Especially the Fourteenth, which guaranteed individual rights as a matter of Federal law, and greatly expanded the reach of the Federal government. For that reason alone it had to be wrong, but on purely legal grounds it was intrinsically flawed because Article V of the Constitution required ratification of amendments by three quarters of the states, and the former Confederate states never properly participated in the approval process. Based on this logic, Luke maintained that nearly all Federal programs enacted since the illegitimate adoption of the Fourteenth Amendment in 1868 were irrevocably tainted.

That's why the country needed to go back to the beginning and return to original intent. Do away with the Sixteenth Amendment and income taxes, and the Seventeenth Amendment and the popular election of Senators. He would have added the Nineteenth Amendment and women's suffrage to his hit list, except Lisa Larkin would for sure have left him. But Lisa or not, the bottom line was clear. The United States needed a constitution that made explicit its bedrock principles of Christianity and Capitalism. Only then could the country realize the full benefits of original intent. Only then could it mitigate the original sin of Theodore Roosevelt's Square Deal and FDR's New Deal, and all the other Big Bad Government that followed.

In truth, of course, Luke's views on the Constitution and his web of conspiracy theories and ad hoc hatreds were not, as he claimed, the product of deep study and thought. He read very little, and his education ended after one misspent year at a junior college. The fodder for his rants was mostly random detritus provided by Hiram Heilman or culled from the Internet by Lisa. Luke contributed a finely tuned ear for the sense and psyche of his audience, but it was Lisa who knew how to spin the wishes of his corporate puppeteers. Only she could take public anger over something like a coalmine disaster and divert it from the mine owners to the pinheads in Washington. No, no, no, she would write out in big block print on four-by-eight cards for Luke to read over the air. No, it wasn't the mine owners' fault at all that explosive gases filled a mineshaft. It was all because the government regulated too much and imposed ventilation requirements that the owners had to ignore if they wanted to stay profitable. If they didn't have to waste time and money fighting the adoption of such petty rules and then defending themselves in court when the Feds tried to enforce them the mines would operate far more safely.

And now she had surpassed herself in the game of Constitutional legerdemain. It was around lunchtime on Monday, the day of Samy Al-Mahdi's abruptly aborted call from Yemen and Stromdahl's frantic early morning calls to Swenson and O'Brien. She and Luke were back in Birmingham, eating in the kitchen of his mansion as they prepared for his next broadcast. They sat on stools pulled up to a granite-topped island in the middle of the room. "Look," she told him. "Look at this. It's Congress that declares war, not the President." She had a copy of the Constitution called up on her laptop, and scrolled down to Article I, Section 8. There it was, plain as day. "The Congress shall have the Power . . . to declare War." There was no such authority given to the President.

He stared several puzzled seconds at the screen. "So what's your point?"

"The point, my little Lukester, is that you need to tell Hiram and Congress to declare war on Iran right away. If Macalester and her Progressives and Democrats won't do their duty, the Republicans have to do it for them."

"And then what?"

"And then, when war's declared and she still does nothing we'll have even more reason to get her impeached. It's perfect."

TWO DAYS LATER, on Wednesday, the last day of the year, Sally held a mid-morning meeting to talk about how she might stave off impeachment, or at least conviction in the Senate if she were impeached. She also wanted to get caught up on where things stood with the investigation. The meeting was impromptu, informal, and small—only her, Stromdahl, and Jane Nelson. She made the invitational calls herself the night before, at once bemused and horrified at the depth of her distrust of anyone else. Had the circle of people she could count on really shrunk to her two college classmates? In Washington, at least, sadly yes.

"No need for uniforms or suits," she told them. "We'll just meet in the Treaty Room." That was the formal name for her private office on the residential second floor. It was her favorite room in the White House; the one she felt was really hers. Unlike Stromdahl, she had replaced her predecessor's heavy mahogany furniture with neoclassical pieces of maple and cherry, light in both form and color and decorated with understated geometric inlays rather than ornate carvings. The peach-colored wall coverings and drapes were also simple and light, and the Persian carpet was of a relatively plain design. It was about as close as she could get to "Minnesota Modern" without completely horrifying her interior designer and the architectural historians on the White House staff.

Before her two advisors arrived she lit the oak logs neatly stacked on the fireplace grate. Briefly she thought back to the days before tablet readers when old newspapers served as kindling material. Now newsprint was mostly dead, and the fireplace had a gas flame lighter that for safety reasons wouldn't work unless the flue was open. The more senior members of the White House domestic staff loved to tell the story of how the Obama girls once caused evacuation of the entire building when they started a fire without checking the chimney opening.

Stromdahl showed up first, again dressed tweedy and informal. He poured himself a cup of coffee, and took a chair next to Sally's in front of the fire. "Jane will be here soon," she said without explanation.

He looked around the room and his eyes fixed on the music box on Sally's desk. She followed his gaze and asked if it was he who'd left the present. Never much at giftwrapping, he'd taped the card to the outside, and apparently it had fallen off before Sally opened the gift. Yes, he admitted, he was the guilty party. "Hope you like it. I thought it kinda brought back some good memories of old times."

She reached over and took his big right paw in both her hands. "Yes it does. Thanks." She was about to give him a chaste little kiss on the cheek when security announced over the speakerphone that Senator Nelson had arrived. Moments later she joined them by the fireplace. She wore a casual outfit and looked like she'd come straight from shopping or maybe a trip to the gym.

The year before Nelson might have given the two of them a knowing look and asked slyly what they were up to, but that was before Sally ascended to exalted high office and became the embodiment of the nation. One did not kid an embodiment about her hanky-panky, no matter how chaste. Instead Jane just asked if they'd had a good Christmas.

"Yeah," Stromdahl said. "All things considered."

"It was very nice," the President said. She stole a glance first at Walleye and then the music box on the desk before putting another log on the fire. Then she got right down to business. Just where had Rumbo come up with his latest Constitutional fantasy? Congress had declared war only five times in the country's entire history, and not once since World War II. And always on the President's request and never based on this kind of flimsy nonsense.

"But he's right that they can do it," Nelson said.

"Oh, I know that. But how do they get anyone to take it seriously?"

The Senator took a sip of coffee and stared a second or two at the now-crackling fire before speaking. "Well, first of all, no Constitution will work if we turn it into a playbook for political games. Which is what's happened since the Tea Nuts grabbed control of the Republican Party. And the Supreme Court hasn't helped either. Not when it finds that corporations can have political and religious beliefs just like real live people. And that for all intents and purposes anyone can spend as much as they want to get their guy elected." She paused and took another sip. "But it's more than that. The money counts only because elections have turned into competitions between polling and marketing teams instead of candidates and ideas. Remember, when the Tea Party got started it ran people who didn't try to hide what they thought about the Second Amendment and violent defiance of authority. Or about absolute bans on abortion and even birth control. They were honest and they got hammered. And the Democrats, God bless them, always go to mush and run away from their own accomplishments if the polls say they aren't popular."

"Yeah," Sally said. "Now both of the old parties spend all their campaign time and money trying to distort what the other side says and then going totally evasive on what they actually stand for. And the voters know it's all advertising agency fluff. That's why they don't trust any politician. That's what we tried to change with the New Progressives."

"Right. And look where that's got us."

Stromdahl interjected to bring them back to the problem at hand. "It got us here, waiting for the Republicans to declare another stupid war. You really think they'll do it?"

"Who knows," Nelson said. "Look, it's stupid but easy. Takes only a simple majority, which they have in both houses, and it's a stick in the eye for Iran without any real consequences. With Sally as President we're not actually going to launch nukes or invade. The Tea Nuts can throw their little temper tantrum and not get spanked." Impeachment and conviction, she continued, would be much tougher for them. "I think I can hold off at least the Senate if we've got anything to slow down the rush to judgment."

"Anything more from Al-Mahdi?" Sally asked.

Stromdahl shook his head no. Nothing since the aborted call two days before.

"So what else have we got?"

"Nothing huge, but maybe something big enough to buy us time. O'Brien tells me there's a possible lead on the trucks."

"You mean the SUVs," Nelson said.

"No, the trucks they used to get the SUVs close to the targets. Least that's what we think happened."

"How does that help us?"

"Well, remember when everyone was all set to blame Muslim terrorists for the bomb in Oklahoma City? Turned out to be Tim McVeigh. Could be the same sort of thing again."

"Yeah," Nelson said. "But McVeigh could never have done eight bombs at once. He had trouble organizing four people, and was so dumb he got caught right away. This thing took a lot more money and brains. Two things the McVeighs of the world don't have." As O'Brien kept saying, the complexity and sophistication of the mall bombs smacked of very well-financed and organized terrorists or some hostile government.

"True enough. But just before I left to come here O'Brien called and told me someone else saw an SUV drive off a truck. In California this time."

"And they saw the driver?"

"Just one person saw it. But yes. This time he did. Both drivers."

THE DEVOUTLY CATHOLIC O'Brien held no doubt that the concatenation of coincidences had to be the work of God, and the President would not overtly disagree. Though her adherence to Catholicism lapsed when she faced the choice of the Church or birth control, and ended when she started asking about the ordination of women, she could not accept a world of random chaos. And anyway, as Stromdahl pointed out, whatever she or O'Brien might believe, there was no dispute that John Dugan's strangeness verged on the Biblical.

For as long as most people remembered he had roamed the Sierra Nevada with all his worldly possessions on his back. The local Indians called him "Pack that Walks Like a Man." His white beard reached to his belt buckle, and his even whiter hair was equally long. Assuming he started his peripatetic hermitage in his early twenties, he now had to be at least seventy, and he wore thick black plastic-rimmed glasses that could have been his father's.

The Park Service cited him several times back in the 1980s for camping without a permit, and his Forest Service rap sheet went back to the early 90s. But both agencies had long since given up trying to enforce upon him. He scrupulously avoided building fires or harming any flora or fauna, and far as anyone could tell he was completely benign. He neither fished nor hunted, and apparently lived off the freeze-dried meals that typical backpackers could tolerate for a week or two at most. There was much speculation whether this diet was evidence of his craziness or its cause.

People also speculated about where Dugan got even the meager amount of money it took to buy his equipment and supplies, but the answer, though not widely known, was neither mysterious nor bizarre. He grew up in Dutch Flat, a semi-ghost town in the Sierra's western foothills, and along with an almost equally strange and hirsute older brother he inherited a modest but adequate fortune from their artist parents. The brother had for years run an antique shop on Main Street, and John returned every now and again to replenish his supplies and the small amount of money he carried with him.

Early in the morning on December 20, the Saturday when the bombs went off in the afternoon, he was headed toward the Flat, walking west on a snow-covered gravel road that paralleled a small creek near the Emigrant Gap exit on Interstate 80. He was surrounded by majestic white firs and ponderosa pines, and by the sound of the wind and the burble of the creek. Except for the traffic noise from the highway and the truck tire tracks in the snow it was almost heaven.

The tire tracks really pissed him off. The gravel road was supposed to be closed for the winter, and he felt a sense of proprietary rage that he, who obeyed all the rules that really counted, should have his pristine and solitary hike disrupted by such an intrusion. Then ahead of him he heard loud voices, and he left the road to circumvent any unwanted human contact. From a hill above the road he saw two men pull a ramp from the back end of a bobtail truck, and one of them climb inside the cargo space to drive out with an old SUV, obviously overloaded and not likely to make it back to I-80 without slipping into a ditch. The driver of the SUV vigorously pointed all this out to the other man, who said he'd take the lead driving back to the highway, but he'd watch carefully in his rearview mirror so he could give a tow with a chain if necessary.

"So did they make it out?" Dugan's brother asked.

"Don't know," Dugan replied. But apparently they did. The next day when he hiked back whence he came there was no sign of either vehicle. And the tire tracks had turned to slush in the warming sun.

ACCORDING TO O'BRIEN, all that was just the first coincidence. The next was even harder to explain without God's intervention. Dugan usually vanished for a month or more at a time, with no radio, phone, or any other device that might link him to civilization. Though he was a firm believer in nylon and Gore-Tex, except for his food and basic camping equipment he wanted nothing to do with modern technology.

But this trek through the wilderness was cut short when he slipped crossing a fast-flowing stream and lost most of his supplies. So like it or not, ten days after his first December visit to Dutch Flat he returned for a second. And then came still another coincidence. Neither of the Dugan brothers ever watched TV or paid any attention to the news, but from his customers the older brother learned about the mall bombs and developed a fascination about who did it. His parents' old TV was now on almost constantly, and he watched with very conflicted emotions. The destruction of commercial decadence had to be good, but not the accompanying death of thousands, or even one. Sometimes things were hard to figure out, which is why he occasionally wondered if maybe he should join in brother John's decision to opt for the simple wilderness life.

John himself pondered the news for several hours before he made the connection to the violation of his sacred solitude on the road in the forest. "I seen on TV about the SUVs and the trucks," he told the sheriff when he got around to calling. "And I think I also seen somethin' might help you."

The Sheriff called the FBI and now they had another piece of the puzzle; actually a few pieces. First, Stromdahl told Nelson and the President, the license plate on the truck was from Kansas, and the three initial characters were SGY. "Dugan also thought that was followed by a number—seven hundred something."

"What else?" Sally asked.

"Well, Dugan said the truck driver looked like Stonewall Jackson. Not sure why he made that comparison, but that's what he said."

"What does that mean?"

"He had a black beard, jeans held up with red suspenders, and he wore an old-style ten-gallon hat. Black and round on the top."

"Sounds to me more like a cross between a lumberjack and a cowboy," Nelson said.

"Yeah. I think the beard was the only real Stonewall Jackson thing. That, and he definitely didn't sound like someone from the Middle East. So maybe it really is like Tim McVeigh again. At least close enough to slow down the impeachment express."

"What about the driver of the SUV?" the President asked.

"That gets even more interesting. Guess what Dugan says he was wearing. A Santa suit."

"And he was white too?"

"No. Dugan said he was very brown."

"Did he have an accent?"

"Nope. Neither of them did. Didn't sound African American or Asian or anything except like someone from the Northwest."

Nelson frowned. It wasn't enough to stop Heilman completely, but maybe she could hold onto enough Democrats to stave off a conviction in the Senate if not the rush to impeach in the House.

Chapter 16

The Dabwa convoy made it back from Aden to Anwar's mountain village shortly before sundown on Tuesday, the thirtieth. Earlier in the day an unmarked black helicopter swooped down on them as they travelled north from Damar, but it never fired and quickly fled eastward when the convoy stopped and three of Anwar's men hopped out with shoulder-held anti-aircraft missiles.

"Who was that?" Samy asked.

"How would I know?" Anwar said. Probably not the government, which had only a weak army that controlled nothing but Sana'a and sometimes Aden, and never trifled with the tribes of the northwest mountains. And not likely any other tribe, because helicopters were a precious asset not so lightly risked.

"Who, then?"

"Perhaps this Ferguson you so revile."

Samy turned the idea over in his head for a few seconds. Just who the hell was Ferguson really working for? And what the hell was he up to? Would he murder an American to cover up his torture of innocent Arabs? Would he kill Samy out of long-simmering spite for reporting the slaughter of innocents at Haditha and pushing for a court martial? With Ferguson, anything was possible. And, of course, maybe it wasn't him at all. The goal of figuring out who really was responsible for the container and the mall bombs remained as elusive as ever.

Wednesday morning the helicopter appeared again, this time hovering at a safe distance above the ridgeline at the head of Anwar's home valley. It landed there and a young bearded man in a *keffiyeh* and a long white *thawb* got out and took the rocky path downward to the village square. He walked with his hands up and his palms forward to show he had no weapons, and he bowed and spoke politely to all he encountered. Once in the square he asked where he might find Anwar and was directed to his house.

He spoke Arabic with a strong trace of the Hadramati dialect indigenous to the vast south central part of Yemen, the part where Samir Akbar reputedly had his hideout. He told the man guarding the door to Anwar's house that he was looking for Samir Al-Mahdi.

"Who has sent you?" the guard asked.

"Tell the most honorable Dr. Al-Mahdi I am sent by an old friend from America. Imam Samir Akbar."

ON NEW YEAR'S DAY, which was Thursday, Samy finally acquired a new battery for the black phone. The mashing of all the keys on the touchpad while it was under the dead body had drained the original down to nothing, not even the emergency reserve, and in the village there was no way to recharge it. But one of Anwar's men found a replacement in Sana'a, and after three days out of contact, Samy was at last able report that he remained among the living.

The call roused a grumpy Stromdahl at 5:00 a.m. in DC, less than four hours after his return from a somber New Year's Eve dinner with the Swensons. He took it while sitting on the edge of the bed in his skivvies and a T-shirt, hunched forward, with his head supported by his left hand and the phone held in his right. The only light came from a small lamp on the nightstand.

"Where are you now?"

Samy explained he was back in his uncle's village, and he told the story of how they outran and then outgunned their pursuers after the attack in Aden. "And then yesterday Sami, who's now Imam Akbar, sent a helicopter to take me to the Hadramaut, but . . ."

"Who sent a chopper? To take you where?" Again the connection was not the best.

"Sami A, but a rocket took it out. This is all fucked up, but I think I'm getting close to an answer. I gotta figure out how to get there on my own. And then how to find him."

"Get where?"

"Wadi Hadramaut, where Sami A has his hideout. It's like in the middle of Yemen, south and east of the desert. It runs southward down to the coastline near Al Mukalla. Everyone knows he's out there somewhere. But that doesn't tell you much more than saying someone's hiding out in Texas. The Hadramaut's a big place."

"Hadramaut hell. You get your ass outta there and get home."

"Can't. Not done yet." He proceeded to tell how he narrowly escaped death a second time. "See I was supposed to fly back in a helicopter with this guy to meet with Sami, and the two of us, me and the pilot, walked up the hill to where he'd landed. The chopper was a four-seater, but he came alone. So I got in like the co-pilot's seat, and then after he started the engine I remembered I left the phone with my uncle so he could find a battery. But I figured I'd need it when I got to Sami's and I'd just have to find a battery somewhere else. So I hopped out to go back for the dead phone, and when I was maybe halfway down the hill the chopper blows up. Someone fired a rocket from the next ridgeline over. Then today Anwar's guys finally did get me the battery, just about an hour ago."

Stromdahl didn't quite follow the telephone battery story or what exactly the helicopter was all about, but he did reach a clear and obvious decision on Samy. There wasn't going to be another Luis Hernandez die for him. "Shit. Get outta there," he ordered.

"Look Skipper, Sami A wants to talk with us. The pilot told me the guys from the fruit company and the shipping company are with him. The ones Ferguson didn't torture and kill. Like the guy at the dock said too. Those are the freakin' people I came over here to find. Ain't no choice. We talk with them it probably solves the whole mystery. That's why someone's tryin' so hard to keep me away from them."

Or maybe it was Akbar trying to keep Samy from learning anything by luring him into a death trap. Or maybe the chopper was sent by someone else entirely. None of the maybes sounded very good to Stromdahl. "Bullshit." he said. "You get the fuck out of there. That's a direct order."

"I'm a civilian."

"You're an idiot. And you're gonna be a dead idiot and I'll have to explain it all to your wife and she's gonna kill me. Get your ass home."

"I'm not hearing you so good. The connection's fading. What did you say?"

Stromdahl yelled again that he should come home, but this time there was no answer. The connection had been broken, and he was left staring at the phone and shaking his head in regret for ever getting Samy into this mess. All the memories of Private Hernandez flooded through his mind and he slammed the bedside phone down hard enough to break it. Then he got dressed in his workout clothes and headed to the gym to pump iron and pound the punching bag.

"WE'VE GOT TIME," he told Swenson on the phone later that morning. "The game doesn't begin till four." In a football world turned upside down, Minnesota was playing Duke in the Sugar Bowl for a chance to go to the semifinal round of the playoffs. And again there was to be a TV viewing party at the Commandant's Eighth and Eye mansion. Swenson was invited, and now Stromdahl wanted him to come two hours early to figure out how they could rescue Samy from his own folly.

The CNO was not thrilled at the prospect. Today was the last day of his new grandson's first visit, and Al-Mahdi was a lost cause. Or at least on a mission now beyond control. "What's to talk about," he said. "We've picked up the phone signal again. We know he hasn't left the village yet. But so what. He doesn't want to come home, and we couldn't help him much if he did. And anyway, why the hell does our Samy want to meet with his old bud the bad Sami in the first place? The other day you were telling me Akbar must be the bomber because all these people ran away to hide with him when Ferguson came around. Now what? Have you decided it was Iran after all?"

"No. I haven't decided anything. Look, we don't know who it was. Could be Iran. Could be Akbar trying to make it look like Iran, which ain't his friend. Hell, could be some of the super-hardliners in Israel trying to make it look like Iran. *Nagaf* even.

Or none of the above. But Samy's right about one thing. Talking with the people who shipped the nitrates is the best lead we've got."

"Oh, so you really do want him to go find Akbar?"

"No. I want to go myself, and I need your help to get in and then get out."

A long silence preceded "No" as Swenson contemplated the alternatives of immediate arrest, further reasoning, or maybe commitment to a mental ward. "And what the hell do you think you'll do if you get there?" he finally asked. "You're six-eight and blond, and you ain't hardly traveling incognito anywhere in Arabia."

"Peter the Great did it in England, and he was just as tall and didn't speak the language. I do speak Arabic, you know."

"Yeah. And the King knew Peter was there and helped him. And your Arabic sucks. Even I can tell you speak it with a Midwest accent."

"That's just it. I'll go undercover as a Norwegian businessman."

"What kind of business?"

"I don't know. Maybe engineering. I'll say I was in Sana'a and wanted to go sightseeing. To the Hadramaut, where they think Akbar's hiding out."

"Sightseeing? In Yemen?" Swenson could not believe they were having this insane discussion. The answer was no, no, a thousand times no. No matter what.

"Yeah. Why not sightseeing? It's a beautiful place with lots of history. I've seen on the Internet. They've got ten-story mud-brick buildings that are thousands of years old. Like Manhattan in the desert." Stromdahl's enthusiasm almost sounded genuine.

"Wally, you don't like going to Manhattan in New York. And that's beside the point. You're nuts. The answer's no. I'll see you at four. Go Gophers!" He clicked off and went back to playing with his grandson.

Stromdahl was sitting at the desk in his study, already dressed for the big game in gold-colored pants and a Minnesota maroon blazer. For the second time that day he was staring at a phone gone dead after he'd been cut off. Samir Al-Mahdi's mission to Yemen continued to go badly.

CHAPTER 17

As much as Swenson wondered why Samy wanted to meet with Akbar, Samy wondered even more why Akbar wanted the meeting. If in fact he now sheltered some of the men who sent the nitrates to Newark it seemed clear they were his people, which meant he had to be behind the bombs as well. But why had Jihad in Yemen not basked in the glory of its grand success? Why did all the obvious clues point to Iran? Was this, like the drone, a scheme to misdirect Americans into doing Akbar's killing for him? And did he now want to use Samy to help sell the lie?

"You will learn from him only what he wants you to learn," Uncle Anwar warned. "Only what he wants you to tell the world. And why should you think that will be the truth?" Anwar looked around the room to invite agreement from the five tribal elders he had brought in for advice about assisting Samy in his plan to travel to Wadi Hadramaut. In particular, Samy wanted to go to Shibam, the famous city of ancient ten story buildings. Akbar would not be there, but Samy figured that would be the best place to connect with his people. Anwar, however, did not want a repeat of the misbegotten trip to Aden. At the very least he needed counsel and concurrence from the elders before backing another of his great nephew's harebrained adventures.

It was Friday, the second day of the New Year, and they were all seated on plain tan cushions in the big room on the second level of Anwar's house. It had a smooth and polished mud brick floor covered with reed mats and flat woven carpets broadly striped in muted browns and grays, and tasseled at the ends. For furniture there were only two low tables and a wooden chest, and not a single piece of art or decoration hung on the thick stone walls. But no one could doubt the position and prosperity of the building's owner. Fine brass ewers and pottery and an old copper and silver *hookah* were displayed in wall niches. The door was richly carved and painted, and the stonework covered with a gleaming white lime plaster into which elaborate arabesque patterns had been cut and molded with great skill and art.

There were six windows, two each in three of the walls, and at one hour past high noon enough sunlight streamed in through the intricate latticework of the shutters that the seven men needed no lamp or candle. Anwar removed the *hookah* from its niche, filled it with *shisha* tobacco, lit it, and passed it around as he and the elders contemplated Samy's problem. All of them nodded their agreement with Anwar on the likely mendacity and treachery of Akbar or any other Sunni.

"But remember," Samy argued as politely as he could, "it was our cousin in Aden who first told us where the clerks ran to hide. Surely we can trust him. And Samir Akbar and I were once like cousins. No, like brothers. He will not harm me."

Anwar said nothing. He took a hit of smoke from the *hookah* and passed it on, and his face remained impassive. One of the elders nodded sagely and said Samy's points were sound, but they went only to the reasons for the proposed trip, not its intrinsic difficulties. "In these times, if you take our trucks and weapons much east of Sana'a, you can be sure they will invite a fight rather than prevent one."

Another elder said they could get Samy no more than halfway from Sana'a to Marib, where the eastern edge of the mountains met the western edge of the desert. And if he made it to Marib he'd still have to go twice again as far to reach Shibam.

Anwar shook his head at the mention of Shibam. "And what will you do even if you get there?" he said. "Akbar lives in side wadis that feed into the Hadramaut and in the mountains above the wadis. Not in houses but in caves. And he moves from cave to cave every day. Not the government nor your CIA nor al Qaeda have found him, and you think you will succeed by going to Shibam?"

"I think he will find me. He already has."

"Yes, and it got his helicopter blown up. How does he know you are not the one who did it? Perhaps you do not now want him to find you."

Perhaps not, Samy conceded. Then he played his trump card. "We have no choice if we are to avoid a holocaust."

In the end Anwar and the elders reluctantly agreed and gave him a beat-up old Land Rover, a fake Yemeni ID card, a two-day supply of food, and a Kalashnikov. The weapon might be necessary, they said, and it would attract little attention. Everyone in Yemen was armed.

The eldest of the elders also hit upon a plan for bettering the chances Akbar would find Samy. He recalled that in one of the country's brief outbreaks of peace the central government had tried to ease tensions between the Sunni tribes and the Shia by arranging a meeting among their leaders. A meet-and-greet sort of thing suggested by American consultants and no more successful in the Arabian Peninsula than most other Western ideas on the practice of politics. But there was one man from Shibam he thought he still might call.

"He likely knows how to contact Imam Akbar, and can alert him to your impending arrival."

"Are you certain he will not betray us," Anwar asked. "I do not want to tell my brother's son I abetted the killing of his son."

The elder tilted his head to the side and held his hands out, palm upwards, as if handing off the decision to the others. "I know only that this man has no love for either al Qaeda or the government. And he will speak with me, which means like Akbar he favors cooperation between our sects."

And what if the call was intercepted?

With hands still held out he looked upward. "As our honorable guest has said, does Allah give us any other choice?"

So it was that on Friday evening the elder made his call, and so it was that Saturday morning, the third of January, Samy headed eastward. Anwar and three of the armed pickups went with him a few kilometers past Sana'a, after which he was on his own. He sent a text message to tell Stromdahl of his plans and then turned off the phone to conserve the battery, though it still sent out a signal of its location.

IN THE ANCIENT past Marib was the capital of Saba, otherwise known as Sheba, a thriving empire with emerald green fields irrigated by the dammed eastward flow of Wadi Dhana, and famous for an affair between one of its queens and Solomon. It grew rich by taxing caravans carrying incense from east to west, where the resinous scent was used to mask the pernicious smells of everyday life in the days before refrigerators and sanitation. Marib always smelled real good. Camel drivers refreshed there after traversing the desert that separated the city from Wadi Hadramaut, or fortified themselves before entering it on the return trip to Oman and the Persian Gulf.

But large floods destroyed the dam and invaders destroyed the empire, and by the time of Muhammad the old city's population had shrunk far below its peak of fifty thousand. It fitfully survived another millennium and a half until the modern civil wars shattered what was left, and except as an archeological site its days were done. The much lesser new Marib lay a few kilometers north of the ruins, a dusty, scruffy patch of earth once home to a small refinery that closed when the local oil wells went dry. It was a place of low buildings and lower expectations, shoddy and forlorn like a busted boomtown in the American West. All it lacked was a saloon and horses. Instead it had four coffee houses and lots of camels, and it stank to high heaven of camel dung.

Samy arrived there without serious incident shortly before dusk. He'd been stopped three times en route, twice at army checkpoints and once at a barricade erected by Shiite rebels. But his flawless Arabic and traditional attire raised little curiosity, and the Land Rover bespoke no wealth. Though it was the fancy hardtop variety favored for ferrying tourists across the Serengeti in Africa, it was far past its prime. The exterior was all dents and peeling paint, the seats were torn, and the air conditioner had long since gone defunct. It drew only sneers at the checkpoints, and at each a small payment sufficed to obtain passage. Samy noted wryly that the army charged more than the extorters against whom it was supposed to protect.

According to the tourist books, Marib had but one hotel, a

four-star jewel in a pretty rough town, as the books would have it. Of course they ignored the many hostelries that with a manger would have looked familiar to Joseph and Mary. Samy selected one of the most substantial, where he took a room and then went out in search of food. As luck would have it, this was the day of a monthly camel auction, and vendors selling lamb kebabs and other treats were still out working the streets even after dark.

He bought two wood skewers of lamb and two pieces of flat bread, all neatly wrapped in hygienically suspect old newspapers, and carried the greasy prize back to the inn. Briefly he thought back to Stromdahl at the Cardiac Arrest, and figured now he was no better. At least he did not have any French fries. That line he had not crossed.

When he walked through the front door he found that the desk clerk had shut things down and apparently gone to find his own dinner. A crudely lettered sign sitting on the counter vaguely said he'd be back soon. Please to wait. But a tall, broad-shouldered Westerner dressed like a tourist or archeologist in khakis and a wide-brimmed floppy desert hat was nonetheless pounding on the bell. Though the hour was late he had on dark aviator glasses that obscured his eyes. When he heard the door open he turned to look at Samy and cocked his head to the side as if in partial recognition. After waiting an odd second too long he asked in bad Arabic what time the clerk had departed. His accent was English or American, and he wore no beard and expressed great impatience with local business hours.

"Don't know," Samy said, also in Arabic. "Was open when I left half an hour ago."

"Are you then staying here?" Again the accent, and phrasing too formal to be fluent.

"Yes." *What else*, Samy thought.

The man said nothing more before turning abruptly back to pounding on the bell. Samy went up to his second-story room to consume his grease feast and finally get some sleep. He awoke early on Sunday morning, the fourth day of the year, and made his way downstairs, where he found the missing clerk back on duty. Who was the tall Western guest last night, Samy asked.

"What guest?" the clerk replied. "You took the last room, and no one has come in since."

"Are you certain?"

The clerk gave him a funny look. Of course he was.

By eight o'clock Samy was back on the road, first a short jog south past the ruins of the old city, then eastward across the desert toward Shibam. The day was still cool, for a change the Rover's engine started and ran smoothly, and save for the rush of air through the open driver's side window he was alone in a world of peace and quiet; left elbow hanging out, right hand on the wheel, and his head and body leaned back for comfort. Silently he praised Allah, out of habit though not belief.

Twenty minutes and ten miles east of the ruins a dusty but late model white SUV caught up with him, then fell in behind, about a hundred yards back. Maybe a Nissan instead of the usual Toyota. He quickly sat up straight and put both hands on the wheel, and repeatedly checked the mirror. Could it really be the tall man from the reception desk? He couldn't see for sure through the SUV's windshield, but the hat and sunglasses were right, and the driver had no beard. Samy swallowed hard, clenched and unclenched his hands on the steering wheel, and glanced at the Kalashnikov on the passenger seat to make certain the magazine was locked in. It was good to go.

Five miles farther down the road he spotted four Bedouin tents pitched near the shoulder to his left. Two old pickups and ten camels were parked nearby. Whose side would the nomads take if he stopped to confront his unwanted company? Probably no one's, but he figured witnesses might deter immediate abduction or murder. He turned abruptly, slammed the brakes, and jumped out the driver's door. Assault rifle in hand, he crouched down on one knee so the Land Rover would provide at least some cover and he could get off the first shot.

The dusty white SUV slowed down almost to a stop, but stayed on the road. Samy crouched lower and made sure the safety was unlocked. As the driver's window rolled down and the vehicle came to a full stop he sighted on it, ready to fire if a hand with a weapon appeared. The door opened a crack, then shut again, and Samy dropped to his stomach for a more stable firing position. What he would have done first thing in his Marine Corps days. *Getting old*, he thought.

The tall man looked out through the window at the Land

Rover and smiled and waved. And then he rolled the window back up and motored on by. With the Kalashnikov dangling down along the side of his leg and his finger still on the trigger, Samy stood up to watch him vanish in the distance. In his head, thinking in English, he'd reached the midpoint of "what the fuck was that" when someone from behind tapped him on the shoulder and he reflexively jerked the trigger and fired two shots into the ground not an inch from his right foot.

He wheeled around with the barrel raised again and almost smashed it into the face of a young Bedouin who had come over to see what was going on. The boy, no more than twelve, yelped and leapt away, then headed straight for one of the tents.

"Wait," Samy shouted. "I'm not going to hurt you."

The boy stopped and turned around, and in language far too profane for one of his age and pious upbringing demanded what the hell Samy thought he was doing. "Why the fuck are you spooking the camels with your gunfire?"

"Sorry," Samy apologized. "You scared me."

The boy shook his head. "I do not think it is I who caused your fear."

IN SHIBAM the book did him in. The one in English at the new tourist hotel in the new part of the city. No hotels were allowed in the old walled city, where the ten-story mud brick towers stood only a few feet apart, separated by alleys only wide enough for three men to walk abreast and too narrow for cars or trucks.

The new hotel, appropriately called the Hadramaut, was the brainchild of a Yemeni hotelier who learned his trade at Cornell and then set out to provide a sort of Las Vegas or Disney-style imitation tower to give his guests the timeless experience of mud brick life with all the comforts of the twenty-first century. The rooms had plastic imitation bricks and plastic imitation plaster walls, and he added every modern amenity possible in a city of seven thousand located in one of the remotest places on earth. His success had not yet surpassed middling, but he persisted, and one of his selling points was the wealth of historical and geographical information available for free. A veritable museum library, his website boasted. Videos and apps for electronic devices, along with books for when connectivity or electricity failed, which here was fairly often.

Samy idly picked up one of the books and quickly became absorbed, even though he knew a lot of the stuff already. Like how big Yemen was. His students at Georgetown sometimes thought of it as a tiny toenail land at the end of the Arabian Peninsular foot, but the truth was its area exceeded California's and almost equaled that of France. He also knew the country had not a single river, only the wadis, hot and dry except when it rained. Then flood waters surged through them and swept away all in their path. Many of the wadis started in the mountains and ended in the desert, where the scorching sand vaporized the last drops of flow like futile tears in hell. A few, like Wadi Hadramaut, eventually conveyed the water to the sea.

All that stuff he knew. What had him so fascinated with the book was the history of Shibam; how there were two theories of its origins. One school had it that people needed to huddle close together behind the walls to defend against the marauding ancestors of the Bedouin. Others believed it was simply a matter of terrain. In the wide swath of Wadi Hadramaut there were but a few hillocks high enough to provide refuge from the floods.

And then there were the various religious historians who loved to spin tales of Noah's Ark, and how the ancients would have thought about such a thing only because of their intermittently flooded life in the great wadis of Yemen. He was deep into the part about how all species on earth had once lived in the country when a young traditionally dressed Arab walked up and addressed him in almost perfect English.

"I see you are reading a book in English. Are you Dr. Al-Mahdi?"

Samy answered without a thought about the strangeness of hearing the first of his native tongues spoken so far from home. Why wouldn't someone who worked with Sami Akbar know English as well as Arabic? And wasn't it great that making contact turned out to be so easy. "Yes," he said. "Have you been sent to get me?"

"Of course. Who else? Why don't you get your things, then follow me. You can leave your Land Rover here."

Suddenly very eager to see his long-ago best friend again, Samy complied right away. He fairly raced to his room, repacked the few things he'd removed from his two duffels, stuffed the Kalashnikov into one of them, and came back down to the lobby.

The young man smiled and took the bags and led him out the front door to a waiting pickup truck. Three more men, all armed with assault weapons, sat in the bed. The man with the bags put them in the rear seat of the extended cab, then held the front passenger side door open for his guest. And then, before Samy took another step toward the truck the man fell to the ground, shot squarely in the middle of his forehead.

Samy heard the gun's report a millisecond later as he dove down to squirm for cover under the truck, oblivious of the sharp-edged gravel that tore a hole in his shirtsleeve and gave him an ugly bleeding gash on his elbow. *Holy shit*, he thought. *Like the bad old days in Iraq*. Except worse. The truck bed above him reverberated with the sound of automatic weapons fire as the three men who'd been waiting there shot back. Rapid gunfire also poured from the inside of the hotel. As best he could sort out the din, there apparently were two attackers inside.

The firefight continued off and on for several minutes that seemed like forever, and he never did hear the three pickups that pulled in behind the building after the shooting began. But he did notice how after the first minute or so the sounds from inside the hotel suddenly grew louder and more intense, though the fire no longer was directed outward at the truck. Then it all stopped for a few seconds and suddenly resumed with the fire from the hotel more intense than ever and once again aimed at the three men in the truck bed. Samy could almost feel the bullets slamming into the sheet metal, like when his body armor once absorbed a slug in Haditha. He suddenly lost all interest in trying to see what was happening and squirmed farther under the truck to get away from the side closest to the hotel.

Above him he heard two of the men in the bed cry out as they were hit. One of their weapons fell to the ground within his reach and he pulled it to him. He stayed under the truck but crawled back toward the hotel and fired a single short burst in the general direction of the building, then stopped to conserve what ammunition remained. *Stupid*, he thought. *Really stupid.* His brief lack of discipline had cost him several precious rounds. The shooting above him was now down to one weapon firing sporadic single shots, and within a few seconds even that ceased. He'd need every round he had.

Unseen by Samy several men rushed from the hotel lobby

and managed to overpower the lone survivor in the pickup bed. And then one of them shouted in Arabic that Samy should hold his fire and come out.

He gripped his newfound weapon and prepared himself to go down in a blaze of bullets if not glory. "Who are you?" he demanded.

"We have come from Imam Akbar. You can come out now."

Samy stayed put, completely unclear about who was who or what side was up. He thought about firing a shot or two to warn everyone off, then rethought better of the idea. He couldn't see a thing to aim at except the feet of the men now surrounding the truck, and if he shot it would only invite return fire sure to kill him. "And how do I know you were sent by Akbar?" he shouted.

Without a hitch the man who had asked him to come out now spoke in English. "The imam said to tell you Batman Seven on two. He said you would know the meaning of this phrase."

"What?"

"Batman Seven on two."

It was Sami Akbar's favorite football play, a fly pattern up the middle on which he scored ten touchdowns one year. Samy Al-Mahdi tossed the assault rifle away and crawled back out into the open. Five men faced him, the muzzles of their weapons only half-lowered. They were all dressed in khakis, and for a second or two Samy wondered if they weren't army troops. But the clothes were too neatly pressed.

Amazed he wasn't shaking with fright and that he could still speak in any language, he continued to use English. "Mind telling me what just happened?"

The apparent leader of the five answered. He was well over six feet tall, but slender and almost slight. Except that his beard was neatly trimmed at six inches and his hair at one, he looked eerily like Osama Bin Laden. But he spoke with a voice more professorial than military or prophetic. "It is a complicated tale best told later. My name is Omar, a servant of Allah and the great Imam Akbar. Please come with us."

They walked around behind the building where their pickups and their drivers were waiting. Samy had forgotten all about his bags, but someone else brought them and tossed them into the bed of one of the trucks, again an extended cab model. He climbed into the rear seat, as directed, and almost jumped right back out.

Sitting next to him, bleeding and semi-conscious and trussed up with rope was the tall, broad-shouldered man from Marib.

Perhaps to distinguish himself from the prisoner, Samy reverted to Arabic. "What is he doing here?"

Omar, now in the front passenger seat and ready to get going, also went back to Arabic. "We will explain later. And also, I must ask, have you a phone?" When Samy paused Omar said he would search if he had to. "Telephones are not allowed at our camps. Their use invites detection and American drone attacks."

Reluctantly, Samy handed it over. Omar flung it out the window and made sure the driver rolled over it on the way out.

CHAPTER 18

Except for bike gear, Wallace Stromdahl detested high tech toys, and if pressed to explain his troglodyte leanings he'd point out that most new stuff either didn't work right or went obsolete too quickly to make the learning curve worthwhile. He remained bitter about the time he'd once spent figuring out how to program Sally's VCR only to have her replace it a month later with a DVD player. Deep within his Minnesota Marine Corps heart of hearts he thought computers and electronics, like cutlery or Chippendale, should last forever, or at least as long as a well-maintained car. Good farmers and good Marines always extracted extra years from their equipment, and disposable or short-lived things undermined this fundamental virtue.

So when he started toting around a smart phone device shortly after they went on the market it surprised everyone, and most of all him. Until then his practice was to acquire new gadgets only if they'd defied obsolescence for at least two years, a practice that regrettably led him to delay the purchase of many things until just before they went obsolete. Now he had the mini-tablet, which he thought was especially cool and neat. Since the Corps had started providing his devices he'd gone through about one a year and at this point was on his ninth or tenth.

Like all its predecessors, he kept the latest little jewel with him wherever he went—in the field on inspections or maneuvers, in the gym, on his bike, and on the small table next to his bed. Around headquarters people joked that he likely took it with him into the shower, but in truth that happened only once or twice. Usually he retrieved his messages immediately upon getting up in the morning, and deferred the shower until he'd read or listened to them all.

When he turned on the little tablet first thing on Saturday, January 3, he found the text message about Al-Mahdi's trip to Shibam. *Shit!* Immediately he got onto the web to find out how far the city was from Sana'a so he could estimate when Samy might get there. His best bet was Sunday the fourth. And what then? How would Samy hook up with Akbar? How would he be received? How the hell would he get out?

This time he called the President instead of Swenson. "I've got to go over there to bring him back."

"You'll do no such thing." She sounded like his mother or his second grade teacher, a didactic speaking habit that predated her election as President. But now that she was elected he no longer could chide her about it and thus had no response.

"Besides," she added, "we've got another problem. Rumbo and Heilman are saying the truck thing out in California means there's more proof Iran did the bombings, not less. Jane Nelson and I are over here meeting about it now."

"Yeah. I saw Heilman's press conference yesterday. Pretty unbelievable."

"Believe it. They're smelling blood."

The South Carolina Senator had concluded that the California truck driver's beard and the skin color of the Santa, plus their unaccented English, confirmed the Iranian mall bombers must have conspired with duplicitous American Muslims. No one at the now bombed-out California mall had actually heard Santa speak, but the man Dugan had seen and heard must be him.

Heilman was now ranting that the Iranian-inspired fifth column had to be stopped. But President Macalester was just sitting on her hands, he said. And so he was calling on Congress to declare war against Iran, and if Sally didn't act on the declaration right away, for the leaders of the House to hold an impeachment vote the same day. Do it all at once—declare war, impeach in the House, convict in the Senate, and be done with it. For most normal people the end of the holidays meant Monday, January 5, but Congress always took extra liberties for itself, so Tuesday would be the day of the declaration, or maybe Wednesday to allow at least a show of debate. But no later than that. War had to be declared and Macalester had to go immediately thereafter. Maybe not the same day, but by the end of the week at the latest.

Jane Nelson's voice now came over the phone, loud and tinny. Again, she and the President were using a speaker. "The bastard's lining up Senate votes for conviction on the bill of impeachment even before the House passes it; before most Senators are back in town. He's planning to have us at war and Sally gone before next weekend. And then they'll give us a new constitution and deport the Iranians and other Muslims. We'll be free of them all. And totally unfree."

On Sunday, not twenty-four hours after the latest message from Samy, irony in the form of an Iranian would turn in their favor, but at the moment they had little reason for hope. It looked for sure like Sally's time as President was about to end.

AMIR KARIMI ALWAYS seemed to have a consulting contract or two going on. Artificial intelligence work like automated pattern recognition or fuzzy data integration. Big picture across the board sorts of things with a multitude of applications. He did weather prediction for NOAA, market modeling for Wall Street, and target acquisition programs for the Navy and Air Force. The FBI had him looking at computerized fingerprint analysis and the logic of complex investigative reasoning, fascinating subjects with potentially great but as yet not fully realized utilitarian benefits.

The income from all this consultation was a more-than-nice supplement to his professor's pay at MIT, and without it he and his family could not have afforded their spacious house in Cambridge. It was light years from his orphaned origins in 1979, the year the mullahs turned Iran into a theocracy and systematically liquidated the likes of his college student parents, who had the temerity to demonstrate for true freedom. He was two months old when they perished, and only nineteen years later did he manage to escape to the U.S.

"So now it's happening here," he said to his wife, Sofia. It was Friday, January 2, and also the second day of what was supposed to be a long New Year's holiday weekend. But holiday or not, he was hard at work, and had come home only because he needed a short break. They were sitting together on a sofa in their basement rec room, watching a news clip of the Senate Majority Leader's latest ravings about the need for a Christian Capitalist Constitution and a crackdown on all Muslims. Especially Iranian Muslims.

At five foot two, Sofia was only a few inches shorter than Amir, and when they sat upright their feet barely reached the floor. They also looked a lot alike, as if from the same Mediterranean fishing village. Her roots went back only two generations further than his, to Italian immigrants who'd come to New Jersey right before World War II. She and Amir met at Princeton in 2000, and he ruefully recalled that while he could not vote, he urged her to support Bush. She'd laughed and asked what the hell he knew about America after only two years in the country, but to her infinite regret she did vote Republican.

"Canada," she said, without taking her eyes off the TV. The topic was not new to them, but this time she was deadly serious. A few seconds later she muted the TV and unleashed her all-too-regular diatribe against the Tea Party. The Christian original intent of the Founding Fathers was just too dumb to believe, she said. But the rightwing Republicans were about to inflict their version of it on everyone, along with Ayn Rand's crackpot economics. At Princeton she'd studied history and read what many of the Founders actually had written about their beliefs. She had the facts on her side, but with the Tea Party that never mattered.

Sometimes, when she suffered a lapse in patience and judgment, she would argue with their neighbor, who was maybe the only openly Republican person in Cambridge. "You know," she'd say, "a lot of the founding fathers weren't Christian at all. They didn't really give a hoot about any organized religion." The neighbor would always shake his head no, and brush her off.

"No listen. Jefferson and Tom Paine hated religion. And Franklin, Madison, and Adams were more Deist than Christian. Washington and Lincoln too." Then, if she was really into it, she'd shift to his hottest hot button. "And you know your big hero Ayn Rand was an out-and-out atheist."

"Well, she's about economics, not God."

"So God has nothing to do with economics?" On that they might actually agree.

"No. I never said that. *Atlas Shrugged* is about free exercise of free will. It's really very Christian when you think it through."

And there the argument would usually end, because Sofia had no answer to such malleable malarkey. Rand was actually about only one thing: herself. For all her supposed logic and materialism, she never accepted either modern physics or evolution because they contradicted her conviction that her self-declared philosophy derived from pure logic. She started with the intrinsic premise that individuals were completely and absolutely responsible for their own lives, and thus there was no room for God, the evolutionary adaptation of Darwin, or the physical uncertainty of Heisenberg. Or for any communitarian impulse to assist others. Certainly there could be no assistance from the government. She had her own religion, and she was the deity.

Amir simply smiled and told his wife she got prettier when she got angry, which of course only made her angrier and prettier. At forty-three she still looked great, except for a few gray hairs and wrinkles she was no different from the little soccer player who could almost beat him at his own game. They both played on their varsity teams in college. She relied on wispy quickness, he on strength and power. He had a thick body and thick, heavy legs that made him seem even shorter than his actual five foot five. So he was always on the lookout for short, pretty women; especially if they had dark eyes and dark hair like his. Since he first asked her out he'd never lost the feeling of joy and wonder that she didn't turn him down.

"Not so fast on Canada," he said. "Not just yet."

She twisted her head to the left to give him a good hard look. "Why not?"

"The crazies haven't taken over yet."

"Sure they have. They got the House. They got the Senate. They got a majority on the Supreme Court. Everything but President. And that's coming next." She pointed at the screen for emphasis. "It's like a done deal."

"Maybe not completely done."

"What do you mean?"

He looked away without responding. He was close to an

answer, but at the moment he couldn't tell anyone. Not even Sofia. No matter how pretty and angry she might be.

Secrecy was always a concern on Amir's consulting projects. He worked on them only out of a small, windowless office specially outfitted for security in a nondescript three-story cinder block building on Washington Street, just north of the MIT campus. Guards, cameras, fancy ID cards, and check-in logs were standard. But not round-the-clock FBI protection like he had now.

At first he didn't believe it when he got the call on December 28. "Right," he said. "The FBI is calling me at home the Sunday after Christmas. And not just the FBI, but the Director himself. Right." He hung up and went back to watching the Patriots' football game with his twin teenage sons.

When the phone rang again only seconds later he noted the caller ID did say Federal Bureau, and when he answered the voice did sound like Danny O'Brien sounded on TV. "Who is this?" he asked crossly.

"This is Director O'Brien," Danny said. "Can we meet this evening?"

"Where?"

"Your off-campus office. I can be there by eight."

"How do you know about my office?"

"Well, for one thing, you already do work for us. And we checked with MIT. But I've got a new job for you."

"What kind of job?"

"Let's talk in your office. Eight o'clock. That work for you?"

So they'd met. He and the Director and a tall, thin middle-aged female agent with a narrow, pinched face and short hair dyed auburn to hide the gray. He already knew her from his other FBI work. The agent did most of the talking at first, and said they wanted Amir to figure out a way for a computer to review billions of electronic images to find pictures of a dark blue truck with very little lettering on it.

"So this is about the mall bombs?"

"Yes."

"And where do the images come from?"

"Does it matter?" O'Brien jumped in to reply.

"How can I say if I don't know?"

The look on O'Brien's face acknowledged Amir was right,

and he glanced back at the agent and told her to go ahead and explain. She said they were from just about every toll booth or weigh station camera anywhere in the country. Anything that took pictures of vehicles on the road and stored the images electronically. "We don't have them all yet, but we're working on it, and you can figure out how to do the searches with the files we've already put together."

"Find the dark blue needle in the haystack. That it?"

"Yes," O'Brien and the agent said together, a bit too brightly.

"You're not serious."

"What's not serious about thousands of dead Americans," O'Brien said.

Amir shook his head in agreement and understanding. And resignation. He went to work that night, and with only brief breaks for food and fresh air he kept at it round-the-clock. Three straight days of nothing. And then late on New Year's Eve he got the word to change the search criteria.

"How so?"

"See if you can find an image of a truck with a Kansas license plate. Begins with SGY, and maybe has a seven in it somewhere."

"Is this the blue truck?"

"No. A different truck. Gray or white, and this time a bobtail, not a semi."

He said thanks, that was all very good. Then he hung up the phone, thrust his arms up in the traditional signal for a touchdown, and shouted yes. Letters and numbers were haystack needles his software was very adept at finding. With renewed purpose he worked through New Year's Day and the wee hours of the next morning until he couldn't keep his head from falling onto the keyboard. Reluctantly he went home to get some sleep, and when he woke up Sofia called him down to the rec room to watch Heilman's threat to deport them both.

After their discussion about Canada and the Tea Party he turned off the already-muted TV in disgust. "Well, I gotta get back to work," he told her. "Got a deadline I sort of have to make."

It still took him a while to adapt his software to the task at hand, and not till Sunday morning did he hit pay dirt, almost a week since he started. He called O'Brien right away.

"SO TELL US all about it," the President said. Again she'd convened a meeting in the Treaty Room. Right after Sunday lunch. It was at O'Brien's request so he could pass along Amir Karimi's great discovery. Though no one said anything explicit, it was clear O'Brien had entered the President's trusted circle, which thus now numbered three. He had arrived first, and the other two, Jane Nelson and Stromdahl, showed up only minutes later. As when the Commandant, the Senator, and the President had met in the room a few days earlier, everyone dressed casually, but this time there was no fire, and they simply gathered around a coffee table with a fresh pot of coffee and a plate of ginger cookies, which Sally had baked herself.

They were fresh from the oven and still hot, and the homey smell belied the moment's gravity. She took a small one and offered the plate around. Stromdahl recalled baking had always been one way she relieved stress if she didn't have time for the gym. But while she created the calories she also had the willpower to resist them. She lost weight during final exams and he consumed her cookies and invariably put on five pounds and then tried to blame her.

Apparently equally susceptible, the Director took two before nodding at Stromdahl and commencing his report. "Well, looks like the Commandant was right about checking every surveillance image from the Interstate system. Looks like the trucks came from Idaho. We got lucky. That's one of the states that really went crazy on budget cutting back in the twenty teens, and they've had to start charging all kinds of fees to stay even barely functional. So they've got lots of toll booths."

Jane Nelson shook her head and said she remembered when the Republicans changed the Interstate Highway Law to allow tolls everywhere. "It was a compromise. What they really wanted to do was privatize it all. That's Heilman's answer to everything."

O'Brien allowed himself a slight grin. "Well, whatever the reason, they did us a real favor on this case."

Stromdahl asked a very different question. "Did I hear you say trucks with an 's'?"

"Exactly." The Director was more than a little exultant, and really playing it to the hilt. "Exactly. Let me tell you the whole story."

"Go ahead," the President said. Her brief glance at Nelson and Stromdahl told them to shut up and stop their interruptions.

"So, we would have done this quicker, but Amir had to re-tool some of the software he uses for our fingerprint project. Anyway, once he got it working he scored right away on the Kansas truck. On December 18 it passed through a toll booth on I-15 a few miles south of Pocatello, Idaho."

"Going which way?" Sally asked.

"South."

"And you're sure it was the same truck?"

"Not one hundred percent, but darn near. We've got an Idaho picture that shows Kansas plate number SGY-715, and the truck is dirty white or gray, like our friend Dugan saw." At this O'Brien stopped for a couple of seconds and another small smile. "Turns out Dugan's back in the mountains again, so we couldn't find him to look at the picture and confirm."

The President, Nelson, and Stromdahl also smiled at the thought of Dugan wandering aimlessly with his backpack.

"But we don't really need Dugan," the Director went on. "There were 358 other Kansas SGY images for the week before December 20. Five of them look like the same truck as it went south on I-15 to Salt Lake City, then west on I-80 towards the coast. Utah has weigh stations, and Nevada and California have scales and toll booths too. But there aren't any booths in the National Forests, and the cameras at the toll island between the mountains and San Francisco weren't working. So the last picture we have is just west of Reno. From the timing, they must have spent the night of the eighteenth near Elko, Nevada, and the night of the nineteenth somewhere in eastern California. Not much doubt it's our guys. And I've got a hunch they started out somewhere near Pocatello, because we didn't find any images taken on the roads to the north, east, or west of there."

He paused and looked around the table to make sure they'd followed him, and to pick up yet another cookie. He took a small bite, and held the rest of it in his hand as he resumed. "'Course we can't be completely certain about the origin thing because there's a lot of empty space up there. But let me tell you what else Amir found. Once he zeroed in on the five toll or weigh station locations that spotted the gray truck, he went back to check for dark blue semi trucks at each of them."

And? His three listeners leaned forward in anticipation as O'Brien took another bite of the cookie before telling them what

Karimi had discovered. The President moved her hand in a circle like a small water wheel to signal that he should keep going. Chop, chop. Speed it up. "So what did he find?"

He gulped down the piece of cookie in his mouth. "Images that look just like the description of the semi. There's one from the Pocatello toll booth, taken on December 16. Later the same day it showed up at the weigh station near Ogden, but not at any of the other places where we got images for the Kansas truck."

"Did you get a license number?" Stromdahl asked.

"Yeah, but it doesn't do us much good. They're fake plates on both of the trucks. Just like on the SUVs with the bombs. We can't tell for sure till we find the trucks, but odds are pretty good they were stolen too." Also just like the SUVs.

"So where did the blue semi go after Ogden?"

Another cookie bite, a big grin, and then the answer. "Now Amir sort of had the same question. So he looked at images along I-80 and I-70. And sure enough, based on the license plate number and the color, it looks as if a semi like the one near Baltimore left from somewhere near Pocatello at about the right time, went south on I-15, east on I-80, then south on I-25 to Denver, then picked up I-70 for the rest of the trip."

"So what the heck's going on in Pocatello?" Sally asked.

CHAPTER 19

"Hayden Lake," Nelson said very quietly. "Maybe they've come back to Idaho."

Stromdahl cocked his head half an inch leftward and his face took on the hard-eyed skepticism of a debt collector fed one lame excuse too many. Wrong geography; wrong history; wrong idea. Pocatello was in Idaho's southeast corner; Hayden Lake way off in the panhandle, and the craziest of its crazies were so long gone Nelson hadn't even remembered what they were called.

"You mean the Aryan Multitude," he asked more sharply than he should have. "Didn't they get run out of there like twenty or thirty years ago? Any of 'em even left?" The last was a scoff, not a question.

Like quarreling children in search of parental justice they both turned to O'Brien, who ignored their friction and answered Stromdahl straight up. Yes and no, he said. Hayden Lake had in fact been the Aryans' headquarters. A bunch of slack-jawed slope-headed white supremacist lowlifes whose hate-filled meanderings did not surpass a toad's capacity for thought. But when they attacked four people who sinned by being black or brown or college students the victims filed a civil suit, and an Idaho jury awarded millions in damages. And then, in a truly wonderful twist, the plaintiffs took the headquarters property as satisfaction of their judgment, and wound up owning it. The not-so-numerous Multitude dispersed like toxic mold spore, but till now no secondary infection had really amounted to much.

Nelson shook her head yes at the Director and held up a hand to forestall any further comment from Stromdahl. "And haven't they been spotted in the Tetons and Yellowstone," she asked. "Not all that far from Pocatello. I'm almost sure. Not too long ago. Right?" She looked at the President, then back at O'Brien for confirmation.

Yes, he said. Spotted but now pretty much harmless. Every now and then a few of them would get drunk enough to bait some blacks or Hispanics or Indians. The usual result was the Aryans got the tar kicked out of their sorry hides.

But Nelson persisted, and bored in like the prosecutor she once had been. *Whooee*, Stromdahl thought as he picked up a second cookie and watched. *Redhead against redhead.* "And most of the men have beards," she said. "Because they think they're like Biblical prophets. Right?"

"Right."

"And didn't they once even try to hook up with al Qaeda, because they both hate Jews and the government?"

Right again, O'Brien conceded. But the attempted al Qaeda connection was long ago. And it never came to anything.

Yes, she nodded. Yes, yes. She was now on her stride, wise to something the other three had yet to grasp, summing up the evidence for the jury. "But hear me out. Let's go through it again. We've got bearded people who hate the government and most of their fellow Americans. We whites are just the biggest group now, not a majority. So you've got motive. Looks like they were carting explosives around the country. So you've got means. And the opportunity sort of speaks for itself. I'd get a conviction every time."

"I hope not on that evidence," the President said.

A wry crinkle in Nelson's eyes broke the train of her peroration. "Me neither. But it's not much less than Heilman and the CIA have on Iran. Maybe just as much. And it's enough for me to pry away the Senate votes we need to stop a conviction if there's an impeachment. At least for this week." Crinkle gone, she shuddered. It might even be true. O'Brien nodded in concession and did not dispute her logic. Stromdahl just shook his head in admiration at the depth of her political and forensic skill in weaving the facts into the fabric of her choice.

THE MEETING DONE, the President walked Nelson and O'Brien to the Treaty Room door, but asked Stromdahl to stay. He went to wait by the window, whence he looked out on some of the city's most iconic sights. The must-see things on every tourist's list, like the South Lawn and Ellipse, the Washington Monument and the Mall, the dome of the Capitol and the Smithsonian. Just out of view were the monuments to Lincoln and Jefferson, the cemetery at Arlington, and the Iwo Jima statue erected in honor of the Marines. They were all symbols of the country's triumphant and exceptional history and nationhood. Where would it go next?

Sally quietly moved beside him, on his right. She slid her left arm around his waist, and joined him in gazing outward. He briefly looked down at the top of her head and took in its clean just-washed smell, same as when first they met. Some things never changed. She always washed it every morning and after every practice or workout, and when they were late getting out of bed in their apartment he had to use the kitchen sink to shave. And they were late fairly often because she liked to wake him up by climbing on top to make love, which always lasted longer than she expected.

Neither of them said a thing as they now looked out the window, and he ever so lightly reached around to put his right hand on her right shoulder but made no move to pull her closer. Thus they stood for minutes, staring at a world they thought they knew but maybe didn't. And then abruptly and without a word, she stood on tiptoes and reached up with her free arm to pull his head down to hers for a not-so-chaste kiss. He bent awkwardly to accept the smooch, left hand at his side, right hand still barely touching her.

She moved her head back an inch or two and laughed. "Walleye, you've always been too darn tall." She then kissed him again, more quickly and lightly, and gave the shorthaired top of his head a playful rub. "I never did really thank you for the music box. That was very sweet of you."

He blushed and mumbled a lie about how he'd happened by the store while walking down the street. No big deal. A spur of the moment kind of thing. Nothing more. But a nice reminder of times past, wasn't it. He hoped she really liked it.

They let their arms fall away from each other and she went back to her desk, where she stood next to her chair, picked up the little wooden box, and opened the lid so it would play. Of course she liked it. Loved it. Best present in a long, long time. It was at least a hundred years old, and the wood was intricately carved and inlaid with a level of skill now almost extinct. Its shiny brass and steel mechanism was visible through a small piece of glass just beneath the lid, a sort of cross between an oversize watch movement and a miniature industrial machine, like maybe a diorama of a loom or printing press. For several entranced seconds she watched the drum's slow rotation before snapping the box shut and looking up.

"But that's not the reason I asked you to stay."

What then?

She sat down at the desk and pointed him to one of the visitor's chairs in front of it. Jane Nelson's spin on Idaho and the bearded truck driver was just a short reprieve, she said. Unless they could find the bombers and capture or kill them, her Presidential days were numbered. Was there anything new from Yemen?

"No. Samy reached Shibam, which is in the middle of nowhere. At least his phone did. Then it went dead again. We lost the signal this morning. Really need to send someone to get him out of there."

Her hand went up like a traffic cop's to stop him before he could suggest again that he go himself. "No. Don't even think it. All I need is the Commandant of the Marine Corps held hostage. No."

They volleyed a quick "but" and "no" back and forth and then went silent, and she turned her head to look out the window once more, like maybe some magical answer was flying about and waiting to be let in. Only after several seconds did she turn back to speak.

"Walleye, I hate to say it, but they're gonna win. And we'll become the first modern democracy to fall of our own stupidity." Once more her hand went up to forestall a response. "I know. I know the Germans voted in Hitler and the fascists. I know almost every country south of us has gone through enough dictators for two baseball teams. I know that kind of stuff. But never like this."

She paused another second, then nodded at the window and gestured toward it with her hand, as if it were a chart at a press conference. "You know, everything you see out there is government. You can't have a country if government is the enemy. At least not a democracy. The government is us. That's the whole idea of the social contract." It was all about cooperation, she said. Early humans cooperated to survive, and that was the beginning of societies. Then we evolved into tribes and cities and nations. Always by cooperating more. By doing more complex things that required more cooperation—and more government—to work right. And the purpose of cooperation and government had long since shifted from just survival to also include making a better life for everybody.

He gave her a wary look as her ruminations started to sound more and more like one of their never-ending political debates back at the U, when she'd regularly accuse him of unevolved Neanderthal Republican ignorance or worse. She always made clear, however, that it was his social evolution that bothered her, not his biological advancement. She conceded he was a modern homo sapiens, which is exactly what made his political views so inexcusable. He should know better. Darwinian evolution, she'd say with punctilious precision, was about heritability, variability, and selection based on adaptation. The possibilities were defined by the limits of biochemistry, and historically there seemed to be progression from lesser to greater biological complexity. But, she hastened to add, only as a result of adaptation, not as some teleological goal.

At this point his eyes usually glazed over. He never understood why a poli-sci major was so fascinated with biology, nor why she felt so compelled to explain it all to him. No, listen, she'd say. It was important. "It's because social evolution started with the cooperative nature of humans, and that's from our biology. From Darwin." But the social forms of cooperation were a matter of human creation and ingenuity, and their evolution was not Darwinian.

"I guess evolution's not working so good lately," he now said. "Or cooperation."

She smiled. "Government's not working so good either, which I guess is the whole point. What the Ayn Randers want, so they can kill it and let greed rule the world. He won't say it in public, but Heilman always tells his caucus we'd be better off if we just let the devil take the hindmost. You get sick and it's tough luck. Just die if you can't afford a doctor. And kids shouldn't expect a good education unless their folks can pay for it."

"You think they really believe that crap?"

"That's just it. They do. Heilman wants to run the country like a corporation, where the wealthy own all the shares and get to call all the shots to maximize their profits. No regulations, no taxes, no nothing. But we're not going to stay exceptional very long by trying to pollute our way to prosperity. Or by making most of our people poor and telling them they, too, can buy in to get rich. How do they do that when the deck's stacked a mile high against them and they start with next to nothing?" If people didn't think they were getting a fair shake they wouldn't trust society and they'd stop cooperating. And then everyone would lose. "If ninety-nine percent of us are poor, there won't be anyone to buy what the one percent wants to sell."

"So why," he asked, "is Heilman winning if we're supposed to be evolving the other way?"

"I don't know. Evolution's not a straight-line thing; it doesn't have a predetermined direction. Even if you understand it you can't always control it. And right now things are completely out of control." She shook her head and went silent again, and Stromdahl, too, said nothing. He sat still and gave her space to gather her thoughts, and when she resumed she went to a whole new subject.

"So those racist pigs are hiding out in Yellowstone." It troubled her that the purest piece of America could be so defiled. "Remember when we went there?"

Of course he did. In late June, the summer after they met. Before his Marine training and football practice. He bought his first good road bike for the trip, and bragged that with the right equipment he'd finally outride her. Not hauling his big ole butt over the hills, she'd taunted back. And not in the flats either, he found out once they got going. Not even when an arthritic old black bear chased him down a hill. Sally sped off and then couldn't stop laughing while Stromdahl spun his pedals faster and faster to get away. In his haste he'd neglected to shift into a higher gear.

"How do you know it had arthritis?" he had asked when they got back to their campsite.

"Easy. Because it couldn't catch you."

"Very funny." He growled, not at all amused.

They now laughed together at the memory before Sally returned to her governmental philosophizing. "Thing was, even you said Yellowstone was exactly the kind of thing a government should do. Parks and public education and food inspection and drug safety and protecting the environment. Busting trusts and regulating banks. Ensuring equal rights. You were for all that stuff; said most of it was actually started by Republicans because they believed in good government. But these Tea Party guys want to end it all. Every bit of it. They'd privatize the parks so people who don't use them aren't forced to subsidize the people who do. That's what they say. No one should ever be taxed to benefit someone else. Not even for disaster relief."

Rumbo liked to explain it with a simple example of the Smiths and Joneses, two neighbors who lived on a dark cul de sac somewhere inside his head. What if Mr. Smith needed a car to get to work and Mr. and Mrs. Jones had an extra car they used only rarely. Would we allow Smith to just take it because of his need? Of course not, Rumbo would bellow. That would be theft, forbidden in the Bible and forbidden in the free market. But how was it any different if the government taxed the Joneses to pay for public transportation that the Smiths used? Why should the government be allowed to steal by arbitrarily transferring wealth from one citizen to another? Tax money spent on anything but the bare essentials was nothing but transfer payment theft and it was fundamentally, biblically, totally wrong.

"I know," Stromdahl said. "It's not only Rumbo. There's a few people at the Pentagon just as nuts. Mostly the ones who listen to him. They seem to think higher taxes on the rich are like Robin Hood robbery to let the poor avoid working."

"I guess they forget that Robin Hood was a hero."

"And they forget how they get paid and how they're organized. The military is one hundred percent paid for with taxes. And it's maybe the prime example of how a complicated organization needs rules and regulations to work right."

Sally gave her head a rueful shake. "Never mind that a society has to be fair for people to buy in and participate."

"Well, for the Rumbo crowd fair's just another four-letter expletive. He spits it out like it's about to gag him."

"Yeah, I know. But I guess Smith and Jones and all the rest of us are about to find out what the Tea Party really means. We're about to go to war against all of Islam and more than a century of social progress."

She shook her head, stood up, and walked back to the window, where once again she stared out at the country's great symbols. Stromdahl walked up behind her and put his right hand on her left shoulder. "It's not what the country wants," he said. "More than half went for you in the last election, and add in the Democrats it's like seventy percent."

"That's just it. Heilman's people know they'll likely lose the next time around, but forget what the country wants, right now they have the votes in Congress and they've corrupted most of the state legislatures. So they'll change everything while they have a chance. They figure they don't even need Congress or a majority to toss out the Constitution. They'll do it with a special constitutional convention, which the Constitution allows. And then there'll never be another vote. It's like a legal coup. Only thing we could do is some kind of coup of our own, which would be even worse."

He moved his hand to her other shoulder and pulled her next to him. "It's not over yet," he said. To himself he thought of Samy and hoped like hell he'd still come through.

ON JANUARY 5, during the Monday morning Luke's Truth broadcast, Rumbo went into full-throated chortle mode about the latest news from Idaho. "Now let's get this straight. We have thousands dead from bombs. Thousands of Americans." He put strong emphasis on "Americans."

"We know the explosives came from Iran," he continued. "And we strongly suspect that trucks carrying the explosives were driven by people who once wanted to join al Qaeda. So obviously they've now joined Iran instead. And we have a President who does what? She does nothing! Nothing at all!"

"My fellow Americans, the time has come to act. Now! Today! It's not just the life of our great country that's at stake, it's our national soul. Are we a land that loves freedom and the Lord, or a land of measly socialist Islam-loving mice? That's the choice our Congress has to make. Not just impeachment. Let us pray they make the right choice." By the end he was shouting like a bible-beating preacher at a summer tent revival, and even over the radio people could see the sweat flying from his brow and his finger jabbing the air in reprobation.

But Hiram Heilman was worried. "We've got the votes to declare war and get her impeached in the House, but I've lost half the Democrat votes we need to convict her in the Senate," he said that afternoon.

He and Lisa and Rumbo were sitting in the great room of Luke's golf course nouveau chateau, where the three of them had assembled for an emergency meeting. The outsize edifice was built of stone and glass and supposedly designed to blend into the landscape during the day and light it up at night. Like a combination limestone jewel box and a grand beacon of freedom, an acolyte architecture critic once gushed. Rumbo, who loved in-your-face ostentation, actually preferred a less positive review that called it a return to the robber baron excesses of the late 1800s. Surrounded by a carefully thinned-out stand of oaks and dogwoods, the palatial monstrosity loomed over the golf course from a flat-topped hill not a chip shot from the ninth hole. The east wall of the great room was all glass and faced the green. The west wall was also glass and looked out on a croquet lawn and beyond that onto the leafless trees in the woods.

The room had a high cedar plank ceiling with exposed rough-sawn pine beams painted brown, but the décor was hardly rustic. Lisa favored high-end antique English furniture and antique Persian rugs, and she spared none of Luke's money in buying the best and rarest. He had no taste of his own and took more pride in the exorbitant prices he'd paid than in what he'd bought. Right now he and Lisa, dressed in matching tan golf slacks and matching red golf sweaters, were seated on a damask-covered Chinese Chippendale sofa that faced the lawn. Outside the sun shone high and bright in the mid-afternoon western sky.

The Senate Majority Leader, just arrived from Washington and still wearing his standard charcoal gray pinstripe suit and red tie, sat in a gold brocade-upholstered wingchair to the sofa's right. Lest there be any doubt about the political significance of the tie's color, it was dotted with small white elephants. The remains of a late lunch were spread out on the coffee table. Plates with bits and pieces of two club sandwiches for the men; smaller plates with half-eaten slices of cherry pie; Lisa's empty salad bowl; a half-full pitcher of ice tea; and a basket of white bread rolls with one left. After two bites of his dessert an agitated Heilman leaned forward in the chair and voiced his doubts.

When Rumbo smiled and tried to tell him the Senate votes would come back into the fold, he rejected the reassurance with a jerky nervous swipe of his hand. "The polls are turning against us too," he persisted.

This harried distraction was quite at odds with his carefully crafted elder statesman image. Tall and broad shouldered, with intense steel gray eyes, a square-jawed craggy face, and perfectly trimmed prematurely white hair, he was the kind of man who wore western wear or Savile Row suits with equal ease. And then there was the voice, deep and slow and upper crust southern, a voice acquired naturally while growing up on an old plantation outside Charleston. Everything about him said big-time serious, and his staff had long since lost track of how many times he'd been called the Senator from Central Casting. By his own attentive reckoning it was ten thousand one hundred seventy-seven, if he included "movie star good looks" in the same category.

Rumbo continued smiling. He had great faith he could sway the polls, and that would grab the attention of the wayward Senators and bring them back. In the House, as Heilman had said, they were solid already because the impeachment part of Presidential removal required only a simple majority, not two thirds. "Don't worry," he said. "Things are going our way, not theirs. Your poll was done before my show today. Our e-mails and calls are like ninety-nine percent in favor of impeachment. Cool down."

Heilman pulled out his phone and went to his recent e-mail messages. "Not what my folks say back in DC. They say people aren't so keen about using nukes, and they're afraid that's what will happen if we impeach and convict and go to war. Here. Take a look yourself." He passed the phone to Lisa, who took a glance and handed it to Luke.

Not to worry, Rumbo said again. He'd take care of it. Just give it a few days. He had a plan.

Unmollified, Heilman simply shook his head. He never had really felt quite comfortable around Luke, and they were very much an odd couple. Odd as odd could be. A blubber-ball slob and a fastidious fashion plate. But the convergence of their politics was the oddest thing of all. Though he grew up in South Carolina on the banks of the Ashley River, the Charleston of Heilman's ancestors was on the Kanawha in West Virginia, and their wealth and political proclivities came from coal, not cotton.

His grandfather returned from World War II and bought up old coal mines as fast as he could, then squeezed a profit from them by busting unions. Later on the company enhanced its profits even more by ignoring every safety and environmental rule on the books. The Heilmans figured the fines and death benefits cost less than compliance. They made so much that they could afford to buy up oil and gas holdings, too, and in the early eighties changed the company's name from Heilman Coal to Heilman Energy. It took a temporary hit when some of its assets in the Middle East were nationalized, but quickly worked around the problem with judiciously placed bribes.

When granddad amassed his first billion he bought the South Carolina plantation, where he moved his family and started raising racehorses. He had money to burn if he wanted, but never on doctors, whom he scorned as a pack of worry mongers out to warn Americans into weakness and surrender. Caution and medical advice were the sorry refuge of candy ass liberal weaklings. And so it was he went down with all vices blazing at the ripe old age of fifty-two. Heilman's father took over, and while he was personally more attentive to medical reality, he continued the company's virulent business traditions and waged an unrelenting war against the tax man, regulators of any stripe, and union organizers. He also won four Kentucky Derbies and a Triple Crown, and organized the South Carolina Ayn Rand Society. He made it into his late seventies before stepping down as chairman, and he remained on the board of directors, ornery as ever and eager to drive a Tea Party stake through the heart of both the Democrats and the upstart NAPsters.

Hiram's older brother now ran the business and regularly fed millions to Tea Party Republican causes. Since the Supreme Court ruled that corporations could make unlimited and anonymous political contributions he had effectively bought twelve Senate seats and ten state governorships. And the Heilmans weren't done yet. The Presidency itself was within their grasp, and their willingness to work with Rumbo was ample evidence of just how badly they wanted it.

LUKE MOST DEFINITELY was cut from a different cloth. Whatever else people might accuse him of, no one ever said he was to the horse farm born. His father got no further than the eighth grade, and for work started out driving trucks at a soft coal strip mine near Jasper, Alabama. He moved on to Birmingham to work as an itinerant mechanic when his fellow coalfield workers ran him off for scabbing during a strike.

Luke inherited his father's hatred of unions, taxes, and government, but not his overt racism. In high school a black football tackle with a deep sense of justice and a deeper abhorrence of bullying was the only protection he had against ridicule and harassment for his own flabby failings, and while he resented the dependency and secretly looked down on blacks, race was the one out of bounds area on his spiteful target list. Somewhere in his inner psyche he feared the tackle would track him down if he went racist on the air.

So Rumbo's family connection to coal was not exactly the same as Heilman's, and neither were his hatreds. Luke was all about God, guns, and getting rid of gays and the government. More or less the red neck, red meat "G" things. Hiram and his brother were into the sophisticated "E" things like economics, employment, education, and environmental regulation. Their professed "G" thing piety was not contrary to their prejudices, but except for getting rid of government neither was it part their philosophy. They most definitely were not truly religious, though in South Carolina Hiram did have to attend church to assure his re-election.

THE HEILMANS' REAL GOAL was to get government altogether out of the "E" things so wealthy "job creators" could work their market magic. They despised miners and others who labored for a living as the losers of the world, not entitled to anything but the lash of the master. That's what economics was all about. If such lowly people wanted better in life they should get motivated and become masters themselves.

How exactly the lowly were supposed to rise, and how a world with only wealthy masters might work were points they never discussed. Early in his Senate career a young female reporter once caught Heilman in an unguarded moment and asked what he thought the minimum wage should be. He didn't really take her seriously because of her youth and gender. "Zero," he growled. Some people might want to work just for the experience, so they could better themselves. And why should the government stop them.

"Sort of like '*arbeit macht freie*,'" the reporter followed up, quoting the slogan the Nazis used at their concentration camps. Work will make you free, it meant.

"Of course not," Heilman shot back. "I never said anything like that."

"But it would be fine with you if someone indentured himself, is that it? Agreed to work for just room and board?"

The Nazi reference really had Heilman ticked off, and his temper displaced his judgment. So for once he gave an almost-honest answer. "I don't believe in slavery or servitude," he said, "because it costs too much if you're responsible for feeding and housing your workers. We can hire people for less than that." Perhaps realizing how bad that sounded, he quickly added that the cost of labor should be set by market forces, which would help everyone by creating incentives to work. Incentives were the key, and government assistance destroyed them. Like a Congressman from Wisconsin once had said, a safety net can quickly become a hammock.

The reporter was incredulous. "Wasn't that Baron Trevelyan's reason for refusing to help the Irish during the potato famine, and didn't two million people die?"

Heilman was about to say the worthwhile Irish were the ones incentivized to leave for America, but finally bit his tongue and walked off.

When the reporter published her article Heilman took a lot of media flack, but Tea Party bloggers praised his "blunt honesty about how government assistance to the poor is what really causes poverty." Nothing should be free, they said. Not even education. At the time Sally was only a month into her Senate career, and she couldn't believe any Senator could really be that dumb. Free public education was as American as apple pie. So during a break in a committee meeting she attempted a rational conversation with him. "Doesn't society need followers and doers as much as leaders? And don't we have to educate people if we expect them to work?"

He hated any mention of society because it sounded dangerously close to socialism, but he did attempt an answer. "Yeah," he said. "We need people with the brains to figure out how to be makers, not takers." He told her he was a bedrock believer in the Randian eat-what-you-kill world where the non-productive received no help. Ever.

"That's what you really believe?"

"Yes."

"So you're a social Darwinist then?" How could a Tea Party Christ and God type have anything to do with any kind of Darwinism, either biological or social?

"Yes," he said again. "Only the productive and fit should survive."

But Darwin was about species, not individuals, and didn't a cooperative species have an advantage over a species of strong individuals who did not cooperate? And wasn't that sort of Christ's message as well?

At this point Heilman's patience with his pesky woman colleague was running very thin. She was even worse than the reporter. Exasperated, he answered with an emphatic yes. Of course cooperation was important. That's why the country needed workers who listened and did what they were told. He wanted order and discipline. That's what was required for reaping riches from the masses by letting the wealthy take all the profit from their labor. What the Chinese had perfected and what Americans needed to compete with them. That was the key to beating China; not education and research.

"So we should go communist? What happened to your free market and all the incentives?"

No, no, no. She'd missed the point completely. America was free, China was not. Americans had property rights and the freedom of contract, the most fundamental freedom of all. Property owners should be free to do with their property what they wanted. Develop it. Build polluting factories on it. Even defile and destroy it. They should be allowed to sell property to whom they saw fit. Or not sell it if they didn't like the cut of a buyer's jib or the color of his skin.

And workers should be free to take on any job they wanted,

with no government interference. If a miner was willing to contract to work in an unsafe mine, he or she should be free to do so. If a child was willing to contract to do menial labor, he or she should be free to do so. If people wanted to buy unsafe products, they should be free to do so. It was their responsibility to figure out if a toy or power saw or car was or wasn't safe enough for them.

What the country needed was more property rights and more contractual freedom. When Sally asked about the freedom of workers to contract with each other to form unions, Heilman stormed away muttering something about illegal monopolies. Of course his own business empire was of the legal variety.

On Luke's Truth, Rumbo pushed both the "E" things and the "G" things, but Heilman never felt sure Luke really understood the importance of contract theory, property rights, economics, and discipline. And right now he was worried the Birmingham bumpkin was equally blind to the political reality in Washington. The Senate vote on Macalester was going to be tough as hell and likely hotter. But they now had a golden opportunity to change the country forever, and they could not mess it up.

CHAPTER 20

Tuesday, January 6, began fairly well for the President. Shortly after nine o'clock Stromdahl and O'Brien called the Oval Office to let her know the FBI had finally completed its DNA analysis of the long strands of hair found inside the Dallas Santa's wig. Not an Iranian. Anything but.

"Took us a while," the Director explained, more a boast than an excuse. "Had to figure out one of the genes. Not at all typical. A recessive thing found only in Scandinavians who have blue eyes and really blond hair." Groundbreaking scientific work, he preened. Stuff only the FBI could do.

"So maybe it was Walleye," Jane Nelson joked on the phone when Sally called her half an hour later. "That's rich. No impeachment this week."

This time it was Sally who said not to use the fishy nickname, but she had a lilt in her voice that belied the admonition. Nelson was right. The hairy new evidence was one more thing that could slow impeachment down if not stop it. Then she laughed outright. "But Walleye has no hair. None. One of his Marine Corps things. I've never seen a hair on his head longer than half an inch."

"What about the trip to France?"

Sally's voice went monotone and cold. "That never happened."

Ah, but it had. The summer after she was first elected to

the Senate she went biking through the Loire Valley to see the chateaux and taste the food and wine and generally decompress. Her looks had become quite a problem. The tabloid types suddenly took an interest in the Senator from glam and wouldn't let the story go. Even if they had to create it out of nothing. Who was she dating? No one. Could not be true. She must have a secret flame. Where did she buy her clothes? Mostly online. Could not be true. She must have a favorite couturier. Who did her hair? What was her favorite restaurant? Where was she last night; and the night before; and where would she be tonight? She needed a break.

And so did Stromdahl, who was on leave and awaiting confirmation of his third star after leading the famous raid on Pakistan's four reactors, a precursor to the raid on Iran. It became necessary when India's troublesome neighbor came apart at every tribal and religious seam, and the contesting warlords fought like drugged-up dervishes over the nuclear spoils. Several tribes actually broke into storage compounds and stole the bombs, but the Indians were able to get them all back.

The reactors were a different matter. The Indians and the warlords fought one another and the remnants of the Pakistani army guarding the nuclear facilities, but it took the Marines to finally break through and completely eliminate any possible capacity to make rogue bombs. The weapons-grade fuel was flown out and the reactors were permanently disabled. And while regrettable, only ten Americans died.

So the general richly deserved his time off too, and when Sally told him about her French plans and said she was going alone he took the hint and arranged a coincidental vacation for himself. Their well-planned serendipity was known only to a very few and acknowledged to no one. Sally dyed her hair darker brown and Stromdahl let his grow out and dyed it too, and even sprouted a mustache. And they used names that were not theirs. Just where the passports came from was an even better-kept secret than the trip.

But Sally now defiantly denied it ever had occurred. "Walleye's never even been to France," she said. "It was just some long-haired hippie who sort of looked like him." They both laughed at the thought, their mood lightened by the latest turn of events. Republican Majority Leader Heilman had lost four of the seven turncoat Senate Democrats, and the House was holding off its impeachment vote until a conviction was more certain. And the declaration of war seemed totally forgotten.

Then came the afternoon, and the smile of good fortune faded faster than the winter sun in the howl of a Minnesota blizzard.

THE NEW YORK CITY transit cop who first saw the body assumed it was only a drunk or a drug addict sleeping off his latest binge. But the cop was new to the force and still bent on following every precaution and doing everything strictly by the book, and that's what saved his life. He called in to report his whereabouts and what he was about to do before he walked down the subway station stairwell to roust the miscreant, and when he didn't answer his sergeant's return call on the radio a few minutes later, the regular New York Police Department sent a backup unit to check on him.

With their siren blaring and lights flashing, the two officers in the car raced to the scene, leapt out, and ran to the top of the steps. There indeed was the transit cop, down at the bottom, lying on top of the body he'd spotted, vomit all over his face and his pants fouled with his own urine and feces. But he was still twitching and breathing, still alive. "I'm going down," one of the rescuers shouted.

"No!" Too late his female partner grabbed at his arm to pull him back, but he was gone, and within seconds he, too, had collapsed. The partner called for a HazMat team, then ran to the trunk of the car where she found a gas mask meant for use in riot control to protect against pepper spray. How would it perform for something more toxic? She gave it a leery look, and held it in her left hand as she ran back to the steps and looked down again. Her partner had thrown up and passed out next to the rookie transit cop, but his breathing remained strong. The rookie was not doing half as well. He was gasping desperately for air and apparently about to breathe his last. And there was no sound of a siren that would signal the approach of the HazMat truck.

The female officer was a five-year NYPD veteran named Loretta Munoz, thirty years old, five foot six, and twenty pounds overweight. She was the mother of two, wife of no one, and now faced the most serious life-and-death decision of her career. Would the gas mask work? She gave it another doubting look, took a deep breath and let it out, and went back to the trunk to retrieve an oxygen cylinder. Once more she perked her ears up in hopes of hearing a siren. Once more there was none. So she put on the mask and headed down the steps.

The HazMat team found all three officers alive, but passed out near the dead body that first attracted the rookie cop. "Looks like Munoz saved the first two by giving them oxygen," the team leader reported. He stood on the sidewalk in his bulky white protective suit, and was speaking on the radio built into the mask. "I think it's some kind of poison gas, and it got to her through her skin. Looks like they'll all make it though."

As he spoke the citywide air raid sirens went off and the highest level alert crackled over the radio in the truck. Shut down everything immediately. The whole public transportation system. There had been Sarin subway attacks in Chicago, Atlanta, San Francisco, and Washington. Hundreds feared dead. New York surely next. Shut it down and clear it out. Now!

No, the team leader thought. *The alert had it wrong*. New York had already been added to the list.

To the Upper East Side residents who lived along Lexington Avenue it seemed a thousand-times-a-thousand police suddenly descended on their quiet neighborhood. In the middle of the afternoon the subway station was little used, and no one had seen the now-dead man enter the stairwell alive. And there were no images, because the surveillance camera had been vandalized the night before. Not likely a coincidence.

Detectives went door-to-door in all the nearby buildings in search of witnesses or some other camera that might have captured a picture. All they came up with was the bantam little maître d' at a French restaurant across the street. He recalled that a panel truck had stopped for maybe five minutes at the head of the subway station stairs, right next to the sign for Lines 4, 5, and 6. The driver and a helper took a big cardboard box out of the back, he said, but he couldn't see where they delivered it. From their level of effort it probably was pretty heavy.

"And you thought that was unusual?"

"*Mais oui*," the maître d' said. He had a perfectly waxed French mustache and spoke with a perfectly refined false French accent, apparently an imitation of Inspector Clouseau's. "The only store it could have gone to, he closed right after the Christmas. And I would have seen if they carried such a box up or down the street to another place. And if they took it someplace else, why they stopped where they did? They were double-parked anyway, which I found very bad. That is why I watched. But if they were going to park not legally, why not as close as possible to where they had to make their delivery?"

The two detectives questioning him exchanged glances. "When was this," the senior detective asked.

"Around one-thirty, I am sure. I remember because I just had seated Monsieur Harrell and his wife, and that is when their reservation was. *Toujours* they are on time. Always."

Was the box big enough to hold a body?

The maître d' frowned and shook his head no.

"You sure?"

He shrugged as Gallicly as he could. "Maybe if the body he was curled up." The maître d' hunched over and folded his arms across his chest to illustrate. "Maybe if the body he was like this."

And what did the truck look like?

A big delivery van. Tan or maybe white. Dirty. He didn't know what make.

Was there any logo or lettering on it?

Another Gallic shrug. He did not remember.

What about the license plates?

"New York, I think. Or maybe New Jersey."

And the license number?

Again a shrug.

Had he seen the men go down the subway stairwell?

Of course not. How could he have? The truck was in the way.

THIS TIME the White House emergency meeting was much bigger. It included even Heilman, who came in his capacity as Majority Leader, and it took place in the Cabinet Room, not the PEOC. Once again Gronkowski blamed Iran, and advocated loudly for launching nukes immediately on Tehran and other selected targets. "What are we waiting for?" he argued. "It's like they shot themselves with their own smoking gun."

Yes, Heilman said. What more evidence did the President need? The police had quickly determined that the dead man in the stairwell was a Columbia University graduate student named Shapur Moktiar. He carried an Iranian passport, went to Mosque every week, and was studying biochemistry. So he'd easily have known all about making Sarin and had access to all the ingredients. Plus the messages on his phone were filled with tirades about jihad and how to launch simultaneous attacks on soft targets that would have big economic consequences. Like shutting down malls and subways. And in his backpack the police found an empty canister still contaminated with Sarin residue and equipped with a timer set to release it at the same time as the gas attacks in the other cities. Something must have gone wrong, and this terrorist scumbag had inadvertently killed himself. It was the residue that felled the three cops.

"For God's sake," Heilman shouted. "Mohanjani's over there laughing his ass off at us, and we're doing nothing. What's wrong with us!" He swiveled his head around the room, and challenged anyone to give him a good answer.

"All true," O'Brien said in a taut but quiet voice, "except he was a plant. Killed and put there by someone who wants us to think it's Iran. He was sharing an apartment with three other grad students, about as ecumenical as air or water—a Jew, a Catholic, and a Hindu woman who apparently was his girlfriend. They all say he loved it here and wanted to become a citizen. And we think his phone was hacked. The dates on the messages don't match up right."

"Bullshit. He was a sleeper. Just like the bastards who hijacked the planes on 9/11. Those guys even drank alcohol for cover. And I'd check out the Hindu girl. Bet she was in it with him."

O'Brien let him finish, then laid out the other evidence. The crime scene stank worse of puke and piss and excrement than any the FBI forensic team had ever investigated, but when they looked closely it was clear none of the vomit had come from Moktiar, which meant he'd breathed the Sarin before his body was deposited at the subway station. And, what about the truck and the cardboard box seen by the maître d'? Moktiar was a victim, not a terrorist, and his murder was likely part of a plot to bring on a war between the United States and Iran that neither country wanted.

DeSales, the National Intelligence Director, added that NSA surveillance had intercepted communications between Mohanjani and his chief of intelligence about the Sarin. The Iranian president was furious, and made clear that if his country's operatives had done this they should be shot. Whatever his public bluster, he did not want a war with the United States. "And remember," DeSales said, "when he was a kid he was part of the human wave attacks in the war with Iraq, and he was gassed and almost died. He hates gas more than he hates us."

Heilman waved his hand in great dismissive disgust. "Shit, the three cops who went down there were floundering around like drunk seals. How the hell can you tell whose puke was whose? And you're telling me you want to take the word of some faggot fake Frenchie who can't even remember the color of the mythical truck. Get real." And how did O'Brien explain the fact that only a week earlier, on the day before New Year's Eve, chemicals had gone missing from Moktiar's lab at Columbia. Exactly the kind of chemicals used to make Sarin. Why Columbia had not reported the theft was a side issue of no small moment. Probably part of some vast liberal pinko Islamic conspiracy. End of argument. Bomb, bomb, bomb. Bomb, bomb Iran. It mattered not that in fact Moktiar himself had promptly told the New York City Police all about the missing chemicals, which is why the University had not. And whatever Mohanjani personally felt about poison gas was irrelevant.

WEDNESDAY MORNING Rumbo took up the bombs-away cry on the radio, and late in the afternoon both the House and Senate followed his advice and declared war on Iran and, for good measure, all its followers and sympathizers. What they meant by the latter was not entirely clear, though according to Heilman the President most definitely fell into the sympathizer category. As the pundits quickly pointed out, if that were true, the country had just declared war on itself. For sure the first great battle would be over Macalester's impeachment and conviction.

She, Stromdahl, and Nelson convened that night in the Treaty Room for a sort of last supper before the now inevitable end. Steak, potatoes, broccoli au gratin, and bread, but no wine. A shared pint of chocolate ice cream for dessert. When done pecking at their food they huddled in front of the fireplace as if to glean some measure of cheer from the dancing flames and the smell of burning oak. But in truth there was little if anything to warm their mood.

"So when does the House actually do the deadly impeachment deed," the President asked Nelson.

"Probably early next week. And I think I can delay a conviction vote in the Senate for another week after impeachment, but not any longer. That's it."

Sally picked up a poker and prodded the logs to keep the flames dancing high. "*Apres moi le holocaust*. If I make it to the twentieth that'll be exactly one year in office. Then it's bombs away."

From force of military habit, Stromdahl always kept his shoulders up and his back straight when he sat in a chair, but even he slumped a little at the thought of the impending disaster. The Congressional Republicans might have declared the war, but his Marines would have to fight it, and the prospects for a quick and easy victory were anything but certain. "How sure are we that Iran has no nukes to shoot back?" he asked.

"Who knows? I've been asking Gronkowski for months, and I can't get a straight answer. I think they really screwed up the raid two years ago, and one reason they want this war is an excuse to go in and clean up the mess. They're hoping a quick strike will take out all the nukes they left behind. Even the Israelis know better. Their ambassador's been pleading with me not to launch."

Ruefully the Commandant shook his head. "They should have let us do the raid if it had to be done. Like we did in Pakistan. Never did understand why they didn't."

Sally's Republican predecessor had made the choice, Nelson pointed out. But, she added, the real instigator was Heilman, who was determined to skirt around the Geneva Convention with any prisoners they took. The Iranians had planted spies everywhere, he said darkly, and only with enhanced interrogation methods could they loosen the tongues of the spymasters in Tehran. And he knew the Marines would not deviate from the rules against torture.

"But the raiders didn't go anywhere near Tehran. Or the Iranian Intelligence Ministry," Stromdahl protested.

"Are you sure?" Nelson asked. "We've really got no idea what they did over there, except they screwed it up and probably lost the nuclear material for four bombs. Or more."

Stromdahl got up and paced back and forth a few steps,

then went to the window and stared at the brightly lit obelisk of the Washington Monument. What would George have done, he wondered.

THE CHRISTMAS SNOW was two weeks gone in DC, and on Thursday, January 8 the temperature was back to a normal 45 degrees. Warm and sunny enough to bring out a multitude of joggers and strolling couples along the old canal towpath in Georgetown. Too many for another secret meeting between the chiefs of the Navy and Marines. So Stromdahl and Swenson went instead to Great Falls Park across the District Line in Maryland, and met at a quiet, isolated spot where the canal widened into an elongated little lake fittingly called Widewater. Stromdahl had a thing about the canal, and this spot in particular, because he often rode his bike there.

In Georgetown the towpath ran along the north bank, but near the university it switched over to the south bank for the rest of the way to Cumberland, and from this vantage point the little lake looked like a pristine mountain tarn. Behind it were steep, tree-covered hills that could have come from a Swiss or German postcard. When the leaves turned orange and gold in the fall photographers hiked there in droves to take pictures. Now the trees loomed barren and without color, and in the late morning of a winter weekday there were no hikers of any kind. The view to the south was very different. Between the towpath and the river was a rocky but relatively flat piece of land covered with brush and only a few stunted and disfigured trees. In the summertime it was known for poison ivy, copperhead snakes, and large snapping turtles, but none of these threats was much of a worry in the winter cold.

Stromdahl rode his bike and again arrived first. He went to the lock at the west end of the lake and chained the bike to a tree as a sign to Swenson. Then he walked across a wooden bridge to the north side of the canal and crunched through the fallen leaves to a place on the hillside where he could see Swenson's approach as well as any unwanted company. After about ten minutes the admiral appeared, gawking around like a first-time tourist. Stromdahl descended and went back across the bridge to meet him. Together they walked through the brush on the south side of the canal to a large, flat rock by the river, a place where the rushing water would make it impossible for anyone to eavesdrop.

They were wearing pretty much the same civilian clothes as at their first canal meeting, except Stromdahl had a strap around his right trouser leg to keep the fabric from getting caught in the bike chain, and he had on biking shoes instead of boots. "Thanks for coming," he said simply.

"What is it this time?" Swenson barked. He knew an unwanted request was imminent and tried from the outset to make clear his displeasure.

"I need some help again."

"Samy?"

"Yeah. I gotta go find him."

"Wally, he knew what he was getting into, and he's probably dead already. What are you gonna do?"

"Maybe find Akbar then. If we don't get an answer on the container and the bombs, Heilman takes over the country."

"That's not our official business."

"Sven, I'm going. One way or another. And all I want from you is a Norwegian passport from Navy Intelligence and a phone like we gave Samy so I can let you and the President know if I learn anything. That's it."

"So, the old passport trick again? Like when you all went to France?"

"Yeah."

"And the President, she knows about this?"

"Hell no. She's already ordered me not to do it. Says I'll make things worse if I get caught."

"Smart lady, our President. You oughta listen."

"Gone lady if I don't go."

Swenson stared out across the river at Virginia, at least a football field away. He picked up a small rock and tossed it as far as he could, maybe a hundred feet or so. "You think this is where George Washington threw the silver dollar all the way across?"

"You believe that old myth?"

"No. But I think it's more likely true than the likelihood of you getting in and out of Yemen alive."

"Maybe Washington had a bionic arm."

Swenson threw another rock, no farther than the first. "Well, you've got a bionic knee. Maybe we'll use that."

"What do you mean?"

"Wally, as God is my witness I ought to turn your ass in. I don't know why I haven't already. I pretty much figured what you wanted, and I talked with my intelligence guys. We'll get you a phone. And a passport too, though that's a twist I hadn't expected. It can be Norwegian if that's what you want. And we're going to implant you with a signal device so we can at least figure out where they blow you up or bury you over there. If we lose the phone signal we won't lose you like we have Al-Mahdi. They won't find the implant when they scan you at the airport because it'll just look like all the other hardware inside your leg. We'll put it into you tonight, at Navy Med. And we'll show you how to send a distress signal if you need help. I'll bring your passport and phone too. You'll have to leave your little tablet behind."

Intrigued by the significance of the implant, Stromdahl asked if it meant Swenson would send someone to come retrieve him.

"You get to the coast, I'll send a SEAL team if I can. That's the best I can do. I can't send in choppers over someone else's territory on my own." He paused a few seconds and shook his head in wonder at how far he actually was willing to go, then simply asked when Stromdahl was leaving.

"Tomorrow?"

"What name do you want on the passport?"

Stromdahl thought about it for a few seconds and looked away, toward the hills. "How about Amundsen. Gunnar Amundsen. 'Bout as Norwegian as you can get."

"Fine. Done deal. Now let's get back to work. I've got to make up a good excuse for where I've been the last two hours. And you better figure out how to cancel your latest football party." On Saturday Minnesota would play Rutgers for one of the two spots in the championship game. The world was truly upside down.

CHAPTER 21

Stromdahl always had an uneasy relationship with his bicycles. Not that he talked to them, or imbued them with imagined evil spirits or malign intent. But he did often speak profanely of their propensity to break down under the heavy load he imposed on their various parts. He weighed at least half again as much as the biggest riders in the *Tour de France*, and caused stresses at the outer limits of most design parameters. Especially was he hard on tires and wheels, and his mountain bike had been in the shop since a rather spectacular Thanksgiving Day crash. It had a blown-out inner tube, a rear rim twisted into the shape of a taco shell, and a bent axle that no longer turned at all. The flat tire he could have fixed himself, but not the wheel hub and axle, which required an expensive special tool and parts that were even more special and on back order.

Thus, of necessity, he took his road bike to the meeting with Swenson, and now, on the way back into DC, he was cursing its skinny high-pressure racing tires. Like rabbits with a hotfoot they skittered perilously side to side in the loose gravel of the towpath, and in the wet patches they bogged down and stuck in the mud with the abrupt finality of a lawn dart thunking into the turf at the end of its flight. The mud killed all momentum, and before he could get his cleated shoes clear of the pedals he found himself sprawled on the ground. He went down twice before he made it to Georgetown.

But the bike did go fast when he got to cranking along the better parts of the trail, and it took him less than fifteen minutes to reach the university. He slowed down to avoid pedestrians as he wended his way through the campus, and then sped up again for the few blocks to the Al-Mahdi townhouse on Volta Place. *Was this the right one? Yes, it had to be.*

He'd been there twice before when Samy held holiday parties for his graduate students, and he remembered it was at the end of a Georgian row more than two and a half centuries old. It had flower boxes under the mullioned windows and intricately wrought brass lanterns on either side of the door. An alley on the right side separated it from the next row and led to an old carriage house in the rear, now used as a garage. Yes, for sure this was the place. But would Ayan be home? He tethered the bike to a nearby lamppost, walked up the three marble steps, took a deep breath, and knocked. He guessed someone was inside because of a light in one upstairs room and slight movement of a curtain.

Indeed Ayan was there, but only because she'd left her little store to retrieve her tablet, which she never forgot but on this day had forgotten and needed right away for one particular phone number. She hadn't even bothered to take off her coat or hat, and was standing by the desk in the cluttered little office next to the master bedroom when she heard his knock. Had she not paused to turn on the tablet to make sure its memory contained the vagrant phone number she would have been gone, back to Sheba's Treasures, her aptly named boutique. An art history degree and countless contacts among the artists and artisans of Yemen had made starting it as natural as motherhood and certainly less painful and difficult. Georgetown lacked neither money nor artsy pretension, and its residents were in constant competition for things stylish and unique. Middle Eastern diplomats and U.S. Senators and high-priced lawyers and lobbyists were all attracted to her ever-changing stock of carved and inlaid furniture, ceramics and glassware, and paintings and tapestries. Just about everything but rugs, a market too saturated and unsavory for her taste.

She peered out the second-story window and got a good look at Stromdahl as he stepped back from the door and surveyed the block, as if to make sure he was at the right place and still alone.

Who was he, she wondered. She saw the biking helmet on his head and the strap around his right leg, and then the tethered bike. Was he some kind of messenger? Not likely. He didn't have a pack, and he was too old for that and had mud all over his jacket and pants. And a messenger would not be scoping out the area like he was afraid of getting caught. So she didn't go down to let him in. And when he persisted in knocking and then went down the alley to go pound on the back door she was about to call the police. Her hand was on the phone when she recalled Samy's description of the meeting in the library right before Christmas. Could it actually be the Commandant? Still on the second floor, she walked to her studio at the back of the house and peeked out one of the two windows to make sure the man was really tall enough to be Stromdahl. Yes, he was very big. She opened the window a wide crack and asked who he was.

Once again he glanced around to check out the area. "Wally Stromdahl," he said in a barely audible loud whisper. "I really need to talk with you. Why don't you let me in so I can explain."

He entered through the kitchen door, and immediately she demanded all he knew about Samy. "Let's sit down," he said. "It's complicated."

She gave him a truly hateful look as she led him past the granite countertop island. From the kitchen they went through a short hallway to the living room, which was like an extension of her boutique. The walls were hung with the work of modern Arabian artists, and the room smelled of oil paint, like an art gallery. Stromdahl sniffed at the odor, but didn't bother to look at the paintings. His eyes stayed on Ayan, as if meeting her gaze might soften it. He removed the muddy jacket, asked where he might put it, and also if she had a towel or something he could use to protect the furniture from the dirt on his pants. She snatched the jacket, went back to the kitchen, and dumped it on the floor near the door. No mud room like in Michigan. Then she shed her own coat and hat, hung them in a closet, and returned to the living room with the requested towel, which he placed on the seat of a chair that faced the fireplace before he sat down.

Wow, he thought. It was his first good look at her in several years, and he'd forgotten what a knockout she was. Her customers at Sheba's Treasures were convinced she was Sheba herself, the real Sheba, not just a namesake. Eighty or ninety percent were men who came to ogle and flirt and then bought presents for their wives or girlfriends. Stromdahl felt a big pang of guilt for separating her from Samy. He couldn't admit, even to himself, that the separation might be forever.

She sat in a chair to his right, on the other side of a small end table. Her face was fraught with both hostility and desire for news about her husband. She didn't bother to ask why Stromdahl had come, and went straight to her only real question. What had he heard from Yemen?

"Less than I'd like."

"But what?" She equally feared and craved the bottom line answer.

"Well, from the last contact with him he made it to Shibam. Four days ago, on Sunday. We were tracking his phone, and we know he was at the Hotel Hadramaut, but then the phone went dead and we don't know where he is now."

Her eyes asked if he was alive.

He paused and looked away, then turned back. "I've got to think he's okay."

"But you don't know."

"No."

"So why are you here?"

"I need a little help."

"You what?"

"I need your help to get him back."

"What?" She was still skeptical, but the edge had almost left her voice. *What did he want?*

"No. I really need your help. I'm going there myself to get him."

"You?"

"Yeah, and I'm going to need help from his uncle Anwar."

"Thought you needed my help."

"I do. To help me with Anwar. See, I can't call him myself. Who knows who might intercept the conversation at his end and get suspicious? Heck, who knows how he'd react to me. So I want you to call and tell him you're coming and you'll be landing early Sunday morning in Sana'a. That's the eleventh."

"Thought you said you were going."

"I am. All I want is to get him to the airport on time. He'll come to pick you up and I'll tell him then what's really going on. You got a picture so I can spot him?"

Yes, she said. Yes she did have an old family photo. And what was really going on, she asked.

"Good question. Won't know myself till I get to Shibam and figure it out."

HE TOOK THE SAME late-night flight from Cairo to Sana'a that Samy Al-Mahdi had taken two weeks earlier. Again it landed in the wee hours of Sunday morning, and after a brief burst of activity the small airport returned to the empty somnolence appropriate to the hour and place. The passengers hustled through the dusty cinder block and concrete arrival hall, and everyone seemed quickly to connect with friends, relatives, or taxi drivers. No one looked at all like the photo of Anwar, and within half an hour the only people in sight were Stromdahl, two soldiers on security duty, and two young men, tallish and thin, not much more than twenty or twenty-five, and dressed in jeans, Grateful Dead T-shirts, and rumpled sport coats, one dark blue the other dark green. They had medium-length beards, only roughly trimmed, and wore *keffiyehs*. All in all as awkward and unstylish a combination of Eastern and Western attire as ever he'd seen.

The two young men kept looking for someone else to appear, and had no interest in the tall fair-skinned man dressed in safari khakis and a floppy wide-brimmed hat. Ten minutes passed before one of them pulled out a phone and started asking the person on the other end if he or she was certain of the date and flight number. "You're positive." "Yes, I understand." "We'll wait for her then." He put the phone back into the inside pocket of his jacket and turned to his buddy. "She's supposed to be on this flight," he said. "And we're supposed to sit tight till she gets here."

Stromdahl overheard the airport end of the conversation and his Arabic let him glean the gist if not the specifics. He waited till the soldiers wandered almost out of sight and then strolled over to the man with the phone and asked, in the best Arabic he could muster, for whom they were waiting. The response came in English, accented but clearly learned in someplace British. "And who, might I ask, are you?"

"A friend of Ayan Al-Mahdi. And you?" He, too, used English. The two young men exchanged glances, and moved a few yards away to confer before sidling back to answer. "I am Bashir Al-Mahdi," the slightly taller and slightly heavier one said. He nodded at his companion. "And this is my younger brother, Abdul."

"So you are here to meet Ayan?"

Again glances back and forth, and again Bashir spoke. "What is your name, friend of Ayan?"

"Gunnar Amundsen. I'm from Norway." He showed them his passport.

"I don't think Ayan has friends from Norway. She is American."

"We met in America. I know her husband, the professor at Georgetown."

Back and forth glances again. "And why are you here?"

"I have business in Sana'a, but I also want to see Shibam."

"And why, then, do you inquire about Ayan?"

For this question Stromdahl had no ready answer except a mumbled repetition that he knew her husband. Bashir frowned and grunted and pulled out his phone for another call. "Yes, I know what time it is." "No she's not here, but there is a Norwegian named Amundsen who says he knows her." "Yes he is very tall and big." "Yes, I'll ask him." Without switching off the phone he turned to Stromdahl and effortlessly changed back to English. "I am told to ask, were you in the American Marine Corps?"

Long pause. "Who's asking?"

"Anwar Al-Mahdi. "

Another long pause and a very cautious yes.

Bashir handed him the phone. "Anwar would speak with you."

Stromdahl shook his head no and waved off the phone. "Let's go outside and I'll tell you more. But not on the telephone."

"I will call you back," Bashir said into the phone. "This way," he said to Stromdahl. "We will take you to see Anwar, but not till daybreak."

THE LATEST ITERATION in the venerable line of Toyota Land Cruisers was parked not far from the main entrance to the airport terminal building, bright yellow and innocent of dents or scratches or rust. Bashir opened the front passenger door for Stromdahl, who held up his right hand to signal they should slow down and wait a minute. Wait till he understood better who they were. "Why is Anwar not here?"

"We are his grandsons. He sent us instead because we live nearby, in Wadi Dahr. And he says that your description fits a Marine general about whom Samir always spoke very highly. So why were you expecting Anwar to come?"

At this Stromdahl finally had no choice but to fess up his identity and his purpose, and only hope the grandsons would understand and help. "You know your cousin Samir has gone missing in Shibam. I'm the one who sent him, and I'm here to bring him back." He explained the ruse of Ayan's call, and why he didn't want to reveal anything over an unsecure telephone.

Yet again they exchanged glances, and this time Abdul replied, in English nowhere near as good as his brother's. "Anwar, too, wants the Samir back, but has learned not about where he is. We think the Akbar has him, but nobody is knowing." Did the general have more information, and what was his plan?

"I know only that he made it to his hotel in Shibam. And I have no plan except to go there and see if I can pick up a trail. Ask around about Akbar. Hope maybe one Samir or the other will contact me." In his heart, if not his head, Stromdahl was convinced Akbar would not harm an old high school teammate and Marine Corps buddy, and that somehow he would even help get Al-Mahdi out of Yemen alive. Meanwhile, the Commandant had morphed into a Norwegian engineer and tourist interested in ancient mud brick buildings.

Abdul and Bashir huddled yet again. Get in, they said. No matter what might be decided about Shibam, for now they had to go to Wadi Dahr to wait for daybreak, and once there they could confer with their father, Anwar's son. The same son with whom Samy had stayed his first night in the country. Stromdahl looked around the nearly empty parking lot. The bright lights and the hum from the transformer on one light stanchion made human presence and activity seem imminent, but there was no one in view. No people and no moving cars; no sounds except the transformer hum and the heat exchangers for the terminal's air conditioning.

Neither of the brothers carried a visible weapon, and with the element of surprise he was sure he could take both of them out with a few well-placed blows. But why? And what then? After a final glance back at the terminal Stromdahl got into the yellow Toyota. With Bashir driving and tires squealing they roared off into the uncertain night. Stromdahl's admonition to slow down induced only grins and greater speed, and he said nothing more.

A MAN AND WOMAN met them when they arrived at the house in Wadi Dahr. They were the parents of Abdul and Bashir. The mother disappeared when she saw her sons came with no female guest. The father was tall like his sons, but stouter throughout. The thickness of his chest and shoulders more than balanced his expansive belly, and he looked powerful, not fat. He had a long gray-flecked beard and wore a *thawb* and skullcap. His eyes were quick and intelligent and darted back and forth between his sons demanding an explanation. He pointed once or twice at Stromdahl, but made no eye contact.

"He is a Marine Corps general, and he has come to find our cousin Samir," Bashir said. "The call from Ayan to Grandpa Anwar was but cover for his trip."

The father looked askance at Stromdahl, frowned, and shook his head in doubt. "A general comes by himself on such a mission?"

"It is he who sent Samir, and he feels personally responsible."

The expression on the father's face suggested acceptance of the plausibility if not the truth of this explanation. "So he will go to Shibam?"

"That is his plan."

"And how?" They all three looked to Stromdahl for enlightenment on this crucial point.

He spoke again in Arabic, for the father's sake. "I was hoping I could borrow a truck or car."

The father's scowl said not likely, but instead of outright rejection he nodded at his sons. "Show this general person to his room and let us talk together more."

CHAPTER 22

They came for him at five-thirty, after he'd slept only two hours and well before Sunday's sunrise. Just the sons. Stromdahl never saw the father again. "All of us are going," they told him.

"All of us?"

"Both of us and you. If we leave early we can make it in one day." They were now dressed, like their guest, in khakis, though they still wore *keffiyeh* head gear and had on old Nike athletic shoes instead of boots.

"Make it where?"

"Shibam," Abdul said in his fractured English. "You are Norway tourist and we your guides are." He smiled and pointed at himself and his brother. The family, it turned out, had among its businesses a tour company, mostly meant for Saudis, but occasionally for others too. That's why they owned the yellow Land Cruiser. And it would not be a big deal for a wealthy European to hire two guides and such a vehicle for some private sightseeing.

Stromdahl grinned back. That would work, he said, and he followed them to the kitchen for a breakfast of flat bread, honey, and yogurt. Nothing hot. No need to disturb the household or take time to light the balky propane stove. By six they were on the road, Bashir at the wheel again, Stromdahl riding shotgun, Abdul right behind them; the Toyota speeding along far too fast in the faint pre-dawn light. Two Kalashnikovs leaned between the front seats with banana-shaped ammunition clips locked in, reminders that in the years since the slow motion revolutions of 2011 and 2015 the country's splintery existence had only worsened.

Bashir took his right hand from the wheel and rubbed the short flash suppressor snout of one of the rifles. "You know how to use this?" he asked.

Stromdahl nodded yes. Of course he did. But at the moment he was more worried about keeping the two young men awake. Long years of military duty allowed him to function fine on little sleep, but the Al-Mahdi brothers weren't doing real well. And so if only for self-preservation he started talking as he watched for any sign Bashir might be dozing off.

"Where did you learn your English?"

"Sheffield."

"England?"

"Yeah. Went to university there."

"What did you study?"

"Civil engineering. Got my degree two years ago. I work for a construction company in Sana'a now. And I teach at the university too."

"What about your brother?"

Abdul answered for himself. "One year at Sheff, then I get thrown out." He laughed, as if proud of his expulsion.

Bashir filled in a few of the lurid facts. "Abdul spent too much time chasing girls. Said he wanted to find a liberated Englishwoman who'd come with him to Yemen. Not many like that, but he had a very good time trying out all the possibilities." He glanced back and shot his brother a combined look of amusement and disapproval, with maybe a dash of jealousy blended in.

Stromdahl peered at the younger brother and tried to imagine him as a lothario. He did have the eyes and face for it, even with the beard. Bashir was less pretty but maybe more handsome. "And what about you?" Stromdahl asked.

"I want to find a liberated Yemeni woman who will come live with me in England."

"He lies," Abdul said.

"Yes, I lied about that. I want to stay here and work to make things better. Maybe make Yemen the paradise of the world again.

But we have no more oil and never enough water, and it isn't easy." He paused and shot Abdul another glance. "And the right woman I still can't find."

"He means he can't find another Ayan."

"Ayan?" This Stromdahl didn't quite get.

Abdul reverted to Arabic to explain. "Yes. The Ayan you were supposed to be when you arrived. She comes every few months to buy things for her store. Everyone loves her. Even Anwar." He told how she always had a perfect sense for the undefined boundary between tradition and an evolutionary modicum of liberation. She wore long black *abaya* dresses and headscarves, but never a veil, and took care to defer to Anwar even while tweaking him for his old-time ways. Like the younger men, he basked in the attention of the beautiful wife of his great nephew, and held her up as the example of what a modern wife should be.

"But you would never let your wives or daughters go freely to the markets as she does," his grandsons pointed out to him. Or travel alone, or start their own businesses, or most of the other things that made Ayan who she was.

"No, but your mothers and sisters now go on their own anyway because of her example." Anwar would smile when he said this, his dismay diminished by his admiration for Ayan and grudging acceptance of his dwindling ability to control his children and their children. In his house everyone dressed properly and prayed properly, but in most of Yemen outside the Dabwa Valley redoubt the timeless way of life he'd always known had just about run out of time. And even in the mountain fastness it was fading quickly as battery-powered electronics trumped the lack of electric lines and connected people to the outside world.

"And you," Bashir said to Stromdahl. "You are lover of your President, no? Very beautiful, your president." In the air he traced with his finger the classic shape of female curves. This gesture and his lopsided grin showed that by love he did not mean affinity for Sally Macalester's politics.

"No," Stromdahl boomed emphatically. Then he looked a little sheepish. "I mean yes, she's beautiful. But no on the rest."

Bashir grinned like a schoolboy who'd been given all the answers before a final exam. "But CNN says you lived together in college." He pulled out his phone and started one-hand thumbing his way to Internet proof while he continued driving.

Stromdahl summarily snatched it away. "That was a long, long time ago."

"And the French magazines, they say you took a trip there with her in the last few years. Is that not true?"

Stromdahl stared straight ahead and said he'd never even been to France. With anyone. "That's an old rumor that just won't die. Keep your eyes on the road."

AT THE UNIVERSITY of Minnesota he took a double major in American History and Scandinavian Studies, and of engineering he was mostly ignorant except for some rudiments learned in the Marines. Thus was he prepared by education for only the Norwegian half of his new role as engineer from Norway. But as a real engineer Bashir was completely committed to the charade, and insisted that they stop to see the dams in Marib. Both the old ruins and the new replacement.

No true tourist, he said, would pass through without visiting these parallel wonders of the ancient and modern world. So Stromdahl really had to do it if he wanted to play the tourist role. Especially if he wanted to be an engineer to boot. And besides, it wasn't even ten o'clock, and the side trip would not take all that much time. Bashir spoke with an easy self-confidence that suggested the concealment of Marine Corps Commandants was old hat for him, but his assurance was born of pride, not experience. He wanted to show off his country, its grand and glorious past, and the hope for its future. As he saw things, it was all about water. And Marib.

Like Samy Al-Mahdi before them, they drove east to the shabby new Marib, then south past the ruins of the old. But there they deviated from Samy's route. Instead of heading farther south to turn east on the road to Shibam, they cut back to the west and up the Wadi Dhana on a thinly paved road with more potholes than asphalt. Near the mouth of the wadi were the remains of the old dam, originally a simple earthen dike built a thousand years before Christ.

The first dam was no more than a dozen feet high and maybe a third of a mile long, but over the centuries various governments improved and raised it, and by the sixth century of the Christian era it was almost fifty feet high and over two thousand feet long. Water from the lake behind it irrigated a green valley oasis of twenty-five square miles, in its time truly one of the wonders of the world.

Bashir stopped the yellow Toyota by what looked like stone battlements—a tower connected by a wall to the hills that bounded the wadi on the south. The three of them clambered out and he proceeded to give an animated little lecture. These were once the sluice gates, he told Stromdahl. He pointed northward across the flat valley floor to a similar structure on the other side. The earthen dam was built between them, he explained.

"And what happened to it?"

"The rains here come only twice a year, brief but very hard, and every now and then the water rushing down the wadi was too much for the dam to hold back. It washed over the top and took with it part of the embankment. And always the government mustered the people to repair it. Always until one time they didn't. And then later floods washed away more and more, until only the sluices remained."

He pointed at the tower and the wall. "We were left with the stones and once again the desert. The Koran tells us the story: 'But they turned aside, so We sent upon them a torrent of which the rush could not be withstood, and in place of their two gardens We gave to them two gardens yielding bitter fruit.'"

"So you've memorized the Koran?" Stromdahl had a vague uneasy feeling Bashir might be from one of the radical madrassas that spit out terrorists faster than McDonald's made burgers.

Bashir laughed. "Only that verse. It tells the whole history of my country. The things that good rulers accomplished and fools let fall apart." Through neglect and inaction, bad governments had wasted Yemen's resources, like the water in the wadi that evaporated or flowed to the sea when there was no dam. "But come," he said. "We have more to see. You will notice the fields here are again green. We have a new dam better than ever. Built about fifty years ago, and kept safe and maintained through all our wars. Everyone understands it's our life and our future."

THEY GOT BACK into the Toyota and drove two more miles west to an embankment that loomed a hundred twenty feet above the dry stream bed. The road zigzagged upward, back and forth across its steeply sloped face, then along the dam crest to a turnaround circle at the southern end. Bashir stopped before the circle, at the midpoint of the crest, and they all climbed out again. A stiff breeze blew downstream off Marib Lake and Stromdahl barely had time to reach up and catch his hat before it blew away.

Bashir laughed at the foolishness of wearing headgear not secured with an *agal* rope, and faced into the wind and spread his arms to embrace its untamed force. He breathed deeply to take in the smell of the water and then looked back the other way and grabbed Stromdahl by the arm to direct his attention eastward, down the wadi. The ruins of both the ancient dam and the ancient city were barely visible in the distance, and the flat land that separated both from the big new dam was a continuous swath of green. Not lush like a rainforest, but abundant with orchards and vineyards and farm fields. "Now you see how much the water brings back life," he said.

Eagerly he explained that ancient wells, long dry, flowed once more with water that seeped from the lake into the aquifer. And pipes and channels conveyed the precious fluid from the lake to fields far downstream and beyond their view. If ever again Yemen became a real country with a real government, it would build more dams and again be paradise.

Where before he had displayed no more maturity than a first-year frat boy, Bashir now was serious far past his years. A prophet for the new Yemen he hoped one day to help build. It would be a place where schools educated people about dams and other water conservation things like drought-resistant plants and drip irrigation. And medicine and democracy. And more. It would be a land of enlightenment, a beacon to the world.

Of course his engineering proclivities caused him to gloss over several complicated parts of the country's long history. And Marib's. Things like the breakup of the Sabean Empire. And conquests by Romans, Abyssinians, Persians, Turks, and assorted others. All matters of more than passing consequence. And then there was the rise of Islam and its warring sects. Marib was located right where Yemen's Shia and Sunni populations crunched together as inexorably as tectonic plates, and the fault line, though religious rather than geologic, was far more active and dangerous than any quake zone in California or Japan.

And how will the engineers fix all that, Stromdahl asked gently.

Bashir kept his gaze riveted down the wadi, and waved at the verdure as if it answered everything. Religion, he said, was like chaff left behind in an ancient granary. Maybe of archeological interest, but little else. For him, hard cold tangible facts like dams and water counted far more than overheated debates about abstract ideas like God.

Stromdahl doubted that Bashir had ever mentioned his disbelief to Anwar, and he suppressed an avuncular chuckle at the simplicity of the young man's ideals. Was it not true, he asked, that such abstractions motivated men to create useful and beautiful tangible facts more often than the other way around? And what purpose had life without belief in God?

Bashir responded by asking what good purpose there was in belief. From what he knew of the world, people and governments often seemed immune to reality. And he quickly added that economics more than religious wars had done in Marib. When sailors figured out the winds and currents of the Arabian Sea, ships became the preferred means for transporting frankincense, and the coastal cities prospered at the expense of their interior cousins. The Sabean kings, however, would not change. They tried to keep the camel routes open and neglected the dam. And in the end they lost both.

Even today, he said, most people eschewed the direct road from Marib to Shibam and drove south to the Gulf of Aden, then east along the coast to Al Mukalla, where Wadi Hadramaut emptied into the sea. From there they drove back north through the wadi to the famous city of ten-story towers. But the paucity of traffic on the more direct bee's line route did have the advantage of discouraging unofficial toll takers, who grew bored waiting for victims to waylay. He figured that in the afternoon heat they'd get through without any problems and soon reach their destination.

"WHAT'S THAT? Roadwork?" At four o'clock they were most of the way across the desert and only thirty miles from Shibam when they saw the trucks ahead of them, stopped and straddling the pavement. Nothing heavy duty, just three dented pickups, maybe blue or black, but so coated with dust no one could tell for sure. And they weren't there for roadwork, whatever Stromdahl might wish or ask. There were no picks or shovels or any other excavation equipment in view; no surveyor's transit or tripod; no activity of any kind except armed and watchful waiting.

Bashir slowed down and stopped. "Roadblock," he said without elaboration. From a distance of maybe two football fields they could make out a group of Bedouins standing in and around the pickups. Each truck had a machine gun mounted in its bed, and two of the guns were manned and casually trained on the yellow Toyota.

"Turn around," Abdul pleaded from the backseat.

Bashir looked up into the rearview mirror. No use. A fourth truck, also with a machine gun, had cut off any possible escape.

Abdul swiveled around to confirm the bad news. "Oh shit."

Stromdahl reached instinctively for one of the assault rifles, but Bashir stayed his hand. "Take it easy. Probably just want money. Keep your hands up where they see 'em. Stay calm. Don't go spooking anyone. Be cool." But sweat was beading on his own forehead and he was anything but cool himself. Not he nor anyone else believed a dozen men would wait in the searing afternoon heat of the desert for the slim monetary pickings likely to pass by.

In the rear seat an even less cool Abdul wildly looked around for an escape route across the sand. Sit still, his brother ordered. They couldn't outrun bullets. As if to punctuate the point for him, the fourth truck pulled up close behind and honked to urge them toward the others. Bashir slumped in resignation and started inching forward.

When they were twenty feet short of the roadblock the apparent leader of the Bedouins stepped toward them with an ubiquitous Kalashnikov raised and pointed. Like the others, he was dressed in traditional desert garb. Briefly he removed his left hand from the weapon and motioned for them to stop, then re-aimed and walked slowly forward to the driver's side door, eyes riveted on his quarry like a mongoose scouting out a cobra.

"Everyone out. Hands up."

Three of the other Bedouins ran up and took the two weapons from the front seat of the Toyota. "Phones and identification papers," the leader demanded. Even Stromdahl recognized his accent as something different from the speech of the nomads. Into whose hands had they fallen?

The three captives handed over their documents and electronic devices, and one of the supposed Bedouins did a complete frisk to assure they'd held nothing back. All clean, he said, and then threw the phones hard onto the asphalt and turned them into smithereens with the butt of his weapon. The leader took the papers, glanced quickly at the brothers' IDs, and tossed them into the Toyota through the open driver's side window. The Amundsen passport he gave a more careful look.

"You speak Arabic, Mr. Amundsen?" He was very polite, and whatever his origins he obviously was educated well enough to read something written in the Latin alphabet.

"Some," Amundsen answered.

"You from Norway?"

"Yes. Oslo."

The leader looked again at the passport and compared it with a picture he pulled out from a pocket on his robe. He looked hard at Stromdahl, then back at the documents and once again at Stromdahl. "I think you are not Amundsen," he said. "And you will come with us." He motioned for three of his men to tie Stromdahl's hands and put a hobble rope on his feet and a black hood over his head. There was no chance to resist or run.

"Where are we going?" Stromdahl demanded, as if it was he who was in charge. He hoped his captors had been sent by Akbar and not al Qaeda, or God only knew who or what else.

"You will find out soon enough," the leader said.

Stromdahl gave a start when a hand grabbed his belt and someone led him to one of the pickups. He heard the door open and felt several pairs of hands push and shove him inside. Must be the rear seat, he thought. The cushion was narrow and hard, and they had him on his back with his legs tucked up so he'd fit. Slam, slam, slam. Three doors closed and the engine started, but they did not move. Blinded and alone in the rear seat, he could tell from the conversation that both front seats were occupied. Then a window went down and a third voice spoke with the driver.

"And the others," the new voice asked.

"Put hoods on them and tie them up. Not too tight. Just enough so we can get away. And puncture one tire. Only one. With a knife or a screw driver. Don't fire your weapons. We have no wish to keep them from reaching Shibam safely, but we also want to give them no chance to follow us."

Five minutes later they were rolling down the road. Headed east, near as Stromdahl could discern, and not especially fast. After ten or fifteen minutes they stopped and turned right. He heard the four-wheel drive engage and they bounced along roughly. Whether across rocky terrain or a badly rutted dirt road he couldn't tell. From the sound of the engine and the angle of the seat they seemed to be climbing, and from the drop in temperature apparently passing through the shadow of steep hills or a cliff. Maybe in a canyon.

How long since they'd left the road? How fast were they going? Which direction? He tried to estimate each of these parameters from the feel of the ride and the engine noise, but soon gave up. They were somewhere south of the highway, which he knew because they'd turned off to the right while heading east. And he figured they had not gone back to the west, where the land was flatter. Otherwise he was lost, and as night fell, colder and colder. "How much longer?" he asked.

There came no reply, but a few minutes later they stopped, pulled him out, and tied a rope around his waist to lead him up a steep and rocky path. At first two men walked with him, one on either side to keep him from falling. Though he couldn't tell for sure, as the path grew steeper it also apparently narrowed, and soon there was only one man by his side and then none. But someone ahead of him kept tugging him along. Unable to see and hampered by the hobble rope, he stumbled and slipped with every step.

And then he stepped over the edge and dropped into the void, tumbling down a slope that was more cliff than hill. Thoughts of the Grand Canyon flashed through his head. The memory of a Christmas trip there with Sally, and the ten-foot fall he took. That time he landed on his pack and broke all their tent poles but none of his bones. So they had to sleep in the open in the middle of a blizzard, with only the collapsed tent for protection. He saw it all in his mind, the image of himself and Sally together. And then his head hit the hard ground of Yemen and all went black.

He woke up with his hands free and the hood off but the hobble still on his legs. Darkness had fallen, and the only light came from a single small electric lantern. The leader, a tall man who looked like Osama Bin Laden, sat next to him and was trying to get him to drink tea. His name, Stromdahl had learned, was Omar.

"Well, now we know you are not a mountain goat," Omar

said with a smile. "You are lucky the man holding your rope was able to slow the fall."

They were sitting on rocks arranged in a circle at a wide spot in the path, no more than eight or nine feet, but enough room to spread out a little. Omar pointed first to the trail and said they did not have much farther to go. Then he pointed over the edge, into the abyss where Stromdahl had almost tumbled. Very lucky, he repeated.

Stromdahl reached around to feel the throbbing lump on the back of his head. Big as a baseball and sore as hell. He tried to turn his head from side to side and realized his neck was going to be very stiff. But all his hands and feet moved and he had no numbness. Maybe he'd survive.

"So where are we going?"

Omar laughed. "You will know when it is time. For now we have to get moving again. Can you walk?"

"I guess so, but not all tied up." He pulled his feet apart to demonstrate the limitations imposed by the hobble.

"Yes. Of course. We will remove it if you tell me you will not try to escape."

"Where the hell would I go if I did?"

Again Omar laughed. "Imam Akbar tells us that he knows you from long ago. And that your name is Stromdahl and you are a Marine. And he says Marines always try to escape."

Aha, Stromdahl thought. *These are Sami's people. Good.* He also thought that only damn fools who get caught need to escape. To Omar he said nothing. But his silence apparently was taken as acceptance of the terms for removal of the hobble, because it was forthwith taken off.

CHAPTER 23

Samir Al-Mahdi sat in a canvas-backed camp chair at a rickety old card table, the foldup kind with steel legs and a vinyl-covered fiberboard top. The only thing on it was a tattered paperback English-language biography of the great Kurdish leader Saladin. Samy must have been reading it when Stromdahl and Omar walked in. The book was open but face down, as if to hold his place, and his hand remained on it when he leaned back and looked up to greet them. "So what took you so long?" he demanded with a faint smile.

"Had some trouble finding the place," Stromdahl answered, deadpan straight and dry. "This ain't exactly the Georgetown campus, you know." Omar, who had led him into the cave, quickly vanished without a wave or a word and left them alone together. Though the cave's entrance was nothing but a two-foot hole in the face of a cliff, inside even the likes of Stromdahl could stand up straight.

Three large electric lanterns illuminated the chamber, and he could see that it was about as big as a good-sized living room and obviously had been occupied for quite some time. It had the lived-in smell of leftover food and stale laundry, and the flat woven *killim* carpets conformed smoothly to the uneven dirt floor. They'd been there long enough to wear thin over the high spots.

The furniture had a settled-in look, too, semi-neat and shuffled around to maximize the space. Stromdahl saw military-style beds and trunks for half a dozen people, a big armoire with heavily carved doors, and an additional table made of unfinished wood and loosely held together with pegs rather than screws or nails or glue. It was covered with neatly stacked maps and charts. On the flatter parts of the walls were a big round clock with a plain white face and large black numbers, a poster-size calendar, and several pictures of Yemen's famous architecture. Briefly he wondered how all these things could possibly have squeezed through the entrance hole, but quickly realized there must be a larger way in, maybe now sealed off.

Samy sat up straight, removed his hand from the Saladin book, and pointed to a second canvas-backed chair on the other side of the card table. "Take a seat," he said with exaggerated geniality. "I had some trouble finding it too. This place isn't so easy to get to on your own. Guess that's the whole point of a hideout." Then he turned more serious. "You got any idea what the fuck's going on?"

"Hell no. That's what I sent you to find out."

"Well, I only know what Omar tells me." Samy paused and looked over Stromdahl's head at the clock and the steady and nearly silent movement of the second hand. "What's today? Sunday?"

"Yeah. January 11. Pretty late though. Almost Monday morning."

"Shit. I've been here more than a week. Kind of lose track of time without any windows." He pointed at the book and said he was halfway through his third read. "Nothing else to do. Sami sent it. Thinks he's the next Saladin. The one who'll save Islam from the evil Christian West."

"Have you seen him yet?"

Al-Mahdi shook his head no. He'd seen only Omar and a few of his men. Two of them occasionally slept in the cave and several others guarded it on the outside, as Samy had discovered when he tried without success to take a fresh-air walk.

"So what all happened?"

"When?"

"Since you got to Yemen."

Samy leaned forward, put his elbows on the flimsy tabletop,

and commenced explaining what he could about his strange and not yet finished journey. Yemen, he said, was filled with spies and informers, and every passenger on every arriving flight was someone's suspect. "Looks like I got spotted and reported three times. To the Jihad, to al Qaeda, and to Ferguson. Same for you, I'd guess."

Stromdahl squinted his eyes and wrinkled his nose at the mention of Ferguson.

"You heard right," Samy said. "Ferguson. Omar says he's the one who sent the freaking container. Then he came back to Aden to kill everyone who might know he did it. How all that worked I haven't figured out yet. Don't know why they didn't just kill the witnesses in the first place." He paused a second and frowned a little. "Maybe had to wait till the ship left or something."

Stromdahl's mind had fallen several lengths behind. "Wait a minute. Ferguson sent the container?"

"Yeah."

"Ferguson!"

"Yeah. And they came after me because they were worried what I might have learned about it when I was in Aden."

Now the tale was turning stranger yet, and Stromdahl wasn't catching up. "Hold on. You told me on the phone you thought he was the one the CIA used to get the confessions about Iran sending it. Now you're saying he did the sending and then got to do the investigating too?"

No shit it was strange, Samy said. Apparently Ferguson had used his Red Sand and CIA connections as a cover for the murders he committed to cover up what he actually had done himself with the shipping container, if that made any sense. "And I guess they didn't know how much I learned from the guy at the docks in Aden so they tried to kill me and Anwar on the way out of town."

This part, at least, Stromdahl sort of understood. "You mean what happened while I was on the phone with you the first time?"

"Right. You heard the beginning of the chase. Anyway, thank God Anwar's men were waiting for us outside the city limits. Like I told you when I called again from the village, they blew the bastards away and later on scared off a helicopter Sami sent to pick me up. Haven't figured that one out either. How he got a chopper, I mean. Not sure who blew it up when it came to the village. Omar says al Qaeda, but hell, could just as well have been Ferguson."

Stromdahl said nothing, but his puzzled frown told Al-Mahdi to explain more.

"See, it's like this," Samy said. "Omar thinks al Qaeda wanted to kidnap me to bargain with Sami, or maybe just for ransom money. And Ferguson's guys decided that instead of killing me they'd follow me so they could find Sami and maybe still get rid of all the witnesses who'd gone to hide with him and Jihad."

The frown grew deeper. How the hell could Omar know what Ferguson's people were thinking or how they'd changed their minds?

"Because they caught one of the bastards, that's how. Says his name is Jones, but that's probably just bullshit. I saw him at the hotel in Marib, and he followed me east to the hotel in Shibam. And then someone from al Qaeda spotted me there, and faked like he was sent by Sami A and the Jihad so I'd leave with him, but Jones and another Ferguson guy started shooting to rescue me and I damn near got killed in the crossfire. And then Sami's guys arrived, with Omar. And now I'm here. Jones too. They caught him in the hotel shootout. Omar says they've got him stored in another cave. He admits he was following me, and one of the shipping company clerks saw him with Ferguson back in October when they brought the container to the loading dock. So the picture's pretty clear about who did the shipping."

Stromdahl's jaw went slack. Clear as mud maybe. Joyce's *Ulysses* was easier to follow than this story, though reading Joyce's supposed masterpiece was probably far more hazardous to a person's sanity. One of his first arguments with Sally had been over its literary merit, and he was definitely on the side of "none."

Samy laughed in sympathy and tried once again. "Kind of messy, ain't it. See, Ferguson and Jones didn't actually drive the container to the dock, but they watched to make sure it got on the ship. And at least two clerks were down at the docks and saw them sitting in their car. Ferguson and the Yemeni security thugs butchered one of them later, but the other clerk ran away to hide out with the Jihad. So we got the container piece of the story from him."

"What about the other clerks? From the fruit company?"

"I'm not clear on that one yet. I don't think the fruit company actually had anything to do with the container. Maybe Ferguson just stole some shipping papers from them. But who knows."

"All right. So Jones is working with Ferguson and they shipped the container. And Jones followed you. I think I get it. Now tell me again what happened at the hotel in Shibam?"

"Omar says the al Qaeda guys tried to trick me into going with them. And Ferguson's men wanted to save me so I'd lead them to Sami A. And then Omar and his guys came in and took care of 'em all. Simple, right?"

"Yeah, simple. So al Qaeda, Jihad, and Ferguson were all after you at once and all fighting with each other? That it?"

"Yeah. What I've been tryin' to tell you."

"Shit."

No one could make this stuff up, Samy said.

Stromdahl, now at least somewhat back on track, moved on to the next question. "Okay, what does the other Sami want?"

"To talk with you. Omar says he knew you'd come after me. He thinks you're like Richard the Lionhearted or something." Once again he pointed at the book. "A worthy enemy of the new Saladin, but not the winner."

"How did he know I'd even sent you?"

"Guess we'll have to ask him, if we ever get a chance."

OMAR AND FOUR other men came for them a couple hours later, at about two o'clock Monday morning. Akbar, he explained, moved from cave to cave every night, and waited many months before returning to a cave once visited. "He lives simply, like a soldier. Not like Bin Laden, who lived always in luxury while sending others to die." Though nearly two decades had passed since Bin Laden's death, Omar spat out his name with utter contempt, then waved his hand at the carpets and other comforts of Samy's quarters. "Our imam was a Marine, and even a place like this he would not use. This is only for guests."

"So when do we see him?" Samy asked.

"Very soon. Before the sunrise. We leave now." With profuse apologies he tied their hands behind their backs and put black hoods over their heads to further assure the secrecy of his leader's whereabouts.

Deprived of sight they only heard the men moving furniture

and one of the rugs, then the creaky hinges of the trap door, to which they were guided. Sit down on the floor, they were told. Scoot to the edge. Now slide down, the bottom of the tunnel is not far beneath your feet. There you go. It was too small for them to stand up, and with their hands tied they had to scoot along on their butts to reach another cave and eventually emerge into the night air.

They suspected they'd made it outside when they were able to stand up again, and quickly knew it from the outdoor smells and the sound and feel of the wind. Omar led them to an SUV or a pickup, in which they rode for about half an hour, more uphill than down. Stromdahl guessed from the engine noises there were at least two other vehicles with them.

When the caravan stopped they were led, still blindfolded, fifty yards up another steep and rock-strewn path. Several times they lost their footing, but Omar admonished them not to curse or speak at all. After about five minutes they were jerked to a halt and they felt hands pressing down on their heads to ease them through the low entrance to the cave Akbar was calling home for this night. Only when they were inside did the blindfolds come off.

It was for sure a Spartan place. The part in which they stood was lit by a single battery-powered lantern; the old incandescent kind. It cast barely enough light to see the walls. For furniture there was only a single crude wooden table that looked like a Goodwill reject. The ceiling was high enough for most people to stand upright, but Stromdahl had to scrunch down until he found a spot near the center where it was a bit higher. Omar left them alone for a few minutes to go deeper into the cave, and he came back with Samir Akbar, who stood in front of the table and looked past them as if the chamber was a mosque filled with the faithful and he was in the pulpit.

THE PROCEDURE for the meeting with the great imam became quickly apparent. He spoke only in the form of prayer and only to Allah, but they were allowed to listen in. And during the times he went silent so he could hear what Allah had to say to him, they could converse with Omar, but only in Arabic. If Akbar caught the gist of their exchange and wished to make a response he would weave it into his next prayer or entreaty.

And so the meeting went, the purity of Akbar's holiness as clear as the intensity of his madness, and likely one and the same. He looked not much like the young man they'd last seen two decades before in North Carolina. He now had a beard, long and scraggly and gray. Not trimmed like Omar's. His hair, too, was long and gray, but mostly concealed by a black turban that along with his plain white robe gave him the look of a prophet somehow trapped into working as a swami in a carny magic show. But what most drew their attention was the empty socket for his left eye and the disfigurement of that side of his face. Omar had not exaggerated his leader's combat exploits. Yet whatever his wounds and whatever hardships he'd endured over the years, Akbar stood ramrod straight and walked with the sure stride of the athlete and Marine he once had been.

"Praise be to Allah," he intoned. "We have visitors from America who come to crusade against us, and others more evil who come to make a holocaust. And the Americans now with us hate the holocaust-makers as much as they hate Islam."

There was a pause. Stromdahl and Al-Mahdi exchanged glances, and the Commandant began to affirm, in English, that if released they would indeed track down Ferguson. Omar hissed to be still and not blaspheme with the devil's tongue. Akbar paid them no heed, and his gaze turned upward, at the heavens beyond the mountain of rock above them. Suddenly he lifted his hands even with his ears to gesture as he spoke in response to his God.

"May it please the great Allah, we will do as is said, and help the crusaders for now, and share with them the truths we have learned about the evil one named Ferguson and the crimes he has committed. We will tell them how the one called Jones stole papers from the fruit company to make a false shipment to America, and how the two of them came back with the hated CIA to kill and destroy all witnesses and evidence."

Again there was a pause, and Al-Mahdi, with his fluent Arabic, whispered loudly to Omar to ask why the clerks had chosen the Jihadists' caves as a refuge. Akbar showed no sign of having heard, but went on to thank Allah for making Jihad a sanctuary from both al Qaeda and the latest feeble attempt at Yemeni government.

And then he invoked Allah's blessing for the departed soul of Jones, who apparently had expired under extreme duress without revealing anything more than they knew already. "So, oh great one, we know not who sent this plague of evildoers upon us, nor why they seek to foment attack upon Persia. We only ask your guidance on how we may discover the rest of the truth and prevent the nuclear flames from consuming us one and all."

He paused once more, and Stromdahl used his Midwestern Arabic to ask Omar if Ferguson was still at large in Yemen. Omar shrugged his ignorance as Akbar again began to speak.

"We will do as you say, oh Allah, and pursue the Ferguson devil back to America. And as you command, we will return the two Americans called Stromdahl and Al-Mahdi to their homeland so they can finish the task there and track and kill him for us. We ask your wisdom on how we may help them make this great journey to do your will."

This time Stromdahl jumped in with pretext as flimsy as his Arabic and asked Omar to tell the imam that he and Samy needed to get to the coast. "If we make it there, Allah and the Navy will send boats to get us. I promise."

For the first time Akbar, however slightly, seemed to acknowledge their presence. His eyes darted briefly downward before he looked back up and asked Allah's blessing for a trek to the sea. "As you have commanded, they will travel to Al Mukalla today and leave Yemen before the sun rises tomorrow."

He turned to walk back into the depths of the cave, and Omar went back outside to organize a vehicular convoy for the trip south to the Gulf. Samy and Stromdahl thought they were once again alone, but from behind they heard the voice of Akbar, this time addressing them directly and in English. He spoke first to Samy. "I have not forgotten, Professor, that we once were brothers in sports and arms, and I wish you no harm. When Allah, blessed be his name, brought you to Yemen and I learned of it, I knew the purpose was so we could work together to stop the madness. And I knew the general had sent you. But a true Muslim cannot live freely in America, and you should come home for good and fight for what is right. For a land where Allah rules and the West is vanquished."

Samy started to answer, but Akbar's hand went up to signal silence. A great imam might deign to speak to someone, but that did not invite reply or conversation, and his eyes shifted to Stromdahl. "And you, my general, may Allah be with you as well. But understand we help you only to preserve the world for His dominion. You will save it so we can later defeat you, just as Saladin drove out King Richard and his Crusaders. Such is His will. And our victory is certain, because we have kept our faith, and you in the West lost yours long ago."

And then, without another word, he turned around and left for good.

THEY REMAINED STANDING, with their eyes fixed for several seconds on the cavernous void into which Akbar had vanished, an apparition from their past who only briefly took on substance before he dissolved once more into mystery and shadow. "What the hell was that all about?" Stromdahl said. "He'll let us loose for now but then he and Allah come back and get us when it suits them. Like we're fish in some damn catch-and-release lake in Minnesota. Don't think I want to be the fish."

Al-Mahdi pointed at the walls of the cave. "Trust me. This ain't Minnesota. And you're already caught. Sami thinks you're one damn big fish."

"I suppose that makes you the bait. Like he said, he figured I'd come get you. And now we'll both get released to go out and kill some other kind of fish he doesn't like."

"That we don't like either."

"Yeah, that part's fine. The enemy of my enemy thing. I get it. But then afterwards Allah kills us and Sami Saladin takes over the lake. Or the world. Except maybe you get a chance to repent and move to Arabia. And he does it all from a cave in damn near the poorest place on earth. Makes perfect sense if you're totally nuts."

"Or if you're totally sane and believe everything is Allah's will. You know, I never told you this before, because I mostly forgot it, but before Sami went over the hill he told me he had a girlfriend in Jacksonville. A local."

"And?"

"A North Carolina Baptist, so he wasn't exactly a hit with her folks. Her father went ape shit. Told her what the fuck was she thinking. A Catholic he could take. A Greek Orthodox. Even a Jew. But not a Muslim. Told her right in front of Sami, like he wasn't there and counted for nothing."

"So's that why he went off the deep end?"

"No. That's the thing. What I just remembered. He said the

old man was right. It showed how all the Christians had learned to get along, except in Northern Ireland. Even with the Jews. And when all the Muslims learned the same thing then they could beat the West at its own game. I think that's when he got his Jihad idea."

"And now he preaches tolerance except for us. So the Muslims can work with each other to fight an intolerant war. And you still say he's not crazy?"

"No crazier than our ultra-Christians. More dangerous, maybe, but no crazier. They'll tell you flat out that Gandhi went to hell because he wasn't a Christian, and Hitler may have made it to heaven if he accepted Christ as his savior. No church, no salvation; go to church and you're forever saved. That simple. All that counts is belief and faith. And Sami sure as hell believes. Just not in Christ."

For his own part, Al-Mahdi had no belief in any god, except as an idea created by man. But he did believe in the power of belief, and accepted religion as a more or less beneficial thing. A source of common purpose and tradition, and of shared ideas of right and wrong. "But if you understand God as something within us, you don't see traditions as divine laws that can't be changed. You can stop mutilating and abusing women. You can stop whipping people for getting haircuts. Or for not getting haircuts. You can stop all that."

Stromdahl had heard it all before during the Georgetown seminar, and he never did agree, then or now. "Yeah," he said, "and Sally—the President—you know she sees it the other way around. She says people may need faith in God, but not the organized religion that perverts it. When we were in school she said every church has something wrong with it. The Catholics wouldn't let her use birth control and Jerry Falwell wouldn't let her vote Democratic. So she'd chuck religion and you'd chuck God, and you're both wrong."

Samy looked surprised at this revelation about Macalester. Didn't she regularly go to church? Yes, Stromdahl said. A different denomination every week, and sometimes to a synagogue or mosque. Or a Hindu or Buddhist temple. But she belonged to no congregation and never would. And anyway, Samy was missing the point.

"Which is?"

"The both of you have it half right and half wrong. We need both faith and religion." Samy was a tag-along religious free rider. Without Popes and preachers and imams who really believed in God, Christmas would become just a shopping holiday. Ramadan just a few days off in the middle of summer. And sermons nothing but cheesy speeches like those given for motivation by failed or retired football coaches.

"Look," Stromdahl went on "God is real even if He's just in our heads. He's real for what the belief makes us do, and if the belief's not something people hold in common, if we don't have religion, faith doesn't mean so much. A cathedral like Notre Dame or Chartres, that's amazing. Couldn't have been built without both belief in God and a church to organize the believers. Without both God and religion the Mormon choir becomes just a big version of Lawrence Welk. Without God and religion you don't have the Minnesota Lutheran charities that saved thirty thousand Muslim refugees from Africa and Asia. You don't have any of those things without both faith and religion."

Maybe so, Al-Mahdi said, but how then sort out the saints from the Akbars of the world. And how then keep the Akbars and Heilmans and Rumbos from waging wars to convert and slay the faithless.

Stromdahl granted it wasn't easy. For two hundred fifty years the exceptional genius of America had been to make it all work. But the balance between God and religion and freedom was always in danger, and one bad election or impeachment could tip it irretrievably beyond repair. And that's why he was now stuck in a cave in Yemen trying like hell to help Sally Macalester hold it all together.

CHAPTER 24

Omar never liked running the gantlet to Al Mukalla, and getting there with a big blond passenger wasn't going to make things any easier. Kind of like trying to hide an albino giraffe in a herd of wildebeest. One of the drivers suggested that they color Stromdahl's skin and disguise him with a wig and a fake beard, but they lacked the required costume parts, and there was no way to conceal his size. Or his accent if he had to answer a question. Omar also thought of putting the general into a crate, but that idea wouldn't work either. If the Bedouin, al Qaeda, or renegade tribesmen waylaid them, a big box, like the big man, would attract exactly the kind of attention they didn't want. Anyone would assume an oversize crate had to contain weapons or some other especially desirable contraband.

And yet, if they got to the highway that ran south through the bottomland of Wadi Hadramaut maybe they could make it all the way. The tribe that controlled it had some years before concluded that reasonable tolls levied on many vehicles reaped greater profits at less risk than violent extortion and expropriation of the few cars and trucks that otherwise would take a chance on getting through. Crude recognition of the tie between cooperation and economics. But could even these tribesmen ignore the likes of Stromdahl? And what about the trip from the caves to the highway? While

Sami Akbar's Jihad controlled the high cliffs, the hills between them and the wadi floor swarmed with bandits and al Qaeda, and the only way to traverse them safely was in force.

Thus Omar's choice was to assemble a well-armed convoy, bigger even than the escort Anwar had assembled to take Samy to Aden. He deployed fifteen pickups. Eight were equipped with machine guns or rocket launchers, and seven carried extra troops. Counting drivers, the total came to more than a hundred men, and if trouble found them, trouble would regret it.

Samy and Stromdahl rode as passengers in yet another big SUV, an older-model Toyota painted a flat desert khaki tan and battered and streaked with dirt. If not for its oversized passenger and the armed trucks with which it traveled it would never have attracted more attention than any other piece of the desert landscape. But its windows were of special thick glass, its dusty, rusty skin concealed even thicker plates of steel, and it lumbered along like a drunken elephant. Which is exactly what the driver called it when he apologized for the bone-shaking ride.

For this trip they were neither bound nor blindfolded, but there was little to see. They departed well before sunrise on Monday, January 12, and all the vehicles proceeded with taillights and headlights taped over except for slits no wider than the hair on a gnat's butt. Omar sat between them in the middle bench seat, and there were two bodyguards behind them and one in front, riding shotgun.

The trucks crept single file downward from the caves in the cliffs, every one in first gear and every engine straining as if eager for the free-running release of third gear or fourth. But the rocky, rutted trace was more footpath than road, and steep enough to challenge the surest-footed goat. And without the braking power of engine compression the trip would fast have ended in a fatal plummet.

"How long will it take?" Stromdahl asked. Nervously he glanced out at the dark hills flanking them on either side. If this were a western movie they were the wagon train plodding through ambush gulch, and he could only hope the local Indians had not spotted them.

Omar leaned forward and admonished the driver to continue cautiously and not to shift out of first even on the flatter stretches. "As a bird flies it is less than 150 kilometers to the coast," he said, without taking his eyes off the truck in front of them. "And Allah willing not more than three hours once we reach daylight and the highway." They could go faster, he added, if they had night vision equipment like the Marines.

Right, Stromdahl thought. Like he'd be supplying that to Jihad anytime soon. He also thought they'd be a helluva lot safer once they reached the flat land of the wadi floor, where daylight and long vistas of visibility would let them spot the enemy from a distance and allow them to bring their superior firepower to bear. "How long to the highway?" he asked.

THE FIREBALL ERUPTED in front of them before Omar had a chance to answer. A white-hot flash and a thundering explosion blew up the lead truck and blocked the road. Then came an eternal second of silence before the tidal wave of cacophony and chaos. Gun muzzles flashed from the hills above them, instantly followed by the sharp crackle of rifle fire and the jackhammer pounding of machine guns. In the hell of the kill zone bullets slammed into the trucks, whistled past, or found their human targets. Next came the rockets and mortars, and in the brief gaps in the deadly fire the cries of the wounded and urgent calls to take cover.

The men moved quickly, with the automatic deftness pounded in through constant drills and training. Even in the heat of the moment Stromdahl had to admire the Marine-like quality of their discipline. Without command the survivors dispersed from the burning trucks and by the light of the towering flames took what cover they could find in the boulder-strewn gulch. Somehow they managed to get two of the machine gun trucks behind rock outcrops, removed one of the rocket launchers from the bed before its truck exploded, and within a minute started returning fire heavy enough to hold their own.

Omar, too, acted with decisive purpose. Their driver and the front seat bodyguard were dead from flying shrapnel that smashed through even the thickened windshield, and the SUV had more scars on its outer skin than a teenager on chocolate. But two rockets had missed, and the occupants of the two rear seats remained unharmed. How long till the next rocket found it's mark? Omar reached over Samy, opened the right door, and pretty much carried Samy with him as he jumped out. Stromdahl found the left door jammed shut and also went out the right side and joined them on the ground. All of them hunkered down as low as they could get, and together they belly crawled to a group of rocks clustered as if intended for a fortress. The rear seat bodyguards had gone the other way and joined one of the machine gun crews.

"You all stay here," Omar ordered. He left them with a Kalashnikov taken from the dead bodyguard and scrambled off to take stock of their not-so-promising situation. Two bullets slammed into the ground behind him, and would have done him in had he not been dodging back and forth like a hyperactive jumping bean.

Samy took the rifle and cautiously stuck his head above the rocks to see what immediate dangers lurked around them. "Shit. Can't see a thing." As he ducked back down a bullet ricocheted not a foot from where he'd stood, then three more struck the surrounding boulders.

"Stay down," Stromdahl said. "They sure as hell can see us." To test his theory he grabbed the rifle from Samy, took off his shirt, and draped it over the stock, and with his hands on the barrel end held it aloft above the top of the nearest boulder. Almost instantly a round slammed into the stock and sent the weapon flying from his grasp. He picked it up, determined it was still useable, and waved for Samy to follow him as he started to crawl toward another cluster of rocks about ten yards away. "Come on. They got us zeroed in here."

When they reached their new redoubt Samy leaned back against a boulder and started to laugh. "Reminds me why I got out of the Corps," he said. Then he laughed again. "Also reminds me why I got in. This is great. Just like in the movies."

Stromdahl gave him a dour look and said nothing. He checked out their cover, sat down against a rock facing Samy, and flashed back to Camp Porcupine and Hernandez. And silently he prayed for another intervention from above. Instead a barrage of rockets and mortar rounds cascaded down on where they'd first taken cover, and they were showered with dirt and bits of shrapnel, fortunately too small and slow to do any harm.

"Shit," he muttered. "Movies be damned."

Ten minutes later they spotted Omar crawling back to the first rock cluster and called for him to join them. He had a bad flesh wound in his left leg and news not so good. Of his hundred men maybe sixty were left, and all were pinned down and running low on ammunition. Come daylight they'd be toast. Shit, Stromdahl said again, and then he started clawing and scratching at his right knee like it was itching him to death.

"What's wrong," Samy asked.

"Nothing. Just trying to send a signal."

"What?"

"Sending a signal. Long story. Tell you later." It was what he'd intended to do when they reached the coast, but now he could only hope the SEALs would be willing to venture inland to rescue him, and that they'd figure an inland signal meant they had to come in force. With renewed intensity he pushed and prodded at the implant in his knee till something felt right, and then he lay back and exhaled loudly.

THE HELICOPTERS arrived much sooner than he dared to hope. In truth he figured they'd never come because Swenson had said the only rescue the Navy would do was an extraction from the coast. A small SEAL team or two. Nothing more. But within an hour of the knee signal, and only minutes after first light, a company of Marines in helicopters swarmed in, preceded by attack choppers that caught the enemy in the open just as they were leaving their positions for a final attack.

Thus did their time in Yemen end. Not at Al Mukalla, but in the hills to the east of Wadi Hadramaut, early on a Monday morning, before the work week had properly begun. The rout was total, and the death count beyond grisly. Almost half of Akbar's men had been killed and some forty of the attackers, most of whom did not look at all like Yemenis. None of them carried papers, and there was no clue where they came from, but it was clear they were well-financed. Their equipment included night vision scopes for their Belgian long-barreled rifles, the latest in U.S.-made rocket launchers, and sophisticated radio gear. And one of the Marine helicopter pilots swore he saw a white-headed man fleeing eastward deeper into the hills. The pilot fired at him but was pretty sure he'd missed. Maybe Akbar had been wrong about Ferguson's departure for America.

IT WAS STILL SUNDAY night back in Washington, but when Swenson learned about the signal from Stromdahl he rushed to his office, which is where he was waiting when the choppers returned to the carrier. Since the Navy Intelligence people had lost contact with Stromdahl's phone they'd kept track of his location through the passive knee signal. It went dead for two spells, when he was in the caves, but otherwise worked fine. Thing was, it did not tell them if a rescue would be timely. They could only hope he'd activate the "come fetch me" signal too, and that they could reach him. Now it had happened, and the Commandant was safe aboard a Navy ship.

"So Ferguson's in this up to his hair roots," Stromdahl reported.

"Ferguson? No way!" Even over the radio the depth of the CNO's shock and disbelief rang loud and clear.

"Yeah. Ferguson. I shoulda killed the son of a bitch in Iraq." Stromdahl actually had come close at their first meeting after the Haditha murders, and he'd always regretted his restraint.

"So you're telling me Ferguson's behind it all."

"No. I'm saying he did it all. Or a big part of it. Question is, who's he working for?"

"Thought he was working for the CIA."

"Not on this one, I don't think."

Either Swenson didn't hear, or the answer didn't register with him. "Shit. You're telling me the Marines just rescued the Jihadists from the CIA. That's fucking rich. Can't wait to hear from Gronkowski about this one." He seemed more delighted at the irony than angry about it.

"Yeah. That's pretty good, isn't it." And how was it, Stromdahl asked, that Marines came to get him and Samy instead of the SEALs. And how come they arrived in force and far inland from the coast. "Thought you said you couldn't do all that without the President's approval."

There was a dramatic delay before Swenson's answer. "I couldn't, so I got it," he said tersely.

"You what?"

"Went to her and told her what was going down. Told her two days after our meeting at Widewater."

Stromdahl shook his head and smiled at the timing. A two-day wait meant Saturday, when he was already in the air and couldn't be reeled back in. "Shit," he said. "You didn't really tell her."

Swenson laughed and said of course he had. "And she told me to go get your ass wherever you were. So she could prosecute the

hell out of you. And she said to use Marines instead of SEALs."
Again he delayed a beat or two for dramatic effect, as if waiting
for Stromdahl to ask why. He continued only when it became
obvious a question from the Commandant wasn't imminent. "She
said she couldn't have you rescued by the Navy. Said you'd never
live it down."

"Sally said all that?"

"Well, most of it. She said to make sure we had a big enough
force, which meant we had to use Marines."

"And the rest of it?"

"Not exactly. She did say you'd be happier to see Marines
than sailors."

This time it was Stromdahl who laughed. "Shit, I'd have been
happy to see the Army. Even Peter Sellers and the Ruritanian
army. It was pretty damn close." But unlike Camp Porcupine and
Luis Hernandez, this time Al-Mahdi made it out with him. That's
what really counted. That and Swenson's report about the football
playoffs. On Saturday Minnesota had beaten Rutgers and was set
to play Alabama for the national championship.

CHAPTER 25

What with an expedited plane change in Germany and the seven-hour time difference between Yemen and the U.S. East Coast, they got back to Washington early Tuesday morning; all patched up and cleaned up, and dressed in starched and pressed camouflage utilities given to them on board the helicopter carrier. How an old-style double-extra-large Marine shirt happened conveniently to be on hand was never clear, though from an odd button replacement and a worn spot on one elbow Stromdahl suspected it was one he'd left with Sally years before on his recuperative visit to Minneapolis. She found it amusing to roll up the sleeves and wear it around the house. He thought it was really sexy, especially when they cuddled up and she let him take it off.

He wasn't certain of the shirt's provenance because the name strip was gone. It also lacked any rank insignia. But when they landed at Andrews Air Force Base everyone saluted the Commandant without hesitation or a second look. He was pretty damned hard to miss.

Four Secret Service SUVs, black as night and shiny as the sun, awaited them on the tarmac. They were the new kind of hybrid, meant to run mostly on electricity, and Stromdahl, who grew up with the roaring engines of farm and military machinery, found their quiet whirring sound unsettling. Sort of like a dog without a bark, or the Fourth of July without firecrackers. The quick and silent acceleration always took him by surprise. "Where we going?" he asked.

"White House," the senior agent said. He sat in the front passenger seat, and gave them only a quick glance over his left shoulder as he spoke. He was a lean but thick-bodied African American, of slightly more than average age and height and dressed in a dark blue suit not tailored well enough to hide the bulge of his shoulder holster. Nothing, tailored or otherwise, could have hidden the walkie-talkie earpiece and microphone he wore, or his darting eyes, ever alert even on the air base. Samy asked him what time it was and he pointed at the dashboard clock without once breaking off his constant scan of their surroundings. They could see the time for themselves, he said, and when they looked it was quarter past four.

At the main Andrews gate the guard took one glance at the badge flashed by the driver of the lead vehicle and waved them all through without peering inside any of the other three. So he never saw Stromdahl and Samy, who were riding in the second SUV. The caravan immediately turned west onto the Capital Beltway and proceeded exactly at the speed limit for the eight miles to the Anacostia Parkway, which took them north past the Navy Yard and dumped them onto the Southwest Freeway. They exited on Fourteenth Street, zipped across the Mall and then jogged left past the Treasury Department to reach the White House East Gate.

THE PRESIDENT, Jane Nelson, and Danny O'Brien sat waiting for them in the second-floor private office. Nelson and O'Brien were dressed in the mismatched attire of people roused from sleep to flee a fire, but Sally wore well-pressed tan slacks and a Minnesota maroon sweater, and every hair was perfectly in place. The FBI Director had shaved, but not well, and there was a noticeable patch of reddish stubble on his right cheek. The Senator's red hair was pulled back into a short ponytail, held half in place with a yellow rubber band she'd found in her purse on the way to the White House.

Sally stood up and grasped Samy's right hand in both of hers and thanked him warmly for all he'd done. She then turned to Stromdahl and gave him a long hard look, equal parts reprove and admiration, and maybe a trace of long-dormant fondness if not love. What he once called her "Oh Walleye" look. It quickly vanished and she got down to the question on which the country's fate and hers now hung.

"I guess you've heard already," she said.

Heard what? Swenson had told them about the Minnesota football win over Rutgers, but that didn't seem very relevant. What else?

The game was Saturday, she said. Monday night, while they were flying radio silent over the Atlantic, the House had finally voted on impeachment. And the Senate was to vote early the next week on conviction. "Jane got us a few days of debate time, but no more." She glanced over at Nelson and gave her an atta girl nod.

Stromdahl said nothing, and Samy let out a soft whistle. They were now down to the last out in the bottom half of the last inning in a twelve-to-nothing game, and the count was oh and two with a flamethrower on the mound. But while that meant their task was damn near impossible, it also was as clear and direct as the batter's job in the ballgame. Get on base or else. And then score. It now looked like Jake Ferguson was at least one of the perpetrator puppets connected to the mall bombings, and they had to find his puppeteer. And if they were wrong about him or couldn't crack the case and track him down before the conviction vote, they were all probably goners.

Of the five of them, Samy especially had no doubts about Ferguson, who was the purest form of evil, a man who sinned for pleasure and without provocation, guilt, or remorse. Had Samy believed in God and God's opposite he would have called Ferguson the Devil incarnate, but when he said as much to Stromdahl the Commandant disagreed.

"No," he said. "Satan was at war with God and sought dominion over the souls of men. Ferguson never had any more thought of heaven or hell or souls than a shark eating its way through a school of fish."

Now, two decades after Iraq, the shark had surfaced, and all of Samy's guilt as well, as if the two of them had come up together from the deep for a final reckoning. In his mind the tortured ghosts of Haditha were crying out for vengeance, justice having long since failed them. "I'm not done with this," he said. "Not till I personally send him back to hell."

Stromdahl swallowed hard, still remorseful both for the Haditha victims and for sending Samy there to become Ferguson's unwitting accomplice. "First we have to find him," he said softly. He paused, then continued in a slightly stronger voice. "And if we're going to save the President we need to find out who he's working for."

Their best hope was O'Brien, who'd been pulling every string he could to get an answer. But so far he didn't have much. He started out by repeating what he'd learned earlier in his efforts to unearth Ferguson's connections. He told them it had been five years since Red Sand and Runyon, its founder, had officially dumped the SOB, and how after that the trail supposedly went cold. "But Runyon and I go back a way, and I don't think he'd out and out lie to me. I also don't think he's Tea Party nuts, just Republican nuts."

"So?" The President asked the question that was in everyone's mind. Where the heck was he going with this?

"So I called him in for another little talk. Told him Ferguson seems hell bent on keeping us from the truth about the container, and probably sent it. Told him about Aden and Shibam and Akbar and asked what he thought might be going on."

"And?"

"He said he really didn't know a thing, but he'd heard some rumors when a few Red Sand guys left to work with Jake. Said Jake formed his own little group of misfits, mostly other Red Sand rejects, but also some next-generation South African *apartheid* types and some of the Israeli ultra-right guys from *Nagaf*. 'Bout as toxic a human mix as anyone could conjure up. If they got pissed at the U.S. there's no telling what they might do."

"And Red Sand had nothing to do with them?" Nelson gave voice to the incredulity they all shared.

"Not officially. But Runyon does admit he occasionally suggested folks contact Jake for work Red Sand wouldn't do."

"Like what?"

"He wouldn't say. I suspect assassinations. And he went all over the map when I asked if he told people how to contact Jake. Went all to mumbles about that and said something about there were others at Red Sand who personally kept in touch with the bastard."

Samy jumped in to ask about Ferguson's connection with the CIA's investigation in Yemen.

O'Brien shook his head and said Runyon's information wasn't all that up-to-date. "What he knows goes back a couple years, to the reactor raid. And he claims he only heard about that secondhand. Says he heard the CIA used Jake and *Nagaf* when the Israelis asked for help on the raid."

The President frowned. Why would Israel use people they were trying to hunt down? For that matter, why would the CIA use them?

"Runyon figures the Israelis didn't know who all the CIA was sending. And he figures maybe the CIA didn't either, though that one's hard to swallow. Says maybe Gronkowski used his hero Jake, and Jake brought in *Nagaf* on his own. You believe that, there's a bridge in Brooklyn I'll sell you. But here's the bottom line. If it was *Nagaf*, they're probably the ones who ended up with the plutonium. And that scares the hell out of me. Runyon too. I think that's mostly why he talked. He said if *Nagaf* sets off nukes on its own everyone comes down on them. Especially the Israelis, who'd be desperate to keep Iran from bombing Tel Aviv to get even. But if we start bombing, then the *Nagaf* guys can blow up whatever they want and it all gets lumped in with us. They settle old scores, take back the land Israel returned to the Palestinians, plus more. And when the fallout settles, both literally and actually, they own half the Middle East."

Stromdahl wasn't buying it. "That makes absolutely no sense at all. None. Zero. No one's that crazy."

"I'm just reporting what Runyon says. He's pretty sure about Jake and *Nagaf* doing part of the reactor raid. The rest of it he's just guessing like the rest of us."

"What about the mall bombs?" Nelson said. "And the Sarin. Doesn't this all mean Ferguson was behind all that too? To get us into a war with Iran? Would he really do all that?"

"Runyon thinks so. Says we have no idea how crazy Jake is."

Stromdahl and Samy quickly looked at one another. They knew he was capable of anything. But was Gronkowski part of it too? Samy turned back to O'Brien and pointed out it was the CIA that sent Ferguson to Yemen.

Stromdahl shook his head. "I don't think they'd be blowing things up here at home and killing ten thousand citizens. Not even with the Gronker in charge. Not even if all the people were liberals or gays. What's Runyon say about that? And about killing the clerks and all in Aden?" He paused briefly, but resumed before anyone else could speak. They also should remember, he said, that the nitrates in the container were never used to make a single bomb. It wasn't clear where the actual bomb materials came from.

O'Brien's face acknowledged the uncertainty. "Look, like I just said, the truth is Runyon doesn't really know what's happened since the reactor raid. I think the malls and the Sarin thing and Yemen are all really a mystery to him too. He said we'd have to ask Gronkowski, whom he doesn't much like."

"Who does?" Stromdahl said. But maybe he had a way to get inside the CIA without going through the Gronker. He'd get on it right away.

THE MARINE CORPS Alumni League started some time after World War II and had more members than there were Marines on active duty. It did pretty typical plain vanilla things like helping with the Corps' museum at Quantico, working with recruiters, and lobbying Congress for military funding and veterans' benefits. Nothing very eye-catching or newsworthy. Its current president was Edward Elliott Chase, who went through advanced infantry training at Quantico with Stromdahl. Back then he was everyone's choice as most likely to make general.

He seemed well on the way to fulfilling this bright prophecy until the week before finishing his infantry training when he met Lydia DePew at a party in Georgetown. Like every other man who'd ever laid an eye on her, he fell instantly into infatuated love. Her mother was a former Mississippi beauty queen, her father was a big-time investment banker from New York, and the combination of genes and money produced a real-life Barbie Doll with big brown eyes and a perfect pouty mouth a whole lot sexier than any child's toy. Lydia was playing at being an art dealer at a little place on Q Street, but she lived only to be noticed and adored. And she demanded equal physical perfection in any man she dated.

Chase had all of that in spades. When he was an All-American halfback at the Naval Academy the sports writers called him a cross between Brad Pitt and Jim Brown. And then there was the added allure of military adventure and dress blues, which he was wearing at the party because he'd stopped by on the way back to Quantico after a formal dinner at Marine Barracks. A friend of another lieutenant was living in Georgetown for the summer, partying away at his father's townhouse, and Lydia got wind it was the place to be that night. She and E.E. were married only six weeks afterwards, right before he left on his first deployment with the Fleet. Almost instantly they rose to near the top on tabloid lists of the most beautiful couples in the world.

They made it through two promotions and two kids in seven years before her father got sent away for a Ponzi scheme and the money dried up. E.E. needed a new profession, she said. Maybe he should go to law school. And so he did, at Georgetown. But when she found out the track to partnership required long years and longer hours and didn't pay so much, she arranged another kind of job opportunity with a family friend who ran a hedge fund. It all came to an end when they were on the train to New York for the interview and she started gushing about how they'd soon have enough that they'd never have to stoop so low again. Her kind of people always took private planes, she said. *And my people never do*, Chase thought.

Six months later their divorce was final and he had custody of the children. He went back to working his way up the ladder at a big DC law firm, where he was now a top litigator and still turned heads with his looks even if his hair had gone from black to steel gray and wrinkles had started to crease his face. And through it all he missed the Marines. Except for the kids he would have rejoined, and about a year after his split from Lydia he got active in the Alumni League to keep as much contact as he could. So he wasn't totally surprised when the Commandant called him Tuesday morning and said to get over to Eighth and Eye right away.

They sat together in the library, with guards posted at the doors to assure their privacy. "Ed, I need your help," Stromdahl said.

Obviously perplexed and uncomfortable, Chase looked away and tried to puzzle out what was going on. The country was about to fall apart in a spasm of Tea Party stupidity, and he guessed Stromdahl's request had nothing to do with appropriations or pensions. But what? E.E. handled commercial litigation cases for big corporations and kept his politics to himself. And he knew about the Commandant's ties to the President, for whom he had not voted. So he chose his words with well-honed lawyerly caution.

"I'll do what I can. Tell me what's going on."

Stromdahl sensed the hesitation, and realized he had no choice but to lay out the whole truth. "This isn't about the League, it's about the country," he said. "Where do you stand on impeachment?"

"I voted Democratic last time. First time ever. I've always been a Republican. Either way, I'm not a big fan of Macalester."

"You want her gone?"

"Yeah. But not impeached. And I don't want the Tea Party running the country. So what's this all about? You all planning a coup or something?"

"No." He paused a few seconds. "Look, you don't have to agree to help, but you do have to promise that what I'm about to tell you stays completely secret. Okay?"

Chase ran it through his head and looked at the door, like he wanted out. After a second or so he turned back to Stromdahl. "I won't do anything illegal. Or wrong. If this ever hits the Internet I want to be able to look my kids in the eye the next day. So if you want, I was never here and I'll leave now."

"I promise it's not illegal. And unless your kids are big fans of Rumbo and Senator Heilman, they'll be proud as hell of you."

Another pause; another look away. Then he turned back and simply said he'd hear Stromdahl out. "But one thing sounds crooked and I'm gone."

The Commandant held his right hand out, palm forward, a signal for Chase to stop. "Don't worry. All I need is for you to arrange a meeting this afternoon between me and Tom Garvey. Remember him?"

"Yeah. Went through Quantico right after us. Really a good guy. Got out to get married and wound up at the CIA. Right?"

"Right. He's now the deputy director, highest-ranking career guy over there. And I know he's in the League. I just checked the membership list. I want you to give him a call and tell him you need to meet this afternoon. Tell him it's about a League committee or something. Whatever it takes."

Chase frowned, obviously not comfortable with the idea.

"Look, I don't care what you say to get him to the meeting, but I want him in your office by four o'clock. Can you do that?"

"I can try. But what the hell for?"

"Because at about three o'clock you're going to receive a crate. A piece of machinery or something that's evidence in one of your cases. You tell me what we should call it."

"And what's really going to be in it?"

"Me. I need to meet with Tom, but he'll spook if I call him or if he thinks there's any way Gronkowski might find out. And I don't want any rumors starting about how he and I were at your firm at the same time. So can you do all that?"

STROMDAHL CRAWLED OUT OF THE CRATE and stood behind the door when Chase and Garvey walked in, and when Chase pulled it shut the Commandant took a quick sideways step to close off any attempt at escape. Garvey was an inch shy of six feet, twenty pounds overweight, and soft from too many years of office work. He'd long since lost all of his hair except for a well-trimmed gray halo, and he looked every bit the contented grandfather of three that he was. For him Stromdahl was as physically immoveable as Gibraltar, and he knew right away he was trapped.

For a millisecond, his body tensed and his eyes went back and forth between his two captors; a burst of panic so palpable that Chase moved to block his path to the tenth-story window. But in an instant Garvey deflated and went dead calm and held out his hand as if all was well with the world and he'd just bumped into Stromdahl at lunch. "Hi, Wally. It's been a few years. How are ya?"

"Been kinda busy lately. Lot going on."

"Like a trip to Yemen?"

Stromdahl gave a start and looked at E.E. Chase. "Maybe you don't want to hear all this," he said. Chase nodded and said he was just about to leave, and they waited till he was gone before continuing.

"So how'd you all learn about that?"

"We hear a lot."

"From Jake Ferguson."

"Can't say."

Stromdahl stuck his tongue against the side of his cheek and thought for a few seconds. Then he sat down in the big leather chair behind the big antique desk and motioned for Garvey to take one of the visitor's chairs. Chase was a traditionalist, and except for a computer and a telephone his oak-paneled office and mahogany furniture would have looked perfectly at home in any century since the seventeenth.

"We need to talk," Stromdahl said.

Garvey remained standing. "No we don't. I'm not far away from retiring with thirty years. I mostly like my work. And I'm not going to screw it all up." He turned to leave, but hesitated when Stromdahl raised his voice a notch and told him to wait.

"Tom, you walk out you're screwed for sure. I'll call Gronkowski and tell him what a wonderful meeting I've just had with you and Senator Nelson. You can go back and try to explain that to him."

This time the eyes turned wary and hostile, but not panicked. He put his right hand on the back of one of the Queen Ann chairs to brace himself, and stared back at Stromdahl with an intensity close to hatred. He said the Commandant could go fuck himself, yanked the door open, walked right out, and slammed it shut behind him. After about two minutes there was a knock, and before Stromdahl could respond E.E. Chase walked in and told him not to leave yet.

"Is he still here?"

Chase made a gentle motion with his hand, as if patting the head of a five-year-old. "Chill," he said. "Just wait a few minutes."

Stromdahl nodded his assent and sat back down at the desk and tried to read the news on his Marine Corps mini-tablet to kill the time. Fifteen minutes later Chase returned and motioned for him to follow. Garvey, Chase said, was waiting for him in the men's room.

"What? Is he some kind of a Senator from Idaho or something?"

"Don't think so. But he'll talk with you there. He was worried the office might be bugged, and he wanted me to clear the floor before I brought you to see him."

"So what did you tell people?"

"That the big box I got might have something toxic in it, and they should leave. Best I could think of. My secretary managed to sell the story, not me." He allowed himself a smile and added he wasn't so sure, but what the contents of the box might not actually be toxic. Stromdahl just gave him a jaundiced glare and asked where the men's room was.

GARVEY WAS SITTING on the sink countertop, his feet dangling above the tiled floor. He said this time Chase should stay with them. He wanted a witness. Stromdahl glanced back and forth between the two men, said that would be fine, and leaned against the wall by the door. Chase sat down next to Garvey, and they all just stared at one another.

"What can you tell us about Ferguson?" Stromdahl finally asked.

"A lot and not so much. Nothing certain. And nothing that goes public. Like Deep Throat. Agreed?"

"Agreed."

Garvey paused a few seconds, and looked back and forth at the other two men. Then he started his tale. "First thing you need to understand is this is all about Hiram Heilman, not the Agency. Gronkowski does pretty much whatever he says."

Stromdahl nodded in encouragement. Not a surprise, he said.

"So two years ago Heilman tells us to use Ferguson on the Iran reactor raid, and bingo, it's done. No questions asked. No control. No one from the Agency goes along. Just him and whatever crew he put together. And no one involved like you and the Marines, not even after your success in Pakistan. Crazy."

"And *Nagaf*?"

Garvey shook his head yes. "Probably who Ferguson used. We're still trying to figure that out ourselves."

"What about Yemen?"

"The recent stuff?"

"Yes."

"You mean the CIA stuff about finding who sent the container?"

"Yes."

"Same thing. We got a lead about it on our own. Nothing to do with Iran. Then Heilman comes again and says use Ferguson and go hard after the Iranians." Garvey paused, apparently uncertain how to continue.

"And you did again?"

"Yeah."

"You got any idea why?"

"Why we agreed or why Heilman wanted to use him?"

"Both."

"We agreed because Gronkowski's a political hack. And he hates all Muslims and thinks Jake's some kind of hero for what he did at Haditha. Not sure what Heilman's up to, but I got a good idea."

"Which is?"

Garvey looked over at Chase, then back at Stromdahl, and then he stood up. At first they were worried he was about to flee, but instead he started pacing while trying to get his thoughts straight. "Well," he said, "this is what I think. I've got no evidence, but I know Heilman, and he's mad hatter nuts."

Another nod of encouragement, and this time a faint smile. No shit the Senator was nuts. "And?"

"And I think he's behind the mall bombs and the subways. Not sure where he got the nitrates and the other chemicals for the bombs, or the Sarin, but we're pretty sure they weren't imported. For sure the nitrates. Whoever did it all had some source here in the States."

"Where?"

"No idea."

Chase was now standing too, face agape, no idea which side was up. "You saying a U.S. Senator just killed ten thousand U.S. citizens? You're the one who's crazy."

"I said that's what I think, but I really believe it's what went down. And it scares the shit out of me. Think about it. He's always talking about blowing up the government, and he means it. Don't forget, he's the king of the Ayn Rand crowd, and her characters are all the time burning or blowing up their own property to keep the moochers from stealing the heroic work of the great capitalists. That's their fucking religion." But however much he despised Heilman, his passion had its limits, and he hastened to add that "I'm not getting into that religious war. I'm keeping my head down. It's not a fight I'll ever win."

"So you've got a Deep Throat at the CIA who thinks Heilman's crazy, which is no news. And maybe, perhaps—of course we're not sure—but maybe he's crazy enough to blow up eight shopping malls. You can't give us Deep Throat's name, and oh yeah, the best evidence of Heilman's craziness is he quotes from *Atlas Shrugged* and really believes it. And with that I'm supposed to stop the vote on convicting Sally. Know what, you're the crazy one!" Back in their student days at the U Stromdahl and Jane Nelson never got along too well; because of his Republicanism, and maybe rivalry for Sally's time. And once again their frictive differences were grating on each other like sand on sandpaper; the rough kind.

To get her the latest anti-impeachment ammunition he'd gone straight to her Senate office after the meeting with Deep Throat Garvey, but she wasn't buying the story any more than Ed Chase had bought it. What the hell, most of her Republican colleagues carried around well-thumbed copies of Ayn Rand's book and quoted it more readily than the Bible or the Constitution. Did Stromdahl really think they'd turn on a fellow member of their cultist congregation?

He sighed and slumped in his chair, unprepared to defend a message based more on hope than conviction. "Guess we better call the President and let her know," he said glumly. They also patched in Danny O'Brien.

"So what's next?" Sally asked. "Can the FBI find out what Heilman's been up to?"

Yes, O'Brien said, but not likely fast enough to beat back the Senate vote. And if word leaked out the President was using the Bureau to investigate a political rival there'd be hell to pay. More fuel for the impeachment fire.

What else, then?

"Pray," O'Brien said. "Pray real hard."

CHAPTER 26

On Wednesday, January 14, prayer or not, the evidence got a little better. Stromdahl was in his office at Marine Corps Headquarters when Linda Ferrell called at about eight in the morning. "Well, sir, I was right."

"Right about what?"

"The container, sir. And the nitrates. The bomb stuff wasn't smuggled in. It was made right here in the old U S of A."

He pulled the phone receiver away from his head and gave it a dubious look. "Where you calling from?"

"Coast Guard, sir. On a secure line."

"You sure?"

"Yes sir. Same one I used last time." When he continued to hesitate she repeated that they were fine. "No need to worry, sir. I double checked. Really."

His acceptance of her explanation was grudging and only half-convinced. But apparently convinced enough. So what about the nitrates, he asked.

"Well, the Ag Department regs are pretty tight, sir, and I didn't think anyone could make or ship as much as went into the bombs without there being a record. So I did some checking on my own."

"Thought we did that already."

"Only sort of. Our guys checked every chemical plant that makes nitrates, and every shipment from a farm store or a warehouse or anywhere else. But there's one lead they never quite followed. In Idaho. Don't know why it took so long to see it. Like it was right under our noses."

The last vestige of Stromdahl's aggravation vanished as quickly as a politician's promise, and his voice had the urgent edge of a man face-to-face with destiny. "What about Idaho?"

"There's a chemical plant that makes pesticides for potato farmers. And get this—it's near Pocatello." The news of the truck sightings right after Christmas had been broadcast far and wide, so she knew all about the significance of the Pocatello location. Now she waited half a second to let Stromdahl absorb it too.

He gasped out an exclamatory "no."

"That's right, sir. Pocatello. Pocatello, Idaho." The company was called IPC, she said, for Idaho Potato Chemicals. It didn't make fertilizer, but did grow potatoes on a few experimental farms to test its products, and over the last year or so had been buying more nitrates than ever before. "I think our guys overlooked it 'cause it was like a chemical plant to chemical plant sale. Probably didn't think it was suspicious. But buying this much doesn't really seem right."

"Was it enough for all the bombs?"

"More than that. A lot more."

"So who owns IPC?"

"That's even more interesting. A company incorporated in Bermuda. Closely held; probably a subsidiary or something. I can't find anything more than that on the web." She paused a beat or two, and when he said nothing she blurted out the plan she'd formed. "Sir, I want to go out there and look around myself. I'll say it's just a regular inspection. Something they won't suspect."

He looked at the clock on his desk and saw he was already ten minutes late for an important staff meeting. He did, after all, still have the Marine Corps to run. So he ended the call after telling Ferrell she should come down to Washington right away. If need be the President herself would patch things up with her Ag Department boss in Newark.

After Ferrell hung up Stromdahl called O'Brien and told him to find out all he could about IPC. Then he called the President. And then, though the staff meeting loomed and he abhorred and never tolerated lateness, he took a few minutes more to see what he could learn for himself on the Internet. Like Linda, he found nothing on IPC except a website extolling the lethality of its pesticides and explaining where they could be purchased.

Linda's discovery was a big break in the case, but its meaning was not yet clear. And it very shortly was eclipsed by something even bigger yet. After lunch the Commandant received another call, this time from a most unlikely source. The most unlikely he ever could have imagined.

LISA LARKIN had pretty much given up trying to do anything about Luke Rumbo's eating, drinking, smoking, and drugging habits. And what the heck, the soft core side of drugs was her thing too. But otherwise she did her best to keep Luke under some semblance of control. She fed him good material for Luke's Truth, tried to feed him healthy food, and monitored his e-mailing and social networking like a mama hawk guarding the nest. It wasn't hard because he could barely turn on a computer or any other electronic device by himself.

One of her regular self-assigned tasks was checking his e-mails to ferret out blunders before he took them public, and to make sure she kept ahead of them she periodically went through a delete-a-thon on his in and out boxes. Thus it was that the afternoon of January 12—"Impeachment Monday"—while Stromdahl and Samy were still flying home, she was clicking through the Lukester's inbox as the two of them waited in his mansion for the crucial roll call. They were monitoring events on TV, but with only half an eye. She was still in her pajamas and sat in one of the chairs in the great room with a tablet in her lap. Luke, also in pajamas, was in a chair closer to the TV, randomly clicking through the channels to see what various people had to say about the impending vote. His own pre-recorded comments already had gone out over the air, and on a pad of paper he was sketching out his triumphal post-impeachment rant.

"Hey," Lisa said, "come over here and tell me about this one."

He leaned forward and set aside the pad of paper, but answered without bothering to get up. "Which one? What's it about?"

"The Sarin subway attacks."

"What about them?"

"It's not the what but the who and the when. Hiram Heilman

sent it. Said you needed to be ready to get on the air to tell everyone how Macalester is letting Iran get away with mass murder."

"Uh huh. What's wrong with that? That's exactly what she is doing. That's why we're impeaching her." He relaxed back into the chair and reverted to channel surfing. Lisa had already gone well past his normal attention span, which was only slightly longer than a newborn cat's.

She paused, uncertain how best to say what had her so upset. "Luke, please pay attention for a minute and listen to me. The e-mail was sent two hours before they found that dead Iranian guy in New York, and it says New York was one of the cities that got attacked."

His face wrinkled into an annoyed frown as he tried to comprehend the significance of what she was saying. At some level he saw the logical flaw, but couldn't get his mind around it.

She connected the dots for him. "So how did Hiram know in advance?"

His blank look made clear he still wasn't getting it, but he sat up straight and was paying full attention.

"Luke, he wouldn't have known unless he was in on it. I think he did the Sarin. And the malls. Or had someone do them."

"No way." He waved her off and shook his head. It simply couldn't be.

"No listen, honey, he's always talking about blowing things up and starting over; about how it doesn't matter if we have to lose a few moochers to take the country back from the socialists and pinkos. And he's been saying for years how a war with Iran would be just great 'cause then American companies could get back the property they lost way back when. He keeps saying that blowing up government is always good, and I think he's gone and done it."

"No." Again Luke protested, but much more weakly. Then he rallied. Shopping malls weren't government. What was she talking about?

"I think he did it," she repeated quietly, without addressing his argument. "I think he's cooked this up himself. All of it." Deep down she detested the Senator, who scorned and condescended to women while his eyes and libido wandered worse than a tomcat's or a rock star's. About every other week he suggested maybe she should take a little romantic trip with him while Rumbo was off doing something else, like attending a cigar smokers convention. Heilman was more corrupt and cynical than even her preacher husband, whom she also hated, but only half as much. Her husband, after all, was a mostly harmless religious fake.

But for all that it took Lisa a few days to figure out what to do. She really did want Macalester gone, yet her discovery about Heilman would almost surely bring impeachment to a screeching halt. On the other hand, if it went through and Heilman's crowd took over the country he'd just as surely beat the rap on bombing the malls, and that would be bad too. Finally she split the baby and decided to wait a day or two. At least let the House take its vote, then call Wallace Stromdahl, who was supposed to be the lead guy on all things related to the mall bombs. She wouldn't talk to anyone but him, and even with her Wolfe Network connections couldn't manage to get through until the middle of the afternoon on Wednesday. Like everyone else in the country, she had not the slightest inkling of his weekend trip to Yemen and what he'd learned there.

THAT EVENING THERE was another White House meeting, with the President's inner circle doubled to six by the addition of Ferrell, Al-Mahdi, and Swenson. Stromdahl brought in the two former Marines, and the President asked the CNO to join them. They met this time in the Oval Office, as much because Linda wanted to see it as for any other reason. The kitchen staff brought in a buffet, but it went untouched as they all huddled to decide their next move. Ugly extra facts were fast turning new hope to old sand, and with the Tea Nut vultures circling Washington they had no one to turn to but themselves.

O'Brien told them his people hadn't yet found anything about who really owned IPC. It was like untangling Martian DNA or looking for Jimmy Hoffa's body. But they did learn the company had bought up several farms over the last two years, which could explain the increased nitrate purchases. Ferrell's slam dunk evidence suddenly wasn't looking so slammy and dunky.

And Senator Nelson said neither Deep Throat's wild suspicions nor the date and time on an e-mail were going to derail Hiram Heilman. The impeachment train was hurtling down the track to conviction way too fast for anyone to pay attention, and the Tea Nut types were immune to facts or logic. The e-mail could easily be a fake, they'd say. Or maybe someone just set the clock wrong on a server or something. Who knew.

What the hell, at this point the accusation against Heilman might even give him a boost. Waffling Senators would think it all some kind of last-minute gimmick concocted by the President to save her political ass. What they needed was evidence that would fill up a TV screen and stop everything like a giant boulder on the tracks. Smoking gun evidence that the bombs came from IPC, or smoking cannon evidence of Heilman's guilt. And there was neither gun nor cannon nor smoke in sight.

They all went silent and stared at the floor until Ferrell cleared her throat and raised her hand. "That's why I want to go out to Idaho and take a look myself," she said. "I still think it's not right. No test farm ever used that much fertilizer."

Again it was O'Brien's lot to dump unwanted facts on the idea. He pulled out a folder filled with maps and aerial photos of the IPC plant and shuffled through them to find the picture he wanted. He laid it on the President's desk and asked what Ferrell planned to check out.

"Their records, sir, and where they've been storing the stuff. That sort of thing. Stuff that'll show it couldn't have been used as fertilizer."

"Well, here's the problem. Take a look at this picture. The plant's mostly pipes and tanks and things, like a giant outdoor chemistry lab." With a pencil O'Brien pointed at the maze of exposed piping and machinery. "There's an office and operations building by the main gate, on the south side, and then there's this." The pencil came to rest on the image of what was easily the largest structure on the site. It appeared to be a steel hangar-like building and it occupied the western third of the property, to the left of the gate as a person drove in. The west, south, and north sides of the building were within a few feet of the perimeter fence. The picture was a high oblique shot taken from the south, and they could see the walls were painted white and the flat roof was black, probably some kind of membrane. There appeared to be no windows.

What is it, Ferrell asked.

"Well, we think that's the research building, which is where the nitrates almost surely would be. Or where they were. And you can see here how it's got a small gate of its own, on the south side like the main gate, and there's an internal fence on the east side that separates it from the rest of the plant. If you look real close you can see a security guard at the smaller gate, right by the door to the big building." The pencil moved again. "And look here. Probably dogs in the space between the walls and the fences. It's like a moat, and it all kinda confirms something fishy's going on. But you're not likely getting in there no matter what badge you flash."

"We don't know that till I try."

"And if it doesn't work we've tipped them off and they destroy the evidence and we're SOL." Not a chance they should take.

What about some kind of surprise assault, Nelson asked. Just rush the place and overpower the guards. Couldn't they do that?

"Remember Waco?" O'Brien said. "Things don't always go as fast as you think, and we're not sure how many people are inside. Or if there's any evidence left. Or how we'd know it was evidence if we found it." He was obviously just started on a long list of "no we can't" reasons. And, most important, if they came up empty a raid would just pour gasoline on the impeachment fire. Another example of government abuse.

Stromdahl broke in to stop him. "Look, we've got just a few days till the Senate votes. We've got no other lead. And no other choice. We have to hold."

Say what?

"It's a Marine thing. At Belleau Wood in World War I a Marine company was cut off and surrounded and down to two or three men. The commander sent a message to his battalion commander. 'We will hold.' His name was Clifton Cates, and he had no choice. He later became Commandant." And like Cates and his Marines, they now had no choice either. They had to do something to find out what the hell was going on at IPC, and they were running very short of time.

"Well, Cates' odds in World War I were lots better than ours now," Sally said. "But Walleye—General Stromdahl—and Ms. Ferrell are right. This is our Belleau Wood; our only choice. We've got no other way out. We have to do something."

O'Brien bent his head forward and pressed his fingertips against his eyes while the rest of his hands covered his face. "Listen," he said without removing his hands or looking up. "Just listen. We've no idea what we'll be getting into. We've looked at aerial photos taken at different times of the day, and based on the number of cars in the parking lot and where they park, the research building is pretty much manned round-the-clock. That in itself probably shows something ain't quite right, but it also means you'll have company if you get inside the building. You gonna be ready for that?"

Again the room went silent, and Stromdahl picked up one of O'Brien's aerial photos and started studying it. After a minute or two he set it down and picked up the folder, which also lay on the desk. He looked through it slowly, and went back and forth between three images that particularly caught his attention. "You got a magnifying glass?" he asked the President.

She opened a desk drawer and pulled one out, the square kind with a built-in battery-powered light. She handed it to him like a knife, handle first, except she took care not to leave fingerprints on the glass lens. "There you go."

He mumbled his thanks, then went back to the first picture and pored over it intently. What was he looking at?

The roof, he said. If they could sneak on top of it, maybe they could break in at night through one of the vents. Like O'Brien, he pointed at the image with a pencil to show what he meant. "We could use tear gas to disable anyone inside."

"That's a big building," Swenson said. "You'll need a lot more tear gas than you can carry onto the roof. What do you do if it's like a hot landing zone?"

"We shoot back."

"And if we're wrong about all this?"

"We can't be." But the Commandant knew that if they had to shoot anyone it would be an ethical and moral Rubicon they might not be able to cross without drowning.

"So say you make it in," O'Brien rejoined the debate. "You won't have much time, and you won't even know what you're looking for." He remained darkly skeptical.

"I know," Stromdahl said softly. "We just have to hope like hell we find something. And that we can get out."

STROMDAHL'S EDUCATION in science and mathematics went only slightly deeper than his engineering training, but since high school he'd been fascinated with randomness. The concept, not the probability and statistics stuff, or the equations that took up whole pages in textbooks. How, he thought, could things be random if God planned every detail down to the last snowflake? Maybe nothing was random for God, and all the world's uncertainty was just human ignorance and misunderstanding. Or maybe God created randomness for purposes as mysterious as all of life. Maybe His plan was about constant change, and randomness was His method. Stromdahl's church was not into denying scientific facts, and he readily accepted the idea that life evolved through the natural selection of random mutations. Evolution made perfect sense to a farm kid whose sister won 4H prizes for breeding better dairy cows.

In the Corps he soon developed a different and more practical view of things random. Military history taught that on the battlefield the winners screwed up ninety percent of what they planned to do, but the losers screwed up more. Victory went to those who could best adapt to the chaos. So training was not about eliminating randomness but learning how to hammer it down when inevitably it raised its ugly head. And battle plans and preparation were about simplifying things to avoid it as much as possible.

But a raid on IPC, conducted in darkness and in wind chill worse than dry ice, would require exquisite complexity, absolute perfection, and likely divine intervention. Not even a one percent goof rate. Plus, if word got out in Washington, where there already was a deathwatch on Macalester's Presidency, they'd be screwed. The imperatives of secrecy limited them to five raiders—Stromdahl, Swenson, Al-Mahdi, Ferrell, and O'Brien, who threw in his lot out of loyalty but not conviction. Senator Nelson volunteered too, but admitted the most lethal weapon she'd ever touched was a broom she once used to chase a possum out of her garage. Of course they'd also need pilots to fly them to Idaho, and maybe a few other helpers along the way, but these adjuncts would not know the larger purpose of the mission.

"Here's what we'll do," Stromdahl told the group gathered around the President's desk. "From the pictures the plant's in the middle of the woods. Trees everywhere. Whoever built it wasn't thinking about defense against an attack. Maybe about secrecy and seclusion, but not a raid. So sneaking up shouldn't be all that hard. But we need to get a look inside to see how it's guarded."

Ferrell would go to the plant, he said, just as she'd suggested, except not as an Ag inspector but someone from Homeland Security, who could ask innocently about things like floodlights and alarm systems.

He pointed again with the pencil, this time at the plant's perimeter. "I want you to check out stuff like this. Looks like the fences have concertina wire across the top. I want you to see if they're electrified. And find out how we can kill the power, and what happens if we do. Will that douse the lights and give us cover of darkness? Find out where the guards are located. That kind of stuff."

And then?

He pulled a map from O'Brien's folder to show them what all he had in mind. IPC was located twenty miles south of Pocatello, less than a mile west of I-15 on a parcel carved out of a Federal forest preserve. The plant was at the end of a two-lane private road that looped south along a creek, then back north to the small parking lot just outside the entrance gate. The northern fence line was only a few yards south of a large hill, the top of which could be reached by way of an old logging road they could enter from the highway.

"Look here. We can get to the hill without anyone seeing us. It's on the opposite side from the gates. And it'll give us a great view of the plant. So we can use it as our base of operations." They'd drive Humvees painted civilian white to blend in with the snow. Two would be enough to carry the ladders and ropes and other equipment and supplies they'd need. He, Al-Mahdi, Swenson, and O'Brien would go to the hilltop directly. Ferrell would join them there after her reconnaissance. Then they'd finalize the plan and go into action.

And when was all this going to happen?

He thought it through for a few seconds. Late Friday night or very early Saturday morning. "We've only got a few hours left today. Tomorrow's Thursday, and it'll take us a few hours to get our stuff together and arrange for our flight and for some vehicles from the local Marine Corps Reserve unit. We can spray-paint them white ourselves. Ferrell can go out tomorrow, first thing in the morning by commercial air. So she can do her reconnaissance even before we get there. We'll fly in on Friday, hook up with her on top of the hill, then make our move."

And what exactly would that be?

"I'm hoping we can kill most of the lights." He pointed to a power substation on the map, located in a small clearing about a mile north of IPC. "From the way the wires run, it probably serves the plant, but Ferrell can confirm that tomorrow. If Admiral Swenson can disable it, Samy and I will bring a ladder down from the hill. We'll cut a hole in the fence, pull it through, and then use it to climb up onto the roof. We'll remove a vent cover and rappel down a rope to get inside."

What about the guards and dogs? And people in the building?

"We'll all carry pistols with silencers, and we'll shoot the dogs if we have to."

And the guards, and people inside?

He exhaled audibly before answering. If the plant wasn't really being used to make bombs, shooting the guards would mean the murder of complete innocents. "If they shoot at us, we shoot back. And I do the shooting. No one else."

They all looked at each other and nodded their heads to signify comprehension if not agreement. "So," Swenson said, "you and Samy are on the roof. What then?"

"We'll pry off a vent cover or blow it off if we have to. Then we'll dump in tear gas canisters and go down the ropes. We'll have gas masks." The same shooting rules would apply, but they'd hope the element of surprise and the gas would make gunfire only hypothetical. "So we'll just tie 'em up."

"And where will the rest of us be?" O'Brien asked.

"You and the chief will sneak through the woods to the south side of the plant, near the research building gate. The chief will continue to the power substation and you'll watch to see if anyone's about to surprise me and Samy while we're inside. Or if anyone tries to escape. You can cut them off or at least get some pictures so we know who it is. Sergeant Ferrell can stay on the hill and give us an alert if anyone's coming on the other side of the plant."

But how would he and Samy get out?

"We can climb back up the rope and go back out through the fence. Or just walk out the front door if the coast is clear. I just hope we find enough to prove how the bombs were made and who made them." God alone knew what actually would greet them.

CHAPTER 27

Herman Reinkuhler was born in Pocatello, raised in Pocatello, and like his father, took his engineering degree in Pocatello, at Idaho State. He'd managed the IPC plant for five years and planned never to leave. Though he grew up inside the little city, he had a farm boy bulky body and farm boy crew-cut hair. His face was round and ruddy with a small button nose, and he was totally indifferent to style or appearances. He ignored all of his wife's suggestions about new clothes, glasses with a lighter frame, or tossing out the plastic pocket protector he used with his work shirts. Yet for all of it she had to love him. How could she not? He was the nicest, most amiable oaf anyone had ever met.

Early Thursday afternoon, dressed in a goose down parka with a periscope hood zipped above his nose, he went to the front gate to greet Linda Ferrell. The sky was cloudless, but wind gusts whistled through the chain-link fence and the chill factor was low enough to make a polar bear wince. Linda, too, was dressed in down. She wore a balaclava under her hood, and except for her eyes, not a square millimeter of skin was exposed. They shook hands without bothering to remove their gloves, and he said something she couldn't hear through all the protective layers. She pointed to her right ear with her right hand to signal her temporary deafness, and he simply flapped his right arm as a sign she should follow him.

Hunched up against the cold they walked like stiff penguins to the office and operations building. Inside the heat was turned up to eighty and the sealed-up smells of wet winter clothing and a coffeepot meltdown filled the air. Reinkuhler stopped to check a few readings on one of the control panels and exchanged complaints about the weather with an operator defiantly dressed in a short-sleeved Hawaiian-print shirt. "Warm front coming in next week. Maybe get us up to ten," the operator grinned.

Reinkuhler clapped him on the back and laughed before waving for Linda to follow him into his office. The door stood half open and revealed a good-sized room filled with the clutter of piled paperwork and assorted parts. A four-inch pipe elbow sat on one chair, and some computer motherboards on another. Two other chairs were empty, but he remained standing and didn't offer a seat. Instead he grabbed a hard hat from the top of a steel bookcase and handed it to her. "Should fit under your hood," he said. From a drawer in his old steel desk he pulled some protective goggles and earplugs, which he also gave to her.

"You'll need these to go outside," he told her. "We've been expecting you. The bulletin you all e-mailed this morning said Washington was sending someone here pretty soon. Didn't think it would be this fast, though." It took her a few seconds to recall that "you all" meant Homeland Security, of which she was now supposedly a part.

She flashed back to a small debate between the President and Stromdahl about how to give her the best cover for her mission. "There's no way we're telling Rogers," Sally had scoffed when he suggested the ruse. Who knew how the hapless fool might screw things up. So it was Swenson who arranged for Linda's fake ID. But Sally did call Rogers early Thursday morning about redoubled chemical plant security. "You need to send out an e-mail right away to every plant in the country. Warn them to be on super alert, and tell them we'll inspect them all soon as we can. Tell them we'll be sending inspectors like in a day or so."

Who would they use, he whined. What exactly would they inspect? How could they ever do it? "We'll figure it out," she assured him. "Just send the e-mail to get things rolling. That's the first step." She waited an hour and then called his chief administrative assistant to make sure it was done. And to make sure the IPC plant was on the list of recipients. With Bumble she never left anything to chance.

What e-mail, Linda now thought, and she almost blurted the question before she remembered. Yes, they had decided to call Rogers and tell him about the plant inspections if not their planned trip to Idaho. "Yes," she told Reinkuhler, "yes, we're inspecting everything. Can't be too safe." She tried to play it casual to cover her brief confusion and panic, but he just beamed back at her, as oblivious as a pet turtle. He apparently never gave a thought to why his remote plant, which produced nothing especially toxic or explosive, should be one of the first inspected. Or why Linda's face had gone blank at the mention of the e-mail. He was an engineer and an innocent through and through.

Thus did the first little random crisis of the raid on IPC pass without consequence, and once Linda saw that Reinkuhler had completely bought the story she relaxed and played his gullibility for all it was worth. Her bona fides would not be questioned and he would willingly answer any question she asked. "So let's start with the perimeter security," she said. "I see you got chain-link fences with razor wire on top. They electric too?"

Of course, he said. He and IPC always took security very seriously, and the plant exceeded all government standards. Homeland Security was the good guys, not at all like EPA or OSHA or Agriculture. The company's lawyers forced inspectors from those oppressive agencies to follow the rulebook to the letter. Calls in advance of inspections, and court orders and search warrants for anything unusual. "That's our SOP. Those guys show up, they better have all the i's dotted and t's crossed. We stonewall 'em on everything." He grinned broadly at the thought of monkey wrenching government any way he could, and seemed completely unaware how bad he must sound to a visitor from the Washington bureaucracy. Well, maybe a little aware. He did take pains to assure Linda once again that her department and the military were the shining exceptions to the rule about pernicious government.

"Appreciate that. We try to help any way we can. Now what can you tell me about the guards and all? Is it just this one entrance gate?"

"For the production side, yes. The research center is

completely separate. I got nothing to do with it. They got a separate gate."

"Which building do you mean?"

"The big white one on the western part of the property. I'll show you when we go back outside. They got their own fence and guards and guard dogs. Super-secret stuff they do there. New products and stuff. No one gets inside unless corporate says so. No one. That's our orders. Even you'll need court papers if you want to go there. Even me."

She was about to ask more about who corporate really was, but thought better of it and stuck to the security questions. "So is their electric fence tied into yours?"

He looked a little puzzled at this question, but answered right away. "Yeah. About the only thing we share. That and the lighting. We got the backup generator on our part of the property, but they made us move it to a safer location, and it's now got armor plating all around it to protect from an explosion."

Was he ordered to do that too?

No, he said proudly. His idea. Like he'd said, safety and security were important. His family had been in the chemical business for a long time, and he knew the hazards all too well.

"I'd like to check it out. Sounds like a great idea for some of the other plants I inspect. Where is it?"

Bundled again like Eskimos, they went back into the cold and he led her to a relatively open area in the middle of the plant. The generator was protected by an eight-foot berm in addition to the armor plate and looked totally impregnable.

"When does it go on?"

"Any time power's interrupted for more than two seconds. It's really quick." He pressed a test switch to show her just how fast the diesel motor roared to life.

"Any backup to the backup?"

He shook his head no, a bit ruefully, she thought. Not for the plant, he said, though he'd suggested it several times. But the research building had battery-powered spotlights attached to security cameras that scanned the moat-like space between the fences and the building walls. Two cameras at each corner of the building provided total coverage. The images all went to the guard shack by the gate for the research side, where there was a battery-powered TV monitor. So the guard could spot intruders no matter what happened to the electricity.

How did he know all that if the research building was so separate?

Easy, he said. He got curious and asked one of the guards. Looked like something he might want to add to his part of the facility too.

"So Admiral Swenson takes out the substation, and then we got only a few seconds till the lights and electric fence come back on. How we getting around the generator problem? Or the cameras?" Stromdahl was not happy with Ferrell's report, which seemed to confirm every inner fear he'd had about how things could go randomly wrong.

It was late Friday afternoon, January 16, and the gang of five had convened as planned on the tree-covered hilltop that overlooked IPC. Linda ditched and concealed her rented minivan in the woods near the Interstate and trudged up a hiking trail through the evergreens and snow. There were no footprints to indicate recent use by anyone else. Dusk was about to become darkness, and the plant's labyrinth of machinery gleamed and hummed before them like a space station dropped into the middle of the arctic tundra. The land was unremittingly white except for the black asphalt of the entrance road and the parking lot, but the constant noise belied the surroundings. It sounded like a hive of monster bumble bees had taken flight in a perpetual swarm.

They huddled together in one of their two Humvees to get out of the subzero wind, but moisture from their breathing and fumes from their coffee mugs quickly fogged all the windows. Stromdahl and O'Brien were sitting in the two front seats and kept wiping the windshield so they could see out. Every fifteen or twenty minutes they'd turn on the engine long enough to run the heater, which wasn't working real well. Even at full blast it barely raised the temperature above freezing.

Linda pulled her parka tighter around her body and tried to stop shivering so she could answer the Commandant's pointed questions about the electricity and the cameras. But despite the cold she grinned like a fox about to steal twenty eggs. "Oh, I got all that covered, sir. Not to worry."

"How's it covered?"

"Well, the guy who runs the place—guy named Reinkuhler— he got called away while he was showing me the generator, and I sort of topped off the fuel tank."

"So?"

"I topped it off with water, which is heavier than the diesel and sinks to the bottom where the fuel line connects. I thought the hose would freeze, but it was heated. So anyway, I don't think their emergency power's gonna last real long. We just wait for the lights to go out, then come back on for a bit, then go out again. The second time they'll stay off." So there. She was very pleased with herself.

"Any guard at the power substation? You check that out too?"

She smiled and snapped her fingers. That part would be easy. It was completely unguarded. Only thing was the building was fairly substantial and the locks were thick and strong. "It'll take a pretty big charge to blow off the doors, then you'll have to set off a second charge to disable the transformers." The wires were too high to reach easily, and given the high voltage level there'd be no way to cut them safely. Explosives were the only way to go.

Swenson asked how long it would take the power company to realize it had lost the substation and send a crew to repair it, but Ferrell was ready for that angle too. "I asked what kind of service arrangement the plant had with them. Reinkuhler told me a crew would have to come from Pocatello, and it usually takes about half an hour. Probably a bit longer when it happens on the night shift."

And what about the cameras? And the dogs. Had she seen the dogs?

Yes she had. There were two dogs. Really big German Shepherds with longish hair that seemed to bristle at any provocation. They patrolled the moat and barked whenever she looked their way. If she took a step towards them they snarled and bared the biggest, whitest fangs she'd seen on any beast since taking her children to see the grizzly bears at the Bronx Zoo. But again she had a solution. "What if I go down the hill first. Ahead of you guys and before we knock out the power. I'll set the dogs off, but so what. I'll just go up to the guard shack and knock. Tell him my car slipped off the road and my phone's out of juice. Tell him I'm hurt and need help. I'm a woman, and I'm small, and I won't seem like much of a threat."

"Then what?" Swenson asked. "I'll still have to knock out the power to kill the electric fence, and when that happens he calls for help. He'll alert the guys in the building, and maybe the state police. We won't have even the half hour before the power company gets here."

"Not if I mace him first."

"What if he stays inside the little shack and just calls someone to come help you. Then you've made things worse."

"Oh I'm gonna be hurting real bad. I won't be wearing a coat or gloves. I'm gonna be a real emergency. He'll open the door and let me in, trust me." And once she'd lured him into this mistake she would knock him out with the mace and the coast would be clear.

Stromdahl turned his head so he could see Linda, Samy, and Swenson in the backseat. Her idea wasn't any crazier than the rest of the plan, and it was simple and direct enough that it might just work. He turned back so he could see the plant and counted seven vehicles in the lot. "So how many people in the plant, and how many other than the guard in the white building," he asked Ferrell.

"Only two in the plant. Reinkuhler told me that in the winter they just lock the gate and run a skeleton shift at night. No guard on that side. So if you assume one person per car, and one car for the guard, there's at least four inside the lab building."

"What will they do when the power goes off?" Swenson asked.

"If they don't suspect anything more than a power failure, I think the plant-side people just call the power company to confirm they're coming."

"What about the other four. Or five. Or six. What'll they do?"

They all looked at each other, hoping for an answer of any kind, but especially an answer that would not reduce the thirty minutes they could count on. No idea, Linda said.

"Maybe we don't have to kill the power if Linda takes out the guard first," Samy suggested.

No, she said. He was forgetting the electric fence.

Could they dig under it?

Not with the ground so cold and frozen.

Stromdahl turned to Samy. "So how long from power failure to rooftop? Think we can do it in two minutes?"

"We can try."

"We gotta do more than try. If we're lucky it'll take 'em that long to find a flashlight, or adjust to the emergency lights if they have them inside. Probably do. So let's say two minutes, and they won't know it's only two of us, especially with the tear gas we'll throw in. We'd still have a chance."

"Sounds like that's our plan," Swenson said. "Linda takes out the guard. Then I take out the power station. The generator comes on but sputters out, and Wally and Samy race for the roof and go in through one of the vents. What about the dogs?"

"I'll get them after the guard," Linda said. "I've seen 'em in action. They'll be gnawing on the fence trying to get out and get me. I'll take a pistol with a silencer so the shots won't alert anyone."

The five of them glanced at each other and nodded their assent if not agreement. The plan was set. Good, Stromdahl finally said. Despite the random surprises, the raid might still work, like an improvised trick football play that succeeds despite itself.

At eleven o'clock Swenson and O'Brien drove down from the hill in one of the Humvees, very slowly and without lights. They relied on the glow from the plant, night vision goggles, and Swenson's memory of the map. Aside from bouncing off a few trees they made it without a problem. O'Brien got out near the entrance road and walked along it for a few hundred yards, then ducked into the woods and found a spot where he could safely watch the research building and the little guard shack at its gate. Swenson continued along the trace of another old road that led to the power station. When he got there he reported on the radio that he was ready to blow it up and waited for the go ahead.

Linda meanwhile crept down the hill and skirted around the west end of the plant. She took a deep breath, shed her jacket, hat, and gloves, and ran to the guard shack. Inside, the guard sat at a small desk and faced two monitors that cycled through images from the eight cameras. Every minute or so he'd look up at the screens, but his eyes and mind were focused on a porn video he'd downloaded to the personal tablet on his lap. He jolted upright and scrambled to turn it off when Linda banged on the door.

"I need help," she shouted. "My car crashed. I'm freezing. Let me in."

He didn't have to stand up or move to see her through the window in the door. "What's wrong?"

"My car crashed. I was just going to the store and I didn't have a coat. Let me in." She was genuinely freezing and shook so hard she had trouble getting out the words.

"Just a second." The guard double checked to make sure his tablet was off, then took one step to reach the door and opened it.

The blast of mace sent him reeling back into the tiny space and his flailing right arm hit one of the monitors and knocked it off the desk. Gasping for air, he fell onto the floor with his back against a small filing cabinet located opposite the door, which he still faced. His legs were splayed in a vee in front of him, his eyes were rolling wildly, and his hands clutched at his throat. Linda took a few steps outside, pulled out the gas mask she had strapped around her waist like a fanny pack, and put it on before going in to hit him with another blast of mace. Then she bound him hand and foot with two pieces of nylon rope.

Her first task was done, but she was now shivering so bad she could barely hold her pistol, much less aim and fire it at the dogs, who as predicted had raced to get as close to her as the fence allowed. They looked almost like wolves, and Reinkuhler later told the FBI that in fact they were half breeds created for their ferocity. Would the people inside the building hear the barking and become suspicious? She had to shoot them to restore silence and to keep them from attacking Stromdahl and Samy when they cut the fence to enter the moat. She had to steady herself, stop shaking, and fire the gun. She had to. Twice she tried and twice she missed. On the radio Stromdahl asked if she was all right, and pressed her to kill the dogs so he could tell Swenson to blow up the substation.

Desperate to get warm she kept one eye on the dogs and stumbled to the wood line to retrieve her coat and gloves. Shaking like a leaf in a hurricane she made it back into the shack to put them on. Even inside in the warmth she dropped the coat twice before she managed to insert her arms into the sleeves. The guard had revived enough to watch her, and between gasps to ask who she was. When he saw the gun stuck in her belt his eyes begged her not to shoot. She ignored him, ran back outside and finally dispatched the dogs. All clear, she reported to Stromdahl.

So far no truly ugly randomness had intruded into the plan,

and Stromdahl was buoyed by a rising tide of hope. At eleven-thirty he told Swenson to knock out the electricity. Boom once, boom twice, and it was done. The lights at the plant flickered out briefly before the diesel generator started. Then they flickered and went out permanently as the engine coughed and sputtered and died, and the only illumination came from the moon and the stars and the eight battery-powered camera spotlights.

What about the two operators from the production plant, Stromdahl asked O'Brien on the radio. Had the barking penetrated their building, and had they emerged to see what had happened? Not to worry, the Director said. He'd seen one operator come out from the office building door with a flashlight in hand, then just turn around and go back inside. "Guess he figured everything except the electricity was okay when he didn't hear anything else. Just gotta hope they don't call anyone but the power company."

With the dogs gone the silence was deafening, an interlude pregnant with imminent violence and chaos. How long would it hold? At 11:35 Al-Mahdi and Stromdahl, ladder in tow, raced to the fence and snipped through the heavy gage wire with a pair of bolt cutters. The only sounds were the crunch of the snow as they ran forward and the dull clunking clicks as they severed the wires. It took half a minute. Three seconds more and they had the ladder leaned against the building. They bounded up in five seconds each. Less than a minute gone and they were on the roof.

Stromdahl pulled out a flashlight and spotted one of the vents. No randomness yet. It was almost too easy. Less than two minutes gone. They were ahead of schedule without a hitch. And their luck got better yet. They found the cover only loosely held on with three easily removed bolts, and inside it was completely dark. No sign anyone was in the building despite the cars outside. Or maybe no one in the room they'd penetrated. Either way, they dispensed with the tear gas and dropped a rope so they could enter.

But then randomness and chance intervened and their luck turned very bad. When Stromdahl went to lower himself down the opening was too narrow. Even Samy could not squeeze through. "Fuck," Stromdahl muttered.

Samy pointed to another vent that looked bigger. They ran over and found the bolts rusted and immoveable. They were now three minutes behind schedule and desperate for a way in. Maybe just go back down the ladder and break in the front door and hope no one was waiting for them, Samy suggested. Did they have any other choice?

BUT BEFORE THEY reached the ladder to climb down O'Brien's voice crackled over their radios. "Hit the deck. Now. We got company."

Four big SUVs raced into the lot, and out of them piled twenty men armed with rifles and grenade launchers and more. They paid no attention to the main plant, and most of them went into the research building. Four waited outside, scanning the building and the landscape, and two others ran to the dead dogs and went inside the space between fence and building to check out the perimeter security.

Up on the roof, through the open vent hole, Stromdahl and Samy could hear the men talking inside. Samy pulled Stromdahl toward him, so they could see each other in the moonlight. "Ferguson," he mouthed silently.

Stromdahl nodded yes.

"That's Ferguson," Samy whispered. "I'd know that voice anywhere." He signaled with his arm that they should crawl back to the ladder to get off the roof and get away.

Stromdahl waved him off and shook his head no. Then held his hand as if to cup his ear, a sign they should wait and listen more.

Samy looked nervously toward the ladder, then back at Stromdahl and finally shook his head yes. They both crept closer to the open vent hole and loosened their parka hoods so they could hear. What first struck them were the accents, some Israeli, some hillbilly. And Ferguson's, which betrayed his New Jersey roots and sounded like the voice of a movie mobster.

"Spread the charges out so everything goes up at once," he ordered the others. "And bring in the gas cans and spill the gas everywhere to make sure it burns. We want the whole damn place to go up fast."

"What if they're still on the roof?" one of the Israeli voices asked.

"Who gives a shit. So they fry. Get to work."

Stromdahl silently berated himself for not thinking things through better. The security camera feed must have gone to some off-site location, not just the guard shack. He should have known.

Then from inside they heard another Israeli voice. "What about the hot stuff. Do we want to blow that up?"

"That shit's gone," Ferguson laughed. "The boss had it sent to DC two days ago. Get a move on. We're done with this place anyway. Good riddance." Again he laughed.

Samy tugged on Stromdahl's sleeve and again signaled they should get down. The Commandant glanced one last time at the vent, then shook his head yes. They crawled back to the ladder and Samy started down two rungs at a time until a shot shattered the silence and sent the ladder a full foot sideways. He was certain it would tip off to the left, but it stayed upright even when struck by a second shot and a third. And somehow not a one hit him.

He stepped down one more rung, leaped off, and flattened himself to the ground like a squashed amoeba. Three automatic bursts sprayed the area around him and ricocheted off the steel wall of the building, but again nothing hit him. The shots had come from the northwest corner of the moat, and seemed to come from two weapons, one automatic, the other not. They had Samy pinned down, and though his pistol was drawn and his right glove was off so he could shoot it, in the weak illumination from the battery-powered security lights he saw nothing at which to fire.

A minute passed, and another with neither a sound nor any sign of movement. His hand was fast progressing from pain to numbness to immobility in the cold. He had no idea what Stromdahl was up to, even though his silhouette was still visible on the roof. Was the coast clear? Oh so slowly Samy reached to his right and shook the fence in the hope he could draw fire that would reveal a target for him. Nothing happened. And when he looked up he saw that the moonlit silhouette of Stromdahl had disappeared.

He could hear his heart beating and nothing else except the wind. Suddenly the firing recommenced, directed at the roof, not Samy. First two weapons firing, both now on automatic, with pistol shots interspersed, then one weapon on automatic and two more pistol shots, then silence again. He worked the fingers of his right hand to restore the feeling, aimed his pistol at the corner, and tried to make out a target. Still nothing. And then a pebble hit him on the back of his head, and another. He hardly felt the first because of his parka hood, but the second was bigger and actually hurt.

"Samy," Stromdahl said in a loud whisper. "Look up. I got 'em both. Now stand up and hold the ladder straight. I'm coming down." Together they crawled out through the hole in the fence and made a mad dash to the north for the woods.

AFTER CONFERRING ON THE RADIO, the gang of five regrouped next to the Humvee that Swenson and O'Brien had driven down from the hill to the south side of the plant. It was concealed in the woods, about a hundred feet from the entrance road. Swenson pointed in the direction of the research building, now out of their sight, and said they should rush it, in hopes the element of surprise could yet allow them to complete their mission.

What surprise, Stromdahl said. Ferguson knew they were there. He'd most likely seen them on the security cams. And he had men posted out front to watch for an attack. Plus they were about to blow the place up.

Maybe it's time to call in the state police, O'Brien said.

Not if they wanted to save the evidence in the building. The police would never get there on time.

"Yeah, but if the police catch Ferguson or some of his men, maybe they'll talk."

Not bloody likely.

What else then?

Don't know.

Their debate ended and everything went moot when the four SUVs raced past, wheels spinning and engines roaring. Seconds later the sky flashed bright orange and white from a chain of explosions and stayed bright from the flames that consumed the research building. Randomness had intervened big time, and their quest had failed. The news media would report a chemical plant accident in Idaho and no one would ever make the connection to the mall bombs or Heilman. It was early Saturday morning, and in two or three days, on the nineteenth or twentieth, the Senate would convict Sally Macalester and she'd be gone.

CHAPTER 28

When he thought about it later, Stromdahl figured maybe the random twist that saved the day at IPC wasn't really so random after all. More likely a matter of preparation and training; proof positive of the old Marine Corps maxim that those who plan and sweat in peace don't panic and bleed in war. But then again, he did have to wonder at the odds the IPC plant would be one of the rare few to exceed OHSA regs and the fire code, especially in a regulation-hating place like Idaho. And this strange anomaly got him to further thought about divine intervention, in which he didn't quite completely believe but sort of accepted on faith as at least a possibility. If God could step in and change events at will, then why was there ever war or disease or the likes of Jake Ferguson? On the other hand, how else explain his own survival against the odds in Afghanistan?

And how else explain Herman Reinkuhler's fanatic fixation on safety and fire protection? Any other plant manager and the whole place would have been totally destroyed, and along with it every shred of evidence. But Herman was the one selected, whether by God or the company, and he had a special history. His father, too, had been a chemical engineer, and died in an explosion when Herman was ten. So at IPC the younger Reinkuhler insisted on not one but two tanker trucks filled with fire-quenching foam.

Bigger trucks than required, and everyone who worked there had to be trained how to use them. Really, seriously trained. Plus he had an arrangement with the Forest Service to send in helicopters with even more foam if the trucks were not enough.

Within seconds of the first blast the two operators on duty ran to the garage building on the east side of the plant, drove the tankers to the west side, and began pouring foam on the flames, and less than fifteen minutes later four choppers started ferrying in more and more of the gloppy stuff, one overhead, one refilling and the other two either coming or going. The trucks and choppers kept the fire from spreading to either the production part of the plant or the surrounding trees, and while they couldn't save the research building, the wreckage was cool enough for investigators to start poking through it within hours. The only thing that came even close to surviving was a thick-walled reinforced concrete room in the northwest corner, the one farthest from the entrance door.

"THEY SAY IT'S LIKE a walk-in safe," O'Brien told Stromdahl on the phone from his office. The five "Idaho Raiders," as they later came to call themselves, had made it back to DC about ten on Saturday morning, and even before they arrived the Director had arranged by radio from the plane for an FBI forensic team to go to Pocatello. The first elements flew in from Denver before noon, and right away they found the room.

Stromdahl was back in uniform and back at Marine headquarters, where he was trying to make things seem normal by plowing through the backlog of papers piled on his desk. But for once even he could not force his mind onto the task at hand. What difference did anything make since the raid had failed? The whole country was about to fall apart. He took O'Brien's call right after lunch. "So what's in it?" he asked.

O'Brien rolled his words around like a wine lover savoring some rare vintage. "Computers," he said. "Two of 'em." Two. Both melted like hot butter and blackened like burnt toast. But the hard drives looked like maybe they'd survived. "They're on a plane to the lab in Virginia. I got our best computer forensics guy standing by."

The lab was in Quantico, right next to the Marine base and not an hour's drive from Stromdahl's office. "I'm on my way," he told O'Brien.

"What? You think you'll make him work any faster? And how do you explain your reason for being there? No one's said this is terrorists yet. Or that it has a thing to do with the malls. Just a bad accident at a remote little pesticide plant. Officially I sent in our forensic team on the chance it might be sabotage or a criminal violation of the safety rules. You go to the lab and you'll blow our cover. Chill."

"Tell your guy whatever the hell you want," Stromdahl shot back. He was not at all chilled, and about as willing to stay away from the lab as a drunk from a tavern.

It was late Saturday afternoon when he showed up at the gate in his chauffeured staff car, dressed in his four-star uniform and expecting to be waved on through. But the guards wouldn't budge, and only after he called O'Brien and had him talk with the security people did they allow him past. "The computer guy's named Mukerjee," O'Brien told him, "and he's kinda touchy. So take it easy."

"What's he touchy about?"

"You'll find out. Just take it easy."

Mukerjee was not at all physically prepossessing, but in the lab he was a towering presence. He stood somewhere south of five six, was maybe forty-five or fifty years old, wore oversize glasses, and had a small paunch that was exaggerated by his otherwise slight frame. He could not have weighed more than a hundred twenty pounds even in his winter clothes. His equally diminutive parents were Muslims from the Indian part of Kashmir who emigrated to escape the perpetual violence when he was three years old. When he was in the third grade he saw one of the Bureau-endorsed hagiographies about J. Edgar Hoover, and from then on his only goal in life was to be an FBI agent. But he always had poor eyesight, and when told his vision would disqualify him from anything except lab work he selected one of the few universities that gave degrees in forensic engineering. He loved his lab more than his family, and he made it very clear that a Marine general was about as welcome there as a mother-in-law in the kitchen.

"I'll let you in," he told Stromdahl, as if talking to a nosy child, "but you'll have to sit at one of the empty benches and leave us alone." The hard drives were heavily damaged, and he wasn't sure he and his team could read anything from them, much less do it quickly. And Marine Corps Commandants did not impress him one jot. He made a point of saying he was a pacifist vegetarian who believed as much in Gandhi as Allah.

"You sure he's the best?" Stromdahl asked O'Brien. He'd moved to an unused part of the lab, and was whispering into the microphone attached to his ever-present tablet.

"Yes, I'm sure. What got your goat? The pacifist thing?"

"No. The can't-do-it-quickly thing."

O'Brien laughed. "He's always like that. Biggest pessimist I've ever met. But he also always proves himself wrong. You tell him what we're looking for?"

"No. He asked and I told him we don't know, except we think the computer was used by terrorists." Stromdahl paused and added that they really didn't know much more. He had no idea what to expect.

"GENERAL, SIR, wake up. Wake up." By four in the morning on Sunday Stromdahl had finally loosened his tie and succumbed to sleep in a part of the lab where the lights were off. With a big book as a pillow he was lying face up on the floor next to a lab bench. But now the lights had suddenly come on, and he squinted into them as he raised his head and frowned at Mukerjee, who was kneeling next to him and staring straight down into his eyes. Their noses were only inches apart.

"What's going on?" he asked in a voice thickened by fatigue and confusion. He didn't recognize the little man and was trying to figure out just where the hell he was.

"We have found some things. Come see." Like a mahout leading an elephant Mukerjee tugged at Stromdahl's sleeve to guide him to a desktop computer on which was displayed an image of one of the bombed-out malls before it was destroyed.

And there were thousands more mall images. Copies of architectural plans obtained from city and country records. Pictures showing the locations of security cameras. Analyses of the most effective locations for parking a truck bomb. And more, like the proper formula for mixing the explosives, and instructions on detonation with phones.

"Damn."

"Yes sir. And take a look at this." He clicked on another file and up popped a set of plans for the Capitol Building.

"That what I think it is?"

Mukerjee nodded yes, and clicked to an analysis of how to bring down the dome.

"Damn. What's that about? You think they planted a bomb that didn't go off?"

"Don't know. How would they get it in?" Mukerjee added that maybe they'd learn more from the second hard drive.

"Yeah," Stromdahl said. "Go look at it now." After the little forensics expert scurried off the Commandant called O'Brien and told him to lock down the Capitol and send over a bomb squad. "Check out all the structural stuff that supports the dome. Looks like that's what they were after."

"You sure? Why didn't they set it off with the others?"

"How the hell do I know? Maybe it was a dud. Or maybe they planned it this way. Maybe there's nothing there. But get hold of the Capitol Police and do a sweep." As soon as he clicked off with the Director he called Sally and told her they needed another meeting as soon as possible.

MUKERJEE PUT copies of the images from the first computer onto an external drive that Stromdahl took to the White House for a seven o'clock breakfast meeting with the four other Idaho Raiders, the President, and Senator Nelson. They were in the Treaty Room again, gathered in a semicircle around Sally's desk, on which sat a large-screen monitor.

"At least the Capitol's clean," O'Brien reported. "Nothing suspicious anywhere near the dome. Or anywhere else."

"Oh great," Nelson said. "So Castaneda will have a dome when he gets sworn in as President. How the hell does this help us now?" She pointed at the collage of mall images on the screen. "What's to say we haven't just discovered that the Iranians did their dirty work in Idaho? Heilman's gonna use this to speed up impeachment so we can launch and stop them before they do more damage. He'll say they're after the Capitol too, and God knows what else."

She and her staff had been working like hell to peel away any votes they could in the Senate, but at this point conviction seemed a near certainty, and Senators out to protect their political hides would go along with it no matter what. Unless they could pin down Heilman's complicity they would remain dead in the water on stopping the vote to convict. They still had nothing more than Deep Throat's anonymous speculation and Lisa Larkin's suspicion about the e-mail to Rumbo.

O'Brien tried a more positive spin. "Well," he said, "we do know from Deep Throat that the good Senator was forcing the CIA to use Ferguson. And we saw Ferguson in Idaho."

"But Deep Throat won't go public," Stromdahl said. "I can't even give you his real name. Or hers. And we only heard Ferguson. Or thought we did. It sounded like him, but I can't be sure."

"I can," Samy said. "It was him."

Not enough, Nelson said. Not a smoking gun. And without both gun and smoke, Heilman would claim the story of his involvement was just a pinko socialist smear. He'd also say that the evidence about the chemical plant showed how devious the Iranians were, more proof the U.S. had to wipe them out. He was still the leader of the Senate, and the Republicans would much sooner believe him than the President, especially this close to ousting her. The burden of proof had shifted.

"But it was the crazy Israelis and Ferguson," Ferrell pointed out. That clearly was the truth.

"Yeah. Prove it. We can't find any of them," Nelson said. According to O'Brien's investigation team, the crew doing Heilman's dirty work in Idaho apparently had been living in an old farmhouse about five miles south of the plant, but it was now vacant and completely bare. The team had found a few fingerprints, but the only ones they could identify came from people who'd been in the Aryan Multitude. There was no trace of Ferguson.

"How'd he ever get them to work with Jews?" Samy asked in disbelief.

"Another good question, and one Heilman will raise all over the place if we try to sell this story without any more proof. It sounds preposterous. And how do we know it was Ferguson at all? Because Sami Akbar's best high school friend says he recognized the voice? Come on."

A knock on the door, at first tentative, then stronger, interrupted them. The President got up to answer it herself, annoyed her orders about no disturbances had been ignored. A young female staffer stood outside, big eyed with fright about her transgression.

"What is it?" Sally asked as gently as possible.

"There's a man named Mukerjee on the phone. From the FBI. Says he absolutely has to talk with Director O'Brien. Immediately, he says." The staffer started to explain how she'd double checked the number to make certain the call was genuine, and how she really didn't want to interrupt, and how sorry she was.

But O'Brien cut her off. "He still on the line?"

The staffer nodded yes.

"Where can I take the call?"

"Right here," Sally said.

MUKERJEE, IT SEEMED, had come unhinged. From pacifist he instantly had become an advocate for the most violent action imaginable. "We must kill them, sir, torture them if we must. They must die for this." When he calmed down a little he explained that the second computer had detailed plans for a small nuclear bomb, a suitcase nuke. And also plans for using it. He would e-mail what looked to be the most important files before sending it all over on another external drive.

The Director hung up and repeated Mukerjee's report. Now what?

Al-Mahdi had a small moment of insight and understanding, but no answer. "Damn. So that's the hot stuff we heard them talking about when we were on the roof. That's probably what they had in the room your guys thought might be a safe. And it's gone now, which is why they didn't care about blowing up the building."

Stromdahl whistled softly as the bigger picture suddenly came clear for him. Heilman and Ferguson must have worked with *Nagaf* to steal the Iranian plutonium, which they somehow smuggled into the U.S. and turned into a compact bomb.

"No way," Swenson said. Plutonium required a lot of heavy shielding. It would be almost impossible to smuggle in.

"Unless they sneaked it in like drugs. Or if a Senator brought it in after a junket." Maybe this particular impossibility was actually not so impossible. Stromdahl told Swenson to call the Pentagon to find out if Heilman had travelled to the Middle East at the time the Iranian reactors were destroyed. All records for Congressional travel with the military were maintained in a single database, and it took less than half an hour to get an answer. Yes, the Senator from South Carolina had gone to Iraq right in the middle of the raid, and had over two tons of luggage when he came back on a VIP Air Force plane. Boxes full of important papers, he'd told the aircraft crew. Apparently no one had asked why there were so many papers or how come they weighed so much.

"Members of Congress don't get screened, do they?" Stromdahl asked. Everyone knew the answer. Of course not. "So that means Heilman and his people very well could have the makings for a nuclear device if they wanted to build one. Shit."

"Yeah," Swenson said. "And rumor has it that *Nagaf* includes several nuclear scientists. So if Heilman's in this with them he's got himself some skilled bomb builders."

Then it dawned on Stromdahl what else he and Samy had heard on the roof. "Remember, they said 'the boss sent it to DC two days ago.' Know what, I think Heilman has a little nuke here in DC." As if on cue, the arriving e-mail signal sounded on his tablet, and he saw he had a message from Mukerjee. There were five attached images. Look at number five first, the message said, then number one.

They all hovered behind him and watched over his shoulder as he clicked the fifth image open. On the small screen it was hard to make out, but it pretty obviously was a map of DC with concentric rings radiating from the Capitol. "What's that mean?" Sally asked.

"I think it's about blast radius," Stromdahl said. "The numbers on the rings show percentage blast destruction and percentage thermal destruction. I think Senator Heilman is planning to blow up the city."

"What good would that do if he wants to take it over?" Nelson said. This plot twist wasn't making any sense.

Stromdahl pointed at the picture, which seemed irrefutable. "You asking me to explain the mind of Hiram Heilman? Listen, the stuff from the other drive shows they were thinking of blowing up the dome. Maybe they just decided to escalate a little." He clicked on the blast radius file to check out the metadata about when it was created. "Here. Look at this. It was created on the fourteenth, just four days ago."

"What about the first image?" Sally said. "Open it"

There was a collective "wow." It was a message from Heilman to someone named Moshe Har-Even demanding that he have one of his men bring the "hot beans" to Washington right away. It, too, was four days old.

At last there was evidence good enough to save Sally. "So I can stop the impeachment," Nelson said. "If there's anything left of the city. But why the hell does he want to blow it up when he's about to take it over?"

"Who knows," O'Brien said. "Maybe our raid spooked him; made him think we'd be able to beat him on conviction. Or maybe he wanted to blow up DC all along. The Tea Party types talk about killing government all the time, and some of them take it pretty literally."

It was the President who got them back on track and cut to the chase. "Where's Heilman now?" she demanded. The quickest way to put all this to rest would be to find him and verify what he did or didn't have with him. And grab the nuke if he had it.

"Well," Nelson said, "he says he goes to church every Sunday, but it's a little early for that. And I doubt he's worried about that today."

"How do we find out? You know anyone on his staff?"

Nelson nodded yes. Sort of. Her own chief of staff, Jim Dedmon, certainly did. "I'll call him right now."

Dedmon's fifteen-year-old daughter answered the phone and said he'd left the house for an early meeting and inexplicably had not taken his iPhone with him. "It's still here on the kitchen counter."

"Who's he meeting with?" Nelson demanded.

"Don't know," the girl replied with a sullen teenage mumble.

"Is your mother there?"

"Yeah."

"Put her on."

The daughter said nothing more, and the next sound on the phone was Mrs. Dedmon's voice. "Jim's at the office now. They're meeting on how to stop the conviction vote. You can call him there."

It took three tries, but finally he picked up. "I was next door with Senator Johnson's people," he said. "Checking on where the votes stand." It wasn't looking very good, he added, but maybe they could make it close. Conviction required sixty-seven votes, and he held only a slim hope they could keep the count even that low.

"Forget the vote. It ain't happening. We can prove the bombs didn't come from Iran. But we have to find Heilman. Right away. Who should we call on his staff?"

The mental shift from last-ditch vote counting in a losing cause to no vote at all had Dedmon overwhelmed, and he couldn't see the need to find Heilman as anything but some kind of afterthought. "I don't get it. What happened?"

"What I said. It wasn't Iran. The nitrates came from Idaho. The Iranians had nothing to do with it. So forget about that. You hear me? Forget about the vote. We gotta find Heilman." For fear of causing total panic she didn't explain why Heilman was so important, but Dedmon finally got the message about the need to find him.

"Heck, he was here not half an hour ago. I saw him coming into the office building. He was carrying a funny-looking black case. Sort of like a big bowling ball bag. Looked real heavy too."

The news jolted Jane Nelson so bad she went speechless for what seemed forever, and when she spoke again a current of tension belied her effort to stay calm. "Listen, Jim. Just listen and do what I tell you. Whatever else you're doing drop it. Go find Heilman and do everything you can to keep him there. We'll be over soon as we can."

"What is it?" the President asked.

Like a boxer too beat up to think straight, Nelson set the phone receiver down without hanging up, looked vacantly out the window, and said nothing. After five long seconds she breathed a deep sigh and turned back to her old friend. "Hiram has the bomb. And he's already on Capitol Hill."

Without a blink, Sally went from embattled politician to commander-in-chief. She asked the general and the admiral what the blast radius would be, and how much of the city she should order evacuated. Swenson said the bomb was likely less powerful than the one dropped on Hiroshima, and exploded on the ground instead of in the air the damage wouldn't spread out so much. Evacuate for a mile and a half around the Capitol and tell everyone else to take shelter.

Nelson looked dubious. The panic of an evacuation might

make things even worse. "Don't mention it's a nuke. If you do, everyone will try to leave, even from the suburbs, and you'll have total gridlock. No one will get out. Just say it's more follow up on the lockdown at the Capitol earlier this morning."

The President pursed her lips and thought about it. She wasn't going to lie. People had a right to know. But before announcing anything they needed to alert the DC police to get every officer they could on the scene to make all streets one way heading out of town. Thank God it wasn't a work day. The National Guard had to be notified too. And every Metro train should head downtown to take on the rush of passengers. "When we make the announcement we'll explain that the subway tunnels are probably the safest place to be. Let's just hope we can keep things moving. And we'll have to coordinate with Maryland and Virginia so they know what's coming. Make arrangements for shelters in gyms. But that can wait at least a little while."

She turned to Ferrell and Swenson, and said they should stay with her and help on all the phone calls. "The rest of you get over to the Hill and arrest that bastard Heilman. And get that damn bomb before he sets it off." This close to the Senate vote on impeachment conviction if they asked anyone else to make the arrest it might trigger fears of a coup, and the agents or officers might refuse.

Even Al-Mahdi frowned at the idea.

"You have a question?"

"No. Just wondering if that's legal."

O'Brien rolled his eyes and laughed. "Don't worry. Even a Senator ain't immune from arrest for felonies or treason. And right now we ain't exactly sweating legal niceties."

STROMDAHL AND THE OTHER three assigned to track down Heilman raced to his staff car and headed for the Hart Senate Office Building. He sat in the front passenger seat. The others were jammed into the rear seat, Nelson in the middle flanked by Al-Mahdi to her right and O'Brien to her left. At quarter to eight on a Sunday morning the sky was bright and the air crisp and unfouled by rush hour traffic fumes. And it was cold. Not Idaho cold, but below freezing without much promise of warming very much, and none of them had thought to grab a coat in their rush to leave.

Two Secret Service cars with lights flashing and sirens blaring cleared the way for the Marine green car as it sped unimpeded down the fourteen iconic Pennsylvania Avenue blocks between the White House and the Capitol grounds. Stromdahl glanced briefly at the famous monuments and buildings along the route. The grandiose Reagan Trade Center, the squat and ugly FBI, the National Archives, the Navy Memorial, and the massive stone tower of the old Post Office Building. How much would be left if they failed?

Between Fourth Street and Third, where the truncated triangle of the National Gallery's eastern annex ended museum row, they veered left onto Constitution Avenue, drove past the Capitol, and turned north onto Northeast Second Street, where the Hart Building was located. It was a nine-story marble-clad edifice without a single feature that might give it a trace of character. One critic had recently quipped that it looked like a relic from the old Soviet Union, and conservatives often said it symbolized the kind of deadly dull life socialists wanted to inflict on the country. How fitting it was named for a liberal Senator from Michigan. But inside was different. The two-story duplex offices were the best on Capitol Hill, and conservatives and liberals alike vied for space there.

Nelson waved at the garage ramp guard and handed the driver her pass card to activate the door. They drove in while the other vehicles stayed outside. The car stopped by the elevator bank and she led them onto the members' elevator, which they took to the third floor. From there they headed for her office to find Dedmon. He was waiting for them at the receptionist's desk, munching on a chocolate glazed donut and sipping lukewarm black coffee in a paper cup. A former Milwaukee lawyer, he'd run Nelson's first campaign and come with her to Washington. He was a year into his seventh decade and though he tried to exercise he had the puffy look of someone who worked too many hours, ate too much junk food, and had too little fun. Since leaving Wisconsin his shoulders had rounded and reduced his stature from six feet even to five ten, and his once-brown hair was mostly gray or gone. He put the donut and coffee down and said that Heilman wasn't in his seventh-floor office.

"I just missed him," Dedmon reported. "He left about a minute before I got there."

Which was when?

"Oh, maybe five minutes ago. What's the big deal?" Without knowing the full story he did not share their sense of urgency.

Nelson looked around to see if anyone else was within earshot, then said very softly that Heilman likely had a suitcase nuke. "That's probably what you saw him with."

Dedmon opened his mouth to say something, but nothing came out and he just stared vacantly past all of them.

"Who all did you talk to?" Stromdahl asked.

"What?" The old lawyer had gone from mildly curious to totally overwhelmed.

"You talked to someone, right?"

"Yeah."

"Who did you talk with?"

"Most of his people were there. Counting votes, just like us."

"What did they say?"

"Huh?"

"Did anyone tell you where he was going?"

Dedmon pulled it together a little and nodded yes. "They said Heilman was going to the Capitol building, then flying to South Carolina. Sounded pretty odd, what with the vote on convicting the President only a day or two away, but they'd also said he'd be back before Monday." Dedmon's voice trailed off. "Guess that's not true."

"Listen," O'Brien said. "Did he have the black case when he left the office?"

"Don't know." His body language said he was kicking himself now for not asking.

Nelson grabbed a phone and handed it to him. "You're pals with his chief of staff, right?"

He mumbled "Yeah. We get along well enough."

"Well call him and find out if he had that freaking case. That's the nuke."

Still overwhelmed and numbed by the enormity of it all, he made the call, hung up, and simply said yes. Heilman had left with the bomb. His chief of staff had no idea what it was.

"Let's go," Stromdahl said. "I'll bet he's taking it to the Capitol to plant it."

How could he be sure?

"I'm not. But remember all those plans on the hard drive?

And the blast radius map was centered on the Capitol." Anyway, what better guess did anyone else have? He pointed at Samy and O'Brien. "Come on. Let's see if we can catch him." Then he turned to Dedmon. "You know if he flies out of Reagan or Dulles?"

Dedmon laughed. The high and mighty Hiram Heilman flew on a private jet from a private airport. God forbid that he endure any of the security hassles his constituents faced.

"What's the name of the place?"

"Not sure. Somewhere in Virginia."

"Well find out exactly where and then call the President. I think she's already on the way to Camp David, but get hold of her and get her to close that airport down."

O'Brien shook his head no. "I'll bet he plans to set it off with a phone call, like the mall bombs. And of course he'll want to wait till he's out of town, maybe in the air. If we spook him by shutting the airport, he may go ahead and set it off sooner." That was their dilemma; not simply to capture Heilman, but to grab him with sufficient surprise and swiftness to keep him from immolating half of the city.

Before Stromdahl could agree or disagree, air raid sirens started wailing outside, a sound not faint, yet distant and muffled by the time it penetrated the building's walls. Then the fire alarm went off, much louder and more piercing, as if designed to shatter minds as well as ears. And for those who might attempt ignoring it the lights began to flash and loudspeakers announced that this time was not a drill and everyone should leave both the building and the city. Shit. Sally's damn evacuation was creating just the confusion Heilman needed to evade capture and set off the blast.

Stromdahl gave the flashing lights a baleful look and then said O'Brien was right. They couldn't spook the son of a bitch. But they still had to stop him. Nelson and Dedmon needed to find out exactly which airport he was using. In the meantime the Commandant, Al-Mahdi, and the Director would go to the Capitol to try to intercept him. What was the best way to get there?

"Take the tunnel," Nelson said. "The subway doesn't run over the weekend, but the walkway next to it stays open. If you go outside you probably won't get in because most of the doors are locked. Certainly they are now."

"Good." Stromdahl looked at O'Brien and Al-Mahdi. "Come on. Let's roll."

CHAPTER 29

The guard at the Hart Building subway station was a retired truck driver, pink and fat and well past fifty. Someone who might pass for a real-life Norman Rockwell Santa Claus if he ever grew a beard. Though he carried a pistol, his job was pretty much minding queues and making sure Senators got first priority on the small open-top subway trains when they were running. At the moment he was on the radio with his counterpart at the Capitol end of the tunnel making sure they wouldn't trap anyone on the walkway by locking the gates. He looked up and told Stromdahl and the other two that no one could enter.

"Did Senator Heilman come through earlier this morning," Stromdahl asked.

"Yeah. About twenty or thirty minutes ago."

"Did he ever come back?"

The guard was getting very nervous. Even in the bowels of the building he could hear the sirens wailing and the announcements on the speaker system, and he wanted quit of his duties so he could get away himself. "No," he said. Heilman had not come back.

"Was he carrying anything when you saw him?"

"Like what?"

"Like an odd-shaped black case?"

"Yeah. Yeah. He did have something like that." The radio crackled and the guard at the other end reported all was clear. "Roger," the fat old Santa-clone said. Then he told them they all had to leave. Everything was now officially closed.

O'Brien stepped up and flashed his badge and told him to go ahead and take off. "But leave the walkway open. We'll be needing it."

No, the guard said. Orders were orders. Stromdahl ignored him and started walking through the tunnel toward the Senate wing of the Capitol. "Hey," the guard said. "You can't go there." His hand went down to draw his pistol, which was snapped inside the holster, nice and snug and safe. Washington was not the Wild West and he was no Wyatt Earp.

Samy closed the ten feet between them in a single step, grabbed his hand, and pried it easily from the handle of the weapon. "Now call your guy at the other end and tell him to keep things open."

Again the guard refused.

Samy pocketed the pistol and pointed a finger at the still-visible Stromdahl's back. "You know who that is?"

The guard looked at the big man, then back at Samy. No, he really didn't know. A general with lots of stars?

"That's the Commandant of the Marines, Wallace Stromdahl, and you know the President put him in charge of security after the mall bombs. You know that, right?"

Samy had a tight grip on his upper arm. Tight to the point of pain, which gave him the guard's close attention. Yes, the old man said. Yes, he'd heard a General Storm-something was in charge. Samy gripped even tighter, gave him a not-so-gentle shake, and pointed down the tunnel, where Stromdahl had gone out of sight. "So call your guy at the other end and tell him to leave things open. We'll shut it down for you."

The guard wavered but did not yield. He turned his head toward O'Brien and asked to see the director's badge again. Okay, he finally said. He guessed it was all right. He made the call on the radio and said some general would be emerging in a few minutes. Then he waddled off as fast as he could move his fat drumstick legs.

AT THE CAPITOL-END of the tunnel the guard was younger and

sharper, a light-skinned African American who looked just a few pounds north of skinny. He was a police wannabe awaiting approval of his application to join the city police force. What was going on, he asked Stromdahl.

"Did Senator Heilman come by here about eight o'clock?"

"Yeah. He had some kinda odd-looking black thing."

"Right. Did he ever come back?"

"No."

"Where else could he leave the building if he didn't want to go back to his office?"

"Probably the Senate members' entrance, at the north end." He pointed northward, handed Stromdahl a visitor's guide map, and explained how to get there. It was locked, but people could use it as an exit.

Stromdahl said a quick thanks and ran up a nearby stairwell. Was he supposed to turn right or left at the top? The guard hadn't been so clear on that little point. He pulled the map out of his pocket. Right. Yes, it had to be right. But then he didn't see the cloakroom sign he was supposed to look for. What had gone awry? Ah, the second right, not the first. And again he missed a turn, and the second set of stairs he was supposed to take. God damn it.

He tried to go back to the subway station to ask the guard again, but he couldn't find that way either. He was totally adrift deep within the innards of the building, and so completely turned around he had no idea which direction was which, except he knew up from down. Stop. Stop and think. If ever there was a time for Marine Corps coolness under pressure, this was it.

He'd been to the Capitol many times to meet with members of Congress and attend ceremonial events like the State of the Union speech. Sally's, of course, but also several others. His first visit went back to his high school senior trip, and he recalled his surprise at how the inside of the dome was not visible from the first floor, only the second. The first floor area underneath the rotunda was known as the crypt, but no one was buried there. It was filled with heavy structural columns and statues. The second floor was much more open, with large public spaces. Not at all like the rat's warren in which he was lost. So he needed to go up another level to find something he might recognize.

He spotted an ascending stairway, took the steps two at

a time, and emerged on the House side of the building, near the original House chamber, now called Statuary Hall. It was immediately south of the rotunda, and if he went due north under the dome he'd be on the Senate side. He could go around the Senate chamber, find and take a descending staircase, and he'd be at the members' entrance or very near it. With a clear plan in mind he started running across the polished stone floor, but his leather-soled dress shoes kept slipping and in his haste he fell twice, like a puppy dog trying to run on linoleum. Better slower and steadier. He reduced his pace to a fast walk, made it to a stairwell, and emerged right by the door. It was chained shut and there was no one in sight.

As he turned to leave, yet another guard appeared, an olive-skinned man maybe five eight and in his mid-thirties. He was wearing a uniform more sharply creased and shoes more highly polished than the other guards'. "You're not supposed to be here, sir. We're evacuating everybody."

"I understand. Were you on duty here before the door was chained?"

"Yes sir, but you have to leave. I'll open it to let you out."

"I'm General Stromdahl, and I need to find Senator Heilman. Did he go out this door a few minutes ago?"

The guard allowed himself the slightest of smiles. "Yes sir. I know who you are. Semper Fi. I was a corporal in Afghanistan in 2012. Got out when I lost part of my foot."

Stromdahl, too, had to smile. "Semper Fi Corporal. Did you see the Senator?"

"Yes sir. He went out the door maybe five minutes ago."

"Was he carrying a black case or bag of some sort?"

"No sir. He didn't have a thing. His limo picked him up."

ONCE HE MADE it outside the noise hit him like the thunderclap in a stadium after a game-winning touchdown. Like the time Minnesota and Michigan were tied near the end of the fourth quarter and he blitzed the quarterback, intercepted his pass, and took it to the end zone just as the clock expired. The only time he ever scored. But this pandemonium was more sustained and unrelenting, a cacophonous mix of sirens, honking horns, idling engines, blaring speakers, and the thunking chop-chop-chop of helicopters sent up in the vain hope that if properly observed the chaos might be controlled. He was amazed at how much had been mobilized in only an hour.

The sky remained clear, but a strong subfreezing wind rudely reminded him he had no coat. *Shit. Fucking shit*. He swore silently at everything in general, and then suddenly relaxed and grinned. Not Senator Heilman nor anyone else was getting out of town real fast in this mess. Not unless they sprouted wings or found a helicopter. And the guard had said Heilman departed in his limo.

He pulled out his tablet and called Nelson's office. She answered herself. No one was there but her and Al-Mahdi and O'Brien, both of whom had just walked in. Dedmon had decided to take the subway to his home in Rockville. "Security says we all need to leave," she said. "But they're not making us go yet. FBI's sending over a bomb squad again, and I'm waiting till they get here." She was quite impressed that the Bureau had people specially trained in how to disarm miniaturized nuclear weapons. One of O'Brien's pet projects.

And then?

"I'll take a subway too, then drive to Camp David if I can make it. Sally wants me and Ferrell there. Admiral Swenson's going back to the Pentagon to brief the Chairman of the Joint Chiefs."

"You find out where Heilman's headed? What airport he uses?"

She wasn't sure, but his office had told Dedmon he almost always used the Heilman Energy corporate jet, which flew out of an airpark in northern Virginia.

Where exactly?

"Place called Occoquan. Occoquan Air Park."

He went online with the tablet to check the location. Ah, so, what he'd thought. Just north of Quantico. Maybe a fifteen-minute helicopter flight from DC. "Tell Samy and O'Brien to meet me at the end of the mall," he said. "I got a chopper coming in to pick us up. I'm hoping we can beat Heilman down there."

IT WAS A WHIRLYBIRD designed to haul forty Marines into combat, but this one was outfitted for comfort and seated no more than ten. The pilot was a youngish-looking major whose name tag and looks suggested he was Filipino. "You bring the rifles?" Stromdahl asked.

"Yes sir." He pointed at one of the rear seats, where two were strapped in like passengers. "Got you the pistols too. Two of 'em. Ammo's up front behind my seat." He paused while Stromdahl checked the weapons out, then asked the Commandant where they were going.

"Small airport in Virginia. Occoquan." The map was still showing on the tablet, which he handed to the pilot. "Know where it is?"

"Yes sir. Just fly down I-95 and turn west at the Occoquan exit."

On liftoff they could see the long lines of traffic inching along the DC streets, and as they climbed a little higher they could see that the bridges across the Potomac were the worst choke points. But to the south, the Virginia highway patrol had all lanes of I-95 flowing away from the city and things were actually clicking right along. If Heilman had made it across the river with the first wave of the rush he might be at Occoquan already. "Faster," Stromdahl told the pilot. "Fast as you can go. And call them on the radio and get clearance to land right away."

"Yes sir." He did as ordered, then asked the purpose of the flight.

Would the flight crew balk at arresting Heilman? Stromdahl's eyes found Al-Mahdi's and then O'Brien's. Should they come clean or not? Al-Mahdi gave him a classically ambivalent shrug. "Your call," it said. O'Brien's look was more decisive. They couldn't proceed with the loyalty of the crew in doubt.

"You know there's a bomb at the Capitol," Stromdahl told the major.

"Yes sir. It's all over the news. And we got briefed before we left Quantico." His tone and the look on his face silently asked what that had to do with a small private airfield.

"Right," Stromdahl said, and he hastened to dispel the whiff of doubt that remained hanging in the air. "Well, we think Senator Heilman planted it, and we need to catch him before he sets it off with a phone call."

The major and his copilot, an even younger captain, turned their heads slightly to exchange glances. They nodded at each other, but said nothing and made no move to change their flight plan. After a second call to the tower at the airpark the major prepared to land by banking the bird right a few degrees and dropping to a lower altitude. And then he spoke again to Stromdahl.

"We're with you sir. Should I warn them you'll be carrying weapons into the terminal?"

O'Brien interjected an emphatic "No." And neither should they continue their descent. He pointed down at the ground, where they could see a long line of luxury cars and limos waiting to get past the entrance gate, and a similar traffic jam on the tarmac as planes jockeyed to get onto the apron where they could drop their stairways to take on passengers. "I'll bet it's a madhouse inside the terminal," he said, "and if he sees us before we see him, all he has to do is punch a few numbers into his phone and Washington's gone. Hell, if he's in that line and saw us already . . ." O'Brien didn't finish the last sentence, but even at this distance they would have heard and seen the explosion, and so far there had been neither boom nor flash of light. Their time had not yet run out.

So what should he do, the pilot asked.

"Go higher and go farther south," Stromdahl said.

And then?

And then he didn't know.

BEFORE COLLEGE Stromdahl had been a passable first baseman as well as a football player, and he'd developed a fascination with baseball statistics, especially batting statistics. At the high school level a really good batter might get a hit in forty percent of his trips to the plate, but the percentage of swings that resulted in hits was much less. Maybe fifteen or twenty percent. But no matter the high failure rate, unless the opposing pitcher was having a fluky bad day of wildness, no team could win without swinging. And that was pretty much their situation now. If they didn't land the probability of success was zero.

There was, of course, a small chance that the FBI bomb squad already had found the bomb and disarmed it. He called the President to find out. No, she said. They'd been at the Capitol for almost an hour, and had found the black carrying case in a hallway by the Senate chamber. But there was no trace of the nuke, and the news from the Quantico forensic lab made things even more dire.

"Walleye, they found more plans on the computer's hard drive, and it's like some kind of plastic explosive, except nuclear.

So it doesn't need the case and it's easy to hide. And whoever designed it figured out a lightweight shield that screens out most of the radiation. So we can't find it with a Geiger counter. That's what our guys were trying at first and it got 'em nowhere. Now they're using dogs, but still no luck."

"Which means . . ."

"Which means you gotta catch Hiram right away." And there was one other thing he ought to know. The plans confirmed the detonator was to be activated by a phone call, but there also was a backup timer, and they had no idea how long before it went off.

He turned off the tablet and stuffed it back into his jacket pocket, then looked down once more at the airpark and the traffic snarl in the parking lot. Reagan Airport was close enough to the Capitol that it shut down as soon as the evacuation was announced, and everyone who had any access to a private plane was now trying to use places like Occoquan to get away. It appeared two attendants were waving cars onto a grassy area between the regular lot and the terminal to accommodate the overflow.

Was Heilman already there? They had no way to tell from up above. "We're going in," he said. Whatever cards randomness might deal them, they'd have to play the hand, but if his plan worked they'd nab Heilman in front of the terminal just as he got out of his limo. Stromdahl figured that would give them the best chance to secure his phone before he could make the fatal call.

ONCE AGAIN the execution of his plan went flawlessly at first. They took only the pistols with them. He and O'Brien had the two that came with the helicopter, and Al-Mahdi had the weapon he'd taken from the fat old guard. Samy also took a pair of binoculars that was part of the chopper's standard gear. The idea was he'd hide in some bushes near the entrance gate, spot the limo with South Carolina "Senate Member" tags, and alert the other two, who'd move in for the capture when the car pulled under the *porte cochere* to drop Heilman off.

In his football days Stromdahl could usually take out two offensive blockers by himself, even the monsters who always seemed to play for Wisconsin. So he figured two or three bodyguards wouldn't be all that tough for him. O'Brien would nab Heilman and his phone. Then they'd stuff the sorry-ass SOB onto the helicopter and take him back to the Capitol to show them where the bomb was hidden. If he didn't want to talk, well, then he'd blow up along with everyone else. And if he later squawked about some violation of his rights, so freaking what.

Stromdahl took off his jacket and tie, and they walked through the crowded terminal with eyes peeled for Heilman in case he'd already arrived. The airpark served jets, not props, and mostly jets of the larger tax exempt corporate variety. Its waiting lounge featured dark hardwoods, soft leather chairs, old Scotch, and a smoking area stocked with fat cigars. An all-female serving staff, carefully selected and scantily dressed, had been imported from Las Vegas.

The throng of waiting passengers, well lubricated with free drinks, were focused on ogling the eye candy and maybe trying to take a bite, and three middle-aged guys walking by were not going to divert them, even if one had the temerity to come in dark skin. And if the new guys seemed to be staring a bit hard it was probably at the waitresses and not because they were looking for someone to arrest. Heilman, however, was nowhere to be seen. So far so good. They could intercept him outside the front door just as planned.

And then they reached the door to go outside and there he was. But in this venue the bodyguards were not expecting trouble. There were two, and Samy and Stromdahl easily disarmed them and used the handcuffs they were carrying to lock their wrists together.

The Senator was two steps behind the bodyguards. He instantly recognized Stromdahl and O'Brien and bolted back outside, and as he ran toward the overflow parking lot he pulled out his phone and started punching numbers. O'Brien raised his pistol to shoot, then dropped his arm and sprinted after him. They needed to take him alive and healthy enough to show them where the bomb was. Otherwise the timer would trump everything.

The pause to raise the pistol gave Heilman a good fifty-foot lead. He made it to the parked cars, ducked down, and vanished among them. The lot attendants had guided the overflow vehicles into parallel lanes, like at a rental car return; eight lanes, ten to twelve cars long, with a six-foot space in between to leave room for the doors to open. The drivers were told to leave the keys in the ignition. Valets would bring them to the terminal later on as needed—if anyone ever returned. Or simply park them in the regular lot once it cleared out a little.

Heilman had gone in between the cars at the front of the two lanes closest to the terminal, but when O'Brien reached the spot three seconds later the in-between row was empty. He quickly ran to check the rows between the other lanes. Nothing. Somewhere in the automotive matrix the madman was hiding, crouched down in front of one car and behind another. And no doubt he was punching the little keyboard on his phone.

O'Brien raced down the row between the first two lanes and didn't see him. He ran back the other way in the row between the second and third lanes, and as he was about to go down the next row he heard a car start at the rear of the last lane. It was a red Ferrari roadster with the top down, and Heilman had it going full tilt toward the pavement and the front gate.

Only later did O'Brien piece together what happened next. He raised his pistol to shoot out the tires, but Stromdahl beat him to it. The Ferrari spun out and crashed into a long black Cadillac limo that was headed for the terminal, and Heilman jumped out and started running for a line of trees about a hundred yards to the north. He made ten yards of the hundred before Al-Mahdi's tackle brought him down. The phone went skittering out of his hand and landed in the middle of some nearby shrubs.

So at last they had him, but surely they had failed. In all the time it took to flush him out he must have placed the call they so desperately wanted to stop. And he had. Three times. Each time to the wrong number. In his haste and panic he kept missing by one digit. His hands were big, like Stromdahl's, and he really needed a mini-tablet, like the Commandant's. But he'd come perilously close to success. When they found the phone in the bushes the right number was all punched in, and given another fraction of a second he would have hit the call button and the Nation's Capital would have been nuclear cinders.

CHAPTER 30

Though he was a big man, Heilman was no match for Walleye Stromdahl, who had six inches on him and also had the Senator's hands tied tightly behind his back. Stromdahl grabbed the collar of his suit jacket, yanked him upright, and told him to get out of the helicopter, which had landed only a few feet from the Capitol. "You got no choice. Now go." He gave his prisoner a good kick in the butt to get him in gear.

The pilots looked on, ready and eager to stay and help stifle any resistance, but Stromdahl waved them off, and once he had Heilman on the ground he ordered them to return to Occoquan. They needed to pick up O'Brien and Al-Mahdi, he said, and the two captive bodyguards. Afterwards, if he succeeded in finding and disarming the bomb, they could come back for him. And if not . . . Well, there couldn't be an if not. That's all there was to it.

He kept his right hand tight on Heilman's collar, and nudged him along by kneeing his rear end. "Come on, Senator, you show me where you hid it or we'll die together when it goes off." Heilman twisted around to give him a hate-twisted look, but said nothing.

The FBI people had told Stromdahl he should go to the Senate members' entrance to get in. The black case was found in the Senate wing of the building, and the odds seemed pretty good the actual device was not too far away. So that was the initial focus of their search, and that's where he should bring Heilman.

At the door the ex-Marine was still standing guard, and for the first time Stromdahl noticed his name tag. Hernandez. The shock hit him so hard he let loose of Heilman, who tried to run away, but stumbled and fell. Stromdahl chased him down, yanked him up again, and gave him a good shake; like he was nothing but a rag doll. "Senator, you ain't goin' nowhere unless I say so. Except maybe straight to hell if your fucking bomb goes off." He dragged and prodded him back to the entrance and stared again at the guard's name.

"Something wrong, sir?"

"No. Not really. Nothing at all if we find his little toy." He gave Heilman another rag doll shake to emphasize the point. "But I want you outta here, Hernandez. You understand?"

"No sir. I volunteered to stay. I'm the only one here except the guys from the bomb squad and an Army unit they brought in. And the dogs. There's four dogs." Four dogs and forty people were searching for the bomb, but Hernandez was all there was guarding the one entrance that remained open. He couldn't leave.

By now a good three hours had elapsed since the announcement of the evacuation, and while they still could hear the sounds of distant chaos, Capitol Hill itself had gone strangely quiet. Like nothing the guard had ever heard before. And he wouldn't abandon the building to such uncertainty.

"Corporal, that's an order. Get out of here. Now."

"Sir, I'm not in the Corps anymore. Wish I was, but I'm not. And I'm not moving."

THE AGENT IN CHARGE of the building search was an FBI veteran of twenty-five years. She was a big woman. Big-boned big, not fat. Her hair was short and brown, and her face hard and professional, though pretty when she smiled. Right now she wasn't smiling, and like Hernandez she refused to leave. She'd come to the entrance when called on the radio and was deep into a heated debate with the Commandant. No, she said. His idea was crazy. How was one man with a balky prisoner in tow going to locate the bomb she and all her people had not yet found?

And how would he disarm it? He had none of the training

he needed, but he was telling all the pros to vacate the building. Everyone, including Hernandez, should depart and get as far outside the blast radius as they could. He would go in dragging the defiant Heilman and succeed where they had not. It was totally crazy.

Maybe crazy he said. But not completely. The origin for his scheme was Heilman's smirk back in Occoquan when he overheard O'Brien talking about the black case and the search of the Senate wing. The smirk told Stromdahl the bomb wasn't there, and also told him the Senator's arrogance and physiognomy might offer the best chance at finding it.

But the agent would have none of it. She wasn't pulling out unless O'Brien or the President ordered it. Okay, he said, they'd call Macalester right away. Then he realized he'd left his jacket on the helicopter, and the tablet was in one of the pockets. Sheepishly he borrowed the agent's phone, and after much explaining about why he wasn't calling from his usual number, he got through to Sally at Camp David.

"Just think about it," he told her. "The symbolism has to mean a lot to him." Why else select the Capitol building as the place to blow up the nuke? The effect would be equally devastating if it were simply dropped into a trash can or left behind in a hotel or office. "Heck, he could have left it in the Hart Building garage. But I'm pretty sure he wanted to see a mushroom cloud sprout from the dome. He wanted to be up in his airplane so he could watch it." It would be like a classic scene from an alien invasion super hero movie.

He could hear Sally exhale as she pondered the request. Did she really want to roll the dice and rest everything on Walleye Stromdahl's instincts about the motivation and psychology of a madman? Did she have a choice? "Put the agent on the phone," she said at last. "I'll tell her."

The agent frowned and shook her head no, but said "Yes ma'am" into the phone and then told Stromdahl to go ahead but be careful. "And if you find it, don't move it, don't touch it, don't do anything till you call me." She handed her phone back to him. "Use this. You got it all down cold what you gotta do?"

"Yes ma'am."

For the first time she smiled. "Good luck, sir. And may the

force be with you." She added that despite his orders she and the others would be waiting right outside the building.

IF HE HAD IT RIGHT on the motive and symbolism, the most logical place to hide the bomb was under the dome, in the rotunda or the crypt. He thought about it for a few seconds and decided that the crypt, with its clutter of columns and statues, was the more likely spot. He grabbed Heilman's left arm, and tugged him along with little resistance and not a sign on his face that they were anywhere near close. And when he checked all the obvious nooks and crannies there was nothing unusual or out of place. Maybe it wasn't the crypt.

The rotunda then. That would be next. He glanced around to find the way up and saw the stairs he'd used before. Again Heilman came meekly along, but when they emerged in Statuary Hall Stromdahl thought he felt the Senator tense up ever so slightly. Were they getting close? Yes, it must be the rotunda.

Or maybe not. He never could pinpoint exactly what sign or signal tipped him off; what triggered his epiphany. Was it the statue, or some look on Heilman's face, or some other change when they walked near it? Or just plain blind dumb luck? Whatever it was, he had dragged Heilman close to the statue when he thought he felt him stiffen and resist. Not much, maybe not at all, maybe just because he slipped. But there was something different about him.

When Stromdahl turned to look at him, he was staring clear across the room, as if attempting to divert attention from the real source of his interest. That's when Stromdahl paused to survey things more carefully, and that's when he realized he had the answer. And when he took a step toward the statue and felt Heilman really resist for the first time, he knew he was on the verge of ending the search.

Every state got to send two statues for display in Statuary Hall, though limited space meant some had to be placed elsewhere in the building. Wisconsin's two were Father Marquette and the great Progressive governor and Senator, Robert La Follette. The marble likeness depicted La Follette in a chair, bracing with his arms to stand up, as if about to give a speech.

Of course, Stromdahl thought. Who else would Heilman want more to blow up? A liberal Progressive who'd once run for President as a third party candidate. What better symbol of his success in ridding the country of both its government and the NAPsters.

He took Heilman's belt and used it to tie up his feet, and then looked behind the statue. The light wasn't very good, and he didn't see any sign of a bomb. Then, just as he was about to continue the search elsewhere, he noticed the slightest of smiles playing on the Senator's lips. Ah, the smirk again. The arrogant condescension and hatred for all things liberal and Progressive.

Stromdahl smiled right back. He was at the right place and just hadn't looked hard enough. "It's here, isn't it Hiram?" He prodded Heilman with his foot, but got only a stare in response. A stare that told him once and for all he was right. He went back behind the statue and looked again. And there it was, a plastic-wrapped package attached to the base of the pediment, like a part of the granite. Taped to its bottom was a phone with two wires that went through the plastic, and next to the phone was a timer set to go off at noon. There were only five minutes left to go. That's why Heilman had gone so passive, and why he got so nervous near La Follette. And that's why the arrogant little smile. He'd made up his mind to die in the blast rather than stop it, and he knew the end was near.

The bomb squad agent was furious. She never should have let Stromdahl go in alone. "Now listen," she said. "Don't touch the phone on the bomb. That might set it off. Use the phone I gave you to take a picture of the bomb and send it to me. Then call me back and I'll tell you what to do next."

He snapped a quick shot, but the flash didn't go off, and it came out too blurry to interpret. Shit. Half a minute wasted. He called the agent. "How do you make the flash work?"

"Dammit. Push the button that says flash. Do you see it?"

Yes, he did. He took a second shot, and this time it worked. There were now three minutes left.

Thirty seconds later she was back on the phone. "I want you to clip the red wire from the phone on the bomb and the blue wire from the timer. Got it?"

"Clip with what? I've got no tools."

God damn she never should have let him go by himself. But they were down to two minutes, and it was Stromdahl or nothing. "What's the yellow wire attached to?" she asked.

"Looks like the bottom of the bomb."

"Shit. Wait a minute."

"There's only a minute left."

"Wait," she said again. He could hear her consulting with someone else in the background. Half a minute later she came back on. "Just yank it all off like a Band-Aid," she said. "Now."

He grabbed the phone with his right hand and the timer with his left and jerked as hard as he could. The phone came right off and he tossed it aside. But the tape holding the timer on was more stubborn. Ten seconds left. He pulled again with both hands and at last it came free.

"They're off," he said, and then he sat down next to the statue and just stared at the floor. The agent's phone was at his side, and he could hear her voice demanding to know if he was still there. After a minute or two he picked it up and said yes. What should he do now?

"Nothing. Don't do a damn thing. Just sit there and wait."

It was now five past noon. Heilman hadn't said a word and had curled up in the fetal position. The agent was off the phone. The silence was pin-drop intense. And then the phone he'd removed from the bomb started to ring. Stromdahl went instantly alert again, picked it up, and looked at the caller ID. It was someone from California. "Hello," he said. "You've reached the Capitol. How can I help you?"

"Who? I'm trying to reach Jack Evans. In Sacramento. Must have punched in the wrong number. Sorry." When they later checked it out the story was completely true. The caller never had a clue that he'd come within a few minutes of blowing up Washington, DC.

MONDAY MORNING, January 19, despite the chaotic aftermath in the city, the entire Senate convened to expel Heilman. The vote was ninety-nine to nothing, and when it was done Senator Nelson asked for a suspension of the rules so she could bring up another pressing matter.

Vice President Castaneda was presiding, and he asked what matter.

Why, the bill of impeachment, of course. Shouldn't they dispose of it right away so the country could start recovering from the crisis?

"Anyone opposed?" Castaneda and everyone else knew the answer. Not a hand or voice was raised.

"On the pending bill of impeachment, all in favor of conviction say aye."

There was total silence.

"All opposed say nay."

The chamber rang loud and clear with the verdict, and when the roll was called the vote again was ninety-nine to nothing.

That night, at the Rose Bowl, Minnesota beat Alabama for its first national football championship in what seemed a century or two. The NCAA had withheld a decision on cancelation until one in the afternoon on Sunday, and by then the political crisis had passed. Stromdahl and the President and Jane Nelson got to watch it in the White House theatre and all three went hoarse as pack-a-day smokers before it was done. The final score was twenty-four to twenty-three, and the win came on a fifty-yard touchdown pass with no time left on the clock.

Two Mondays later, on February second, a unit of the Wyoming National Guard on special patrol duty in Yellowstone Park finally tracked down most of the miscreants who'd fled from the Pocatello chemical plant. After a brief firefight they captured eight renegade Israelis and ten members of the Aryan Multitude. One Israeli was killed and a white-headed man, though wounded, somehow crawled away.

The trail of blood led to a small clearing where several snowmobiles had been hidden. He managed to get one started, rode off, and was never seen again. That spring a snowmobile was found abandoned about five miles away from the scene of the battle. Near as the investigators could tell from its condition and bits of clothing nearby, it had stalled and the driver had been dragged off by wolves. No remains were ever found.

Throughout his trial and subsequent incarceration while he awaited execution, Hiram Heilman went silent as a Trappist monk. At the Federal Penitentiary he would occasionally write notes to describe his symptoms if he became ill, and once, early on, he also scribbled a note requesting the complete works of Ayn Rand, which his family provided. When a fellow inmate and former philosophy professor destroyed all the volumes, Heilman was found weeping in his cell as he vainly tried to put the torn pages back together.

Despite his silence, he had his lawyers pursue every possible appeal, and he apparently suffered no pangs of irony about his long-time efforts to hasten executions by doing away with judicial review. And so, without ever speaking another word, he lasted ten years before they stuck the final needle into his arm.

Within a month of Sally's exoneration Stromdahl and Swenson resigned from the military. Anyone who broke as many laws and rules as they had should pay the price, they said. No matter the justification or reason. Swenson became a military news analyst for a cable network, but tired of it after a few months and taught for a while at Harvard. Sally's successor appointed him Secretary of State. Stromdahl wanted totally out of Washington and public life and went back to the family farm to ponder his future.

Ayan Al-Mahdi forgave Samy for getting involved with Stromdahl and he went back to teaching at Georgetown. He no longer had any problem filling even the most esoteric of his seminars. Danny O'Brien continued at the FBI and rejected several offers to run for public office or become CEO at some large corporation. A few years later Sally appointed him to the Supreme Court.

Linda Ferrell returned to her Ag Department job and shunned all publicity. The only time she ever spoke to the media about the bomb plot and her role in thwarting it was when all five of the Idaho Raiders were awarded special Congressional medals of appreciation. When she and her family drove to Washington for the ceremony and stopped at a service plaza on I-95 no one recognized her.

Luke Rumbo continued with his radio show and always played down what Lisa Larkin had done to blow the whistle on Heilman. For a while his ratings fell as fast as the prospects of the Progressives rose. All the polls showed they would win a majority in the House in the next election, and that the country was finally willing to embrace some sensible solutions to its many problems. But old habits and old politics die hard, and by the time the next election rolled around he was happily back at slinging his conservative brickbats in every direction. Only time would tell if the country had really learned its lesson.

For several years people wondered whatever became of Samir Akbar. He vanished from all intelligence reports and there were no incidents linked to his Jihad. Then a year into Sally's second term he emerged from his caves to run for President of Yemen. She decided not to attempt any intervention. It likely would have been futile and all her advisers said it would do more harm than good. Wait and see, she told her Secretary of State.

Wait for what, the Secretary asked?

The President shrugged. Many years before in Israel, Menachem Begin had evolved from terrorist to peacemaker. Maybe that's the course Akbar would take. And in truth there was no better choice. She held no illusions it would really work out that way, but took it as something of a good sign that he'd called Samy Al-Mahdi for political advice.

CHAPTER 31

Of course there followed years and years of Congressional investigations, specially appointed commissions, and media exposés. Not to mention novels, documentaries, and social media commentary. Heilman's mad scheme came to be known as the Christmas Coup, or the Santa Claus Conspiracy because of the elaborate Santa hoax. Why had he used men dressed in Santa suits? And why use the suitcase nuke after the mall bombs and the Sarin attack had worked so well and Sally's conviction was so imminent?

The Senator wasn't talking, and Ferguson was never found, but the Israelis soon started chattering like magpies to avoid the death penalty here or extradition to the new Palestinian state, which sought them for numerous atrocities. They explained that Heilman didn't want to do a nuclear attack in the U.S. because none of them was certain their plasticized atomic weapon would work. His plan was to use the device back in the Middle East to make sure everything went up in mushroom clouds. His secret researchers had been working on methods for extracting oil from areas contaminated by atomic fallout. So after the nuclear destruction *Nagaf* could move in to take things over in the name of Israel. And by then a new U.S. Government, free of Progressives and Democrats, would look kindly on Heilman Energy getting back its long-lost holdings and a lot more. It was perfect for all involved.

Stromdahl apparently had it right about a last-minute decision to blow up Washington rather than lose on impeachment, which Heilman feared after Al-Mahdi and the Commandant made it out of Yemen and then went to Idaho. The Senator knew they'd found out about Ferguson, and rightly guessed the next step would lead to him. The Santa part of the plot got pretty convoluted. Heilman and his people couldn't find any brown-skinned Asians or Middle Easterners they could rely upon to haul the bombs to the malls, and even if they had, they might have been identified from surveillance cameras and then things would have come unraveled. They had to find a way to use *Nagaf* and Aryan Multitude drivers, make them look like Middle Eastern Muslims, and also assure their faces couldn't really be seen. That meant face paint, and to make it less obvious they needed to conceal most of the faces.

The Santa suits were the perfect solution, although the Mall of America Santa messed up and smudged his beard with the skin coloring, and the fool in Texas went and lost his beard and wig. One of the Israelis had come up with the Santa idea, but Heilman jumped right on board. Despite his professed Christian piety, he really hated Christmas. As a true Ayn Rander he believed mostly in greed and selfishness. He certainly did not take well to a holiday based on the principle that it's better to give than receive.

There did remain the problem of how to avoid having someone see the Santas changing or making good their escape, which again could provide a clue that might undo the entire plot. So they scouted out a place in each mall where they could get into regular clothes and wipe off the makeup. Like the restroom at Tysons Center.

The IPC plant, it turned out, had been acquired by Heilman Energy through a whole series of shell corporations. Heilman's brother, who ran the company, claimed he had no idea what was going on there, but no one ever believed him. In the public's mind he was clearly guilty even if there wasn't enough evidence to convict him. How could he not have known? The research facility became the workshop for the entire plot. It had all the equipment for making the fake license plates as well as the nitrate bombs and the suitcase nuke. Plus the *Nagaf* Israelis were doing their research on how to safely re-start oil wells where all the surface equipment had been destroyed by nuclear weapons.

The *Nagaf* captives also filled in some other details. Ferrell had it exactly right on the Newark container. The idea had been for it to be discovered before the mall bombs, not after. The connection to Iran would then have been more obvious, and the declaration of war easier to obtain. Red Sand and Runyon had known that Ferguson had hooked up with *Nagaf*, which is why Runyon backed off the idea of using him to start a secret Red Sand subsidiary. *Nagaf* was too violent and dangerous even for him. Runyon probably also had a pretty good idea that Ferguson and his new buddies had something to do with the mall bombs, but he likely buried his head in the sand to avoid finding out for sure.

In Yemen, it was Ferguson's people who had blown up Samir Akbar's helicopter. They'd decided by then that they wanted to follow Al-Mahdi as a way to find Akbar and the clerks who'd escaped, and there was no way they could do that if Samy got whisked away by air. They almost screwed up when he got inside the chopper, but when he stepped back out to go get his phone they fired their rocket.

The subway Sarin attacks had been planned all along as a backup or additional push to get a war with Iran. The *Nagaf* people identified the poor Columbia grad student, killed him with Sarin, and then took him to the subway station and planted the body as a false clue. They also managed to tamper with his computer and phone, and to steal some of the chemicals from his lab to make things look even more suspicious.

And how on earth did Israelis ever get along with the Aryan Multitude? That one had all the investigators totally stymied. At this the senior member of *Nagaf* laughed and laughed. The Multitude members were so stupid, he said, that Ferguson convinced them the Israelis were a different kind of Jew, the kind of people Hitler would have loved to work with. And considering Fabelman's proclivities, maybe that wasn't completely off the mark.

OVER THE YEARS the religious debate between Stromdahl and Al-Mahdi continued unabated, mostly on the phone and Internet, but sometimes when they visited each other. The former

Commandant said the close calls and coincidences that let them foil Heilman would never have all gone their way without the help of God. What was random for humans was within God's infinite comprehension, and He must have intervened.

Samy would respond with the obvious questions about why such an all-knowing God would allow things to degenerate so far in the first place, and Stromdahl said it was like a test to sort out the good from the bad. Kind of like an evolutionary thing as human society moved from war and poverty to peace and prosperity. The paradox of attributing evolution to God did not escape him, but neither did he think it was really a paradox; more a matter of extreme irony that people wouldn't give God credit for something as amazing as evolution.

They never came to any agreement, but had great fun over it. Sally sometimes joined in and said that while it all proved the existence of God, it also showed the bottomless inability of humans or any religion to understand such an all-powerful deity. For her, it was arrogant to think men were created in God's image, and so she rejected giving the deity form or gender.

When not debating religion and politics with him, she tried to talk Stromdahl out of retirement to serve in some high government post. Shortly after Heilman's conviction she even suggested the former Commandant should come back to Washington, eventually to succeed her as President. The polls showed the country was all for that idea. But he had much different and smaller plans. First a bike trip across the United States, something he'd dreamed of for years. And then maybe become president of the U of M, not the USA. Sally said to hold off on the bike trip until she retired. Maybe she would join him, and then they could live together again in Minneapolis in the apartment she still owned, not far from the campus.

ABOUT THE AUTHOR

Bert Black is a Minnesota lawyer who served in the Marine Corps during the Vietnam War. He lives in downtown Minneapolis with a dog and a cat and memories of his late wife. When not practicing law or writing he is an avid bicycle rider. *Impeachment Day* is his first novel.